Captured in Her Gaze

Jolie Dvorak

Captured in Her Gaze
Copyright © Jolie Dvorak 2024
www.joliedvorak.com
All Rights Reserved

The right of Jolie Dvorak to be identified as the author of this work has been asserted by her under the *Copyright Amendment (Moral Rights) Act 2000*.

No part of this publication may be reproduced, distributed, or transmitted in any form or by any means, including photocopying, recording, or other electronic or mechanical methods, without the prior written permission of the publisher, except as permitted by U.S. copyright law. For permission requests, contact the author.

The use of this work in any form for the training, development, or research of artificial intelligence systems or algorithms is strictly prohibited without the direct and explicit consent of the author. This includes, but is not limited to, the use of text, characters, plot elements, and any other component of the work in machine learning, neural networks, or similar technologies. Violation of this provision may result in legal action.

The story, all names, characters, and incidents portrayed in this production are fictitious. No identification with actual persons (living or deceased), places, buildings, and products in intended or should be inferred.

ISBN: 9798874169886

First edition 2024

Captured in Her Gaze

Jolie Dvorak

Two Hearts Press

Contents

Part One	3
Part Two	135
Part Three	257
About the Author	305
Also by Jolie Dvorak	306
Dear reader	309

Part One

Chapter One

"I don't want to do it."

Thea wiped her fingers on the generous curve of Lollie's arse and followed that with an absentminded slap. She returned to the art table.

There was a groan from the sofa – exhausted *and* exasperated – and the flop of a bare body against the leather. Thea ignored it.

"It's mainstream, commercialised Hollywood bullshit," she said, spitting out each word with contempt. "These are not things that I do."

Thea Voronov was a photographer famous for her art, not empty, overproduced Tinseltown dross.

"For fuck's sake, Thea. That was supposed to take your mind off it, not—"

The whine came to a sudden halt. Lollie was many things – a talented and efficient photography assistant, discreet, capable and organised. Mouthy and crass. She was disrespectful and brave enough to tell Thea exactly what she thought and precisely what Thea sometimes needed to hear. She was also fit, hot and rather a good fuck, and right now, she was naked on the leather sofa in Thea's studio, her chest still heaving, her thighs still quivering from the rush Thea had just pushed through her.

But the thing that made Lollie so very suitable – so very *convenient* – was the thrill she got from obeying Thea's orders.

Thea held up her hand and Lollie shut her mouth.

"I don't want to do it," Thea said again.

She looked at the glossies on the art table. They were agency headshots of two actors. One was a woman she knew well. Older. A friend. A one-time lover. A confidante. Thea's fingers caressed the edge of that print carefully.

The other face was younger. A woman in her mid-twenties looked back at her with a beauty that reached into Thea's soul and tore it apart.

Thea's studio was already set up for tomorrow's shoot – promo pics for a joint campaign for a movie release and a diamond company, not that Thea cared. She and Lollie had spent the last three hours working on it, making sure everything met Thea's exacting standards. Seamless paper drops were spotless, cameras were charged, lights, cables and monitors were set. Of course, Thea insisted that her studio was always maintained at this level of readiness and Lollie knew she'd get her arse whipped if it wasn't.

Lollie *liked* getting her arse whipped, but they'd got the work done. She'd been Thea's assistant for nearly five years, starting as a starry-eyed fangirl, eager to learn the trade from the art world's finest photographer, but she quickly caught Thea's measure. She ran the admin side of Thea's business now – things Thea had no patience for. She wrangled clients, agents, talent and assistants like a pro, but Lollie's real talent was managing Thea's moods.

Thea wasn't ashamed to admit it. She paid the woman enough.

Something about tomorrow's job had wormed its way into Thea's mind and begun to fester.

She looked at the headshot of the younger woman again.

Not something, she corrected herself, annoyed at the admission. *Her*. Memona Swan.

Flawless light brown skin that reflected light like honey. Lustrous jet black hair that glowed like the midnight stars. Hazel eyes incandescent with galaxies.

Memona Swan was the movie world's latest darling. She was a dawning star set to explode like a supernova, with the power of Hollywood's famous StudioOne behind her and a relentless media machine that would see her burn brighter than the sun.

Thea almost felt sorry for her.

She was due in Thea's photography studio tomorrow.

"Almost impossible to believe she's real," Lollie said, softly, coming up behind Thea. "How can anyone be that beautiful?"

She leaned the middle of her back against the tall art table, breezily turning her shoulders to the two actors on the table – megastar of stage and screen, Dame Katherine Cox and the perfect Memona Swan. Lollie was still utterly naked. Thea was fully clothed – her favourite faded skin-tight black jeans and boots, a faded band tee tucked in and crumpled from where Lollie had clutched at it. There was a confusion of chains and jewellery at her throat and an oversized pinstripe blazer pushed to her elbows. Thea liked the power imbalance and Lollie liked to strip. Ordering her to do so was an easy pleasure.

Lollie put her foot up on the table's footrest. It made her thigh stick out. Thea spared it a glance. There was a very pleasing bite mark on it. If she'd been in less of a mood, Thea would have squeezed it playfully, just to watch Lollie squirm, just to hear her beg for Thea to do it again.

Lollie snagged a box of takeaway noodles they hadn't quite finished before the afternoon's work had degenerated into sex. She picked out a baby shrimp and held it delicately between her chopsticks. She frowned at it.

"You made your reputation on commercialised bullshit," Lollie said, mildly. "Don't get all righteous now."

She addressed her words to the shrimp, which Thea thought was wise. Thea wasn't in the mood for anyone's shit right now, especially not Lollie's. If the woman pushed it, if she was deliberately goading Thea because she hoped for a second round, maybe this time with toys, then Thea couldn't promise how gentle she'd be.

Which, again, Lollie would like.

Thea sighed.

The woman was right. There had always been two sides to Thea's work, but it was her dramatic and sometimes quirky studies of celebrities that catapulted her to the top of her profession. Now, she was the world's foremost portrait photographer – as famous as the celebrities who were her subjects. Superstars, giants of the silver screen, musicians, fashion moguls – they all begged to stand before her lens. Their greatness permitted them an audience with Thea in the first place. Once she was done with them, they all emerged shining even brighter.

It was a cycle – exploitative and parasitic. Mutually beneficial but soul-destroying. Ugly.

Thea knew all about the ugly side of life.

This beautiful woman – this Memona Swan – was simply grist for the mill. A beauty this pure was the kind of high-octane fuel that would keep the whole machine running at top gear. Her face, that exquisite pout at the corner of her lips, those cheekbones that were breaking Thea's mind, would fatten bank accounts across the industry – not least Thea's.

There was an innocence in those hazel eyes that had no clue what was about to descend.

"She the reason you don't want to do it, then?" Lollie tilted her head at the photo of Memona.

Lollie was too observant and it annoyed Thea no end. There was, of course, no way she was going to let Lollie know that.

"I'm not interested in photographing the diamond," she tried.

The movie Memona Swan was starring in – the whole reason for tomorrow's shoot – featured a vast diamond. It was supposed to be a historical thing from India, the size of Thea's fist, except in this case it was some kind of created diamond from a company that was as excited as everyone else to be working with Thea Voronov. Both actresses would wear the diamond during the photoshoot and it made for some technical challenges.

"Bullshit. You're scared of *her*." Lollie pointed her chopsticks at the photo of Memona Swan and Thea only just stopped herself from waving them away so they didn't damage the print. She felt protective of the woman even in paper form. She didn't know why.

She shook her head to clear such ridiculous thoughts from it. She was Thea Voronov. She had an eye for beauty and a heart of stone, and the entire industry knew it.

It was a very brave soul who dared to remark on the irony.

"Run me through the schedule again," Thea ordered.

Lollie gave a pleased grunt and swapped her box of noodles for her phone. She thumbed through it, folding her arms under her boobs as she did. Thea took a moment to admire her – full breasts, round hips, classic English-rose skin that always pinked nicely under Thea's hands. She'd put up with the rest of Lollie's impudence if it meant she had something naked and luscious like that decorating her studio.

"Kate in the morning – ten til twelve, then Mem joins for the double until three. You'll have Mem on her own for two hours after that." Lollie paused. "There will be check-ins with the StudioOne people and the diamond company, but I'll handle those. You won't be interrupted," she promised.

Good.

There was a moment's silence. The whole thing was unavoidable at this point. She *could* pitch a fit and refuse – the tantrum would only further cement her reputation as the temperamental genius artist, but she couldn't be bothered dealing with the fallout. Her publicist, Adiatu, would bitch and moan. Her friend and business partner, Jasper, would be less nice about it. And the gig *would* drop an outrageous amount of money into her bank account. Not that she needed it.

She found herself slightly interested in the beautiful Memona Swan, but the girl was likely to be very much the same as every other vacant, greedy starlet climbing to success. Sure, she wouldn't say no if this pretty Mem girl wanted to play. She wouldn't mind having all that beauty at her service at all...

Lollie nudged her with her shoulder. "This isn't like you, Thea. Just take the girl's picture and be done with it."

"I'm fine," she snapped. "It's an easy brief. Simple. You could do it."

"Gee. Thanks, boss."

"It will be good to work with Kate again," Thea murmured, her mind back on the job. She had some ideas beyond what StudioOne wanted that she could try with Kate. Thea was Kate's preferred photographer and they'd known each other for years. In all the ways. "I've always done Kate."

"Haven't you, though," muttered Lollie.

Cheek like that deserved a slapped thigh and the squeak Lollie made snapped Thea out of her mood.

"I think that's just about enough of your attitude."

"Planning on *doing her* again?" Lollie asked, blithe and as cheerful as ever. Nothing got to Lollie. It was a no-strings relationship so low key it was absent the merest thread. "You know she's shagging someone new now? You want me to make up the bed? A hundred quid says Kate won't let you get her into it tomorrow."

The second room of the studio contained a king sized bed. Most of the industry knew that too. Sometimes Thea used it for particular photo shoots. Sometimes she didn't bother taking a camera in at all.

Thea gave a wolfish smile. "If you want to play that game, just hand your money over now." Katherine Cox might be ten years older than Thea but she'd always enjoyed Thea's games. Thea had a very private album of some very intimate photos of Kate and the actor was generally up for adding to it. "All I need to do is leave the black ropes on the pillow and Kate just falls into my bed."

Lollie sighed dramatically and fanned her face. "Oh god, yes. Those photos were magnificent. Dame Katherine Cox all tied up like—"

"You weren't supposed to see those!"

Lollie poked her tongue out. "I'm your assistant. I see everything."

They both laughed. Thea stepped into Lollie's space pressing her back against the art table.

"What's the bet for Memona Swan?" she asked.

It would be one way to get the woman out of her head, she supposed. Her headshot was on the table behind Lollie. Devastating eyes. Flawless skin. Thea wondered what it might look like tied up in black silk rope.

"Ooo, now we're talking," Lollie grinned. She opened her legs to let Thea press a thigh between them. "You think you can pull a babe like that? On a first shoot?" It was a decidedly brattish challenge. "That is one seriously gorgeous woman. Maybe she's straight. Maybe she's vanilla. Maybe she wouldn't like your shit."

Thea's hand crept into Lollie's hair and tangled there. She tugged on her hair and watched her throat lengthen as her head tipped back.

"You think I can't?" Thea growled in her ear. Lollie's skin crinkled into gooseflesh. "I'm Thea Voronov."

"You're cocky as fuck."

Thea pressed up with her thigh. Lollie's eyes rolled back and Thea palmed her breast hard.

"The red satin sheets," she ordered.

Lollie moved her hips against Thea's thigh and Thea dropped one hand to her arse, squeezing the flesh she found there and helping the woman keep her rhythm. She'd help her right to her edge and then command her to stop. Watching her struggle to obey was most of the fun.

"Wuh?"

"They'll go best with Mem's skin tones."

Lollie's eyes snapped to Thea's. Amused irritation just managed to show beneath her lust.

"You think you're so good," she panted.

Thea pushed two fingers inside her without warning and laughed at her moan. Lollie braced herself against Thea's shoulders.

"You know I am."

"Two hundred quid," Lollie muttered between thrusts. It was her turn to laugh at Thea's expression. Goading. "Unless you think you're losing your touch."

That hit harder than she expected. Maybe she was, but she wasn't going to let Lollie get away with that either. Her free hand circled Lollie's throat and, with her fingers still between the woman's legs, she danced her back to the sofa. Lollie collapsed backwards onto it with a delighted giggle and spread her thighs wide. Thea sank deeper inside her and watched each curl of her fingers arch the girl's back. When a few sharp slaps reminded Lollie to beg – just the way Thea liked her to – she added her mouth to her task and showed her how very precisely her touch was still under her command.

Lollie's wails were almost performative.

Was she losing her touch?

Thea was the very best at what she did. Her photography drove the fashion world, the art scene and the film industry. Global media empires begged for her gaze. She had the power to shoot wannabes to instant stardom, she documented the lives of mega-celebrities, queens, kings, billionaires and presidents. Her exhibitions were red carpet events in London, New York, Paris and Milan. All of Europe, all of the arts world fawned over her, grovelled for the focus of her lens. Worshipped her.

And it all felt empty.

Which was why she'd fuck Lollie now then send her home. Maybe she'd retreat to the house, down half a bottle of something twenty-five years old and sleep it off alone. Maybe she'd head out into the streets, into the gritty, forgotten parts of London and take photos of the ugliness of life – the reality of the world that was far more interesting, far more *familiar* than the mainstream, commercialised bullshit she created here.

Lollie drilled her heels into Thea's back. Thea lifted her, pushed her and watched her prettiness mottle and spoil. Stuck in her mood, she even missed the moment to have her bit of fun and deny Lollie hers. The girl sneered and grunted and growled her way through her orgasm, greedy and careless in the way she cried Thea's name. She didn't need Thea. Lollie barely even wanted her. This was just a perk of the job.

Thea wiped her mouth and didn't care either. She was back where she'd started.

She didn't want to do this. She was done with seeing the few things that were truly beautiful turn sour.

Lollie panted for a few moments and then smiled. She reached for the button of Thea's jeans. Her skin was still blotchy.

"Let me," she simpered.

So Thea let her. Held her by the hair just where she wanted her and took her meagre pleasure.

And afterwards felt just as empty.

She wondered about Memona Swan's beauty and if it was just as shallow.

Chapter Two

"For a superstar, you're pretty handy with a drill."

The two friends stood back and looked proudly at their handiwork – a re-re-assembled, third-hand Ikea bedside table with its wobbly wonkiness screwed right out of it. It was good for another few years now.

The words took a few moments to sink through the glow of achievement and settle in Mem's mind. She pointed the drill like a gun and revved it like a badass.

"I'm not a superstar, you dick."

Piper hammed it up. This was a new habit she'd gotten into since Mem's role in her latest movie and she wasn't sure she liked it. She was a goofball, though. Piper clapped both hands over her heart like a 1920s silent movie heroine and struck a pose of melodramatic cheese, her lips open in an O of anguish. Milking it – or maybe mocking Mem's role, she couldn't decide – Piper pressed the back of one hand to her forehead.

"Oh darling, how you wound me," she cried, upper class English accent dialled up to eleven. She collapsed artfully backwards onto the single bed behind her.

As she fell, her foot kicked the tray of screws they'd been using to fix the bedside table. Three hundred tek screws tipped over the wooden floorboards and spiralled around the room.

"Fuck." Piper was herself again.

Mem rolled her eyes. "Idiot."

There was a beat and their eyes met. They dissolved into snort-giggles and knelt to clean up the mess.

Mem Swan was not a superstar. Well, not yet anyway. Right now, she stood on the precipice of fame. Yawning in front of her was a canyon of press junkets, step-and-repeats at red carpet events and the mindless repetition of back-to-back interviews. It was coming. There was no stopping it now.

Which was why she valued the quiet, ordinary moments like these. Preferably without Piper being a twit.

Something else occurred to her.

"Why would being a superstar and being handy with the tools be mutually exclusive?" she asked, archly.

Piper grunted. She was half under the bed reaching for a screw. "I was making fun of you," she said. "Got it!" She emerged with a triumphant grin and tossed the offending screw into the box. "I was making fun of both of us, really. It's a stretch to say that either of us are 'handy with the tools' – lesbian stereotype or no – but we're learning, aren't we? I think we've done really well here."

Mem looked around the small room with approval. It was plain. Not bare – they'd done their best to make sure it wasn't that. Homey. The single bed sported a crocheted blanket in bright granny squares. There was a bookcase, a wardrobe with a mirror edged with stickers that said *You are beautiful*, *You are bold*, and *You are loved*. And the bedside table. All carefully thrifted, lovingly cleaned and repaired.

Piper spread a handmade rag rug in the centre of the room and Mem placed a small vintage vase on the bedside table. There was a short-stemmed yellow rose in it that she'd pinched from the neighbour's garden that morning.

"It's nice," she said. Piper smiled.

"One more room in Heart and Grace House. One more woman we can help," Piper said.

She held up her hand and Mem slapped her palm into it in a happy high five. They gathered up their tools and headed to the next room. The wooden bedframe they'd painted yesterday was waiting to be reassembled. Mem revved her drill.

Piper grimaced. "Not sure why we're fucking around with crappy old furniture from Gumtree though, when you're earning an absolute fortune."

"Because we don't know how long it will last. We've got to make the money stretch as far as we can." Mem had said this a hundred times before.

"Babes, I do the books here. I've *seen* what you've donated to this shelter. There is a tonne more stretch in those deposits of yours, let me tell you."

Mem thumped her, as cheerfully as she could. She hated discussions about money, especially about the obscene numbers she was earning these days, but Piper was her best friend and had been since they were eight. She wasn't going to hide anything from Piper.

"And food and utilities are more expensive and more important. We need to prioritise."

Piper relented. "I know. I'm just having a whinge. I've still got paint in my hair from yesterday. You're going to be in trouble for that for quite a while."

Piper was Black and short with a low centre of gravity. She had a quirky taste in overalls and bright shirts rolled to her shoulders. She wore her hair in an exuberant blow out that floated free around her face, and she'd been filthy mad – in a best-friends kinda way – when yesterday's painting session had degenerated into a paint fight.

She grinned. "I love what we're doing, though. Plus, you're pretty hot with power tools."

Mem shot her with her drill gun again. "Fuck off, Pipes. You know I love you, but I'm not your type."

"I'm willing to look past that to the movie star status and the million dollar paycheck."

Piper laughed. Mem tried to match it.

She failed.

Piper leaned two bits of bed frame together and looked at Mem keenly. "You alright, babes?" she asked, quietly. "Want to tell me about it?" she added, when Mem didn't answer.

Mem sighed. She didn't really. She bolted the bedhead onto the rest of the frame.

A year and a half ago, Mem had been waiting tables at a gastropub in Camden. She'd put a steak and chips down in front of a man who'd stared up at her with his eyes wide and his mouth hanging open. That wasn't a particularly rare occurrence for Mem – Mem was beautiful – but it was what he said next that would change her life.

"You wanna be in the movies?"

She'd laughed in his face. Mem heard lines like that all the time – and this one was particularly lame. People saw beauty as fair game. Inappropriate advances were her lot in life. Her Indian/Pakistani background generally added an extra layer of disrespect, though her beauty confused it. Watching society's cultural biases tie themselves in knots was never a hoot.

But this wasn't a line. It turned out to be an honest-to-god job offer. The guy was directing a low budget horror film and had just lost his leading lady to a better offer. He needed someone fast, and as he said, Mem didn't just fit the bill, she exceeded it so utterly and completely she was going to catapult the lot of them to stardom.

It only took one look at her shitty tips that night and the smell of chip oil in her hair again to call the guy up and accept his offer.

They made that first movie and it achieved cult status in weeks. Mem was just discussing a sequel with the man and wondering if she should get an agent when StudioOne called her.

Then the whole thing kicked into hyperdrive.

What was bothering her now was just more of the insecurity that had been plaguing her ever since she'd started this wild ride. But Piper cared. She was real and genuine – and that was something rare, not just in Mem's new profession, but in her whole life.

"Agh, it's nothing. Just another set of new experiences I have to get used to. Now filming is over, it's all publicity stuff and, somehow, that's kinda harder than everything else."

"No script?"

Mem nodded. "Exactly. I'm not an actor. Never have been. I was just in the right place at the right time, and when someone gave me the words to say, told me what to do and how to be, and there was a running schedule and make-up artists and hairdressers and dialogue coaches, well"—she shrugged—"I was just the product of everyone else's work. A doll. It was easy."

Piper pulled a face. Mem gestured at the bed-end. They wedged it against the frame and Piper slotted screws into the appropriate holes.

"And now?"

"Now media people ask me questions – personal stuff that I never know how to answer – and I get booked with famous portrait photographers for an entire day and I've got no idea—"

Piper held up a hand and narrowed her eyes. "Woah. Famous portrait photographers? Like who?"

"Thea Voronov."

"Bull*shit*."

"Tomorrow. At her house and studio, apparently." Mem grimaced. "All afternoon."

The bed was standing by itself. Together they wrestled the mattress onto the base and collapsed down onto it. Mem flopped onto her back and looked at the ceiling. Piper did the same. They might have been thirteen years old again hanging out after school in Piper's bedroom.

"It's an art shoot for StudioOne, for the diamond company and for some magazine. I don't know which one. It's just me, Kate and this Thea person. Apparently she's one of the best. According to Adiatu, even Annie Leibovitz thinks she's brilliant. Armani pays her millions for perfume campaigns. And I'm freaking out about it."

"Why?"

Mem sighed with exasperation. "Oh my god, Piper, the usual reasons, okay? I'm not— I'm not an actor. I'm not the talent they think I am. All I am is a pretty face. Sooner or later, I'll fuck up and they'll realise that's all I am. A pretty face with nothing behind it. And when I do, you can guarantee there will be someone there to catch it on camera."

There was a silence.

"I tripped down the stairs of my trailer the other day and some pap with a long lens put it all over the Daily Mail. I looked like an idiot."

Piper squeezed her hand. "I didn't see it," she said.

"Sorry," Mem said. "I'm just freaking out. As usual."

Piper squeezed her hand. "Imposter syndrome's got you hard, hasn't it?"

Mem blew a sigh to the ceiling. Syndrome? This was real. She wasn't an actor. She literally *was* an imposter in the role.

"Shut up, Pipes."

"Screw you, babes," Piper said, mild as ever, then her tone got serious. "First up, you're way more than just a doll, so please don't let me hear you say anything like that again. I know you, girl. I know you think people only see you for your beauty, but I know the person inside, and Mem – you're amazing. Look at what you've done here in just a few short months. This place is making a real difference to people who need it, and your heart is all over it. And look at how you've absolutely conquered StudioOne. You're way stronger than you think."

"Don't get all mushy on me," muttered Mem.

Piper dug her in the ribs. "Insightful, caring and confidence-building, you dick, not mushy."

Mem smiled. Everyone needed a friend like Piper.

"And second, don't freak about Thea Voronov. My mum knows her—"

"Oh god, of course she does. Is there anyone your mum doesn't know?"

"—and she does beautiful work. You'll be fine. You've been fine up til now, haven't you?"

Mem had to admit that was true. Every new stage in the movie-making process had been terrifying and Mem woke up in cold sweats most nights thinking about the next day's work, but Piper was right. She hadn't fucked up. Yet.

"And this is your last movie. You're nearly there. We have a plan, right?"

Piper waved a hand around the room.

Heart and Grace House was a women's refuge and shelter. Piper and Mem had built it in a row house in Clapham Common with their bare hands and almost all of Mem's paychecks from her first movie. Her per diem filming allowance from StudioOne kept it ticking along too. They were putting the obscene money back into a good cause and helping homeless women and women escaping domestic violence.

Mem's utterly first world problems were for a good cause. She could do this.

"Yeah," Mem whispered. "We have a plan. And you're right. I'll be fine. I'm just having a wobble."

Piper chuckled and rolled her eyes. "Another one."

It made Mem laugh. "Fuck, you're awful, mate." She sat up and swatted Piper on the arm. "Your supportive friend schtick still needs work, you know."

"Pfft. You're the actor."

Mem howled in outrage and Piper giggled triumphantly. Piper stretched out on the bare mattress with her arms above her head, her eyes closed and a very satisfied look on her face. It was too much for Mem.

She tore one of the new pillows from its plastic wrap and whacked Piper soundly in the gut with it.

"Ooof."

The resulting pillow fight added twenty minutes and a few stray feathers to their work schedule but it was worth it. Mem's mardy mood lifted and the apprehension about the following day's photo shoot fell into the back of her mind. Piper and Mem made up the bed in the new room, complete with a patchwork quilt they'd thrifted from a charity store. They gazed contentedly at their handiwork.

"You know Thea Voronov is one of London's hottest – and most reclusive – celesbians, don't you?" said Piper. "And you're going to spend the whole day with her. I could possibly be jealous."

Mem felt the worry stir in the pit of her stomach again.

"Rumour has it she likes to shag the beautiful women who sit before her lens."

"Thought you were trying to make me feel better."

"You might get lucky, is all I'm saying. After all, some people seem to think you're reasonably attractive." Piper said it with a dead straight face.

Mem threatened her with the pillow again.

Piper grinned.

"Not interested," Mem sighed. And she wasn't. There was only one reason Mem was doing this movie and that was to fund the shelter. Hot celesbians just weren't on her radar. In fact, she wasn't interested in hot anythings. *Everyone* Mem had ever dated had seen her as eye-candy, as decoration for their own style. The hot ones were the worst. Mem could live without it. She had plenty of other things to worry about.

"How do you even know this?" Mem exclaimed, suddenly. "You're a maths nerd. When was the last time you cared about celebrity gossip? Is celesbian even a word?" She pulled a face. "You do remember we're from Clapham, right? I'm just plain old Mem Swan. What hot celesbian is going to be interested in me?"

She bent to pick up their tools and didn't see Piper's doubtful look. As she swept out the door, she didn't hear Piper's long suffering sigh or her sad whisper either.

"Oh, Mem. There's nothing plain about you, babes."

Chapter Three

Dame Katherine Cox was Hollywood royalty.

She was also two hours early.

She knocked on Thea's back door before the usual paps had gathered at her front gate, before even the keenest StudioOne people had arrived. She used their secret code and it made Thea smile.

All the same, Thea greeted her with a condescending eyebrow – and Kate saw right through it.

"Don't be a grump," she said as a greeting, and stepped in close to kiss Thea fair on the mouth. She laughed when Thea took the kiss for herself, slipping a hand around Kate's back and pulling her in to bite at her lower lip. "Hey! None of that. I brought breakfast."

Kate was tall and slim and in fantastic shape for her forty-nine years. London born and bred, she'd started treading boards at three years of age, playing the sweetest of fairies in her parent's West End production of *A Midsummer Night's Dream*. That led to cute-kid roles on British sit-coms, which attracted the angsty-teen roles in low-budget American movies. She landed her first Hollywood blockbuster in her early twenties, nailed it, and had picked her roles ever since. She had more Oscars, Golden Globes and BAFTAs than almost any actress in history and ruled the film industry like an empress.

Thea had known her from the very beginning. She was a friend of Jasper's – their fathers had gone to the same posh boys' school. She might present a polished, sophisticated demeanour to the rest of the world, but Katherine Cox had her own addictions, her own needs.

It just so happened that Kate's desires and Thea's converged – usually in a bed, often with cuffs, velvet and leather, and always with Kate on her knees.

She was an exquisite moaner.

Kate was an old-hand at events like this one. She knew how to avoid paparazzi before the main event and she knew how to snatch moments of peace from the jaws of chaos. More importantly, she knew Mrs Titov, Thea's neighbour over the back fence. She knew how to sneak through the woman's garden to get into Thea's. That was a trick Thea had taught her years ago, when sending the famous Katherine Cox out the front door of her house and into the blinding flash of the paparazzi with rope marks and love bites still on her throat was not the best thing for her career.

But *two* hours before a shoot was keen, even for Kate.

"Not that I don't enjoy seeing you," said Thea, "but what are you doing here so early?"

Kate pecked at her cheek again, then strolled through Thea's house like she owned it. She let Lollie and Jasper in at the front door.

"Business," she called over her shoulder.

"Fuck," Thea muttered.

Thea had barely slept. Images of Memona Swan's perfect complexion had paraded across her mind's eye all night. Fevered dreams about the rest of the woman's body had tormented what little sleep she'd got. She didn't need this.

Lollie pressed a coffee into each person's hands and they headed out to the studio – the barn-type building in Thea's back garden.

This had been planned without her, Thea realised. It did nothing for her mood.

"Eat!" Kate told her, pushing a bowl into her hand. "Superfoods. It's good for you." She tsked at Thea's eye roll. "Someone needs to look after you, love."

Thea took the bowl from her. Kate's eyes flickered down for a moment and Thea noticed the tiniest blush – absolutely endearing on a woman of Kate's stature but evidence of the power she allowed Thea to have over her. They settled at the art table. Thea's bowl contained nuts and berries, all scattered on top of what was probably – knowing Kate – unsweetened yoghurt. A wedge of waffle had been thrust into the yoghurt and the whole thing was drizzled with honey and sprinkled with what looked distinctly like sand.

"What is this?" she asked, flatly.

A long arm wrapped itself over her shoulder and gave her a squeeze.

"It's healthy, Theadora Voronov. Not something I expect you to understand, but why don't you just go with it. Dame Katherine's gone to a lot of trouble."

That was Jasper Fitz-Stewart, Earl of Ravensworth, CEO of Spectrum Media and founder and creative director of Luxe, Adore and X magazines, plus a stable of others. He was Thea's long-time friend and fellow photography nerd, and a complete pain in the arse. A handsome, amiable and annoyingly bloody cheerful one at that.

"Dame Katherine paid a caterer," Thea growled.

"I did not! And don't call me that, Jasper."

Jasper poked out his tongue.

Kate tossed a grape at him. "Enough with the 'dame' rubbish, thank you. I wish I'd never accepted that honour. It makes me feel old."

"You are old." Lollie didn't look up from her phone.

Thea smacked the back of her head.

"What?" squawked Lollie.

"Forty-nine is not old," Thea told her. "*Kate* is not old."

Kate was eleven years older than Thea. It only fueled their dynamic.

"I've never thought I was," Kate said, blithely. She sipped her coffee and shuffled through the headshots that were still on the table from yesterday until she found one of hers. She held it up. "Look at this woman, though. I can see my mother in my face for the first time in my life. This silly 'dame' title just rubs it in."

"Yo mumma's hot too." Jasper ducked when Kate pegged another grape at him. "But that's not what we're here for. Shall we get to business?"

"Please do," said Thea. "Explain what you're doing here two full hours before you're supposed to be." She shot Lollie a death ray. The woman had mentioned nothing of this yesterday. Thea would take great care in extracting a suitable apology from her later.

"CreatedDiamonds," announced Jasper. "They're the company who provided the diamonds for the movie – the big one you'll be playing with today and all the rest of the jewels. First British company in the laboratory-grown diamond space with a very prestigious group of investors backing it. Manufacturing facilities in India and China. Expect their brand to absolutely explode once this movie hits the screens."

Thea blinked at him. "What the fuck is a laboratory grown diamond?"

Jasper chuckled. He snapped his fingers at Lollie and looked very pleased with himself. "Pay up."

Lollie grumbled. "You live under a bloody rock, Thea, I swear. We've been working on how to photograph this damn diamond for days now. Do you even *read*?" And then – instantly – "Sorry." A tenner changed hands.

Thea raised an eyebrow. Lollie, at least, had the grace to redden slightly and fiddle with her phone again. Jasper looked as cocky as ever.

"Lab-grown diamonds are just the same as natural diamonds." Kate played the peace-maker. "Apparently they were ugly brown things back in the day, but the technology has really taken off. Even the best jewellers can't tell the difference now – not without specialised equipment. We've been working with lab-grown diamonds all the way through filming and, well, I've worn plenty of Cartier, Graf and Harry Winston on red carpets in my time and I know my diamonds, but these ones are stunning."

"And they're a quarter of the price," added Lollie, cheerful again. "My sister's engagement ring looks like something from the Crown Jewels and it's an actual, real-life diamond. And her Andy is an apprentice plumber, for fuck's sake. It's not like he—"

Thea held up her hand.

Jasper pulled a folder from his satchel and spread it on the table. Inside was a mix of marketing materials from CreatedDimaonds, print-outs of various news articles and pages of spreadsheets all with columns of numbers. He pushed one particular page towards her but Thea averted her eyes.

"Lab-grown diamonds put genuine jewels in reach of everyone," said Jasper. "Bigger diamonds, higher-quality than ever before. Major industry disruption. Russia produces more diamonds than any country in the world, but with global sanctions against them, their gems aren't making it to market. De Beers convinced the world that diamonds were forever, but nobody wants to declare their love with a tiny rock that fucks up the environment and denies miners in Africa a living wage. Your movie"—he nodded at Kate—"will reveal the power of lab-grown diamonds to billions of people around the world, *and*"—he couldn't stop a grin— "if we ride the wave, all this will make us stupidly rich."

There was a silence. The morning sunlight slanted through the high windows of Thea's studio and lit individual strands of Kate's red hair. A breath of it touched her cheek. It was far more interesting than anything Jasper was going on about.

"You already are," Thea told Jasper. "Rich *and* stupid, actually." She slugged back her coffee and ignored his snort. "I don't see what this has to do with me."

They were all watching her carefully. Plainly, this had quite a bit to do with her.

"CreatedDiamonds want Kate and Mem as brand ambassadors, and they want your lens shooting all their campaigns."

There was a strained silence.

"I don't do—"

Everyone began talking at once.

"You know they're actually green diamonds – environmentally, that is," babbled Kate. "And I'll be committing nearly all of what I earn back into my wildlife charities."

"I've put all my savings into it, and Jasper says shares are rising every day." Lollie's brightness looked desperate.

"All my magazines will be backing this up," grinned Jasper. "It will be just like old times – and there's six zeros in it for you, love. At least."

None of this moved Thea one bit.

She watched the light catch on the droplets of steam rising from her coffee.

"And Memona Swan?" she asked, softly. "What does she get out of this? Seems like this is a simple deal for our respective agents to thrash out with this diamond company's people. Why are *we* having this meeting at all?"

Lollie coughed and looked at her fingernails. Jasper shuffled his papers. They both looked expectantly at Kate.

Thea waited. She didn't know what this shit was but it was beginning to annoy her. She had a full day of shooting ahead of her and she didn't need this cloak-and-daggers idiocy now. When nobody spoke, she shot an impatient eyebrow at Kate and had the pleasure of seeing her flush and lower her gaze, eyelids fluttering, just as if Thea had demanded she drop to her knees for her.

It was delicious, but it didn't explain what the fuck was going on.

Jasper looked between them and groaned. "God, Kate. You're supposed to be the world's finest actor."

Lollie whacked his arm. "She is," she hissed.

"So, persuade the *tsarina* here to do the job for us."

That was a little ripe, Thea thought, considering Jasper was an actual earl.

"It's a package deal, Thea," Kate said, softly. "The diamond company, StudioOne, you, me and Mem Swan. It will be the most enviable collaboration on the planet. I know you'll bitch and moan about it for a little while, but eventually you'll join us because it's Jasper and me – but Mem is the sticking point."

The beautiful Memona Swan who Thea had dreamt about all last night, whose eyes outshone any diamond, whose beauty could turn even the brightest crystal to dust.

She pretended to be interested. "How so?"

"She wants out." Kate shrugged as if the concept was incomprehensible. "She's a lovely girl – really is. I like her a lot. She's talented, a little bit shy, humble and down-to-earth – rare qualities in this industry and for someone so beautiful – but she's said it over and over again. This is her last movie and after this, she's out." She fixed Thea with a look that was a heady mix of complications for such an early hour of the day. "You have to talk her into it."

"What? Why me?"

Kate blinked. There was something pleading in her eyes. Regret too. Maybe an apology. Something that looked awfully like goodbye.

"Why. Me?"

Lollie had none of Kate's grace. "Because you're infatuated with her."

Out the corner of her eye, Thea saw Jasper swat Lollie on the arm. All three of them watched her like she was a bomb about to explode.

"Because she's just your type, Thea, darling," said Kate, gently. "You captured me, back in the day. You created me." She reached across the table for her hand. "Do the same for her."

Thea went very still, then stood up in a burst of movement and strode to the glass door. She stood with her hands on her hips and stared at her garden. She despised being pushed around like this, but Kate had said something that pretty much defined who Thea was.

Thea could dig her heels in and have her ice-queen moment but they all knew she wouldn't. She'd do it for Jasper and Kate. She may have made them, her art might have propelled both of them into the stratosphere and they might have been nothing at all without her, but she owed them.

She'd been nineteen and living on the streets when Jasper and Kate had saved her. Her life had fallen apart – as anyone's would when their father was convicted of heading a crime-ring that spanned Europe. She'd been homeless and alone, and the media had hounded her every move. She'd barely known Jasper then. He'd been an acquaintance at the art college Thea was flunking out of, and a pretentious one at that. Certainly not a friend. But Thea, Jasper and Kate had saved each other – or used each other – a hundred times over since then, depending on how you wanted to look at it.

Of course she'd do it.

She ran both her hands up through her hair and blew out an explosive sigh.

Behind her she heard Jasper and Lollie smack their hands together in a high five. They began discussing strategy almost immediately, Jasper plying Lollie for details on the executives who'd be at the shoot later that day and Lollie sharing everything she knew. She was as canny as Jasper, when Thea thought about it.

She almost didn't hear Kate come up beside her.

A head landed on her shoulder. The gesture had all the softness of late, late nights spent together, both of them breathless, Kate seeking out Thea's gentle side with an unshakable trust that it was actually there.

Why did this feel like an ending?

"Thank you, Thea. I'm glad you're with us."

"You make it sound like you didn't think I would be."

Kate's cheek rubbed against her shoulder. Thea wanted to fall into her but they had a whole day of work ahead of them.

"You'll like her, Thea, darling. I know you will. And maybe—" Kate pulled back to look at her, all cheekbones and earnest green eyes "—maybe she'll be just what you need."

"I don't need anyone," Thea said, automatically.

The doorbell rang. It was the bell on the front door of the house, rigged to ring out here in the studio. The first of the screaming hoards had arrived. Adiatu, probably, and her troupe of publicity monsters and stylists. The StudioOne creatives wouldn't be far behind.

That was enough time wasted on whatever this was.

Thea clapped her hands.

"Lollie! Off your arse! Jasper, get the fuck out of my studio. Katherine, see him to the door. I have work to do."

She stalked off to her circle of screens, flicking on lights and gear as she went. The brilliant and mercurial artist in her eyrie. Untouchable and unapproachable.

To her gratification, they scattered. Kate gathered up her breakfast hamper before she went and paused at the door, looking back at Thea as she did.

Thea hardly spared her a glance.

"You *do* need someone, Thea," she whispered. "Please don't close your heart to this one."

That didn't even need an answer. Thea didn't have a heart.

"Get out, Kate."

Chapter Four

A scrum of photographers was waiting for her.

Thea's house was in Gloucester Crescent in Camden – a four-storey row house in beige London bricks with white corner stones. As exclusive as hell, though Mem thought of the artists and bohemians the place was famous for in the 60s and wondered if that was why Thea was here. Eight men all wielding cameras like weapons called to her from the footpath.

She stepped out of the fancy black car the studio had arranged for her and into the noise.

Vultures.

She'd chosen this, she reminded herself. She could do it. She was here to be photographed. What were a few happy snaps for the paps? She flashed them one of her more dazzling smiles – the one that slayed men in the streets, the one that opened doors and ensured she never paid for a drink at the pub.

"Beautiful, Mem, darlin'," called one. "Look here, luv?"

She knew this man. She'd seen him before at rope lines, hovering at the edge of the crowd control barriers whenever they'd filmed outdoors on location. He was a patronising arsehole, but his photos were always good. He sold to Spectrum Media and the more expensive image libraries, and his pics ended up in all the higher class publications and news services. She gave him her sultry smile. Watched it hit him hard and jam his finger down on the shutter.

Cameras clicked and whirred like machine guns.

"That's our girl," he grinned. "You gonna smile like that for Thea Voronov?"

The group laughed – a low grumble of male voices that managed to sound threatening even though Mem knew they were all mostly harmless.

"Thea is going to fucking eat her alive," she heard one mutter.

"Nice work, well done."

Mem's agent greeted her at Thea's front door – as far as she ever greeted anyone. Business was alway more important for Adiatu. She was a Sierra Leonean power-woman, tall and fierce with a predilection for sharp navy suits, towering heels and an intimidating amount of gold jewellery. Her long black hair was twisted into thick locs and piled on her head like a crown. She was Kate Cox's agent too, and Thea Voronov's, and Kate said Mem was lucky to have her. Adiatu took no shit from paparazzi or fledgling movie stars alike.

Mem hadn't yet decided if she liked her.

"Not bad," the woman decreed, having swept an assessing gaze over Mem's clothes. "You actually listening to that stylist I found for you?"

Mem would have liked to have shown up in her usual jeans and t-shirt, tattered olive-green Converse, and a woollen beanie pulled down to her ears, but today she'd dressed up. It stopped Adiatu's snarky remarks if nothing else. Dark blue skinny jeans and a blazer over a cami so low it looked like she wore nothing beneath it. Appearances, Adiatu never tired of telling her, were everything.

Obviously, she'd known there'd be paps.

Adiatu didn't wait for Mem's answer but led her through to an open, airy kitchen which flowed through to a glassed conservatory, all white walls and generous cane furniture. A cup of coffee was pressed into Mem's hand.

The scene was the kind of ordered chaos Mem was beginning to find familiar.

Costume racks were pressed against the walls. A handful of executives from StudioOne muttered in a group, all serious and suits with phones to their ears. One of the assistant directors from the first unit was in discussion with a woman from the costume team, one of Mem's gowns from the movie held up between them. Mem recognised a line producer too and one of the runners. Portable mirrors and lights had been set up at what might have been Thea Voronov's kitchen table, the surface of which was scattered with large glossy photographs. Neglected cups of coffee steamed gently in the noise.

There were at least twenty people in the room. None of them were Thea Voronov.

That was a tiny relief.

"She's here," announced Adiatu.

Every person in the room looked at Mem.

She was used to this now, though it had taken a while.

"Hi everyone," she said, glad her brightness didn't sound as fake as it felt. "Where do you want me?"

She had three seconds of grace before the chaos swirled around her and pulled her under.

At least she knew the make-up artist.

Benny wrapped her in a huge hug once the hairdressers were done with her.

"Missed you since the shoot finished, darls. I've been working for Adore magazine – you know, with truly beautiful people who don't challenge my skills at all." He grinned at Mem. "Guess I have to work for my money again."

Mem swatted him on the arm. "Shut up, Benny," she said, smiling back. "I've missed you too."

She had. She really had. Benny was Australian and called a spade an ever-loving shovel. His level headedness and kind words of encouragement practically got Mem through the whole shoot.

Working on *The Wolverton Diamond* had been six gruelling months of faking it in front of the cast and crew of one of Hollywood's biggest movie studios. Mem's first movie – the zombie flick with the guy from the gastropub – had been more running and screaming than actual acting. The vibe on set had been casual. It had been a laugh and slightly better money than waiting tables, and that was all Mem had expected from it. But *The Wolverton Diamond* was on a whole other level. StudioOne's retelling of the treasured English tale had filmed in London and Mumbai with a joint US, UK and Indian crew. It was a StudioOne and Britflix collaboration with a budget bigger than several third world countries. Memona Swan in the lead role. Dame Katherine Cox, no less, as her co-star.

No pressure then.

Benny met her most mornings in the make-up trailer – wherever they were – sometimes at four or five a.m. He always made sure she was topped up with coffee and confidence and a good sense of perspective.

He saw through all the bullshit.

And he knew all her tells. He clocked the doubt that must have been showing in her face right now.

"Come on," he said, gently. He was a sensitive soul, really. He held out a chair in front of his mirror and his case of gear. "Let's get some slap on this ugly mug of yours." He ignored the shocked looks from studio officials around them and bent to whisper in her ear. "And don't worry. Thea Voronov is going to go crazy for you."

Memona Swan was beautiful.

It wasn't conceit to say it. Mem had known it all her life.

Sure, every child thinks they're beautiful at one point. If they have loving parents, of course. Kids believe what they're told – *Aren't you the prettiest thing? Don't you look gorgeous in that dress? Oh, you're so sweet I could dunk you in my tea!*

It was deeply problematic, but what five-year-old knew that?

For most kids, reality didn't hit until the end of primary school when the compliments slowed, then dried up altogether and puberty raised its gangly, spotty head. Mem watched all her friends go through it – that gloomy realisation that they were never going to be supermodels. Prince Charming, if the guy was even around, wasn't going to look twice. Most of Mem's friends took it well. Only a few took the emo road. Even fewer went into denial and developed addictions to beauty products and salons. There was something to be said for the internet and social media, Mem thought, despite how much the Boomers railed at it.

There was a refreshingly healthy bunch of ordinary people on TikTok.

But Mem Swan wasn't ordinary.

She had been a beautiful baby, a beautiful toddler and a beautiful child. Puberty had been kind and, if anything, her beauty had only deepened. Ripened.

It taught her who her friends were. Jealousy was a very powerful force.

And it taught her how to hide. When beauty was all people saw, it was easier to simply disappear under baggy clothes, dark glasses and an old baseball cap.

That first zombie movie had blown her cover, but *The Wolverton Diamond* had amplified it a hundredfold. Already Mem's face was recognised globally. She'd seen herself on billboards, on YouTube ads, on the sides of London's red double-decker buses.

There was nowhere left to hide.

Benny pressed foundation onto her skin.

"You met her yet?" he asked, quietly.

Mem shook her head. When Benny tutted and raised an eyebrow, she rolled her eyes. She always fidgeted in his chair.

Her phone buzzed. A text from Piper.

— *Have you seen her yet?* —

"I met her about two hours ago when I was doing Kate," said Benny. "I'm still recovering. Quaking in my shoes, I was. She's fucking terrifying."

"Oh, great."

She tapped out a message to Piper.

— *No, I haven't. And calm down. I'm fine* —

"Just letting you know what you're in for," said Benny, blithely working on her eyes. "She swept in here like a tornado and demanded to know who was doing Kate's make-up and who was doing yours." He waved an eyeliner pen at the general crowd. "That lot dobbed me in like the cowards they are and suddenly I was in the eye of the storm."

Mem held her phone up so she could read Piper's response.

— *You shouldn't have spent all last night googling her* —

That was a fair call. Reading about the woman's many awards and accolades hadn't helped Mem's nerves at all.

"I mean, she actually went through my kit and chucked stuff out. 'None of this, none of that,' she said. 'I want to see them exactly as they are. I don't want to see *you*.'" Benny affected an impatient, angry voice as he imitated her, one hand on his hip with a frown like thunder. "Luckily the AD came to my rescue otherwise I'd still be crying in a corner somewhere."

"She can't be that bad." Mem swallowed. "Can she?"

"We settled on foundation and a tiny bit on the eyes."
Her phone buzzed again.

— You wanted to see how hot she is —

Mem couldn't deny that. Piper's tag of *hot, reclusive celesbian* had been a tiny bit intriguing. At least some of those terms seemed inconsistent, though understandable. Celebrity status had been thrust on Mem and all she wanted to do was hide from it. Perhaps she and Thea Voronov had something in common.

A flurry of messages came from Piper.

— Apparently she started out shooting girlie pics for Jasper Fitz-Stewart and that kink magazine —

— Apparently she has a bed in her studio —

— Apparently she's shagged every celebrity she's photographed —

— Apparently she likes them bound and begging on their knees —

Mem laughed and showed the screen to Benny.

"Apparently someone has a bit of an obsession," he drawled.

Mem's googling had revealed a few things. Thea Voronov's art was extraordinary. Her images and her connections with all the leading fashion magazines meant that whatever Thea Voronov photographed immediately became the next pre-eminent trend. She dominated the art and fashion worlds. Her work was cutting and delicate, critical and astounding. Sometimes repugnant. Always breathtaking.

But her personal history was even more intriguing. Some articles talked about a childhood in the old Soviet Union with rich and privileged parents, nannies and fast cars, the whole family crossing borders with ease. One faded polaroid showed a blond kid laughing in the sunshine on the deck of a superyacht, the French Riviera in the background.

Then there'd been the scandal.

Mem checked the dates. Twenty years ago. A huge police operation that exposed a crime syndicate, dragged down a few politicians and sent Thea Voronov's father to prison for his sins. He'd been a full-on Russian crime baron running a network of drug traffickers and prostitution rings across Europe. Old news articles showed pics of a teenaged Thea looking bewildered as she was evicted from her father's exclusive Knightsbridge home while a media scrum gleefully reported on the seizing of his luxury cars.

The next picture Mem found was just a year later. A police mugshot. Dirty and angry, her hair dank and yellow over eyes rimmed with too much eyeliner, Thea glared at the camera with hatred.

More modern photos showed Thea Voronov was a woman in her late thirties – confident, proud, successful and wealthy. Effortlessly stylish.

And most definitely hot.

Mem looked up and away from Benny's eyeliner pen and found herself looking at a huge black and white print on the kitchen wall.

It was a woman's face – the raw, moody, honest kind of photograph Thea Voronov was famous for. The model was not what the fashion world would call traditionally beautiful. She was in her fifties and the camera had focused on the wrinkles around her eyes. A burst of light behind her outlined her cheek and an old scar there drew the gaze like a beauty spot. But the playfulness in her eyes had been captured perfectly. She was plain – *ordinary* – but she looked like a lover.

She also looked familiar, though Mem wasn't sure why.

The image was in stark contrast to Thea's 'art' shots of celebrities that Mem had seen on the internet last night. She thought about it and held up her phone to eye level again to type in an answer.

— *She makes ordinary people look beautiful. And beautiful people look ordinary* —

Benny saw it.

"Oh, she does that, alright," he murmured.

Piper didn't hesitate in her answer.

— *So you're scared then?* —

Benny saw that too. He put one hand on Mem's shoulder.

"Darls, you're not scared, are you?" he whispered.

— *No!* —

Benny pulled a face at her.

"Maybe a little bit," she admitted.

The hand on her shoulder squeezed. "You've come a long way, Mem Swan. This is just one more step. You'll be fine." He flashed her a quick grin with apologetic overtones and dropped his voice even lower. "Plus, you know there's no way anyone can take a bad pic of you."

Mem nodded. She was overthinking this. She should just straighten her shoulders, lift her chin high and put the most beautiful face Thea Voronov would ever see in front of her lens.

Benny saw her mood change. He nodded at her confidence.

"There you are, darls," he said, loudly and for the benefit of the rest of the room. "It was a tough job, but I've done the best I can."

Mem poked her tongue out at him. He was a good friend.

She had three seconds before Adiatu descended again.

A woman named Lollie Jones emerged from the garden and went toe to toe with Mem's agent.

"But she's not in costume yet," Adiatu started. "StudioOne and I want final approval over—"

"It's not your shoot," Lollie said, bluntly but not rudely. She nodded and gestured to the wardrobe team who scurried to hand her Mem's costume-bag. Mem was impressed. She'd never seen anyone stand up to Adiatu like that.

Lollie was about Mem's age. White and preppy. She wore a casual linen suit in pale pink which she teamed with bright white trainers. Her long brown hair was in a simple ponytail. The impression was all sweetness and light, but Mem got a hint of something steely inside.

"This is it? The big floofy frock?" Lollie smiled at Mem. "You ready?"

"Memona-darling, I'll accompany you," Adiatu declared. She waved an imperious hand. "Follow us, you darling angels from hair and make-up—"

Lollie blocked the door. "No. Just Ms Swan. Thea's orders."

Adiatu drew herself up with a dangerous smile, but Lollie met it with a strength just as impressive. Adiatu surrendered.

"Be wonderful, Mem-sweet. Be your gorgeous, wonderful self," she cried. Theatrical. For the benefit of everyone in the room. Then she dropped her voice. She grabbed Mem's arm. "Thea Voronov will make both of us rich and famous beyond your wildest dreams. Do *exactly* as she asks, Mem. Give her everything she wants." She paused and her fingers tightened. "And if she wants anything more—" Her voice trailed off and her gaze was a suggestive mix of greed, lechery and jealousy.

What the fuck?

Lollie was back in a second.

"Let's get you away from the circus," she murmured, kindly. "Thea doesn't want you stressed."

Chapter Five

Thea Voronov's studio was an old building of stone and wood that sat in the corner of a small garden of flowers and old trees.

It was cool and dark inside – tranquil after the hubbub of the kitchen – and in a small ante-room Lollie pointed to an old-fashioned folding screen where Mem could change.

"Let me know if you need help with zips or buttons or things," she said, and the strident attitude she'd used with Adiatu was gone. Mem decided she liked her.

Through an open archway to another room, Mem could hear the murmur of Dame Katherine Cox's voice talking and laughing with another. She couldn't hear their words but it sounded relaxed and comfortable. She let the sound soothe her, breathing deeply and trying to settle the twist of nerves in her stomach.

She did need Lollie's help with the zip, after all.

"Oh my days, what a dress," Lollie breathed when Mem emerged from behind the screen. "It looks like it's made of light. Thea will adore it."

Mem's nervousness finally got the better of her.

"What's she like?" she whispered, knowing the woman was just in the next room. "Thea, I mean? I haven't really done an art shoot like this before. Test shoots and filming for the movie, but this— This feels very different."

Lollie gave a soft chuckle. "Don't worry. You have nothing to be nervous about. Thea is going to love you."

Mem couldn't help but notice that everyone said almost the same thing.

"Come on," Lollie whispered. "Kate got here early. You can watch for a bit before we go in."

She led Mem into the main studio, a wide, high space rigged with an astonishing amount of lights. Strangely, barely any of them were lit. Instead, an overhead skylight was open to the sunshine, and it cast a thin beam down to a Regency-style settee on a Persian rug where Dame Katherine Cox reclined in its glow.

Kate cut a very suave figure. She was dressed in the costume that accompanied Mem's from the same scene in the movie. In her case, it was a tuxedo and top hat, a white bow tie and two-tone black and white shoes completing the 1930s look. She rested one ankle on her knee. One hand dangled idly over the armrest. The other clutched a long, slender cigarette holder and the smoke she blew from the corner of her lips caught and twisted in the light.

She was the absolute picture of vintage elegance, wealth and leisure – *and* she was Dame Katherine Cox. Even in street clothes Kate was so ludicrously sexy Mem's poor gay little brain had given up long ago. In a tuxedo, it was a million times worse, but Mem didn't even need to pinch herself anymore. Kate was a friend now.

This time, it was someone else who took her breath away.

Thea Voronov crouched at her feet.

And she may have been kneeling, and Kate may have been one of the finest actors in the world, but there was no doubt who was in control.

Thea made a gesture and Kate altered her pose. There was the rapid-fire whirr of a camera shutter and Thea flicked her free hand again. Kate seemed to know what Thea wanted without being told.

Watching her... *obey*... pulled the air from Mem's lungs. She wasn't quite sure why.

But Thea herself—

Something inside Mem rolled over and died.

The woman was lithe and fit. Her long legs were clad in skin-tight black leather pants, the line of her thighs drawn taut by the heels of her black boots. Her shirt was a deep royal purple, the sleeves rolled to just below her elbows. A wide leather cuff with a bank of gold studs graced one wrist. Her hair was almost the same golden colour, just kissing her shoulders, but straight, as if it had been scorched into submission with a flat iron.

She had her back to her, but Mem knew the moment she turned around was going to be devastating.

The pair hadn't heard them come in.

"Oh sweetheart, that's the silliest thing I've ever heard," Kate murmured to Thea.

Thea's answer was inaudible, but she ducked her head for a moment. She might have been looking at her camera.

"Just be on your best behaviour and you'll be fine." Kate looked down and smirked. "Or maybe don't."

The camera whirred again and Thea stood up. She stepped between Kate's knees and reached a hand down to Kate's face. One long finger traced her cheek and Kate smiled triumphantly. The moment she did, Thea slapped her cheek – lightly, playfully, but the act was so intimate and erotic it left Mem with no doubt how very close the two were. They laughed and Mem suddenly felt as if she and Lollie were intruding. She was almost embarrassed to be there – and at the same time, she felt something warm inside her, something deep, something that wanted exactly what Kate had.

She was jealous.

And she hadn't even seen Thea's face.

Beside her, Lollie coughed. "I have our other leading lady," she said, as if the intense little scene they'd just witnessed had never happened.

Thea turned around and Mem gaped. The nerves she'd been desperately holding back all morning breached their feeble barriers and flooded through her body in a rush of dizzyingly hot blood. They spun her head, stole her breath and twisted her gut.

The woman was stunning.

The same flat-ironed hair hung low over her eyes in a long fringe. Her eyes were dark beneath it, rimmed with heavy eyeliner, the sharpest gleam of blue flashing from within. High cheekbones collapsed Mem's mind. The smirk that suddenly twisted Thea's lips only emphasised their severity. Around her neck, a confusion of gold chains tangled with a loose black tie, the knot low on her chest, the tails dragging Mem's eyes down to her breasts. Her black lace bra was clearly visible, the curve of her breasts capturing Mem's gaze like she was helpless. The shirt buttons began below her bra – two, Mem noticed. She couldn't tear her eyes from them even as she knew where the trajectory was taking her. Lower. The shirt was tucked at the waist into those devastating pants, the whole thing accented with a large gold belt buckle.

Hips. Thighs.

Shit.

Mem was staring. Static buzzed in her head. By the time she re-engaged her brain and forced her eyes upwards again, Thea's own eyes had narrowed, and were interrogating Mem's entire existence.

"*You* are beautiful."

Mem had heard that a million times before, but in Thea's mouth it sounded like an accusation.

The silence was awkward.

Great start.

Kate moved first – wonderful, perfect, life-saving Kate.

"Fucking artists!" she cried. She smacked Thea hard on the upper arm and glared at her. Thea barely moved but Kate bustled forward and wrapped Mem in a hug. "Honestly, I don't know what makes them think genius is an excuse for sheer, bloody rudeness, but I swear to god Thea Voronov was absent the day they handed out manners. Lovely to see you, Mem, dearest. Come on, you two, let's try that again. Properly." She whacked Thea again. One of Thea's brows twitched. "Thea, this is Memona Swan. Mem, I'd like you to meet Thea Voronov. She's not normally this much of a prat."

"Yes she is," said Lollie.

Thea gave them both a thin fuck-you smile.

Mem decided to be the grown up.

"Pleased to meet you." She held out her hand and immediately winced on the inside. Too eager. Too gushy. *Please don't make this weird, Swan*, she told herself. *The world famous artist doesn't need to know you're too gay to function.*

Thea's eyes flicked down to Mem's hand and narrowed even further. She didn't move.

"Oh, for fuck's sake," Kate muttered. She nudged Thea with her shoulder.

Thea's fingers closed on Mem's.

Her touch burned like fire. Thea's skin was warm and her fingers were strong. Mem felt the brush of each fingertip on her wrist, light but electric and her eyes snapped up to Thea's.

For one split second, Thea looked just as shocked. Then she smirked again.

"Hmm."

A short little hum, dry and derisive, and Thea's eyes captured hers like a challenge. Just when Mem thought they were going to burn through to her soul, Thea swept them over the rest of her body in a brisk, assessing manner. They came to a sudden, greedy halt at the swell of Mem's breasts, where a diamond the size of Mem's heart sat on the curve of her decolletage.

It was too much for Kate.

"Honestly!" she exploded. She thumped Thea's arm again. "You are bloody awful sometimes, Thea. Get out of here. Go!" She pointed at a bank of screens on a standing desk somewhere deeper into the gloom. "Go do your photographer thang over there if you're going to be like this. Lollie and I will run Mem through the schedule."

Thea didn't look the least bit phased by Kate's outburst. She tweaked one eyebrow at Mem – a definite flirt so confident it was dangerous – and swaggered away to her workstation. Mem couldn't take her eyes off the tight curve of her arse in those leather pants as she walked away.

When Mem looked back, both Kate and Lollie were grinning at her. Kate tugged her to the sofa.

"She likes you," she breathed. "I *knew* she would. Everything is going to be perfect. This will be fun." She smiled, happily, and sat back and crossed her legs. "Lollie, tell Mem what we're doing next."

They had a list of shots that both StudioOne and the diamond company had requested and they worked through those first.

"Generally I'd say we'd be lucky if Thea's patience lasted through something like this, but given the vibe in these, I think we'll be fine," Lollie said.

The requested shots encapsulated the relationship between Mem and Kate's characters in the movie and the modern version of the script had definitely added some heat. They blocked out a few together with Lollie while Thea was busy – Mem curtseying before Kate, the pair of them waltzing together, Kate looking greedily down at Mem as she sat on the settee. Mem's 1930s-style debutante's dress was a meringue of white net and lace, covered in small glass gems, with a tight lace bodice and shoestring straps. With Kate in a slim tuxedo and easily three inches taller than her, the power dynamic was obvious even without the script.

There had been a lot of giggles during filming, and Mem had learned a few unexpected things about herself.

She had *enjoyed* curtseying to Kate.

She'd been... *flustered*... in so many of their scenes. Assistant directors had praised her acting, and the director had gushed over the 'nuance and detail' she brought to her character, but the rise in her own body temperature had been real. Kate had winked at her with a knowing smile.

Mem Swan had always known she was attracted to beautiful women, but she'd had no idea she'd wanted to crawl across the floor to them. It had been a revelation.

She'd gone home and googled the words 'submission' and 'dominatrix' feeling like a total goose, only to have her breathing shallow out immediately and a deeply arousing burn flare between her legs. That led to some sapphic romances of the kind she'd never downloaded before, and – *what the hell?* – three hours lost on an increasingly bleak corner of pornhub. She regretted that a little, and deleted her browser history with sticky fingers, but the next day dawned on a whole new world.

Mem was submissive. She just had no idea what to do about it. With the chaos of her filming schedule, she'd had no time to experiment, not to mention anyone to experiment with.

Dame Katherine Cox had been very kind.

"You should explore that, sweetheart," she said. "I'm afraid I'm cast against type in my role. Can't help you at all."

She had smiled softly at her new girlfriend, the second-second AD, and she had smirked back.

There were power dynamics everywhere, Mem was beginning to notice.

Right now, Kate brought out a different vibe – the cheeky, playful clown act she often brought to the film set. It helped Mem relax. They settled into their usual working relationship and it was just like being back on set.

And then Thea emerged from the darkness with her camera and Mem's pulse rate spiked all over again.

Kate squeezed her hand and they got to work.

Thea had an unusual method of working.

She prowled around the pair of them at first, just outside the circle of light. Mem could feel her there, her eyes analysing and weighing. She stepped closer to examine the fall of light on their skin. She took a few quick shots, then stopped and strode away to her screens. She snapped her fingers and pointed at Lollie, who clearly knew what the artist would need next. The skylight in the ceiling was opened or closed at Thea's command. Additional lights or silver reflectors were set at a distance. With a sharp nod at Lollie a super-focused, super-bright handheld light appeared and was aimed at the diamond on Mem's chest. It spun a million rainbows across her skin and onto the white of Kate's shirt.

Thea looked delighted.

Only once she was happy did she start taking photos.

She was mostly silent as she worked. Mem and Kate took one of the curtseying scenes and Thea paused them or reset their positions with the slightest wave of her fingers or a soft hum. Kate seemed to know all her signals and Mem let her lead the way.

They were an hour into their work when Thea finally spoke.

"Isn't it a kids' movie?"

Her voice was low. She stepped into the light and frowned at them both.

Mem was sitting on the settee, her dress like a floating cloud around her. Kate was standing behind her, proud and aloof, one hand curling down to wrap around Mem's throat, her fingers tantalisingly close to the diamond. In the movie, Kate's character wanted the diamond more than anything.

"It is," Mem said, when no one else spoke.

Thea turned a slow, puzzled gaze on her. "And yet all these shots the Studio has requested involve Kate looking regal and you looking submissive," she said. One eyebrow twitched.

Mem blushed at the word *submissive*.

Thea noticed. Her eyes danced.

"Are you complaining?" Kate laughed.

Thank god for Kate. Thea's gaze couldn't get any heavier.

"Not at all."

Lollie snickered.

"Didn't think so." Kate put on the bored and languid voice she used for her character and waved the cigarette holder. Mansplaining vintage lesbian style. "It's a children's book from the 1920s," she said. "It got an upgrade. StudioOne messed with the details and the time period a little bit, but they gave voice to the latent sapphic overtones that have been in the book for the last hundred years."

She bent and tucked a finger under Mem's chin and tilted her face up. It was a move straight from the film.

Thea's camera whirred, so they stayed in character – Kate all overbearing and arrogant, Mem with her eyelids fluttering.

Really, acting wasn't hard at all when someone like Dame Katherine was leaning over her in a tuxedo with her fingers on her cheek and her thumb on her lips.

Thea stepped back into the darkness and resumed her prowling. When she settled again, it was in a crouch just off centre, her lens looking up at both Mem and Kate.

"I think it's quite a fair interpretation," Mem heard herself saying. "I mean, it's such a well-loved book across the generations – in England and in India. The author herself was rumoured to be queer, so the sapphic vibes are probably genuine. She just couldn't make it overt, back in the day, I suppose." She could hear Thea's camera working but she kept her eyes on Kate. Kate smiled, encouragingly. "If StudioOne didn't acknowledge it, they'd be criticised for suppressing the story's inherent queerness. If they made it too obvious, there'd be backlash from the mainstream. It's a tricky balance. They've taken a nuanced touch with the colonial issues too—"

She trailed off. The chatter of the camera had stopped and both Kate and Thea were looking at her. Lollie was watching too.

Mem hid a grimace. She'd forgotten. Pretty or smart. Not both.

Thea's stare was intimidating.

"All excellent points," Kate said, when the silence had stretched on a fraction too long. "Of course, we haven't seen the finished product yet. Who knows what it will look like once it's been edited and run through post."

She pulled Mem to her feet and swept her into another of the positions they'd rehearsed – a waltz hold with Kate's hand low at the small of Mem's back and Kate's eyes on the diamond. Kate gave her a quick wink and they fell into character. Mem had enjoyed filming these scenes. The blushing, the fluttering eyelashes, the inexplicable feeling that she was happy taking this submissive role for Kate's character didn't feel like acting at all.

Doing it in front of Thea Voronov was something else entirely.

She could *feel* Thea watching them, greedily.

Thea's camera got to work and she stalked the space, catching their possessive little dance from every angle.

"Is your background Indian, Mem?" Thea asked, quietly. Her camera clicked.

"Clapham born and bred, actually," Mem said. "My grandmother on my mum's side came over from Pakistan after Partition. Classic story of a Muslim girl in love with a Hindu boy. She used to read *The Wolverton Diamond* to me when I was little."

Thea stepped out of the shadows and looked pointedly at Kate and Mem's very heated embrace.

"When you were *little*?" She waved her free hand at the pair of them. "And yet the sexual tension in these poses is off the charts. What on earth is this story about?"

There was a guffaw and a snort from Kate and Lollie.

"Are you joking?"

"It's one of the most famous kid's stories of all time!"

Lollie was incredulous. "How can you not know *The Wolverton Diamond?*" She shook her head. "You know Paddington Bear? You know Mary Poppins? You know *The Magic Faraway Tree?*"

"You made that last one up," Thea muttered.

"So how is it you don't know—?"

Kate's laugh was affectionate. "You're missing the crucial piece, Lollie. She knows the movies. When was the last time you saw the tsarina here sit still long enough to actually read a b—"

Thea backed quickly into the darkness but not before Mem saw her face. She looked furious.

"Lollie!" Thea was back at her workstation already. Mem could see the light from her screens glancing off chiselled cheekbones. "This, this and these. Take these proofs out to the StudioOne people." She strode back to the centre of the room as soon as Lollie was gone and turned her ire on Kate. "We're almost at the end of your time here today, Katherine. A word, in the other room, if you don't mind. You'll excuse us, please,

Ms Swan." She didn't wait for Mem's answer, but stalked off to a door on the other side of the room almost immediately.

"Think I'm in trouble," Kate whispered to Mem with a grin.

"Now, Kate!"

The famous Dame Katherine Cox followed meekly.

It left Mem sitting alone on an antique Regency chaise lounge in a tight pool of sunlight in a dress made of rainbows with a million dollar diamond around her neck.

Two absolute truths vibrated through her body and spun through her mind.

One: if the concept of 'being submissive' had been a vague and newly formed notion curling at the edges of Mem's need, it had now burst forth as an all-consuming fire in her soul.

And two: Thea Voronov was a towering, magnificent and downright fucking stunning top and the only person in the world Mem's soul wanted to bow to.

Kate kicked the door shut, but the catch was loose. All it took was a gentle whisper of a breeze from the skylight above Mem's head to rattle the door open again. It swung in a few tiny centimetres, barely enough to be noticeable, then breathed back closed. Moments later, it did it again.

Mem's bedroom door in her parent's house had done the same thing. When she was little she'd thought it was ghosts or monsters, or the breath of the house itself. Nothing had stopped it – not the wads of paper Mem pushed into the catch in her early teens, desperate for privacy, or her father's hopeless handyman efforts later. In the end, it became a comfort. A soundtrack to her childhood.

The notion that Thea might be the kind of woman who was prepared to tolerate a gently breathing door in her studio was a very small conciliation to the weirdness Mem was feeling right now.

Thea and Kate were arguing.

Mem couldn't hear the words but Thea sounded irritated and impatient, and Kate barely seemed to get a word in. Mem wondered exactly what their relationship was if Thea got to talk to Kate like that. Even StudioOne execs bowed to Dame Katherine Cox.

It was quite obviously a physical relationship too – or, at least, it had been in the past. Mem knew Kate was seeing someone new, though.

Anwen was an assistant director on *The Wolverton Diamond,* and Kate had invited Mem back to her trailer to let her in on the secret the pair were hoping to keep from the rest of the crew and the media. The Welsh woman was funny and genuine, and Kate looked relaxed around her. It was more than just an on-set romance, Kate told her, holding Anwen's hand. They smiled soppily at each other.

Mem wondered if Anwen knew her new squeeze was still handsy with Thea Voronov.

Mem was still sitting on the chaise lounge like an obedient puppy. The conversation in the other room showed no signs of stopping, so she got up and wandered around the studio.

It was a bare space. In its deepest corners stood rolls of seamless backdrops. Two wooden ladders that looked as if they'd been made in the 1950s leaned against a wall. An equally retro wooden filing cabinet was labelled with colours – not the words, but coloured sticky dots. Red and yellow on the top drawer, green and blue on the middle, and purple on the bottom. Mem frowned at it for a moment and then realised. Gels and filters for the lights.

Thea's desk with its computer and bank of screens blinked at Mem from the opposite corner. It felt like a sacred space, like an altar to Thea's art.

It drew Mem like a magnet.

She knew she shouldn't look – she was trespassing on Thea's creative process – but she couldn't stop herself. She wanted to see herself through Thea's eyes. She wanted to see how the magic that Thea was famous for worked on her.

She nudged the mouse with the tip of her finger and woke the screens up—

And nearly stumbled back.

Her own image blinked onto the main screen – an extreme close-up of her face, a striking angle, a surprising calibration of light and shadow. A prism of light glistened on her lower lip and drew the eye to it. Below her chin and out of focus, the diamond was a pale stone in comparison. Her eyes were downcast and her lashes fluttered on her cheeks.

It was an exploration of beauty, but at the same time, it wasn't. She could see individual pores on her cheek picked out in perfect clarity. Light fell on her cheekbones and darkness sculpted them more harshly than she was accustomed to seeing. Thea's lens had peeled her and left her raw and honest. Plain.

Mem had never seen herself like that.

It was a long time before she could look away.

On another screen were the posed shots of her and Kate, twelve thumbnails in colour.

These ones, Mem suspected, would make the StudioOne executives ecstatic. They were vibrant yet elegant, the 1930s brought to life with sophistication and grace. Kate was a strong, defiant figure who wore her confidence like armour – a striking contrast to Mem's vulnerability. They were exquisite pictures, and Mem had no doubt she'd soon be seeing them on billboards and movie posters.

But a third screen held a different set of photos.

These were undeniably erotic. In these, Thea had caught the dynamic between *The Wolverton Diamond's* main characters and amplified it a hundred fold. These were a celebration of feminine power and allure – and as Mem looked, she realised most of them were quite candid. She hadn't been acting in that one. Kate was laughing there. *That* was when they'd been horsing around dancing. Yet, it was this level of intimacy that added depth to the sexual charge. Thea had captured their characters' relationship, their own, plus the give and take of the whole situation, and she had unmasked them all.

Thea was a genius.

Mem had to remind herself to breathe.

She took the mouse and scrolled through more. There were more close ups of both her and Kate amid the shots the studio had requested.

There were many, many more of her than of Kate.

A gentle shift in air pressure opened the door behind her.

"—I know what you're like and I know what you're thinking, you wicked thing. There's ten years between you, so be good." Kate's voice. The conversation was gentler now. Playful tones that teased as if this was an old, familiar line.

"There's ten years between you and me – and I'm never good."

"Yes you are, you silly—"

The door closed again.

Mem knew she should go back to the sofa but the pictures on Thea's screens were addictive and, besides, it was dark in Thea's corner. She couldn't be seen from the door. Thea's pictures made her look like an angel one moment, a siren the next.

"—definitely too old for *that*." Kate laughed.

"You've still got it."

Kate's laughter deepened. "Oh, I know. I just bruise more easily—"

There was the faint scent of cigarette smoke – the brand that Kate had to smoke on set and which she blamed for making her take up the habit again – and then the soft thud of the door swinging closed again.

Mem scrolled through a hundred pics of Kate and her together, and then a hundred more of just her. She saw herself as if for the first time. Exposed.

"But she's beautiful. I didn't expect—"

"Oh, for heaven's sake, just do it, Thea. You know you will. When has a conscience ever bothered you before?"

The door made a different noise and Mem tore her eyes away from the screens.

"Like what you see?"

Thea's voice was dry. She leaned against the door frame, her arms folded under her breasts in an aggressive confusion of jewellery and skin. Something dangerous danced in the darkness of her eyes.

It set Mem's blood on fire.

"I'm sorry," she said. "I shouldn't have looked, but once I started, I couldn't stop—"

Thea looked distinctly unimpressed. Kate sailed past her with a blithe smile and joined Mem at the screens.

"Oh, you are brave, Mem darling. Thea would whip me black and blue if I peeked at her work. Aren't you the golden child? Let me look. Did she capture my good side?"

"We still have work to do." Thea was cold.

"Slave driver," Kate grumbled. She draped her arm over Mem's shoulder and walked her back to the sofa. Thea's eyes drilled into Mem's back. "She's no fun at all."

Lollie returned with the news that the execs were thrilled, news that Thea rolled her eyes at. Kate carried the moment, as she always did, praising Thea and then immediately taking it all back with the taunt that Thea's head was big enough without the praise. Lollie laughed a little too knowingly and caught the hard edge of Thea's tongue, and so Kate smoothed over that moment too.

Thea's eyes barely left Mem's the whole time.

They took a few more of the posed shots the Studio wanted until Thea decreed them perfect. Then Kate sailed out, all air kisses and entreaties that they be good, with a significant look at Thea.

It was time for Mem's solo shoot.

Chapter Six

Thea stood and looked at her for a long moment.

The woman had been beautiful on paper, but in the flesh, Memona Swan was utterly sensational. *Precisely* what Thea liked – from the luscious swell of her lips to the sexy, teasing flutter of her eyes. Thea knew she was ruined even as she hitched her best sneer onto her face.

This was a *job*, she told herself. Nothing more. Kate and Jasper wanted Mem in their stable, and they'd enlisted Thea to bend her to their will. It was cruel, it was mercenary, and it was business – and Thea would do it because she owed them.

And because she wasn't above such things herself. Pretty things like Memona Swan were eager to be exploited. That's why they were in front of her lens in the first place.

This one was no different.

Except that Thea couldn't take her eyes off this girl. She was *perfect*.

She let her gaze roam over Mem's face and body without any kind of filter. That playful little pout at the corner of her smile was just begging to be kissed. The toss of her head revealed the curve of her neck – and Thea's lips curled back from her teeth as she imagined biting it, as she imagined the woman rising and arching beneath her. Thea was already picturing Mem's breasts straining against silk ropes and the pretty way she knew she would teach Mem to beg. The rest of her body was hidden by a dress Thea fervently wanted on the floor.

She was almost ready to lose her mind.

Jasper, Kate and Lollie had known, the traitorous bastards. Thea had to give them credit – they knew her tastes too well. Mem was an intoxicating blend of naivety and confidence, intelligence and courage. The way she and Kate had acted today – hours and hours of Mem's fluttering eyelashes, her deference to Kate's authority and her beautiful downcast gaze. Sure, they were acting. They were playing characters. Following a script. Or, at least, Kate was. Thea nearly chuckled. She *knew* Kate Cox didn't suit the dominant role, but fuck, the actress knew how to draw a gorgeous, natural submission out of Mem Swan. Thea's blood had been up all day just watching.

Mem was hungry for it.

Somewhere way, way in the background, Lollie cleared her throat.

Thea dragged her eyes up again, as slow as she liked, damn it – and *there* was exactly the sign she was looking for.

Mem swallowed. Looked to the floor at Thea's feet. Back up. Straight back down again.

Oh, sweetheart, Thea thought. *You want this so bad.*

She allowed her lips to stretch into a greedy smirk. This was going to be easy.

Too easy.

So why was she hesitating? Why did she suddenly feel the desire to be courteous, gracious and ... *kind*?

When had she ever been any of those things?

She was amused when it turned out to be Mem Swan who took the lead. The woman tossed her chin suddenly and swung her weight onto one hip. She put on a silent performance worthy of any of the cheapest, most desperate starlets who'd ever entered Thea's studio.

The cute little act didn't even register at first, but then, as Mem moved more confidently into her rehearsed charade, switched on her charm and quirked her lips in that deliberate, coy way, Thea felt a strange mix of pleasure and irritation.

It was nothing Thea hadn't seen before – a winning combination of bashful smile, flirtatious glance, and a teasing bite of her lip. It was a ploy Thea suspected Mem had used a million times to enchant and sway those around her. And it might have worked on most people.

Thea Voronov wasn't most people.

"Don't pull that shit with me."

She kept her voice low, but she watched the iron edge of her tone hit Mem's act with a rush of satisfaction. The colour drained from Mem's face and the confident play was replaced with vulnerability.

That was far more attractive, Thea thought. Genuine. Honest.

For a split second, Mem looked ready to crumble, to drop to her knees, and the rush of power hit Thea right between her legs.

She decided to play her own game.

"Not unless you think you can really do it justice," she murmured.

A challenge. An invitation. *Step into the dance, Memona Swan. Meet me head on.*

It had been a long while since anyone had dared stand up to her, especially here, in her own studio, where every frame, every light, every angle was under her control. She suddenly found herself thrilled by the possibilities. She knew exactly what she'd like to see Mem do. Knew precisely how she'd make the girl beg. Could almost taste her submission on her tongue.

But Mem's response nearly had her undone.

Her lips fell open and Thea couldn't see anything else. The entire universe halted on Mem's soft intake of breath.

"Okay then," Mem whispered.

It was hushed and brave, but it was filled with promise. Was it Thea's imagination, or did it also sound like a gift, laid beautifully at her feet?

It took more effort than she expected to switch back into professional mode. She snapped her fingers and Lollie pressed a camera into her hand. A prime lens, Thea noted. Good girl. Every detail mattered. Light, angle, focus. Everything needed to be perfect. She directed Mem to the set ensuring her every gesture dripped with authority. Mem quivered at her commands and Thea's fingers twitched on the shutter release. This wasn't just about snapping an image. This would be about capturing Mem's spirit, her essence, and her soul.

She waited until Mem was settled, then hit her with her demand.

"Very well then. Impress me."

Mem's cheeks flushed, but she obeyed, her posture defiant. It was priceless to watch, setting fire to Thea's blood through her lens, Mem straining with every fibre of her body to serve Thea's art. It was going to be a dance of wills, a battle of desires. She wanted to see how far Mem would go, how much she would reveal.

And as Lollie chuckled softly in the background, Thea had the strongest feeling she had found what she was looking for – her inspiration, her art and her reason.

All the things she hadn't known she needed.

It was an almost silent shoot.

When they were done, Thea sent Lollie up to the house with the final proofs for the StudioOne execs, and Mem and Thea were left alone.

Mem had done well. Sure, the required shots had been nothing but artifice, Thea's every creative instinct corrupted by the commercialised vision of the movie studio. It had been a galling compromise, despite having such a delicious partner. A tedious battle between her art and their demands.

Thea didn't do well with obeying other people's demands. She was more accustomed to watching others obey hers.

And Memona Swan had bent to Thea's word like it was hardwired into her soul. She vibrated with it, with an energy that made Thea urgent. She wanted to make this woman quiver with her touch.

They looked at each for one long, heavy moment.

Thea made a decision.

"I have a confession to make, Ms Swan," Thea murmured into the silence.

"Please call me Mem."

A pretty request.

"I almost cancelled today's job," Thea said.

"Why?"

"Because of you." She stepped into the light, almost into Mem's personal space. "Look. Look at you." She scrolled through the images she'd just taken and held out the screen on the back of her camera for Mem to see.

It wasn't a shot she'd ever dream of sending up to the StudioOne execs. Here she had exposed something deeper and enigmatic – not beauty, not in the traditional way – but something that shone out of Mem and was quickly driving Thea insane.

Mem frowned at the screen.

Thea imagined the girl wasn't used to seeing herself like that. Interesting.

She stepped closer. She was pleased to discover she was a good three inches taller than Mem, and the heels on her boots only emphasised the height difference between them. Mem's gaze had trouble rising to meet her own. Her eyes danced around Thea's lips, her jawline, her throat. Thea nearly laughed.

"You didn't want to work with me because I'm—" Mem stopped.

Thea raised an eyebrow.

"—because I'm beautiful?" she finished.

Thea snorted. She stepped quickly away and sat on the end of the chaise lounge with a casual grace. Her long legs stretched out in front of her and she crossed them lazily at the ankles. She smirked up at Mem.

"I find beauty a little tedious, actually," she drawled. "Boring. I mean, when you're surrounded by gorgeous women day after day, like I am, with their perfect smiles and their perfect skin, their perfect bodies"—she dragged her eyes slowly and deliberately over Mem, taking in every inch of her—"I'm spoiled. What can I say?"

Spoiled didn't even begin to cover it. Thea knew what she could get away with and frequently crossed the line. The question was whether Mem would be happy to meet her on the other side. She was delighted when Mem huffed out a nervous laugh.

"Sucks to be you."

Thea grinned at the girl's impudence. The dimple in her cheek was the purest vodka. Thea wanted to slug back the bottle.

She waved a hand. "I can live with it. Sit." She tipped her head at the lounge beside her.

Mem sat in a flounce of dress. The crystals in the fabric tinkled. They cast a million reflections and set Mem's skin glowing. Thea wondered what would happen if she tore it off her.

"Why didn't you, then?" Mem asked.

Thea frowned. Her gaze caught on Mem's breasts. Distracted.

"Why didn't you cancel?"

"I find I am obsessed with you," Thea admitted and her eyes moved up to Mem's face. They lingered on her lips for a very long moment. "I realised I want considerably more from you than just one photoshoot."

There was that perfect little gasp again. Tiny, panting little breaths the woman tried to hide. Thea didn't want her to. She wanted to exhaust her utterly. She wanted to fuck her into tomorrow and capture her devastation on film. Mem drew her lower lip into her teeth – a move that only made Thea want to bite it for her. Oh, she was going to be so perfect.

But a definite streak of cheek was unexpected.

"Not the smoothest line I've ever heard," Mem murmured. The very tip of her tongue poked out between her lips.

There was a beat, then Thea threw back her head and laughed, and all the irritations of the day fell away. She felt... *relaxed*. Comfortable, for some reason, and she suspected it had everything to do with the warmth in Mem's smile. And that eagerness. And oh, that smile. Thea wanted to bask in it. She wanted to see it welcoming her home after a long day, she imagined it nuzzled into her neck as they cuddled on the couch, she pictured it offered to her across a pillow as the morning sunshine streamed across their bed—

She blinked. The fuck?

The smile faded. Mem was confused.

Thea relented.

"You're right," she admitted. "Agh. I've been disagreeable all day. I'd say I was sorry, but it's your fault entirely, Ms Swan. You're driving me crazy."

"Because I'm pretty?"

Thea cocked an eyebrow laden with ridicule.

"Oh." Mem looked at her hands and looked embarrassed. "Sorry. I've never done a photoshoot like this before. Only movies. Kate said I'd be fine, but clearly I've wasted your time—"

She was worried she wasn't good enough?

"No! No. Not at all," Thea said quickly. "Didn't you hear me? You're the most stunning thing I've ever had in front of my lens. *That's* why I'm obsessed with you."

"But beauty bores you."

Thea twisted on the sofa, crooking one knee up on the seat to face Mem. She tipped her head to one side and fixed Mem with a sharp look.

"Our culture plays beauty like a single symphony in the same key, over and over again. Oh, it's meticulously constructed, honed in makeup chairs, amplified by lighting, and polished with digital brushes. It is an army of faces, anonymous and uniform, dressed in different shades of sameness. It sings, yes, but rarely of anything more than the vanity of a society obsessed with a singular concept of perfection. *That* is what bores me."

She stretched her arms across the back of the lounge. One finger grazed against Mem's bare arm. Her skin was warm and Thea's hands were cool. Mem's skin instantly rippled with goosebumps. Thea watched, mesmerised.

"Because it is a beauty that merely echoes," she murmured. "It pretends. It doesn't live. It sells, but it cannot feel." Her finger trailed up to Mem's shoulder and she watched it like she couldn't stop it. "And that's not enough for me." Her voice was a low, hoarse whisper. "I want more."

"More what?" breathed Mem.

"More of you," Thea said, simply. "I want all of this."

Thea paused and hovered her finger millimetres above the rise of Mem's breast – all that perfection and a beautiful soul above it. Mem bit her lip again and it drove Thea crazy. She asked the question with her eyebrows. Mem granted consent with the tiniest of nods. Thea hooked into the V of her dress and tugged.

Mem nearly toppled into her.

"There's something different in you," Thea whispered. "Something raw and glorious. An untouched canvas that is begging for the stroke of a master's brush." She smirked. "Or a camera. I want you, Mem. I want your body, your smile and your soul. I want you as my muse."

Mem was breathing through her mouth. She stared at Thea like she was stuck – waiting on Thea's word. She looked as lost as Thea felt.

"I— I don't know what that means."

Thea wasn't sure either. That wasn't going to stop her from taking everything she could get.

"A muse who can inspire me. Who will share my vision. And my bed, if you're game. Someone to be moulded, adored, and possessed in every frame I shoot."

There was a spark of longing on Mem's face that bravely met Thea's fire with a hesitant flame of its own.

She had her.

"Someone to dive into the depths of passion and creativity with me, without limits and without fear."

Thea was hyper-aware of the effect her words were having on Mem – the sudden dilation of her pupils, her lips parted, her chest rising and falling in needy little pants. She knew *just* the kind of woman Mem was.

"Someone to be mine."

Thea chuckled suddenly, breaking the mood. She had to flick Mem's chin to make the girl shut her mouth. It felt so right she gripped her face and tilted it up to her own. Mem moved under her touch like a dream.

"There's an entire world waiting for you, Memona Swan – not just as a star, but as a masterpiece. *My* masterpiece. My muse. A living, breathing work of art. I could do the most extraordinary things with you." She paused. "*To* you." She let her go – a gesture of trust, giving Mem the space to choose, to deliberately step into the inferno that was Thea's world.

Mem simply breathed. Her eyes were molten chocolate and Thea wanted to drown.

"Well?"

The smile was back. "I'm... *game*," Mem whispered.

Thea felt a grin crack her face, but she had to be certain.

"I will expect everything from you and I can be very exacting," she warned. "Your body and your soul at the service of my art. Do you understand?"

"Not even a little bit," Mem breathed. "But I want to. I want you to teach me— I want you— I want—"

Thea took pity on her

"I have an exhibition coming up at the Tate Modern. We can start with that." She thought about it. "Perhaps we'll get this diamond back and have a bit of fun. I like the way your beauty turns it pale," she murmured, "though I can't imagine the diamond company will think of it that way." Two birds, one stone, she supposed. Mem's tiny, delicate frown was back again. She had to stop this, before she simply dragged the girl into the bedroom and fucked her silly.

Lollie saved her.

"The honchos are happy," she announced. "It's a wrap. They want the diamond back." She stopped dead when she saw the tableau in front of her – Thea and Mem so close they could have kissed, Thea's hand still resting on Mem's breast. Lollie swore under her breath. "Really?"

Thea raised an eyebrow.

Lollie let out an exasperated sigh but she gathered up her screen, some other papers and a bag from under Thea's workstation.

"We're keeping the diamond and the top tier actress for now?"

Thea and Lollie both looked at Mem.

There was a very clear question in Lollie's eyes. A lifeline, if she wanted it. Lollie was making sure Mem knew exactly what she was getting herself into.

This was Mem's one chance to back out.

Thea saw realisation hit Mem like a slap to the face. The woman blinked, panicked, and then stood, smoothing the front of her dress. She looked apologetically at Thea, something like real regret in her eyes.

Something went rotten in Thea's chest. It had been worth a try.

"I really do have to go," Mem said, looking down at Thea still on the lounge. "I mean, if we're finished, of course. It's late, isn't it? I have a family dinner this evening. At my parent's house. I'm so sorry. You know how it is," she babbled.

Thea didn't.

She held her eyes for a moment, then waved a hand in dismissal. Mem sucked in a breath at the audacity of the gesture and blushed in a way that proved everything Thea wanted from her might still be on the table. Thea decided she could be gracious.

"It's been a pleasure, Ms Swan," she said, standing and towering over her. She extended her own hand this time, then seized Mem's fingers and brought them to her lips. She kissed once and nipped at her knuckles before dropping her hand. There was another gasp when Thea deliberately turned her back and stalked over to her computer.

She heard Lollie show Mem out.

Lollie's sauciness when she returned wasn't the least bit unexpected.

"That will be two hundred quid, then," she drawled, holding out her hand with a smug expression. "Crashed and burned with both Kate and Mem, hey boss? You are definitely losing your touch."

Thea slapped her hand away.

"Not even a little bit," Thea grated. Usually she'd whip Lollie til she howled for insolence like that, but she had someone else's body on her mind now. How had the world changed so much in just one day? "The game is still on. Memona Swan has agreed to be my muse."

She ignored Lollie's startled 'wuh?'

"Your stupid diamond deal is in the bag. You're all going to owe me."

Chapter Seven

"How did it go with Thea Voronov?"

Piper had her head in the fridge searching for milk for her cornflakes. She sniffed warily at a carton, squeaked with alarm and dropped it immediately into the bin. She reached for the apple juice instead.

"It was... good," Mem tried. "Fine. It went, um, well. Just a photoshoot, you know. Nothing special."

Piper blew a raspberry. "Bullshit. I'm sorry I wasn't here last night when you got home – it was mental at Heart and Grace yesterday. Totally needed a drink afterwards. I know you were worried about it, though. What was she like? Did you fall on your face? Was it very draining?" She poured apple juice liberally over her breakfast cereal and Mem tried not to gag.

Draining? That didn't even begin to describe it, though if Thea Voronov had put her teeth to her throat and bled her dry, Mem wouldn't have been surprised. Wouldn't have stopped her either. Thea was the most compelling woman Mem had ever met and she had turned Mem's world upside down in just a handful of hours. Mem hadn't slept last night. Her heart was still racing even now.

"Thea was—"

She didn't even know how to finish that statement. She put a hand to her forehead. She was probably feverish. All she could picture were Thea's eyes drilling into her and that proud, confident smirk on her lips. The woman's cocky swagger and that incredible finger she'd dragged over her breasts. The sheer, unfiltered entitlement that flowed from her as Thea outlined precisely what she wanted from Mem.

"She was amazing," Mem said when she realised Piper was watching her curiously. "I only saw a few of the images we produced, but they were gorgeous. I had no idea I could look like that."

"Private session, hunh?" Piper waggled her eyebrows suggestively.

Mem reached out to thump her arm. "I told you I had a private session with her, so don't make it sound like that. Thea was very—"

"Mmm?"

Thea had been *exhilarating*. Everything about her oozed power, and Mem didn't understand it – she didn't even want to analyse it – she just wanted to surrender to it. She just wanted to offer Thea whatever she wanted, whatever she asked for.

No. She amended that thought.

She wanted Thea to take it.

She was wet all over again just thinking about her – at breakfast, for fuck's sake.

"Mem? Babes? Thea was very what?"

There was genuine concern in Piper's tone. It made Mem feel a bit guilty. She collapsed onto the kitchen stool opposite her friend and gave in to the fizzing, bubbling feeling that threatened to overcome her.

"Holy fuck, Pipes, she was incredible—"

"Woah— Did you shag her?"

"What? No! Nearly. No." Mem slumped over the countertop. "Oh god, I think we nearly came close and I— Oh god, Piper, I said I had to go. Dinner with my family! I ran out like a timid little princess. What the fuck was I thinking?"

Piper looked alarmed, a spoonful of soggy cornflakes halfway to her lips.

"The way she looked at me! The images she created. I'd rethink my whole approach to showbiz if it meant Thea Voronov would look at me like that again. She made me feel so... special, so wanted."

"You are special." Piper sounded nonplussed. "Mem? Of course you're special. Why would you think that?"

And Thea had asked her to be her muse. Mem had googled the fuck out of that last night in a frantic wave of desire and still had no idea what it meant, except that Thea wanted it. Thea wanted *her*, and that made Mem throb.

She hoped Thea still wanted to see her after she'd fled the scene like a frightened lamb.

"Are you okay?" Piper asked. "Listen, about Thea—"

"I'm fine," Mem promised. She snapped out of it. There was still a whole schedule of pre-release events coming up over the next few weeks. Life went on, sexy photographers making hot demands or not. "I have a whole day of interviews today. Not looking forward to it but at least I'll be with Kate."

Piper waggled her eyebrows. "Mmmmm. Kaaate," she drooled, apparently glad for the change of subject. "God, you're lucky. Don't know how you control yourself, though. I'd be begging for Kate to ravish me at every opportunity. I admire your self control," she said, cheerfully.

Mem wasn't sure she actually had any. She tipped the last of her coffee dregs down the sink and took Piper's bowl.

"Oi! I haven't finished—"

"Don't eat that. It's gross. Grab a fruit salad or something on your way into Kensington," Mem told her, back in control of herself again. "Be healthy."

Piper looked at her blankly. "I put *apple* juice on it. Wait— Why am I going to Kensington?"

"Imperial College London enrolment. I've been at you for weeks to sort this out. I'm paying your university fees, remember. It's time you did something with that big brain of yours."

"I'm running a women's refuge! With you!"

"You're way smarter than that."

There was the usual grumble, but Mem wasn't in the mood to hear it. Piper had a gift for mathematics, and maybe it was the fact that Mem was making changes in her own life, but it was time for Piper to get off her arse too.

"I'm not sure if—"

But Mem's phone buzzed on the countertop.

"That's my car," Mem said. She ignored Piper's eye roll.

"Ooo, that's my car," she mimicked.

"Shut up, Pipes."

"Love you, babes."

Mem sat next to Adiatu in the back of a luxury chauffeured car on her way to a media call with Kate. Adiatu droned on about talking points but Mem tuned her out. She researched Thea a bit more deeply.

"Her parents were Russian mafia, you know," Piper had said. "People smugglers, gun runners. Full on kleptocrats during the Soviet time and oligarchs living the high life in London after Putin. Her old man did time for it in Belmarsh prison. Well, until someone did him in on the inside."

"How do you even know this?" Mem asked, but Piper had just waved her question away.

"No reason. Just the news." She shrugged. "That happened ages ago actually, but Mum was from Russia, originally. She was interested."

Mem skimmed over all that stuff now. What did it matter who Thea's parents had been? It was the woman herself she was obsessed with.

There were pages and pages on Thea's collaborations with Jasper Fitz-Stewart and the early versions of their magazines. While the history of the UK's most successful LGBTQ+ mags was fascinating enough, Mem found herself thinking that most of their rise was probably due to Thea's art. She could see Thea's eye – her curious and raw, edgy but elegant take – in every now-iconic image associated with the magazines.

Even when Fitz-Stewart expanded his empire into girlie mags, Thea's genius was still there in every picture, her skill and her masterful finesse lending even the most commercial subjects a kind of magic.

During a break in the very tedious media schedule – back-to-back seven minute interviews sitting next to Kate Cox and enduring a parade of journalists who asked identical questions with the air of expecting a unique and personal answer – Mem found herself drawn to her phone again. This time, in her boredom, she utterly failed to stop herself gravitating towards Thea's *other* set of work – her work with Fitz-Stewart's kink magazine.

These articles were intense. Mem scrolled through commentary from models who'd worked on those original photoshoots and who talked about a wild, hedonistic lifestyle in which Thea and Jasper Fitz-Stewart had indulged in every delight. Every fantasy.

"*Legendary in the sense that everything you've heard is true,*" quoted one model. She was photographed in moody black and white, shadows held at bay by her gleaming black latex, the spikes of her collar, and the scales of the snake draped across her torso. "*Thea Voronov? Fucking brilliant. Absolutely merciless. But empowering too, you know? Like, she showed me I could be fearless. Changed my life.*"

Mem scrolled through images unapologetically queer in their eroticness but populated with women who looked strong and beautiful. There was nothing of the usual cliqued lingerie and leather set-ups with suggestive poses framed by society's judgement. In Thea's images, her models moved unflinchingly through the space as if traditional norms were mere trivialities beneath their heels. Thea didn't cater to the viewer. She didn't water anything down. She gave light to the soul being photographed – gloriously kinky, unique, proud and daring.

And sexy as fuck.

Kate appeared at her shoulder with a cup of tea in a paper cup for each of them. She put them on a side table and began stretching – hip flexors and leg raises. She was in an expensive linen suit with heels which she kicked off with a groan of relief.

"I swear if my arse *and* my brain fall asleep we're going to be in real trouble." She tipped her chin at Mem's phone. "God, I wish my bum still looked like that. Good times."

"What?!" Mem blinked at her phone. "Is that you?"

They were looking at a pic of two women, though neither's face could be seen. A gorgeously curved backside was crooked over a corseted lap. It was another of Thea's moody, shadow drenched images, but in this case there were splashes of colour. Mostly in the series of pink stripes across the backside of the submitting model.

"Which one?" Mem asked, and then realised she already knew. That snippet of conversation she overheard in Thea's studio. *I just bruise more easily these days.*

Kate rested her elbows on the back of Mem's chair and leaned in for a better look at the picture.

"Trim, taut and terrific I was then. Look how fabulous my arse is there." She deflated with a raspberry noise and sank into the chair beside Mem. "I hate getting old."

"You're not old. I'm sure your bum still looks this good."

Kate giggled. "And that is exactly why I like you so much, you darling thing." She held out her hand for Mem's phone and scrolled through the rest of the gallery, sighing happily. "So. Tell me. After I left the other day, did you and Thea—?" She selected a shot of another two women – this one an image that left nothing to the imagination – and waggled it suggestively.

Mem was instantly flustered. "Did we—? Um—? We took some more photos?"

"Mmhmm?"

"Not those kinds of photos!" Mem thought back to what they had done, to the deal they'd nearly, maybe, struck and blushed maroon. Was this the kind of thing Thea expected from her 'muse'? Mem realised her heart had stopped beating.

Kate's laugh was rich and warm. She squeezed Mem's knee. "It's okay, sweetheart. I know that look. I'm just jealous."

Mem looked at the phone. "But these are just set-ups, right? I mean, they're poses. They're staged." That wasn't quite what she wanted to know. "Is Thea—? I mean, is she—?"

"Is Thea Voronov an intense and unbending domme who can take you from your knees to the stars with just the kiss of a flogger and have you sobbing like a baby for more? Oh, god yes."

Mem gaped – that was exactly what she'd wanted to hear – but Kate was lost in a dream of her own. She leaned in. The phone was still open between them and Kate's finger flicked slowly through the rest of Thea's images. She was caught in another time and place, and Mem found she was slightly jealous.

"Thea may be many things, but she's not afraid of the force of her desires," Kate murmured, "and she explores them with utter focus. With Thea, it's all about control, it's all about power – maybe because she had so little when she was younger – but she is an absolute goddess when she wields it."

Adiatu called to them from across the break-out room. "Five minutes, darlings."

Kate blinked, snapping out of it and rolling her eyes as soon as Adiatu turned her back.

"And she can be a right stroppy, sulky little bitch when she doesn't," Kate added dryly. She handed the phone back to Mem and sipped her tea.

"She wasn't like that with me," Mem said. "Not at all."

Kate frowned at her. "Bollocks. She was stroppy and sulky all day."

"No, no, I mean, after you left. She wasn't... domineering."

"Are you sure?" Kate was watching her closely. She gave her a small smile.

Mem found she couldn't hold her gaze.

"I was hoping that might happen," Kate said, softly. "She likes you."

"I don't understand," Mem said. "Stroppy and sulky means she likes me?" That made no sense.

"Locking away her dominance. Her authentic self." Kate explained, though it didn't really help. "She was polite, wasn't she? As much as she can be. Her best bloody behaviour. Idiot," she muttered.

Adiatu called again and Kate got to her feet, slapping her thighs and slipping her shoes back on. "Thea Voronov presents a picture of icy control to the world but the woman herself is a mess of contradictions, darling. You'll either never see her again, or she'll follow you around like a little lost puppy until you give her what she wants."

Mem was more confused than ever. "What does she want?"

Kate's dry chuckle said it all.

"She asked me to be her muse."

Kate's eyes lit up. "She did? And you said yes? Oh, you lucky, lucky thing. Now I'm really jealous." Her smile was very knowing. "My advice? Give her everything. Oh, she'll be far too stubborn to ask, so let her think she's taking it. She'll make it worth it. Time of your life."

Mem frowned. That sounded a little mercenary, actually. Heartless. As if Kate didn't expect anything more from Thea than the flick of her whip and some rope burn. Hadn't they been friends for years? That was cruel. Surely there was more to Thea than just kink?

Kate must have seen her expression.

"That was unfair of me, Mem. I happen to know that Thea is crushing over you too. Talk to her. Be brave." She turned away but stopped again with a curious expression on her face. "Come to think of it, there's a strong chance you might just be the one who can cut through all Thea's shit. You two might actually be made for each other."

Mem looked at the picture on her phone again. Was this what she wanted? Kink had never been part of any of her previous relationships. She hadn't even known she was interested.

But even now, she knew it wasn't the latex or the leather. It was Thea.

The thought of Thea sent her pulse through the roof.

Chapter Eight

Jasper Fitz-Stewart, Earl of Ravensworth, CEO of Spectrum Media, photographer, playboy and lazy, entitled traitor to the ideals he had once held true, was being exactly that.

Thea lounged on the expensive leather chesterfield in his magnificently appointed office on the sixty-sixth floor of the Shard and stared at the view. She listened with half an ear to Jasper chewing out a business development manager over the less than stellar results from one of their recent takeovers.

"We're working on pinning down the target advertisers and matching them to the established readership," the poor man muttered.

Jasper sucked a long draw from his coffee and waved him away, his patience having reached its limit.

"Do that," he called. "And send me those figures you mentioned." He heaved a long sigh as soon as the door was closed and slouched back in his chair. "Incompetent idiot," he breathed and fixed Thea with a wry smile.

"You employed him," Thea pointed out. "Since when did you care about shit like that?" She waved a hand at the entire operation – the two floors of Spectrum Media and its stable of eight international magazines, various smaller publications, associated brands and social channels. She couldn't deny it was luxurious, exclusive and fitting for a global media house, but it was a long way from where they'd started. "I hate this place, Jasper."

"I know you do." He grinned at her. "But it's not your place, Thea, darling. I keep all the boring people here – the bean counters and the marketers, the folk who write the mission statements. Your people, and all my creatives, are still back in the warehouse at Camden Lock."

"I still don't understand why we moved."

He looked at her. "It's not really *we* anymore, is it?" he said, gently.

It wasn't.

It hadn't been for a long time.

Thea had met Jasper at one of her lowest points, nearly twenty years ago. He was an art student then – too old not to have graduated yet, but too lazy to apply himself and get a real job. He wasn't the Earl of Ravensworth then, but he hid his heritage from his friends just as he hid his sexuality from his father. He had a rundown terrace house in Notting Hill, and it had stayed dowdy as the area gentrified around it. He gave a spare room to a scrappy, angry young woman with a police record and an addiction who was about to flunk out of her last resort. Art college and Thea didn't hit it off until Jasper shared his love of photography with her. He taught her everything he knew and stood back to watch her soar.

They'd been an incredible team.

Thea drank her coffee and wrinkled her nose at the pretentious brand in its oversized, recyclable takeout cup. Jasper had favoured massive budget tins of the instant stuff once. They'd drunk it from chipped mugs they'd lifted from thrift stores, working long hours on the first magazine of their collaboration. *Fruity* was an angry, defiant rag in those days, not the revered LGBTQ+ publication it was now. Jasper had focused on the critical issues and Thea captured the community in a light no one had yet seen them in. The gay gaze, Jasper called it, and still chortled like an idiot every time. Thea thumped him for it.

It set up a pattern they'd perfected through the rest of his magazines – *Quim* and *Bangz* for the lesbians and the gays, and then *Prynz* and *Forge* as Jasper ventured into more mainstream men's mags. By the time Jasper had inherited the earldom and Spectrum Media was packed into a funky, four-storey warehouse by the canal in Camden, he was ready to expand into the mainstream luxury and style markets too. *Adore*, *X* and *Luxe* came next and Thea worked for all of them, celebrities almost begging to stand before her lens.

It was only then that she realised Jasper's empire was all his and she was merely a cog in its workings.

The best, the brightest and the most coveted cog, but a tool in Jasper's kit nonetheless.

It didn't matter. He was a friend and she had precious few of those. He'd saved her life.

And by that time, of course, she'd made her own name and her own fortune.

She ignored his gentle dig.

"So why am I here?" she asked.

She was in a mood this morning after being blown off for a *family dinner*, and she was keen to take it out on someone else.

"CreatedDiamonds," Jasper said, leaning back in his executive chair and tucking his hands behind his head. A very expensive set of cufflinks glittered at each wrist. "How are we doing?"

Thea stood and moved to the window. The Thames snaked below her, slow, wide and eternal.

"It's only been a day," she said. "And I haven't decided—"

"*You* haven't decided?" Jasper made a *pfft* noise and came to stand next to her. He put his hands on his hips. "I'm not asking about you. I'm thinking about the lovely Memona Swan."

That was exactly what Thea was doing. It was what she'd been doing every minute since she'd last laid eyes on her.

Mem Swan and her unutterable beauty. Her perfect face and those eyes that looked at Thea and saw all the way through to her soul. Her body, gorgeously curved and exquisitely proportioned. Thighs that she wanted locked around her hips, dragging her down, breasts that she was aching to have heave under her mouth. The whimpers she dreamed Mem might make – intoxicating, begging sobs as Thea pushed at her desires.

Her soft, warm skin and her gentle, beckoning gaze that was so, so tempting.

Thea couldn't get Memona Swan out of her mind.

Jasper nudged her with his elbow.

"That good, huh?"

Thea pulled herself taller. "I have no idea what you're talking about," she muttered.

"Did you get her clothes off her? Is she that gorgeous all over?"

"You are a lecherous old fart."

Jasper laughed and looked pleased at the insult. "And you're not? *I've never denied it*." But he wasn't about to give up. "Well?" he sang.

"And a shit stirring pain in the arse."

"Tell me something I don't know." He turned his back to London and leant against the glass with his arms folded. He flashed her the grin

Thea both adored and had spent twenty years wanting to smack from his face. His eyebrows waggled mercilessly. "Oh, come on," he whined. "You know I'll find out anyway."

Thea gave in.

"She's perfect," she whispered. "She's beyond perfect. She's divine."

Jasper's eyes nearly bugged out of his head.

"Woah," he said, standing upright again. "What am I seeing? Are you *smiling*? Are you okay? Should I call a doctor?"

"Fuck off, Jasper," Thea told him. She spun on her heel and went back to the sofa. She was particularly irritated when Jasper bounded back to his desk and tucked himself in like an eager school boy.

"So. You got her into bed then?" He hooted with astonishment when Thea shook her head. "What? What happened? What's so different about this one?"

That was what Thea was still trying to figure out. Part of her wanted to call Memona Swan up right now and beg her for a night together. Part of her wanted to track her down to her home, pack up all her gear and move her straight into Thea's bedroom. Part of her wanted to tie the girl to the bed with black silk rope, drown her in rose petals and never let her go.

And part of her wanted to warn her away.

Run, beautiful girl. Run now.

While you still can.

"Agh!" Thea swooped forward, her elbows on her knees, her fingers running up through her hair. "I don't know! Nothing. Everything. She's perfect – too perfect for the likes of me. And she has a perfect life too. Family dinners, talent and a dazzling future ahead of her. Kate says everyone on set adored her and she's the nicest kid she's ever worked with. And she *is* a kid. I'm ten years older than her and I practically assaulted her—"

"Tell me more."

"You're disgusting."

Jasper chuckled then looked a tiny bit alarmed. "You didn't assault her, did you?"

"Christ, Jasper!"

There was a moment's silence.

"I asked her to be my muse."

That stopped him dead. He blinked and for one soft-arsed moment, he actually looked kind.

"Really, darling? She's that perfect?"

She gave him her best fuck-you smile.

The moment didn't last, of course.

"Or she will be once you've trained her, right? I know you, you kinky devil. You'll be exploiting her perfect beauty in no time."

It just made her moodier.

"Shut up," she grumbled. Toddlers had more equanimity.

"It's alright, Thea, darling. This is you. If anything, you were probably so scrupulously polite it drove the poor girl crazy."

She glared again.

"Well, you have a reputation, my dear. You can seduce any woman you want – and you frequently do – and you use them and drop them like stones but as soon as you meet anyone you truly respect, you're a complete gentleman." He laughed at her. "Kate still goes on about how you open doors for her—"

"I don't!"

"You do and it's adorable. Don't ever stop, darling."

None of this was helping. "Kate is different," she muttered.

Jasper narrowed his eyes at her, but his smile was kind. He always seemed to know just when she needed that kindness. She tried not to resent him for it. He was too bloody clever.

"How so?" he asked.

"Because she knows me too well," Thea sighed. "She knows what I am and where I came from."

"Bullshit," Jasper said. "That is an excuse you've been using for way too long. An excuse not to get close to anyone. Don't tell me you're going to waste this chance with the perfect Memona Swan for the same stupid reasons."

"They're not stupid."

Jasper's patience ran out. He collected up a folder of papers and snapped their edges on the top of his desk. They bore the CreatedDiamonds logo.

"You are Thea Voronov, for fucks sake. Act like it. Shag her, love her, use her – I don't care, but at the very least persuade her to sign up for the sequel film and the brand ambassadorship with CreatedDiamonds. Make yourself bloody useful for once."

"We wouldn't be sitting in this office if it wasn't for my usefulness, you arse." Thea stood up. She'd had enough of this – Jasper and the whole poisonous industry if she thought about it. Was there anyone who wasn't using anyone else? "I just told you I'm bewitched by her. How do you think I bring all that stuff up while I'm in the middle of—"

She broke off when she caught Jasper's filthy grin. She'd been going to say 'loving her' but how could it possibly be love? She hardly knew the woman.

"I've got plenty of ideas," leered Jasper. He stood too and handed her the folder.

Thea stuck two fingers up at him. He chuckled merrily.

"Why do you and Kate want this so much anyway?" she asked, genuinely curious.

Jasper shrugged. "I'm just in it for the money."

"Aren't you always," she sighed. She rolled the folder into a tight tube and ignored Jasper's pointed grimace as she did. "Do you have any scruples?"

That only made Jasper laugh harder. "Oh, more than you, Thea darling. But you'll have to ask Kate about her reasons."

They looked at each other for a moment. Behind Jasper, nine million Londoners bustled through the city and Thea wondered where Mem was and what she was doing.

She realised Jasper was still looking at her expectantly.

"I'm grumpy, Jasper," she said. "Leave me alone."

Jasper smiled again, threw an arm over her shoulders and squeezed her into a half-hug. He walked her to the door and she pushed him off. Not that she didn't love him, but she didn't need a floor full of financial and marketing people thinking Thea Voronov was the kind of person who hugged. She lifted her chin.

"You *are* grumpy and you're revolting like this," Jasper told her. "Get out of here. Get back across the river and go do some work for me. There's a beautiful woman and a Ducati motorcycle in studio three at the warehouse for you to play with. Lollie has the details." He ignored her eye roll. "Go. Make art."

She walked away.

"Party at mine tomorrow night, darling," he called to her back.

"Not interested."

"Be there, Thea. Kate is bringing Mem. I want that diamond contract."

Chapter Nine

Mem was pretty sure Dame Katherine Cox was trying to get her drunk.

"Shots, darlings," she cried. She set a raft of glittering little glasses in front of them and passed one to Mem. "No idea what it is, but it's Jasper's so it's probably expensive. Down the hatch!"

She smashed her glass against Mem's with a massive grin. Mem didn't have much choice.

Ugh. Vodka. A really smooth one.

Mem was already buzzy from the bottle of cheap bubbles she'd shared at Kate's before arriving, and the glass of a far more expensive champagne Jasper Fitz-Stewart, the Earl of Ravensworth, pressed into her hand the moment she'd stepped into his apartment.

It wasn't the booze that had Mem's head spinning, though. She was hot with the thought of seeing Thea Voronov again.

They were gathered on a U-shape of white leather lounges in Jasper's South Bank penthouse, ridiculously luxurious, with a view of the Thames to kill for. Mem was currently level with the top of the London Eye and slap bang in the middle of one of the most stylish parties she had ever had the luck to attend. She wanted to slap herself when the phrase 'you've hit the big time now, babe,' literally drifted through her mind.

Lollie and Kate were chatting with a blond woman from CreatedDiamonds and Adiatu loomed over the back of the couch, keeping tabs on the conversation. Her hand lightly touched the woman's shoulder every now and then, and Mem recognised the distinct signs of Adiatu's calculating greed. Two other women, so slim and leggy they had to be models, whispered amongst themselves. They never took their eyes off Kate.

Mem couldn't focus. Sure, the champagne, and now the shots, were loosening her up quite nicely, but she was a mess of nerves.

Kate had promised Thea Voronov would be there – and since Mem had spent most of the last forty-eight hours with her brain and her body in hyper-drive, she *needed* to see her. She couldn't stop playing back every interaction she'd had with the gorgeous photographer and her heavy stare. She had dissected and analysed every word they'd said, wondering what it all meant. And she couldn't stop this tight, dizzy feeling in her chest, or the dull throbbing ache in her core whenever she pictured Thea – and the way that firm, possessive finger had hooked into her dress and pulled her close.

She'd let her own fingers follow the path that Thea's had taken. She'd slipped them between her legs in a desperate attempt to rub it all from her mind. She'd bravely twisted the cold tap in the shower to full and dived beneath it, daring herself to stay there until she calmed the fuck down – but her mind only imagined Thea daring her instead and she turned the water off, hotter than ever.

Thea wanted her – she knew that – but then Mem had been a Class A Twit and run like a frightened child – to her parent's house, no less, for a family-freaking-dinner. What an insult.

You want a bonnet and a high-lace collar to go with that, Mem, you prude? she asked herself. She just wanted to see Thea again and hope the woman still wanted to talk to her. She wanted to apologise – and she tried not to acknowledge the thrilling flutter in her chest at *that* thought – and explain.

If she was lucky, Thea might still want her.

If she was extremely lucky, Thea might let her apologise on her knees.

Fuck. The alcohol was definitely going to her head. At this rate, she was going to jump Thea the moment she walked in the door.

"Darling Mem, your glass is empty!" Jasper Fitz-Stewart appeared at her elbow and pouted winningly. "Aren't you enjoying my party? Kate! You're neglecting your duties." He threw Kate a playful glare and took Mem's glass. "Let's get you another Dom."

Mem froze. She blinked. *Domme?*

Jasper hooted with delight and held up a bottle. "Pérignon, you gorgeous thing. Oh, I can see why Thea likes you."

Kate smacked him. "Idiot."

Mem wanted to fall through the floor. What was wrong with her? She was hopelessly horny. Jasper chortled merrily and filled her glass with more champagne.

The diamond woman was explaining to the models how laboratory-grown diamonds were of higher quality than the ones that came out of the ground. Mem couldn't have cared less.

"Is she here?" Mem asked him, softly.

"Fashionably late, as always," Jasper said. "Don't worry. She'll find you." His gaze sharpened for a tiny moment before his perfect, amiable grin covered his face again. "I heard someone agreed to be a muse. Sounds promising. You're braver than I am, darling." He nudged her and put on a performance of mock-scandal. If he'd been wearing pearls, he'd have clutched them. "You have seen her work, haven't you? You know what you're getting yourself into?"

Kate reached around her and thumped him again. "Bugger off, Jasper," she said, mildly.

He ambled away, all smiles and effortless charm.

Mem sipped her champagne, then shrugged and considered where she was. She slugged back half the glass. You only live once, right?

"Is he really an earl?" she whispered to Kate. Looking around to watch him schmoozing his guests was really just an excuse to scan the room to see if Thea had arrived.

"Jasper is a pretentious git, and too bloody charming for his own good, but yes, he is an actual earl," Kate said. "We try not to mention it though because his head is big enough as it is. And he's rich as Croesus. This is just his city pad for when he's feeling all glitzy and wants to show off."

"He owns that castle in Hampshire where your movie was filmed," said Lollie.

"He *owns* that?" Mem squeaked. *The Wolverton Diamond* had been filmed in one of England's most magnificent stately homes – the kind of place that made Downton Abbey look like a bungalow. Mem was having a bit of trouble believing the company she was in.

"And a castle in Scotland," said a voice that pulsed through Mem's soul. "It has an actual dungeon."

Mem started so violently she spilled her champagne.

"Taxi!" Kate cried.

She was here!

Thea strode into the middle of their little gathering with a confidence that sang through every fibre of her being. She was in a suit – naturally – but this one fit her like Versace was her bitch and Victoria had sold all her secrets. Her eyes were black-rimmed and dark as sin, and the look on her face dared anyone to fuck with her.

Anyone who wasn't Mem, apparently, because she stepped right into Mem's space.

She didn't even bother to bend down. One finger tracked a very possessive line down Mem's cheek, hooked under her chin and flicked her face up. Mem's eyes snapped to hers. Thea's were dancing. Her smirk was ridiculous. Mem adored it.

"My muse," she said, softly, in greeting. No one else was with them. It was just Thea and Mem.

Kate blew a raspberry. "Still haven't learnt any fucking manners, I see, Thea." She sounded slightly jealous.

It broke the moment. The corner of Thea's lips tweaked like she was glad for the insult and she caressed Mem's cheek very gently for one more moment before she let her go. She flicked her own chin at the two models in an obvious dismissal, and the women got up and left without comment. Thea threw herself into their place, right next to Mem, lounging back on the sofa with a messy grace, crossing her long legs so that one heel rubbed against Mem's leg.

Four inch heels. So black and shiny Mem could see her face in them.

Again: fuck.

Thea placed one palm very deliberately on Mem's thigh.

The whole performance had taken only minutes, but Mem was panting as if she'd run a mile.

"Katherine, you're drunk," Thea said.

"Not quite yet, but I'm working on it." Kate didn't sound the slightest bit remorseful. "This is the first do I've been to in weeks that isn't work. There are no studio execs, no paparazzi – well, aside from you, of course – and it's fucking bliss." She completely ignored Thea's middle finger at the word 'paparazzi' and reached to the table to pluck another bottle of Dom Pérignon from an ice bucket. She topped up her own glass and Mem's.

"Oh, not for me—"

Kate poured anyway. Mem didn't have a say in it, apparently.

"We're talking diamonds," Kate declared. "This is Tash Kirov-White from the company that provided the rock for our movie. They want to give Mem and me a heap of money to make them look sexy. I'm terribly excited about it, but Mem is being a stick in the mud. I thought getting her sloshed might help, but maybe you can convince her, Thea."

Thea's hand twitched on Mem's leg. When Mem turned to look at her, she was glaring angrily at Kate, but she tore her eyes back to Mem's as soon as she saw Mem looking. Her smirk turned lethal and it lit Mem up. Her pupils widened and she pressed harder with her thumb. Her palm was hot on Mem's bare leg.

"Nice dress," Thea murmured into her ear. Her breath spilled down Mem's throat and lifted every hair on the back of her neck. "I like how little there is of it."

"Are you paying attention, Voronov?" Kate tutted.

"Not in the slightest."

Thea's eyes were on the neckline of Mem's dress. Mem's were stuck on the smooth, white expanse of skin plainly on show between Thea's breasts between the lapels of her jacket. Mem wanted to put her mouth to it. She wondered if Thea would let her.

Adiatu had already explained the proposed brand ambassador role with CreatedDiamonds, and Mem had already informed her she wasn't interested. Tash Kirov-White chatted away about opportunities and creative vision as if no one had bothered to let her know Mem wasn't on board. She was keen and engaging, with an Oxford English accent tinged with Eastern European edges, but Mem barely heard a word.

Thea's hand was creeping higher. Her little finger slid under the hem of Mem's dress. Mem could have stopped her, but she didn't want to.

"It's just four weeks until the premiere for *The Wolverton Diamond*," Tash enthused. "We're hoping for a joint launch of our campaign with Kate and Mem on the red carpet at the premiere. And some of your extraordinary images of course, Ms Voronov, on a grand scale, gracing the Royal Albert Hall."

She beamed encouragingly at Thea.

Thea simply stared back. Utterly expressionless. She bared her teeth.

"Be nice," muttered Kate.

"Not even possible," Jasper said cheerfully, appearing behind them and slapping Thea on the back of the head. "But she does take a half decent happy snap. I can personally guarantee CreatedDiamonds a bunch for the premiere, Tash."

Tash Kirov-White looked ecstatic.

Thea pressed her lips into a fuck-you smile which she offered to everyone in the group in equal measure. Mem noticed Lollie smother a giggle and Adiatu's leer turned greedier than ever. Kate, at least, dropped her eyes.

"Have you seen the view from the balcony?" Thea asked Mem, and her hand appeared in front of Mem's face in a distinct order. Mem slipped her palm into Thea's. Her fingers were warm.

Jasper's chuckle was rich behind their backs.

"You're not looking at the view."

"Oh, I am."

Thea had her back to the Thames, leaning her hip against the railing. Her arms were folded and her feet were crossed at the ankles. She gazed at Mem like she was hungry.

The air was cooler outside though it did nothing to soothe the heat that was rippling off Thea Voronov in waves. Mem could *feel* her beside her. It made it very difficult to think. They really had to talk.

Thea got in first.

"How is your family?"

Mem blinked.

"You had dinner with your parents." Thea drawled it, as if she wasn't entirely convinced Mem had been telling the truth. "Not an excuse I've heard before."

She was so unbelievably cocky. Mem barely hid an eye roll.

"Women run from your studio with better excuses?"

Thea looked startled for one split second, before a grin dawned on her face like the sunrise.

"You're far cheekier than I expected, Ms Swan," she said. "I like it." She brushed the backs of her fingers down Mem's arm. Mem's entire body broke out in goosebumps. "Women tend not to run from my studio at all."

"That's confident."

Thea smirked. "A mere statement of fact."

"I really did have dinner with my folks."

There was a sigh and Thea finally turned to stare out over the park to the river. "That must be nice."

"You haven't met my family."

The party buzzed behind them – Jasper's easy laugh rising over music and chatter. They both turned at the noise. Dame Katherine Cox was barefoot on a table, tugging one of the models up to join her. They both vamped up some Bob Fosse moves and Jasper couldn't contain himself. He jumped up too and used a chip bowl as a bowler hat.

Thea chuckled. "Those idiots are my family."

Mem was surprised at the warmth in her tone. The woman was magic when she smiled.

"I like them."

The smile narrowed into smug possessiveness almost instantly and it drained the blood from Mem's brain. "I'm glad you do. We'll all be doing a lot of work together yet."

Mem frowned. "Do you mean the CreatedDiamonds ambassador thing?"

Thea tweaked an eyebrow. She didn't say anything.

"I'm not doing it," Mem said. "I told Adiatu—"

"What if I asked you to?"

Thea's voice dropped an octave and flowed like honey. It trickled through Mem's mind, slipped in a slow, thick cascade down her spine and curled in a hot pool in her cunt. Mem leaned forward. She'd do fucking anything if Thea asked her like that.

"Do you mean, as your muse?" she breathed. "Is that what that means?"

Thea looked triumphant. Her eyes glittered. "I simply feel it would be strategic positioning for you. It's a high class brand. Katherine wouldn't lend her name to it otherwise, and Jasper will do it justice with his media stable." She dragged her gaze from Mem's face down her body and all the way back up again in a slow, indulgent leer. "And I will make you look sensational."

Mem had absolutely no doubts about that. She found she couldn't take her eyes off Thea's mouth, and when the tip of Thea's tongue crept out and brushed her top lip, Mem stopped breathing entirely. The whole of London shrank to just the few centimetres between them and Mem was lost in the power of Thea's gaze. How was she doing this to her?

She blinked and tried to turn her brain back on. That was probably good advice – and Thea would know. Thea Voronov had her finger on the pulse of luxury style. Hell, Thea Voronov *drove* the pulse of luxury style.

Thea Voronov had total command of Mem's pulse too. Mem took a deep breath and didn't even try to disguise the way it shuddered into her.

"I kind of have other plans," Mem managed.

"Other plans?"

"Goals. You know. Projects."

Thea simply leaned closer. She put her lips to the side of Mem's neck and whispered – not into her ear, but into the skin just below it. It burned.

"What if I *ordered* you to?"

Mem shut her eyes. She was torn – *fuck,* she wanted Thea to tear her apart – but she both fervently wanted Thea to order her and desperately hoped she wouldn't, because Mem was rapidly losing all sense of reason. Thea was melting it from her, leaving nothing but need in its place.

"I have a roadmap all planned out," Mem said, weakly.

There was a gentle huff of breath on her neck that could have been a snort of derision, or a sigh of surrender. Thea pulled back.

"Well, if you have other plans."

The door to the apartment slid open and startled them both.

"Voronov! I need you. I have whiskey and a pingpong ball."

Only Mem heard her whisper, "for fuck's sake, Jasper," before she turned and laid on the perfect picture of bored arrogance. "Are you seventeen again, Lord Ravensworth?"

Jasper stuck two fingers up with a breezy smile. "You didn't even know me then, party pooper. Get in here."

Thea gave Mem one more devastating smirk, shrugged and swaggered away.

Mem had no idea what just happened.

The next two hours were almost unbearable.

Not because the party was dull – far from it. Jasper plainly knew how to throw an entertaining bash. The room glowed, and the lights of the city spread like a glittering blanket below the equally expansive balcony. Beautiful people spilled from room to room, the women tall and tanned, all legs and tits, in dresses and jewels more expensive than any Mem had ever owned.

There were faces Mem recognised – from movies and magazine covers – and Kate dragged her to meet them, her voice friendly and loud, her laughter easily soothing over the slight discomfort she seemed to know Mem felt. She squeezed her hand every now and then, with a champagne-fueled grin that told her to be brave and throw caution to the wind.

The fame of each of the people Kate introduced her to may have been intimidating, but Mem's eyes always found their way back to Thea.

Across the room, Thea played a lethal game of beer pong. Not that Jasper stooped to beer or plastic cups, of course. The glasses racked at either end of his mahogany dining table were crystal. The liquid in them was topped up with an aged Balvenie. Thea smiled viciously each time her throw had her opponents drinking, one smile for them, an even sharper one for Mem.

She was performing, Mem realised – and what a show! Her shoulders were thrown back, one hand was thrust into her pocket, and she managed to look more confident than anyone else in the room, more graceful, and casually careless at the same time.

It was an intoxicating blend and it drew Mem's eyes like a magnet.

Others were attracted to it too. Men roared with laughter at her jokes. Women drifted closer, their eyes fluttering. One or two were foolish enough to drape themselves against her, and Thea turned each one away with a sharp mouth. It made Jasper laugh. Thea's eyes simply burned darkly at Mem, and she tossed another perfect shot.

Jasper played to lose.

Later, Thea prowled the room, only settling when Jasper regaled a group with a ludicrous story from decades ago – he, Thea and Kate running like criminals through Camden Markets with the cops on their heels and Kate wearing nothing but a leather collar and a rug.

"Indecent exposure," Jasper explained, "though we were in a Persian rug seller's shop."

"It was a really good shot," Thea protested.

"Do you have any idea how hard it is to run in a rug?" Kate asked the crowd.

"Thea fell in the canal," boomed Jasper.

"I didn't."

"You were *green*," he laughed.

"You stank," said Kate.

"I was pushed." Thea rolled her eyes. There was a smile around her lips that might have been fond. "*You* pushed me, Jasper." She had a lofty pride all over her features, which lasted until she saw Mem watched her. Then, incredibly, she *blushed*.

Jasper hooted, wrapped his arm around her neck and ruffled her hair.

"Fuck off," she muttered into his chest under the cover of everyone's laughter, but Mem saw the quick squeeze she gave him and the soft glance she directed at Kate.

Later still, the playlist moved into some classic Depeche Mode and Kate tugged Mem to an impromptu dance floor in the middle of the sunken lounge. Kate's moves were truly kooky, and for a moment, Mem was dumbfounded. The most sophisticated woman on the planet was all elbows and hips on the off-beat, her whole vibe completely hilarious. With the kind of bullying only a megastar could get away with, she insisted Mem and the leggy models join her, and the vodka, the champagne and the sheer silliness of it all combined into a riotous sense of fun, and suddenly Mem was dancing without a care in the world.

It was a while before she noticed Thea had stopped prowling. She was simply standing, watching, her hands in her pockets, her eyes black, her lips parted.

It was another moment before Mem realised the only person Thea was watching was her.

She knew it was the alcohol, but Mem looked her square in the eyes, held out her hand and crooked one finger. She felt so powerful.

Until Thea took her hand.

Before Mem knew what had happened, Thea spun her and wrapped herself around her. Mem's hand was somehow behind her back and pressed between them, flat against Thea's abs. Thea's other hand snaked around Mem's waist, her fingers brushing the underside of her breast. Thea's breath was hot on her neck, her thigh was hard on the backs of Mem's legs, her hips were tilted up against Mem's arse.

The effect on Mem's body was instant.

She was on fire. Her knees wanted to bend. Her mind simply surrendered and her head fell back against Thea's shoulder. Thea's triumph trickled into her ear and ran down her neck like lava. Thea moved her body for her, and Mem wanted nothing but to be controlled. When the hand straying so close to her breast moved up and took a greedy handful, Mem couldn't stop a groan.

The laugh in her ear was kind.

"Let's get you someplace private," Thea murmured.

Somehow, it was both a question and an order, and Mem knew that Thea would be an utter gentleman if she said no. But she could feel the sheer force of the woman at her back, her heat and her urgency. Mem's brave moment of power was swept away as Thea took control – and the ease with which the woman did it was so fucking sexy, Mem was soaked.

"Yes, please," she managed.

Thea laughed, twined her fingers in Mem's and led her away.

Chapter Ten

There was a hallway.

Mem didn't see it.

Thea pulled her along it and lost her patience somewhere near yet another floor to ceiling window. Mem was aware of her back to the glass and Thea pressed against her, one hand on Mem's hip, the other at her throat, her teeth grazing that perfect spot behind Mem's ear. All of London could see them but Mem didn't care.

Was this really happening?

They fell into a guest room. Thea kicked the door closed behind her and walked Mem backwards to the bed with her hand still on her throat. Mem's legs hit the bed and Thea squeezed – once, lightly – and Mem simply collapsed, something in her mind shorting out, something between her legs flaring with heat. She scooted backwards as Thea straddled her thighs and pushed until Mem was lying on her back. Mem was soaked in a second – and it all moved quickly after that.

"I want you. All of you."

Mem nodded. Thea's need was fueling her own. She was squirming under Thea's legs. She wanted Thea's hands all over her, her fingers deep inside her – fuck, she wanted all of Thea she could get.

"Tell me, my sweet little muse. I need to hear you."

"I—" Mem had to clear her throat. "Yes. I want you too. Very much." *That* was classy. So sophisticated. What was she? Suddenly she had the vocabulary of a toddler. "Please, Thea."

The woman above her seemed to like the plea. Her smirk poured petrol on Mem's need and tossed on a match for good measure. A full body spasm of desire rushed through her, utterly unstoppable, and Mem didn't even try to hide it. She arched her back, gripped the bedcovers and let her body push against Thea's thighs.

A moan wrenched itself from her throat.

When she opened her eyes again, Thea was looking down at her with an open hunger – rapt, avaricious and determined to sample it all. She laughed with delight and narrowed her eyes. Then she dived in.

Her hand slid up Mem's dress and cupped her over her underwear. Laughed.

"Slick," she said, smirking like a conqueror. "That for me?"

Mem fought down her desperation and tried for dignity. "Who else? Don't tease me."

That only made Thea laugh more. "You want me to tease you, you impudent thing." Her fingers played along the edge of Mem's knickers.

Mem struggled to open her legs but her skirt was short and tight, and Thea was still straddling her thighs. Thea's fingers curled around lace and her thumb pressed hard over Mem's clit, but still she waited.

"May I?"

"*God*. Yes! Please."

But this time Thea didn't laugh. She simply pushed the cloth aside and ran two fingers the length of Mem's pussy like she owned it. Her own moan fell from open lips and spilled over Mem, heavy with need. Mem felt a curious thrill of power. Thea's chest heaved. She was struggling to hold onto her own composure and it was such a fucking turn on to watch. Thea needed this too.

Their eyes locked for one frozen moment.

The fog of alcohol seared away on the pressure building under Thea's thumb and Mem was suddenly as sober as she'd ever been.

Thea hadn't kissed her yet.

There was a thumb on her clit, fingers paused in the soaked mess of her cunt, and a burning greed in the woman above her but Mem found herself reaching gently up towards Thea's face. She cradled her cheek and drew her close. Their lips touched.

They were so *unbelievably* perfect.

Thea pulled back with the same astonished surprise and her eyes pinballed between Mem's, confusion and shock overpowering her lust for just a moment.

But *just* a moment. When Mem hummed and tugged her lips back down again, Thea resisted, proud again. She sat up, actually *pinched* Mem's clit and smirked viciously.

"Dress off," she ordered, climbing off Mem's legs.

She was fucking regal too, Mem thought, living for the crisp command in Thea's tone.

There was only one thing to do.

She crawled off the bed, unzipped her dress and let it crumple to the floor at her feet. Her black lace bra hit the carpet too. She stepped out of her knickers – they were ruined anyway – and she stood before Thea in nothing but her heels.

Thea's eyes turned black.

"Oh, darling. You are *beautiful*," Thea breathed.

She stared until it should have been demeaning. She *examined* Mem – not like an artist. Not even like a connoisseur. Thea sat on the edge of the bed and looked at Mem like someone seeing salvation, having never believed she could be saved. Thea looked at Mem like she was *redeemed*.

"Come here," she murmured. For the first time since Mem had met her, she was soft, her voice gentle.

Mem slipped into the space between her knees, and Thea looked up. She was a goddess, beautiful and powerful beyond Mem's wildest dreams, but right now, Thea was the one worshipping. Mem was drained by her gaze.

Thea fell helplessly forward, brushing her lips on the hollow between Mem's breasts, burying her face in them with a sigh. One hand fell delicately to Mem's hip and the other cupped the curve of her breast almost as if she was afraid to touch, and Mem was suddenly confused. What had happened to the woman's towering ego? Just seconds ago she'd been making Mem beg. How had the mood switched from lust to whatever the fuck this was so quickly?

"Is this what it means to be your muse?" Mem whispered, brushing her fingers over the nape of Thea's neck, cradling her close. "Is this what you want from me?"

Thea caught a nipple in her mouth and sucked hard. Mem twitched. One more helpless moan and Mem pulled Thea's face in harder, gripping her wrist as she pinched at her other nipple. Thea was lost. On Mem. It was almost as overwhelming as her urgent lust, but Mem had to know.

"Is this about art or is it about sex?"

Mem saw the exact moment that aloof pride re-entered Thea's body. She felt it too when Thea bit down on her nipple and tweaked the other in time.

"Is there a difference?" She quirked one eyebrow and that glorious fucking attitude was back like it had never left. "Get on the bed, my muse."

A harsh swat landed on Mem's arse. She didn't know whether it was the delicious sting of the blow or the challenge on Thea's face, but suddenly she was whining like a brat. She wanted so much more of this. Thea tolerated her hesitation for all of three seconds, then clambered over her and pinned her wrists above her head.

"Keep them there," she said, then she fell on Mem's breasts again.

Her mouth was incredible. Her teeth grazed and bit. Her tongue was hot and strong, soothing over hurts that Mem instinctively knew were just tiny promises of what Thea really wanted to do to her. Her fingers were hard, and it was winding Mem up like crazy. She wanted those fingers back between her legs. She wanted Thea deep inside her. She wanted Thea to raise her up and never let her down.

A small, dazed part of her mind remembered Thea's question.

"You said you wanted me for your exhibition. Something at the Tate?"

There was a snort. "Are you saying you don't want this?"

Thea's hand crept back to Mem's throat. She squeezed. And stared Mem down.

It was like a bolt of lightning straight to Mem's pussy. Another spasm, and she felt herself gush. Mem whimpered.

"I want this very much."

There was a beat, a tiny sneer, then Thea laughed again. A glorious sound. She tangled her fist in Mem's hair and pulled her head back, breathing into her throat.

"Oh, I know you do. You are so ready for this. You want to do everything I ask, don't you, darling? You want me to own you."

"I do. Oh god, please, yes. I do."

Two fingers slipped inside Mem like they belonged there, and Thea was on her knees over one of Mem's thighs, pinning her down. When she started thrusting, it was at a merciless pace, a look in her eyes both goading and encouraging, demanding and astonished. Mem had never felt so strong, so desired and so wanted, and utterly weak all at the same time. Her body wound itself tighter and tighter. Thea seemed to know and changed her angle to hit deeper, harder. She curled her fingers upwards and—

"Oh!"

That fucking smirk. "Oh?"

"C-close. I'm so—"

And *again*, Thea stopped.

Mem didn't have time to complain because, in a scrabble of movement, Thea spun her over and dumped her face down on the bed.

"Hands and knees."

"Wha—"

"Up!"

There was a stinging slap on her backside then a hot mouth soothing over the hurt, and Mem was astonished at how it felt. No one had slapped her bum during sex – ever – and she couldn't believe the effect it had on her. She nearly shot over the edge right there.

She pointed her toes and hammered her feet against the bed, desperate to hold on.

"You sweet, sweet thing. That really works for you, doesn't it?"

Her smugness was infuriating, but Mem couldn't deny it.

"Doesn't it?!"

Slap.

Her arms gave way and she bit the bed covers, Thea's delighted chuckle ringing in her ears.

"Oh, you are going to be so much fun, darling."

That word did it for her too. She groaned into the pillows.

"*Darling.*" Thea draped herself over Mem and whispered it lushly into her ear, hot and liquid, loaded with tease. How did she know?

"The things I want to do to you, my precious muse. You're going to be begging me—"

Mem couldn't stand it any longer. "I'm begging you now, Thea. Please fuck me. Please."

"Perfect," Thea breathed, and with no warning plunged her fingers back into Mem's pussy, curling them and dragging them brilliantly.

And, fuck, she was amazing.

Thea put her whole body into it, deepening each thrust of her wrist with a grind from her hips. The expensive linen of her blazer brushed against Mem's backside and that sent her spiralling too – Thea was fully dressed, Mem was naked but for her heels – and the power imbalance was exhilarating. Thea's free hand pressed between her shoulder blades, forcing her chest down and her backside higher, the angle intensifying until Mem was mewling with every movement.

And then Thea was draped over her again, her other hand reaching around to rub her clit, hot, wet, opened mouthed kisses at the base of her spine, bites on the flesh of her arse, and Mem was screaming towards oblivion faster than she ever had in her life. One sharp, perfectly timed slap on her backside, right over a bruising bite, and Mem was gone, clenching around Thea's fingers, her legs in spasm until she was bent, rearing up off the bed. Thea didn't relent, chasing her orgasm, demanding she give more. Mem felt herself flipped over, her legs spread, and then Thea on her again, her mouth hot over her clit, the pressure rising all over again. One look down at the incredible woman with her head between her legs, watching her with eyes that drained her soul and Mem simply cried until she gushed again, and Thea was triumphant.

The next thing she knew, she was flat on her back. Thea reclined beside her, her head resting on one crooked elbow. Her phone was in her other hand taking pictures. She looked entranced.

Her smile was kind.

"Exhibition," she murmured, not quite apologetically.

Mem gave a weak laugh. "So *this* is what being your muse means?"

"Are you complaining?"

Damn, she was proud, but Mem could easily forgive her that. "Not one bit." She stretched like a cat. Thea held up her phone again. "I think I want to be your muse for the rest of my life."

She thought it would get a laugh, but it was the wrong thing to say.

Bitterness twisted Thea's lips and she stood up, stalking to the other side of the room in a clattering of heels, her shoulders tight, her hands in her pockets. Mem sat up.

"Thea?"

She stared out the window and Mem looked at her profile. Proud, of course, almost arrogant – stunning in that suit and so elegant – but something was upsetting her.

Mem tried again. "I've never felt like this before," she admitted. What harm could there be in total honesty? She was naked on the bed, she may as well bare her heart too. "I've never felt like this with anyone, Thea, but I'm drawn to you. I couldn't stop myself from wanting you if I tried. And that was"—she huffed out an exhausted laugh—"that was the most amazing orgasm I've had in my life, and if that's what being your muse means then you can count me in for every second of the day, but... but it's more than that, isn't it? Because it feels like more to me."

Thea didn't move. The silence stretched out.

That was embarrassing.

Mem looked on the ground for her clothes. She was just gathering the strength to move when Thea strode back to the bed. She still had her chin up and her hands in her pockets, but she wore a cautious smile.

"I— I feel the same."

Mem's relieved giggle would have been even more humiliating, except that it made Thea laugh too. And she was beautiful when she laughed. The woman sat back down again and trailed her fingers up Mem's arm. It caused every inch of Mem's skin to crinkle with goosebumps, and Thea watched it in wonder. Then she seemed to make a decision.

"It's art *and* sex – if that's okay with you," she said, returning to the same position as before, her head on her hand. Mem scurried to mirror her pose and they lay facing each other. Thea's fingers brushed a lazy, entitled pattern on Mem's boob, circling her nipple and Mem loved it.

"Think of all the famous painters throughout history and the models who sat for them. All those naked masterpieces," Thea mused. "You think they never shagged? Of course they did."

She was comparing herself to the grand masters? Mem went for the safer taunt.

"So I'm a masterpiece, then?"

Thea's lips flattened into a smirk and she flicked Mem's nipple.

"You know you are. It's in the way we look at each other – everyone, always. There's always sex in our gaze, or something weighing and judging at least." She shrugged. "Life, art, beauty, sex. I don't see the difference. But I see you, Mem Swan, and what I see in you makes me hungry." Her voice dropped to a whisper and Mem leaned closer. "I want to taste you and I want to see what that will do to my art. I can't explain it any better than that. I'm greedy and I'm selfish and I want you. Will you have a problem with that?"

Would Mem have a problem surrendering to the most enthralling, captivating woman she'd ever met? Hell no, but she wasn't ready to let Thea win this round quite so easily.

"So, you're going to fuck me and take photos of me?"

Thea's laugh spilled into the room again. Mem decided she wanted to be responsible for it over and over again. She rolled onto her back, raised her arms over her head and stretched out languidly, keen to see how cheekiness worked on Thea. If the open-mouthed grin and the rush to palm Mem's boob and squeeze it hard was anything to go by, Thea clearly loved it. Mem arched into her hand and threw her head back. When she opened her eyes, Thea was photographing her again. She squawked in outrage.

"Essentially," Thea said, mildly. "There are a few other tasks we can add to the job description if you like."

"I can think of a few things," Mem said, her eyes dropping to the V of Thea's suit.

"Greedy wench."

"Don't I get to say what I want?" Mem protested.

Thea seemed momentarily surprised. "Of course you do."

"I want—"

The bedroom door suddenly burst open so violently it hit the wall and bounced all the way back. Jasper copped it in the face.

"Fuck," he slurred.

"I think they just did!" Kate was right behind him, considerably more drunk than she'd been last time Mem saw her. They stumbled into the room and stopped at the end of the bed.

Mem squealed with embarrassment and grabbed at the bedcover, but Thea sat up slowly, leaving her hand resting lightly on Mem's breast. One very imperious eyebrow gave the instruction. *Stay like that*, Mem realised. *All laid out for me. Naked. Perfect.*

Mine.

Mem obeyed and a flush swept over her face and her breasts. Thea's smile was unholy.

"Awfully sorry, old things." Jasper didn't look it. He had a grin wider than the Thames and he raised both eyebrows so high they nearly flew off his head. Kate snort-laughed into his shoulder. They were both so pissed Mem fervently hoped their memories would be foggy by the morning.

She squirmed a little under Thea's hand.

Jasper noticed Thea's phone.

"Ooo! Are you taking photos? Sexy ones? Tiddies?" He wheezed out a burp. "Send them to me?"

"Jasper!" Kate attempted to swat his shoulder, missed by a mile, and dissolved into giggles.

"Inappropriate," Thea chided, mildly.

Mem blew a soft raspberry at her obvious double standards. It earned her a swift pinch to her under-boob. The zing shot straight to her pussy. She smiled serenely back at Thea.

Thea lost patience with her friends. "What are you doing in here? Go away!" She was still the very picture of elegance, Mem thought, not in the slightest bit ruffled by what they'd just done, her long legs stretched lazily on the bed.

Her thumb caressed the side of Mem's breast in a light, slow back and forth. Mem wondered if she knew she was doing it.

Jasper snapped back into action. He swung around and peered at the bookshelves. "My apartment, old chap. There should be a couple of awards in here. *Dame* Katherine's been banging on about how many Oscars and Golden Globes she's got, and really, I'm sure I've got more."

"You can't act," Kate pointed out.

"British Breast Awards." Jasper slurred. "*Presht!* Press awards— fuck it, Design Week Awards. For my magazines. For my *art*."

"Whose art?" asked Mem. "I thought Thea Voronov made you famous."

Jasper turned and gaped at her like Christmas had been cancelled. Kate hooted with delight, and Thea threw her head back and crowed. She kissed Mem's mouth – a fierce taking kind of kiss and Mem opened to her and let herself be kissed.

"Oh, you perfect, perfect thing," Thea murmured against her lips.

Kate watched them with a pleased smile. She clapped her hands. "Out, out, out Jasper. No, you filthy old man, go!" She seized him by the shoulders and propelled him toward the door. "Enjoy, you two."

Mem didn't even hear the door close. She was lost to the hardness in Thea's hands, to the possession in her mouth. She was consumed and owned, and it felt so right.

Chapter Eleven

Thea Voronov was no stranger to self-loathing.

In fact, it was an emotional state she'd carried for so long it had essentially become a second skin – she barely noticed she was wearing it. When she slipped on a silk shirt to cover it and flicked up the collar around her throat, or she shucked on a thousand-pound designer jacket and shot the cuffs like a boss, when she strode through Jasper's building in Camden Lock on heels that set everyone else scurrying to her beat then, *then* she could almost forget it.

Self-loathing made her what she was. Gave her something to rise above. That was what she felt in her best moments.

And at her worst, she knew it was bullshit. She was resigned to it. The shitshow that was her life was simply a parade of opportunities for Thea to deepen that contempt. Innocence to abuse with her camera, society's standards to corrupt with her lens. She was about to do exactly that now, in Jasper's studio three, with three pretty women and a morally bankrupt advertising campaign for a celebrity already as wealthy as sin.

Thea would be paid obscenely for it.

She didn't want to be working today – she didn't even need to be working – but Jasper was being an arse. He knew that despite an incredible encounter with the luscious Memona Swan at his party the other night, Thea hadn't convinced her to accept the role with CreatedDiamonds and he was being petulant.

"You can work for your money," he said over the phone. "Lollie's got everything set up for you. Studio three, if you please."

Thea thought this was particularly ripe coming from a spoiled mummy's boy who'd inherited more country estates than the king, but nothing shut Jasper up when he got like this.

It was easier just to do his precious shoot and line her bank account.

"I think you'll find it's your money, Jasper. Keep that attitude up and my invoice will make your eyes bleed."

He chuckled. "You're worth it, darling."

Exploitation ran in her blood, what could she say?

Ever since she was thirteen and she figured out exactly what it was that happened to all those young women her father brought into their house, or onto their boat.

They weren't nannies.

Some of them had barely been older than she was.

But when the rest of the world figured it out too and Thea's world came crashing down, there'd been enough elements in the media to convince her she was right to be disgusted with herself. It had stuck.

And then she'd gone and seduced the exquisite Memona Swan, drunk, at a party.

She hated herself.

Thea snapped her fingers and everything swirled into action around her.

Lollie had everything under control, as always. Her favourite gear had been brought from her own studio in Gloucester Crescent just a few blocks away and a team of creatives had the set, lights and the talent ready and waiting for her. Thea cast a bored eye over the brief, aimed a playlist at the sound system and got to work.

It was a simple job – so simple Thea wondered why she was even doing it, aside from the fact that the celebrity who was launching the fragrance had paid a small fortune to have Thea Voronov shoot it. Jasper was good for that, at least.

As she'd expected, the three models were young and totally star-struck to be working with Thea. Probably the culmination of their wildest dreams. Thea snapped closeups of the three wrapped around each other, all pouty lips, lowered eyelids and provocative stares. Just this job would propel each of them into the next stage of their careers – take them from lingerie shoots to the catwalks of Paris. They simpered at Thea like they'd be happy to do whatever she asked, like they'd heard all the rumours and were desperate for them to be true.

And, normally, Thea would have given them exactly what they wanted. She'd have sailed through the brief, sent the audience away, and fucked all three women at once right on the piles of lace and roses they were posing on. It would have passed the time. Been a moderately satisfying sweetener in an otherwise dull and uninspiring job.

But something was different today. Thea was impatient. Craving something else entirely.

"Boss?" Lollie murmured when the hours were up and they had the shots they wanted. Thea was regarding the eager tangle of women on the bed with narrowed eyes.

Thea spared her a glance. Lollie knew her fancies well enough to anticipate what usually came next, but Thea grimaced.

"This is formulaic," she said. "Dull. A waste of my time. Who styled this shit?"

Lollie leaned closer and lowered her voice so the execs in the corner couldn't hear. "That would be the celebrity herself. America's favourite diva. You want me to get her on the phone right now so you can tell her her campaign is crap, or are you going to leave that pleasure to me?"

Thea smirked at Lollie's tone. Resigned yet a tiny bit bratty. It was why she liked her.

"No, but let's mix it up a bit, shall we? We'll do my thing. It's what this woman is paying for, after all." She pointed to a lighting tech and crooked two fingers. "Get everyone else out, get me fifty metres of gold tulle and get some rose gels on those overheads."

Lollie gave a happy, subversive grin and a wholly new vibe filled the room. The lights fell, angles deepened, make-up was smeared and the remaining team set to corrupting the brief, and creating something wilder. Something vivid and alive. Something visionary.

This was what Thea enjoyed – asking the eye to look in a new way, forcing the viewer to see beyond expectations and through to possibilities. After a few startled moments, the three models took their cue from Lollie and threw themselves into it and, for a while, Thea was almost enjoying herself. The women's conventional beauty became extraordinary. Thea turned what was simply fashionable into something poetic.

When they saw the proofs on the screens, the models nearly cried at their good luck – and on any other day, Thea would have ensured they repaid her in full.

They were beautiful, but they were nothing compared to what Thea had been drowning in with Mem Swan two nights ago.

Thea strolled the few streets home to Gloucester Crescent, her hands in her pockets and wondering what the fuck was wrong with her.

Back in her own studio, she scrolled through the hundreds of images she'd snapped for *The Wolverton Diamond* shoot the other day and felt her mind unravel even further. Mem more stunning than that diamond. The pretty submission she'd shown to Kate. The signs, clear as day, that she wanted to submit to Thea too.

Thea succumbed and went through the pics she'd taken on her phone in Jasper's guest room. Her equanimity crumbled entirely.

How was this girl doing this to her? Why was Memona Swan's beauty unpicking every careful knot in the painstaking web of work and purpose Thea had built around herself for all these years?

And why did she suddenly want to tear the whole safety net down?

Thea had never been the type to go soft on the talent. Pretty girls were all the same. They only wanted one thing.

Three, she corrected herself, lost in a snap of Mem naked, her head tipped back, her eyes closed, her lips parted. Sex, fame and money. Three things everyone was keen to use Thea for.

There was no real indication Mem was any different.

Then she'd met her, of course, and everything was different. Mem was… Thea's logical brain died at the edge of that thought and something more feral took over. Mem was so fucking perfect, so *angelic* it tore Thea's soul apart. So wet and warm, and the way she sobbed Thea's name… *fuck*, Thea would crave that forever. She'd drive the girl through a million climaxes just to be needed like that.

She swiped further through her photo reel. A darkening bruise on the girl's breast, the taste of her lush brown skin still warm in Thea's mouth. Mem's teeth savaging her lower lip. A wicked twist in her smile, a lust in her eyes that met Thea halfway, drew her in and flung them both over the precipice.

Thea's self-loathing raised its ugly head again. She'd jumped Mem like she couldn't control herself. Fucking a pretty girl at a party wasn't anything unusual for Thea, but this was the first time in a long time she'd allowed her usual self-disgust to actually bother her. She'd followed Jasper's orders and Kate's honeyed entreaties like she was a tool, a gun for hire. Did she really want to manipulate Mem Swan and pull her into the machine? Did she really want to see a woman of Memona's calibre used and cheapened? Sullied and spoiled?

She paused on another photo.

Mem kneeling on the bed, her face tilted up to Thea's, but her eyes fluttering down. Lashes that whispered of temptation, a kiss in the corner of her mouth that was begging to be taken, a body that promised insanity and absolution.

Thea sighed. There was one more issue that confused things.

Mem wanted Thea's dominance. That simple fact was as obvious as her beauty. And while Thea's core was burning even now at the thought of her submission, that shit only fed Thea's self-loathing. It only made Thea more monstrous. She'd already been unfair to Mem. She'd asked her for far more than she'd ever taken from anyone else – even Kate – and it was patently clear the girl had never even been tied to the bed posts.

She wanted to be ... *respectful* ... with this one.

Her lip curled.

Not that she wouldn't love to make Mem beg for her touch, frantic for release. The beautiful way the girl unravelled, stunning even as she fell apart, reached deep inside her, past the monster, right through to a part of herself Thea barely recognised.

Was it her heart?

She snorted.

Monsters like Thea didn't have hearts. And what was to say that Mem was any different from the women in the photoshoot today? Eager to use Thea for everything they could get? Mem Swan was probably just the same.

And yet the girl had blown her off – *her! Thea Voronov!* – for a family dinner.

That was a first. Perhaps it was genuine.

Agh.

She threw her phone aside and snatched up one of her more compact cameras. An ancient thing. Loaded it with film. Back in her house she dug out torn baggy jeans and a tattered old hoodie from the back of her wardrobe. With her hair tucked under a cap and the hood pulled down low she was unrecognisable.

She grabbed her skateboard and headed out into the city.

There was ugliness in London and it clustered around Westminster and spilled over to South Bank. She knew it well – had slept rough with it years ago when her life had fallen apart and every face looked at her with accusing eyes. Now, she captured it on film, as she did often, honouring the grime on homeless hands and faces, recording the dignity and humanity in those who society judged as least worthy.

She caught up with old friends.

She pressed a twenty pound note into the cold fingers of a homeless woman under the Waterloo Bridge in exchange for a photo and snapped the beauty in the woman's smile. The soul behind the dirt.

Thea had been running from ugliness all her life. She knew it intimately. Knew the horror it was capable of.

Memona Swan's perfect features flashed before her eyes again and Thea gave up.

On her phone, she thumbed through her image reel until she found a favourite.

A naked body tangled in Jasper's silk sheets. In the foreground, Thea's hand rested on Mem's breast – a greedy grab at a full, rich ripeness, her own black fingernails digging in. At the top of the image, Mem's head was tilted back, her lips open and bruised with lust, utter bliss on her face.

Thea dictated a message.

– *I want more of this* –

The reply was almost instant.

– *So do I* –

A very smug smile pulled Thea's lips into a line as she considered her response. Her phone buzzed again in her hand. Three more times.

– *So much more* –
– *Oh god yes* –
And then—
– *Please* –

She laughed out loud. Thea liked them eager, but Mem begging exploded something in her chest.

– *I'll pick you up at eight* – she sent. – *Wear something red* –

Chapter Twelve

Mem wasn't the tiniest bit surprised to find that Thea drove an Aston Martin DB12.

The sleek, low-slung vehicle purred to a stop out the front of Mem's house. It was liquid crimson – so dark it was almost impossible to look at, with black windows that hid its secrets.

The vehicle was just like the woman who stepped out to greet her – elegant and powerful, effortlessly classy with the hint of something wild under the hood.

Jasper's party had only gotten wilder after Kate and Jasper left Mem and Thea alone in that spare room. Thea had fucked her again until Mem was certain she wasn't going to be able to walk, and then she'd stood and looked down at her, one hand in her pocket. She was glorious. Utterly unruffled. Ludicrously proud. She'd snapped a few more images with her phone and smiled wolfishly.

"But don't you want me to—" Mem had said as Thea left the room.

"Plenty of time, darling," she'd leered and dragged her eyes over the wreckage that was Mem's body. "You're mine now. I'll call you when I need you."

And she strolled away.

Mem had no idea why that casual prerogative devastated her the way it did. Thea was going to call her, and Mem was going to jump – or kneel, or crawl, or whatever Thea asked – and Mem couldn't wait.

Right now the woman looked sexy beyond words in a three piece suit in teal-green shot silk. Her eyes were dark-rimmed and her hair shone in the twilight. She strode around the vehicle on towering heels and straight up to Mem, but she stopped dead when she finally looked at her.

"I thought I told you to wear red," she murmured. She swept her eyes over Mem's body with a dangerous smile in the corner of her mouth.

Her gaze was definitely appreciative, though there was a hint of mischief too, like she secretly approved of Mem's disobedience. "Do you imagine you'll get away with that, Ms Swan?"

Mem was in a little black dress, short and tight, having had no idea of what Thea had planned for her. She'd decided to play it safe. Red was part of her contingency plan.

She stepped closer and reached lightly for the lapels of that sensational suit. Thea was wearing nothing under the vest. One of Thea's eyebrows shot up at Mem's boldness and she pulled herself even taller. Mem moulded herself carefully along Thea's pride.

"There's red," Mem promised. "It's just hidden."

"You're being pert."

One of Thea's hands reached around Mem's arse and felt through the fabric for the line of her thong. Mem's skirt was so tight she couldn't twist her fingers beneath it but she gave Mem a godless smirk and light slap on her backside.

Mem pouted and swung her hips. "You figured it out."

"Get in the car, Memona," Thea growled, but she opened the door for her with a smooth sophistication. It didn't quite cover her greed.

She was chuckling when she got into the car herself.

They drove to a sparkling tower in Bishopsgate and took the lift to the forty-second floor.

Thea strode right in and leaned coolly against the back wall. Mem wanted to press against her and demand a kiss, but a straight couple followed them in and turned their backs. Bankers, probably. Dull suits.

Mem stood, a little unsure. Lift etiquette had her staring at the couple's backs. Thea's casual disregard for etiquette meant she was just behind Mem's shoulder, leering at her with barely hidden arousal.

The couple talked about their day as if Thea and Mem weren't even there.

"Noticed you managed to slide that big deal in just before close," the man said.

Mem *felt* Thea's amusement flare like a burst of heat behind her and was not the slightest bit surprised when she felt fingers grasp at her hips.

"The Amrohi account? Took a bit of teasing, but got it in in the end."

Thea's fingers didn't stop. One hand snaked around her waist and brushed against the swell under her breast. A silent laugh right in her ear spilled a hot breath down Mem's neck, and suddenly she was tugged backwards, hard against Thea's body, the two of them intertwined.

"It's all about finding the right leverage point, isn't it?"

"Sure," agreed the woman. "And having just the right touch. Gentle at first, and then applying the right amount of pressure."

Thea's hand slipped inside the V of Mem's dress and cupped her breast. She squeezed. Firm. Greedy.

Just the right touch.

God, she was dreadful! Mem grinned and tried to turn in her arms, but Thea's grip on her body was undeniable. The order whispered into her ear was barely audible, but filthy hot.

"Eyes front, baby."

Teeth pulled Mem's earlobe into a warm mouth and Mem struggled not to gasp. Her eyelids fluttered and she stared at the backs of the couple's heads, pleading with fate and the universe that they'd stick with convention and not turn around.

"I've always admired your technique," the man muttered. "You really know how to handle those bigger transactions."

Could these two hear each other?

Mem had to bite her lip to stop the laugh and the moan that threatened to spill from her throat, and Thea knew it. She pinched her nipple through her dress. Hard. It sent a shooting spark of desire right through Mem's body – sizzling down her spine, bursting in her core. She pressed her thighs together and went limp against Thea's body.

Her head tipped back and landed on Thea's shoulder. The biting moved down to her neck.

"Well, I do have a new client who's keen to explore some deep investment opportunities. If you're willing to learn, I'm more than happy to take the lead."

Amusement was rolling off Thea in waves. Her face nuzzled into Mem's hair and her other hand found the hem of her skirt, low, at the back of her legs. Mem suddenly wondered how far Thea was going to take it, and then realised she'd be happy to go all the way, right here, wherever Thea wanted to take her.

She shifted her feet further apart.

She was rewarded with another pinch to her nipple and hard fingers sliding over the satin of her underwear – already wet. Thea's fingers found the lace of her thong. She tugged, pulling the fabric tight over Mem's clit – nowhere near enough for what Mem wanted right now, but enough to wind her up for the rest of the evening. She wondered what the couple in front would see if they turned around, and the mere thought of it – Thea's hands groping at her as if they owned her – had her twitching against Thea's body. She wished the lift was mirrored.

"Show me the ropes, please," the man said. "I'd love that."

And this time it was Thea holding back a laugh and a groan. She pressed her face into the nape of Mem's neck and her fingers into the slick between Mem's legs—

And with a rush that made Mem's stomach flip, the lift slowed and the two people in front of them stepped out on the thirty-ninth floor.

They didn't look back.

"You are—" Mem started as the doors closed again.

Thea let her go and Mem finally turned to look at her. Two fingers tapped at her lower lip and Mem opened her mouth, tasting herself on Thea's fingers.

The smirk on Thea's face was almost unbearable, but Mem took those fingers as deep into her mouth as she could and saw the smirk slip a little. Thea watched Mem's lips.

This was the way Thea liked to play the game.

Mem couldn't wait to show Thea just how much she could handle.

They were greeted by name at a restaurant three floors and several miles above the one the two bankers had visited.

The concierge led them to a table that faced the most spectacular view of London Mem had ever seen. The restaurant was small and their nook was secluded, and Thea's hand was on Mem's arm in a manner that felt distinctly possessive. Mem leaned into it. It earned her a heavy look.

Thea settled into a plush armchair, comfortable in the atmosphere of finery in a manner that was as sexy as fuck. She was angular in the candlelight – it emphasised her cheekbones and the vivid liveliness of her gaze.

"I thought you'd appreciate the seclusion," she said. "Fewer staring eyes."

"But fingering me mere centimetres behind a couple of strangers is completely fine?"

Thea smirked. "You enjoyed it."

Mem couldn't stop a flush. Thea saw it. It was answer enough.

"Thank you—" Mem started.

"You're welcome."

Mem snorted out an astonished laugh. Thea was unbelievable. She brought her own fingers to her lips – the fingers that had just been between Mem's legs – and she licked them, inhaling deeply. Her black fingernails on long, elegant fingers shorted out Mem's brain.

"I meant for the table! You are terrible." Mem laughed. Thea looked so ridiculously proud of herself Mem just wanted those fingers in her again, but this was clearly one of London's most exclusive restaurants. They needed to settle things down or Mem would be begging Thea to fuck her under the table. Or on it. "As Kate keeps telling me," she said, trying for a bit of dignity, "I probably need to get used to it. It's only going to get crazier once this movie is released."

"Someone as beautiful as you, I can't imagine that you're not used to it," Thea said, casually.

"Is that a compliment?" Mem teased. Everyone saw Mem's beauty. Generally, it was all they saw. Thea saw her differently.

"I'm afraid I didn't intend that as a compliment." Thea actually looked ashamed. Mem was astonished. "I was more curious. Surely people have been staring at you all your life?"

It was Mem's turn to shrug.

"You'll have to make do with my eyes on you all evening then," Thea murmured, with a smile that was definitely predatory. "For now, at least."

"Does that mean I can expect other parts of you on me later?"

Thea laughed, delighted. "Sassy little thing, aren't you?"

"I'm not, usually. It's something I'm trying out." Mem aimed a coy smile at Thea and wondered where the hell this was coming from. It wasn't a performance that was ever going to win an Oscar, but it had a beautiful effect on Thea. She laughed again, smirked, and leaned back in her chair looking very satisfied. "Do you like it?"

"You might need to be careful. It could land you in a lot of trouble."

"Promise?" asked Mem.

Her deep, low chuckle danced between them as a waiter came back and poured them both a glass of champagne.

"I'm glad you messaged me," said Mem, when he was gone. "I have to confess, I've been thinking about you almost continuously since— since—"

"Since I took advantage of you at Jasper's?"

And, just like that, Thea's playfulness was gone. She sneered and stared out at the view, looking at London as though she hated it. Her hand crept up to her lips and she bit at the pad of her thumb, hard enough to make Mem wince.

"You didn't take advantage of me!"

She was soundly ignored. When Thea looked back she had trouble meeting Mem's eyes, and she sneered again. Mem reached for her hand across the table and squeezed it.

"You *didn't* take advantage of me," she said again.

"We'd both been drinking. I was oafish. I— I apologise." Thea had to clear her throat and Mem got the impression she didn't apologise very often. "That wasn't what I'd planned, or how I'd imagined—"

"You imagined?"

"Yes, you impertinent thing. Don't tell me you didn't imagine us too. You were desperate for me."

Mem sighed. She had been. She still was.

"You were amazing," she whispered. "I loved everything we did. Everything you did to me."

Thea lifted her chin. Mem wanted to feed that pride. She was marble – chiselled, beautiful and haughty. And... and something bitter.

"I also really appreciated your—"

There was a rude guffaw. "*Appreciated?* I don't think anyone's ever used that word to thank me for a fuck."

What the hell was this?

Mem seized Thea's hand again and held it until Thea looked her in the eyes. She gave her her best smile.

"I mean, I appreciated your advice on the CreatedDiamonds thing – the brand ambassadorship. I really value it, Thea. You have so much experience in this field and I have none, so... thank you."

In the long silence that followed Thea simply stared at her, suspicion sharp and tight behind her eyes, a piercing assessment of Mem that was agony to endure. After a moment, she relaxed.

"Tell me about you, Mem Swan." Her lazy fingers brushed all the strangeness away and she smiled. It looked kind. Genuine. "I've been selfish with you. I asked you for something immense and I've done nothing but use you since. Again, I... *apologise.* I'd like to get to know you." Her eyes lost their steel and she twirled the stem of her glass idly on the linen tablecloth, like this was a reset and they were trying again.

Sulky and stroppy, Kate had said, when she was trying not to be who she really needed to be.

Mem forgave her her prickliness.

"I'm afraid I'm really very ordinary," Mem said. "Average family, average school, average job—"

"Filming StudioOne's biggest movie this year alongside Dame Katherine Cox." Thea sounded playful again.

"Well, yeah. Aside from that."

"You don't like your new career?"

"It's hardly a career. It was an accident. I was waiting tables when the director of that first movie found me."

Thea nodded. Everyone knew that story.

"I don't even like it that much," Mem admitted. "I know that sounds spoiled. So many people would kill to be in my position, but I really can't wait until it's over."

"So you don't want to do the sequel?"

"Oh god, no!" said Mem. "I'm nearly at the end. No more shoots at remote locations at four in the morning. No more hairdressers and makeup artists poking and prodding. No more photographers in my face every other minute—"

She stopped.

Fuck. *Why had she said that?*

Thea was ice.

"Not you, of course, Thea. I didn't mean— I wasn't talking about you. Paparazzi. You know."

There was total silence.

"Go on."

Mem swallowed. "Once it's all over, I get my life back, that's all I meant. Frankly, I can't wait."

Two waiters swooped into the room. They deposited a plate in front of each of them and ignored the uncomfortable silence. One reached for the champagne to top up their glasses, but Thea dismissed him. She didn't take her eyes off Mem.

Mem shifted in her seat. She couldn't get a lead on Thea's mood changes. She couldn't seem to take her foot out of her own mouth. So much for her brave, cheeky sass. What a stupid thing to say.

When the waiters were gone, Thea poured the bubbles herself.

"I understand," she said, finally. A rueful smile curled one side of her mouth. "I spent quite a few years running from paparazzi myself. They are vultures. They don't care who they hurt." Her eyes flicked up to Mem's again, dark with something different this time – compassion perhaps, or solidarity.

"I really didn't mean—"

Thea flicked her fingers. "Don't mind me. I spent the day up to my eyeballs in gorgeous women. Such a trial." She rolled her eyes, watching Mem to see how her tease landed. "I wanted you the whole time and I tend to get irritable when I can't have what I want. Eat."

Mem picked up her fork. She considered Thea carefully. There was enough heat in Thea's gaze to make her confident no damage had been done. She tried an experiment.

"At least you got the gorgeous women," she said. "I spent the day recording a TV interview with an old white man who thinks he's much funnier than he is, and I couldn't stop thinking of your fingers inside me."

Thea choked on her sashimi.

Mem poked out her tongue and handed Thea her champagne.

"So, the sass is back. I think I do like it."

Mem grinned. "Good."

"Don't be cocky, though, darling. That only suits me."

It was an amazing meal. Mem was revelling in an explosion of flavour when she felt a soft foot against the inside of her calf. Thea had slipped off her shoe. Her foot travelled higher. When it nudged Mem's thighs apart and settled on the seat between her knees, it became almost impossible to think at all.

Thea was explaining her upcoming exhibition at the Tate Modern and her plans for working on some shots with Mem when she remembered her voice.

"Working? Is that what we're calling it? I thought we'd established that you just want to get me naked and take nudey pictures of me."

Thea's instant smile was a mile wide. It plucked Mem's heart right out of her chest and catapulted it to the stars. *This* was what Mem wanted – a glowing promise of friendship and connection. Her and Thea, an idea that suddenly seemed so full of potential and rightness, as if the two of them were meant to be together. Mem crossed her legs trapping Thea's foot between her thighs, and had the satisfaction of seeing Thea's delight intensify. The feeling lasted until Thea realised she was being watched and tucked that gorgeous smile right back down into smugness again.

"We need to talk about this attitude of yours," she crooned. "My muse has forgotten the rules."

The danger in her tone set Mem's heart flip-flopping too.

"There are rules? You never explained them!" Mem protested, but her nerve stalled in a messy flurry of blinking and blushing when Thea shot an eyebrow. Instant submission. *Fuck.* How did Thea do this to her? Why did she like it so much? "Think I'm going to enjoy breaking them."

"You've been talking to Kate," Thea drawled. She swirled the liquid in her champagne glass, the absolute picture of idleness. "Is there something you want, Ms Swan?"

Mem remembered what Kate had told her. *Be brave. Let Thea take it. She will make it worth it.*

"I want the real you, Thea Voronov."

"Impudent. Who are you to presume—?" She pulled her foot away.

Mem took a deep breath. "I'll give you the real Mem, if you share the real Thea with me."

Thea's gasp froze time and all eternity hung on the tremble of her lower lip.

"The industry has put me in a box," Mem went on. "I'm the ingénue, the girl next door – but they don't see me. The industry only sees what makes them rich. The only thing a pretty girl can be in this world."

"And what is that?"

"Something innocent. Something to be exploited."

Thea blanched.

"But you look at me differently, Thea. Those photos you took of me at the shoot for the movie— they weren't innocent. What we did at Jasper's wasn't either. I know you wanted more. You were holding back. I was wondering if that was because you thought I wouldn't like it."

"If I did hold back," Thea murmured, leaning forward now, "it was out of respect for your boundaries."

"Thank you." Mem summoned all the courage she had. "But I think— I think I want more. Of you."

Thea went very still. "And what do you imagine that might be?" she asked, archly.

Mem couldn't tell if Thea was angry or pleased, but she loved the sense of danger in her attitude. "This is really very new to me, but I know you like to take control. And think I want to give you—"

Thea held up a hand. It was a simple gesture that commanded Mem's body, shut down all the doubts in her mind and proved her point all in one. She regarded Mem with an enigmatic expression, her other hand tapping a rhythm against her wine glass, complex and fierce, just as she looked.

And so, stepping fully and deliberately into the role she hoped might be hers, Mem dropped her eyes, lowered her lashes, and waited patiently and hopefully, for Thea to speak.

There was a breathy inhale from the other side of the table.

"So, you've seen some pictures and heard some rumours, hmm? They're all true, darling. Taking your control is the least of it. I can whip you to the very edge of your desire, I can flog you until your reason and your sanity sing on the tip of my whip. And when I let you, my sweet muse, when I *allow* you to plunge over that edge into ecstasy you will sob my name til your throat is hoarse begging me for more."

Mem was panting. Her core was burning just at Thea's words – throbbing – and her vision was whiting out at the edges. This version of Thea was setting her on fire.

Thea's voice dropped even lower.

"But I'm not a toy, Ms Swan. I'm not a game. And neither are you. You have to know I want more from you than that. Oh, I'll have your submission in my bed, if you want to give it to me, but I'll demand far, far more. I want your soul, darling. Your essence. And I will drink it from your lips, lick it from the sweat on your spine, from the heaven between your legs. I will possess you. There are no half measures with me."

Mem gaped.

Thea watched her with dark, intense eyes.

"Okay," Mem managed, and fuck it, but it came out like a squeak. She pressed a hand to her burning cheeks, but there wasn't anything she wanted more. She wanted to explore all of that with Thea.

Thea's lips twitched. "Okay?"

The woman might be wilder and more intense than anyone else Mem knew, but even now, cool as she was, the signs were there. Thea was crazy for her too. A nervous and extremely turned on giggle was threatening to break through whatever was left of Mem's poise.

"Yes." She firmed it up. "Told you before I was game. I trust you."

"You might come to regret that." Thea sipped her wine, and watched her again for a very long time, but when she set the glass down, her sudden smile was warm with respect. She seemed to have come to a decision.

"Very well. Why don't we start now? Show me what you wore that is red."

Mem blinked.

"Take it off," Thea said.

"What?"

Thea's expression didn't change.

"Here?"

"There's no one around. Put what you wore that is red on the table."

Mem felt a strange mix of excitement and eagerness – and simultaneously, a distinct sense of naughty disobedience.

She reached behind her back and unclasped her bra through her dress, slid the straps off her shoulders and down her arms. Staring Thea deep in the eye and feeling her face burn, she hooked one finger into the V of her dress and pulled out a red, lacey bra. She placed it on the table.

She poked out the extreme tip of her tongue and felt rather proud of herself.

Thea's face gave nothing away.

"Oh baby. That's not how it goes," she drawled. "I thought you wanted to obey me."

"I do!"

"My delicious little muse is a brat. This will be fun. There's something else you're wearing that is red. Put it on the table."

Mem's heart was beating double time.

"You can't be serious."

"Are you game to test me?"

Her gaze was unyielding.

Mem bit her lip, considering her next move. She wanted this, the thrill of surrender, but she hadn't expected— She didn't know what she'd expected, to be truthful. Despite her protestations, she *was* an innocent, especially in the world of submission.

She decided to trust Thea.

She stood – the restaurant was quiet, after all – and with only a few ungainly wiggles, she slid her red thong down her legs. It crumpled around her feet – her best stilettos. Thea watched her, idly, coolly, but Mem noticed her nostrils flare, and it gave her an idea.

She turned her back to Thea and bent down slowly to pick up the small pile of lace. She kept her legs straight and her arse in the air.

There was a definite curse behind her.

Mem smiled. She was beginning to understand how this worked.

She put the thong on the table atop the bra and sat down again. Her underwear was exceptionally bright against the white linen tablecloth.

Thea's lips twitched in a smirk. "That wasn't so hard now, was it?"

"You have a wicked sense of fun."

"You have no idea," Thea assured her, "but for now, I appreciate your obedience."

The word hit Mem in exactly the way Thea obviously expected it would.

She adored Thea's laugh.

"Let's enjoy dessert, shall we?" Thea said, "and then we'll go. I want to show you how I see you. Will you come back to the studio with me?"

Mem would do anything Thea asked her to.

"Yes, Thea," she murmured.

Thea reached across the table and cupped her cheek tenderly.

"Thank you, darling," she said. Her eyes were soft again. Kind. "You're doing very well."

Chapter Thirteen

A photographer noticed them leaving the restaurant.

Thea saw him from across the street and stepped closer to Mem as they walked back to her car.

"Arsehole at twenty paces," she warned and ducked her own head, but Mem put her chin up and flashed that amazing smile. Thea could see Kate in the move and she felt a curious swell of pride for both women, but all the same, she told the pap to fuck off as roundly as she could. *Protective* – that was the feeling. Mem didn't deserve this.

She kissed Mem's fingers as she handed her into the car, but by that time the arsehole quotient had doubled, and she clocked a third paparazzo in the rearview on the drive back to Gloucester Crescent.

As she pulled into her driveway, the three had become four and they joined a fifth already in the street leaning against a grey van. Two of them she knew, from both sides of the camera.

"Nothing to see here, boys. Why don't you get lives? Go home to your beds?"

Would they never give up?

"Working late, Voronov?"

"Whose bed you going to, Mem luv?"

The flurry of flashes that followed definitely caught Mem's stricken expression.

Thea immediately wrapped her arm around Mem's shoulder and led her inside, but not before giving the paps another mouthful.

"Sorry. That was my fault," she told Mem in the quiet of her hallway, their fingers still entwined. "Stupid of me. Are you okay?"

Mem smiled at her. "Three apologies in one night? I'm fine. Paps are something I need to get used to."

Thea's lips twitched but she sighed. "You shouldn't have to."

She'd planned to take Mem straight out to the studio, but they didn't make it down the hallway.

She needed to get a grip on herself. She wanted Mem so very badly and she'd almost ruined it by losing her shit in the middle of their dinner – the dinner that she'd hoped might show her precious muse that Thea Voronov was capable of being charming and courteous and could woo a woman with sophistication and style rather than simply dragging her off to bed like a caveman.

She'd always known achieving on that ambition was going to be touch and go, but then Mem had pulled that stunt with her underwear and Thea had surrendered completely.

There was also the way Thea's heart stalled in her chest when Mem placed her hand on hers and entreated her to believe she wanted Thea too. It was warm.

Nice.

But the force of Thea's desire had always sailed right past nice. Thea wanted Mem's skin, her body, *fuck,* she wanted to claw her way through the very texture of the girl's vulnerability. Because there was a chance – just a chance – that Mem might be equal to Thea's cravings, and true enough not to run from her when she was done taking her pleasure.

Pleasures Thea was certain Mem wanted to explore too.

Mem confirmed it when she looked hopefully up the stairs and aimed a coy smile at Thea with her chin pressed into her shoulder.

Thea pressed her against the wall.

"Probably time to talk about those rules," she murmured, brushing teasing kisses along her neck, her jaw, everywhere but her mouth. Mem twitched under her hands, practically vibrating under her tongue, but Thea was cruel. She nibbled and nipped, and Mem's body jolted beautifully. She almost laughed at how much it was winding the girl up.

Mem hooked her thigh over Thea's hip and pulled her closer. There was nothing under that dress. That simple fact was driving Thea crazy.

"Theeeaaa." Mem whined it, drawing it out into four bratty syllables. "Please."

That was more like it. Thea knew the game from here.

"Please what, my muse?" She murmured it into Mem's throat.

Two perfect breasts pressed against hers at the word 'muse'.

"You said—"

"Mmm?"

"You said we could— that you would— Um, I want you to—"

This naivety was sweetness itself. "Use your words, darling."

There was a very inelegant grunt. "I'm fucking trying! You know I'm a newbie at this. And you're being such a tease."

Thea pulled back triumphantly. "I know almost nothing at all about you, Mem Swan, but believe me, I want to explore every inch of you. I want to paw through your desires, push at every one of your limits. I want—" She reeled herself in. "But I need to hear you say it, sweet girl. I need your consent."

The word made Mem groan. "Yessss," she whined.

Thea chuckled. She put her hands on her hips and tossed her chin, and died for the way Mem remained helpless against the wall, her eyes following Thea's hands, swirling over her body. "Not quite enough, I'm afraid. You want me to…" she prompted.

"Oh my god, Thea! Please! I really, really want you to… to… *dominate* me!"

It took everything Thea had not to laugh. She really was too sweet – and the way her skin flushed – oh. Thea hid her smirk by leaning in again to the agony of her throat and groaning.

"I can't believe you made me say that," Mem grumbled. "How cringe. I must sound like a— like a hopelessly horny teenager."

Hopeless and horny definitely described Thea right now, but she could afford to be gracious. Just a little bit. She stroked Mem's cheek with one soft finger then gripped her chin. "It was a tiny bit gauche, my muse, but adorable. And communication is a critical part of what we're about to do. It's important we can both articulate what we want."

Mem swallowed. "And what are we about to do?"

Thea knew she was in real danger here. Mem's soft trusting eyes had already slayed her.

"Nothing you're not ready for, but, if you will have me, it will be my pleasure to take control of your body and all your needs and have you submit to my desire."

Mem's head thudded against the wall, her eyes closed.

"Oh, fuck."

"I hope so." Thea laughed again into the heaven of her hair. She could smell her arousal. "You really are a noob at this."

Mem opened one eye. "I hate you. Stop teasing me."

"So, humiliation isn't your thing. Good to know."

"Just fucking take me, will you?"

Thea smirked. "Ask nicely."

Mem pushed her away and looked her deep in the eyes. She licked her lips. "I am ready, willing and eager to submit to your dominance," she said evenly.

Oh, that did it. Thea was burning now, her pulse pounding in her cunt, her blood rushing in her ears. Her hand slid up to Mem's throat and she knew it was all over. The girl had won.

She pressed closer still, felt Mem squirm against the hard wall behind her, scrabbling to position her hips more open and wide beneath Thea's. She tipped Mem's head back and kissed into her without any warning, with the intent and drive of someone who really meant it.

Mem was breathless when she let her go. Her eyes stuck on her mouth, panting.

"It will be my honour," Thea murmured.

She seized Mem's hand and drew her out to the studio.

There was a set of cuffs on the pillow of the bed in the studio.

The simple fact that Thea had been so fucking confident she'd laid them there earlier almost did Mem in right then and there. She'd been wet for Thea all evening. By now, she was practically dripping.

There was a chain too. It hung down from the ceiling in the middle of the bed and stopped a few feet above it.

It didn't take a genius to guess how this was going to go, but all the same, Mem's body figured it out before her brain did. Her heart rate took off, her nipples turned to rocks, her core flashed with heat. So when Thea made one simple gesture at her body with the laziest flick of her wrists,

Mem found herself tearing her dress off in a frenzy. She nearly threw herself on the bed.

But Thea caught her wrist.

"Whether you are in my studio or in my bed, my eager muse, my word will be your law. I will never hurt you or harm you, but I will test your boundaries. I will take you to the edges of your comfort and possibly push you beyond. You can stop anytime you wish, but if you stay, you surrender to my vision, my direction. My control. Do you agree?"

Mem was breathing through parted lips. Thea's eyes caught on them, even in the dim light. She nodded.

Thea shot an eyebrow.

"Yes, Thea."

One finger stretched out and traced the curve of her breast, tickling down the side. "Good girl. That is how you will always answer me. Give me a safe word."

"Thea." She said it without thinking – it was the only word in her head at this stage – and Thea laughed.

"Not my name. I'm going to make you say *that* over and over." Her smile was cruel and kind.

"Diamonds." That won her a hard stare and Mem wondered if it was the wrong thing to say too, but Thea let it drop.

She pointed to the floor. Her meaning was clear and Mem's pulse throbbed in her core in response. Thea didn't step back, so Mem when dropped to her knees right there, her eyes were level with the zip on Thea's slacks. She swallowed.

The view up Thea's body was sensational. Up over that amazing suit, expensive fabric tucked into a trim waist, buttons undone low over her chest, all that alabaster skin – and then she was looking into sharp blue eyes staring down at her, amusement dancing in them like a tease. Suddenly, Mem couldn't breathe.

"Perfect," Thea murmured, almost under her breath, as if she hadn't wanted Mem to hear. Kind fingers touched her chin, a thumb on Mem's lower lip. "You like it down there?"

Mem nodded and the thumb pushed between her lips. Mem drew it in eagerly, suckling until the pad of Thea's thumb was a firm pressure on her tongue. Then she remembered the way she'd been instructed to answer! The panic in her eyes gave her away, and Thea laughed.

"I know you do, darling. Submitting is natural for you, isn't it?" Something soured for a split second, then she was teasing again. "Aren't I the lucky one?"

When she stepped back and threw her jacket off and rolled her sleeves, Mem had to disagree. Thea kicked off her shoes, stepped out of her pants and her underwear with an easy grace and no hint of self consciousness. She was proud. She was glorious. When she stepped close again, she smelled divine. All of Mem's sordid dreams had come true – all of them, even the ones she'd never been game to dream. Thea was exquisite.

"Show me how lucky I am."

She curled her fingers into Mem's hair, short nails scratching lightly at the nape of her neck. Mem would have leant back into the touch, except there was something far more enticing in front of her. She brushed the corners of Thea's shirt open – more pale skin, an impressive set of abs, and a neat tangle of surprisingly dark hair between her legs. For a moment, she simply admired the view. The fingers in her hair clenched.

Mem dove in.

Nothing could have prepared her for how perfect it felt to be on her knees with her face buried in Thea's cunt. The heat of her against her tongue, her scent, her spice, her flavour – they filled her senses and set her throbbing. They made her greedy. The hand gripping her hair, the thrill of the power imbalance – she'd never been so turned on. It all combined and suddenly she was eating Thea out as if her life depended on it, her hands roaming those incredible thighs, reaching around to grip her arse.

"*Fuck*!"

When she looked up, she nearly came right then, just at the view. Thea had her head thrown back. Her breasts were heaving between the lines of her shirt and her other arm was raised above her head. She tugged at her own hair, her elbow pointing at the ceiling. Mem was triumphant. *She* had done this to Thea. *She* was driving her to the edge. The magnificent woman who had ruled Mem's every thought since she'd laid eyes on her was now coming undone on Mem's tongue.

And so quickly!

She felt Thea thicken on her lips, she felt her knees begin to quiver. She wanted to hold her up and lick her through it, but just as she was revelling in her power Thea's command reasserted itself. She was pulled away by her hair, a ragged curse and a laugh ringing in her ears.

"Oh, you clever, clever girl."

Thea sounded dazed, but the smugness was still there. She looked down at Mem and panted, open mouthed, puzzled for just a second then blisteringly entitled. Self-satisfied, that's what it was. Thea was the cat who'd gotten the cream, devoured the canary and was now determined to have her fun – all the fun – with the mouse.

Mem couldn't wait.

The cuffs were soft leather bands that wrapped around her wrists. They clipped together on a short chain.

"Is this okay, my muse?"

Mem loved that she checked in even though it was clear Thea already knew. Mem was addicted to Thea's energy already, the natural way she had of controlling and demanding, all laced with cockiness and blended with care, so that it felt right for Mem to obey. She was drawn to the bed, her arms were ordered over her head and her wrists were clipped to the chain that dangled there. She was still on her knees, but the bed was soft and she was stretched out and exposed. Utterly at Thea's mercy.

Thea stood back and watched her.

It was almost obscene, the way she stared. It was obscene the way Mem's body dripped to be watched, the way she pressed her thighs together and whimpered when Thea seemed prepared to leave her there, trussed up like a toy awaiting Thea's pleasure.

She nearly exploded when Thea gave her a wicked grin and walked right out of the room.

What did that mean?

Had she done something wrong?

Mem wriggled but she was stuck. She heard Thea in the other room – the clatter of something being picked up, the soft click of metal and plastic. Mem closed her eyes and allowed an indulgent spasm of desire to ripple through her. She squirmed and moaned. This was torture. This was delicious and exactly what she'd wanted.

When she opened her eyes, Thea was watching her from the door, one shoulder leaning against the frame, a ludicrously possessive look in her eyes. She was holding a camera.

Of course she was.

"Just for us, darling," she cooed, prowling forward. "I'd ask, but I'm afraid you've already agreed to this. Signed away your soul."

It was only then Mem noticed what was in her other hand.

A crop.

Mem's entire body jolted and Thea laughed.

"I'll go easy on you, darling. I know this is your first time." She crawled onto the bed and left the camera on a pillow. Brought her lips right to Mem's ear. "I'll teach you how to beg properly for my mercy later." She trailed the tip of the crop down Mem's side and smiled at the goosebumps it left behind. It was a soft thing, Mem realised. Definitely a beginner's toy. It was red and black with feathers almost hiding the leather.

It looked beautiful in Thea's hands – and she was absolutely masterful in its use.

Mem hadn't known what to expect, but the rational part of her mind quickly shut down and allowed Thea to take control. It was as if the woman already knew her body and what she wanted before Mem did. If there'd ever been an instruction manual for Mem's body, Thea Voronov had written it. Mem felt known – each delicate, teasing tickle of the feathers, the most careful and perfectly positioned flick of the leather. The sting, the tingle. The hot, wet heat of a soothing tongue over each touch of the toy – and then Thea's eyes—

Mem saw fire. She saw excitement and the control of someone who was ready to take everything Mem had until there was nothing left to offer. And then, incredibly, she saw something far gentler – something astonished that gazed on Mem as if she was precious beyond diamonds, as if Thea could never be worthy of her.

Mem whispered the question. "Are *you* okay, Thea?"

Cocky arrogance replaced the worship like a switch had been flipped.

"Just want to see how much you can take, my muse, so I can use you like this whenever I—"

That shouldn't have been the thing that tipped the scales, but Mem's orgasm hit her in an undeniable rush. She shuddered and moaned – threw a wild, helpless glance at Thea – then tossed her head back and writhed. Thea seized her camera. The chain rattled. Mem arched upwards, backwards, spun from her wrists in their cuffs. The whirr of the camera only set her off a second time, and she cried out – from pleasure, from embarrassment – until she hung her head and panted.

Thea's chuckle was absolutely unbearable. She threw back her shoulders and crowed.

"All that and I haven't even *touched* you? Oh my darling muse, you are perfect."

Mem growled.

Thea let her down. "You are whipped, my gorgeous little sub," she laughed.

"Stop it."

"Whipped for me." Suddenly, it sounded reverent, and Thea laid her in the pillows, kissed her wrists and made sure she was comfortable, all with exquisite care.

Then, without any warning, she put her lips to Mem's core and blew her mind.

She was skilled – oh, she was good. It was only their second time, but everything Thea had learnt from their encounter at Jasper's party, she put to use now with the confidence of an expert. It shattered Mem just a little to know exactly that – that Thea had catalogued all her tells and already fine tuned and perfected her touch so she could fuck Mem with commitment. Two fingers followed without any warning – pushing and thrusting inside Mem and dragging perfectly. She opened herself as wide as she could and a strong arm settled over her hips and held her still – and without even thinking about it, without even wondering why it felt so right and so perfect, she simply let Thea take whatever she wanted, however she wanted to take it.

Thea ravished her, and when the time was right, she ordered her.

"Now, my muse. Give yourself to me now."

And the moan that wrenched itself from her throat startled them both. With all her self control surrendered to Thea's lips and the iron of her fingers, the shock wave rippled out from Mem's spine, lifting her off the bed, Thea riding her hard. The most powerful pleasure she'd ever known shot like lightning through her nerves and collapsed her mind, and all she knew was the wildness in Thea's eyes that locked onto hers and refused to let her go.

Chapter Fourteen

It was midnight, but Thea felt alive.

Mem was unlike any woman Thea had ever seen, any conquest she'd ever taken to her bed. She was the sexiest, most submissive of sirens, her call both a promise and a challenge. Thea found herself inspired – and suddenly she didn't want to wait.

Naked, she rose from the bed and fetched her camera. Mem dozed, wrecked in a tangle of sheets, her lips parted, the flush still in her skin and still so beautiful. Thea threw the aperture wide, drunk on the kiss of light on the girl's skin. Divine. She pulled the focus in tight – that spot, right there, on Mem's throat – the abandon in the arch of her neck, the tiniest tell of uncertainty as her eyes fluttered open, sought Thea's, then widened with remembrance.

That delicious flush of colour, from her face to her breasts – rich and warm. Thea chased it with her lens.

"Do you ever stop?" Mem laughed, weakly.

Thea didn't answer.

"Should I go?"

The girl looked embarrassed suddenly and Thea was ashamed – which wasn't like her. Her hand reached out before she could stop it and her palm landed on Mem's chest, just below her throat.

Mem paused, instantly. Even her breath hitched. The deep pools of her eyes locked onto Thea's, but her whole essence waited – *waited* – for Thea's direction.

It was glorious, having so much power over so much perfection. Thea looked at her hand right in the centre of— not *innocence*, she smiled at the memory of what they'd just done. Definitely not innocence. Mem was exquisite. She'd been beautiful even as Thea had fucked her – her gasps, her pleas and her shrieks. Thea had forgotten herself more than once and used her hard – and oh, but Mem had squirmed and whimpered beneath her and spread herself even wider for her as she did. She was a natural sub, which simply made her all the more ideal for Thea, and which filled her with horror at the same time.

Because it would make bending her to Jasper's little plan all the easier. Monster.

She looked at the woman waiting on her word and realised she had one chance.

"No," Thea said, simply. More honest than she'd been in a long time. "I don't want you to go."

Mem's slow, shy smile sealed it.

She was nothing like anyone Thea had ever had before.

Thea snapped her fingers, loving the swell in her chest when Mem obeyed her without hesitation, sitting up and taking her hand.

"I said I wanted to show you how I see you."

Thea led her into the main studio and flicked on some lights – not many, the shadows in Mem were just as enticing as her brilliance. She dragged a single wooden chair to the centre of the room but held up two fingers when Mem went to sit on it.

"Kneel," she commanded.

Mem froze, confused. "On the chair?"

"At its feet."

"Naked?"

Thea smiled. Dragged her eyes over all that beautiful brown skin. "Definitely naked." She tossed her a cushion for her knees and settled into the position she'd always intended to take – her own arse in the chair, her legs wide, Mem on the ground between her knees.

Mem's eyes fell to the view between Thea's legs and bit her lip hard.

Thea chuckled. She captured *that*, that adorable blush, that deliciously cheeky deference to the game Thea was making her play. Her camera whirred and Thea realised Mem's beauty commanded her too, challenging the artist in her to push to new heights.

She could capture the sublime with this woman, she realised. Show the world what true beauty was and transcend it all. Or she could keep her all to herself.

She blinked that thought away. Slipped one finger under the girl's chin and tilted her face up.

"You like being in front of a camera?" Thea asked.

Mem gave a tiny frown. "I don't actually. I always have been, though." She gave a tiny smile when Thea's camera clicked again and she ducked her head. "It was my mum and dad when I was little, with my dad's ye olde film camera."

"I use a ye olde film camera," Thea said, archly, and then found herself grinning when Mem pulled a face.

"You probably know how to use it though."

"Cheeky."

"My dad was a rubbish photographer. Mum was so relieved when digital cameras came out. They saved a fortune. They only took a million more photos, though." She shrugged and wrinkled her nose.

Thea snapped a handful of pics of that too.

Mem froze.

They looked at each other. With a careful breath, Mem slipped back into her pose again – the submissive pose she thought Thea wanted. Thea *did* want that. She wanted Mem to crawl to this place between her knees of her own volition and beg until her throat was hoarse, but Thea liked this impish humour too. Who was this girl? Thea lowered her camera.

"And yet, here you are."

Mem blinked, as if she suddenly remembered exactly where she was. Thea rubbed it in.

"Naked. On your knees. Between my legs."

This time Mem's blush swept over her whole body. Thea watched, entranced, and like an idiot, only pointed her camera at it to catch the end. They watched each other for a long moment.

"It's just a job," Mem said, eventually. "The movies, the interviews, the photoshoots. I don't want the fame. It's not even me."

Thea reached one finger down to tip her chin to one side. Her skin was hot in the cool night air. Mem moved easily at her touch, not the slightest resistance to Thea's direction. She looked up from under heavy eyelids. She breathed between parted lips. It was intoxicating, but it was a perfect act – the same shit Thea saw every day from other models who knew the same routines. Thea couldn't decide whether she loved or hated it on Mem.

"Liar," Thea said, then let her camera go crazy at the reaction. She smirked. "You're loving this. I can see it in your skin. The camera sees it too. You are gasping for it."

Mem drew a long, steadying breath and stared back defiantly. She was stunning. "I'm gasping for you," she said. She planted a kiss on the inside of Thea's thigh, then looked up and smiled—

—and, god, it was like the sun reversed in its orbit and shone down through the skylight with all the gold of heaven. Thea was transfixed. Her smile! The desire in her eyes, all mixed up in an intoxicating blend of lust, nerves and sass – and something else that Thea didn't quite recognise. What was that? Connection? Warmth? Friendship? Something that certainly addressed Thea as an equal.

She wasn't expecting that.

It felt … nice.

Jasper, Kate, Lollie and their conniving plans could go to hell. Thea wanted this for herself.

She put two fingers under Mem's chin again and drew her higher until she was kneeling up, their faces perilously close. She could taste Mem's excitement. The woman was watching Thea's mouth, teetering on the edge of temptation and Thea wanted to tip her over into feverishness.

"Up."

"What?"

"Do you trust me?" Thea asked.

"You know I do," Mem said.

"How do you feel about rope?"

She tied her in a basic bind, not wanting to go too far on their first time. Mem surrendered to it like she'd been born for it, her head lolling back on Thea's shoulder, heavy lidded eyes following her every move. Thea drew the ropes over her body like a promise, the burgundy silk a kind of magic against her skin. The lush swells of flesh that rose between them tore at Thea's sanity. She explored every inch of Mem with her mouth.

"What is this?"

Thea was kissing a slim, pale line on Mem's left shoulder blade. Mem roused. "It's a scar."

"And I thought you were perfect."

Her wrists were bound behind her back, but Mem's hands were free. One flapped at Thea in mock-annoyance and tickled her thigh. Thea chuckled.

"I like it," her muse said. "I fell off the trampoline when I was kid—well, actually my big bully of a cousin bounced us. My sister and I both came off."

Thea was perplexed. "Isn't bouncing what you're supposed to do on a trampoline?"

"Well, yes, but he *bounced* us. You know, deliberately, to scare us."

Thea had no idea what that meant. She trailed a length of rope slowly and purposefully over Mem's shoulder from behind, knowing it was brushing against straining breasts. Mem's breath shuddered.

"I think our childhoods were very different," she murmured.

Mem seemed to think about that. "I landed on the springs on my back, but my sister broke her finger, and while she was howling with pain and was told she'd be okay, my parents, the aunties and uncles, were all relieved my injury wasn't on my face." Mem hummed. "It was the first time I realised my worth was just my looks. So, I like the scar. It grounds me."

Thea liked it too. She kissed it again.

"I think I understand that," she murmured, tightening some knots. Mem's head found her shoulder again. Her eyes closed. "Beauty is a precious commodity in this world and its value isn't always enjoyed by the person behind it. It gets controlled. Exploited. By people like the movie studio and the media. People like me."

Mem tried to twist in her ropes. Their eyes met.

"That's true, but you aren't exploiting me."

Thea saw her own darkness reflected in Mem's eyes. "Perhaps not right now, in this exact moment, but I have. I expect I will again. Just as you are using me."

That frown was adorable. Thea hooked her fingers under a loop of rope and tugged, and Mem's confusion fled. Her moan was liquid heaven and she squirmed helplessly in her bonds. Thea picked her up in a bridal hold and deposited her carefully on the chaise lounge, all trussed up like a present.

The noise Mem made when Thea got her mouth on her was one she had never heard before – an abandoned, breathy sound wrenched from her lungs as her thighs quivered and strained against her bonds. Her hips made little circles against her lips and Thea dragged her tongue through her and gripped her body, probably too hard. Her mouth flooded with the taste of Mem's climax and it tasted like guilt.

She left the girl panting and fetched her camera.

Much, much later, when the ropes were loosened and they were back on the bed, Thea massaged every muscle and kissed every bruise.

"That was wonderful," Mem sighed. "I had no idea…"

She seemed exhausted, but Thea was still burning with inspiration. She got up off the bed and held up a finger when Mem started to rise too.

"Stay there." She smiled when Mem settled back down without question.

If this was Lollie, Kate or any other woman Thea might have found and used, she'd slap her arse and order her out of her bed. Instead, she padded naked through the studio and found Mem a robe.

She didn't miss the way Mem's eyes followed her as she went. She threw her shoulders back and walked proudly. Let her look. Thea knew she was in good shape. The running and the kickboxing paid off.

Back in the bedroom, she tossed a robe at Mem and tugged her own shirt back on. Nothing else. She left it unbuttoned.

Mem sat up and gave her a tiny frown. The sheet was tangled between her legs and her hair tumbled over one breast. There was a very pleasing bruise forming on the other that Thea had sucked there, and she found herself automatically holding up her phone for a picture. She'd only taken two when Mem's confused frown turned into a very brattish pout and an eye roll.

"Really! Don't you ever stop?" she cried.

"With someone as beautiful as you, no, I don't think I ever will," Thea murmured.

Mem looked suspicious, but she smiled. "Is that a line?"

"You think I need to use a line on you?"

Mem crawled suddenly to the end of the bed and knelt up in front of her. "I think we've discovered that orders work just as well," she whispered. She looked brave and embarrassed in equal measures, and when Thea dropped one hand to her utterly perfect breast and thumbed the mark she'd left there, her breath caught beautifully and her whole upper body heaved.

Thea squeezed.

Mem sighed and pressed into her touch, and Thea nearly dissolved into a thousand pieces. She fought down the heat that rose between her legs and held up her phone.

"Oh my god!" Mem squealed. "Stop!"

Thea grinned and slapped her boob. "Let's look at them."

She strode out to her computer and hid a chuckle at the huff of indignation behind her. If everything went well, she'd take that out of Mem later.

She plugged in her devices and immediately began sifting through the images that appeared on the large screens. Lust flashed through her again as she remembered how *that* had felt, how Mem had moaned when Thea pushed into her *then*. She heard the soft pad of feet behind her and was astonished when Mem put her chin on her shoulder and slipped an arm around her waist, her fingers sliding under Thea's open shirt and tickling her abs.

Thea never let anyone touch her like that.

She wondered why, when it felt so nice.

It only lasted a moment.

"Those are obscene!" Mem exploded, eyes wide.

Thea laughed. "Well, that one is. Hmm, and maybe that one. But these ones are raw, primal. Look what we've caught here—" she gestured to the screen, a blurred image of her own fingers tangled in Mem's hair, Mem's throat taut. "This beautiful vulnerability, the delicate balance between power and surrender. It's a sensual dance as old as time, the light and shadow of control and release, of dominance and submission."

Mem made a tiny squeaking noise. The softness of her breasts pushed against Thea's back. She felt Mem mould herself to her body.

A few clicks of the mouse turned the image black and white, and with the exposure pushed and the midtones deepened the image gained a far more powerful undercurrent.

"Oh," Mem breathed.

"These are profound," said Thea. "I adore them. The elegance, *here*, in the way a body yields – your body, Mem. The way it submits to my touch. They're incredibly beautiful." Thea clicked through more images. She was in danger of becoming lost in them. "I want to work with this some more—"

She was absolutely delighted when Mem tilted her hips up against her backside and blew a soft, teasing raspberry right into her ear. Thea would *never* tolerate that from anyone else.

"That is *definitely* a line," Mem said.

Thea laughed. Again. She couldn't remember when she'd laughed so easily, so carelessly, with a woman in her arms. She realised she liked it – and that look of teasing lightness in Mem's eyes.

But she turned and thrust her hands under Mem's robe, reaching around to grab a handful of that luscious arse, her lips settling at Mem's collarbone as her head fell back with a sigh.

"I want to work with this a lot more," Thea told that divine point at the base of Mem's throat.

Mem shivered. Thea licked over the goosebumps – fascinated – then remembered herself and bit down. Hard. Mem's abandoned moan and the ripple that pulsed through her body set Thea on fire.

"With your camera?" the girl whimpered.

"With everything."

It was a moment before either of them could speak.

"Anything you wish." Mem's whisper sounded as lost as Thea felt.

Thea walked her backwards to the bed.

They didn't make it back up to the house until morning.

Thea found herself walking behind Mem just to watch the sway of her hips through the satin robe. She was stuck on Mem's body – and the warmth of the laugh in her voice when she caught Thea doing it.

"Stop!"

Thea slapped her backside. "Make me."

"I wouldn't dare."

"Correct answer, darling." Thea led Mem through to the kitchen and flicked on the coffee machine. "I will always want to look at you."

In the front room, Thea tweaked the edge of the curtain at the window and they both peered out at three photographers leaning against a car on the opposite side of the road.

"Have they been there all night? They're crazy!"

Thea knew all of them and fought down a vague sense of déjà vu. She briefly considered throwing the front door open and telling them to fuck off. She clocked the wide aperture telephoto lenses all the men were sporting and knew a candid snap of Memona Swan doing the walk of shame from Thea Voronov's front door would be an easy shot.

"They're after you, darling. But I won't let them get you."

She closed the gap in the curtains and took Mem's hand. Pulled her back to the kitchen.

"I can get you around them. Secret gate in the back garden. You shouldn't let them control your life."

"Aren't you one of them?"

Thea froze. Was that how Mem saw her? It was a valid question, she supposed.

"A vulture? A monster?" She sneered. "Maybe I am."

Mem stepped around the kitchen island and into her space. She leaned up against her and slotted her legs perfectly around Thea's. She reached past her to switch the coffee machine off. Thea held herself tall and rigid, and Mem smiled into her neck and dropped a simple kiss there.

"Don't be silly," she said. "You're nothing like that."

She was so innocent, so naive – and so, so soft and warm. Thea couldn't stop her hands from sliding back under Mem's robe. When her palms found Mem's breasts again, Mem's ruined sigh was heavy in the back of her throat. For a moment her thighs clenched around Thea's.

"Do you need to be somewhere today?"

"Nothing I can't cancel."

"Convince me to stay?"

Mem's pussy was hot and wet on Thea's thigh. Thea dropped one hand to her backside and pulled her in.

Thea forgot about breakfast – she almost forgot her own name. Her other hand snaked up to Mem's hair. She tangled her fingers in the hair at the nape of her neck and tugged. She pressed up with her thigh.

"Convince you?" she asked, dangerously.

Mem moaned. "Order me."

Thea smiled. "My pleasure, darling."

It was much later still when Mem insisted she really must go.

Thea watched her dress, then ordered her a car and led her back through the garden to the studio and past it to a small gate in the back fence.

"You'll use this gate in the future," Thea explained. "Mrs Tits is a friend. I trust her."

Mem looked at her incredulously.

"Mrs Tits? The future?"

Thea ducked her head for a moment. She'd assumed.

"If you want to, of course," she said, quietly. When Mem said nothing, she kept going. "I'd like to see you again—" When had she ever been so damn courteous? "No, I want to see you all the time. I want to make this serious, I want—"

Mem's fingers tangled in hers.

"You mean, pursue a relationship, rather than just ordering me to strip in restaurants?"

Thea gripped her chin. "You cocky thing. Don't imagine I'll stop doing that."

She *felt* Mem's pulse quicken under her fingers. Her eagerness was obvious, but still, Thea wanted to hear her say it.

"Well?"

Mem made a show of pretending to think about it.

Thea snorted. "You are a terrible actor."

"Oi!" Mem laughed, and the relaxed sound was genuine and honest and comfortable. It was trusting. "You're right, though. I don't know what they see in me. But, yes. Yes, please, Thea. I'd love to see you again."

Oh, that was very pretty begging. Thea kissed her, committing the softness of her lips to memory, licking into her gentleness.

She led her through her neighbour's garden, past the house to the street and saw Mem into an uber to take her back to Clapham and away from the predatory eyes that lurked in wait.

Thea hadn't felt like this for a long time, but Mem had been an unexpected pleasure. That Mem seemed keen to play exactly the kind of games Thea liked was a bonus.

She'd be careful with this one, she decided. All those beautiful tells were too precious to spoil – the shivers through Mem's body that gave her away, that shy glance and the flutter of her eyelids, the blossom of colour in her cheeks. It all told Thea how content Mem would be – *will* be – bending to Thea's will. She'd teach her everything. She'd savour those delicious little flinches, the way her toes curled, those hopeless, needy sighs.

She went back to her workstation and nearly lost herself in sweet, sweet dreams as she scrolled through sumptuous images and replayed what they'd done.

Then her eyes fell on the damned diamond and she remembered what Jasper, Kate and Lollie had asked of her.

Seducing Memona Swan was part of the job. She had to convince her to do the sequel and sell her soul for advertising too.

Thea's lips twisted like she'd tasted something bitter. It wasn't that she didn't think she could do it – exploiting women for profit ran in the family, for fuck's sake, and she was her father's daughter. Manipulation and control – these were some of her favourite things.

But the idea of *using* Mem Swan had all the signs of spoiling something perfect – and Thea had the strangest feeling that perfection could be hers.

Part Two

Chapter Fifteen

Life became an exhilarating blur of contrasts.

By day, Mem played the role of Hollywood's rapidly ascending star, facing flashing cameras and demanding journalists as they raced towards the premiere. There were interviews and press events for *The Wolverton Diamond*, fittings for designer clothes she'd never dreamed of wearing. Adiatu ushered her from one event to the next, always bright and polished to a glossy perfection, an image crafted for public consumption. Kate was a lifeline, an expert who guided Mem through the strangeness of it all.

Bit by bit, Mem began to perfect her role. Her confidence grew. She stood taller, copying the poise she saw in Kate and the swagger she admired in Thea. Her time spent before Thea's camera as her muse gave her the skills she needed to face the rest of the media machine. Interviews became less terrifying, paparazzi simply a necessary evil. She saw herself on the sides of buses and the covers of magazines and no longer cringed.

She sat through the first showings of the trailers of the movie and had to admit it looked amazing. *She* looked amazing. That heavy stone of dread in the pit of her stomach began to feel more like a seed just waiting to grow and blossom.

It was all going to be okay.

One small issue was the lack of time she seemed to have for Heart and Grace House, and even less time to spend with Piper, but her friend understood. Piper kept her up to date with texts and calls and emails, necessary because Mem was hardly ever home either, especially in the evenings.

Because when the sun slipped below the horizon and the glaring lights of the press cooled and the world seemed to still just slightly, Mem became someone else entirely.

She became Thea's.

Thea's world was a realm of shadows, sharp contrasts and piercing highlights charged with tension. Thea, with her demanding touch and her all-knowing eyes, could command Mem's body with a caress and a glance, and her dominance was both a thrill and a comfort. Mem found an unexpected peace in submitting to the certainty of Thea's desires and the unequivocal way she extracted them from her.

No one had ever looked at Mem the way Thea looked at her. She wasn't sure what a muse was supposed to call the artist she inspired, but as the nights went on, Mem was certain that devotee, admirer or even worshipper could be used to describe Thea's reverence for her. Thea saw through to her soul, to the woman Mem had always meant to be. When Thea touched her, Mem learned how to beg and cry in just the right way – a way that drew Thea even taller, that glorious pride glancing off her cheekbones, something queenly in her eyes. It was raw and intimate, a sanctuary and an escape from the artificial glamour of Mem's days.

And bit by bit, something fun, mischievous and playful made itself known in Thea's gaze at her.

Thea Voronov made her happy.

***

"I cannot possibly call you Mrs Tits," Mem said the first time they were properly introduced.

Yelena Litvina Titov was not at all what Mem expected, but even so, calling her *Mrs Tits* seemed a bit much. Thea had described the woman who lived in the house over her back garden fence as 'a harmless old babushka who does me a favour every now and then.' Mem had been picturing a sweet old thing who baked Russian honey cake. She had not been prepared for motorbike leathers and a vodka still on the kitchen counter.

Yelena had short, silver-white hair cut in a messy pixie and eyes that watched Thea sharply. She smiled at Mem. She'd just arrived home and welcomed them both into her home, dropping her red bike helmet on a side table, shrugging off a black leather jacket and tossing it expertly onto a peg. She led them through to the kitchen. She was slim and agile, and in the kind of shape Mem hoped she'd be at seventy.

"Of course you can," Thea said, blithely. She threw herself into one of Mrs Titov's kitchen chairs and put her long legs up on another.

"Titov is actually my ex-husband's name," the woman told Mem. She flicked a dismissive finger at Thea. "This smartarse uses it to piss me off. It works."

She had an almost stereotypical Russian accent, thick and deep.

"You like it," Thea drawled. "It's a compliment."

Yelena cocked one eyebrow and waited. Mem got the feeling these two had been needling each other for years. They plainly liked each other, though pretending they didn't seemed to be the dynamic.

"It's perky." Thea dragged it out, playing for her audience. "Not like your actual *babushkiny grudi*."

Mrs Tits clipped Thea on the ear. Thea chuckled triumphantly.

"Old grandmother boobs," Yelena translated. "You be careful with this one. She's a bitch."

"Takes one to know one," Thea grinned.

"Boil the kettle, Fyodora Grigorievna Voronov. Make yourself useful."

Thea's mirth dried up in an instant at her full name and she narrowed her eyes at Mem, daring her to laugh. Mem looked between them and giggled. She couldn't hold it in. Thea's smirk promised her she'd pay for it later.

Mem couldn't wait.

She liked this side of Thea – the casual, standing-at-the-kitchen-counter side that was nowhere near the domineering goddess she wanted to worship all the time. For some reason that caused Mem to throb in exactly the same way as when Thea ordered her to bed, she found Thea just as sexy in the kitchen as she was everywhere else.

Mem would take it.

Fuck, she'd take anything Thea wanted to give her.

Mrs Tits leaned back against her kitchen counter with her arms folded while Thea made tea. She watched Mem with a smile that seemed to *know*.

"I still don't think I can call you Mrs Tits," Mem said.

"Lena, then. That's the name my *friends* use." Lena aimed a pointed look at the back of Thea's head. Thea blew an exasperated sigh at the ceiling and tapped a teaspoon in a rapid rhythm on the countertop in irritation. Mem laughed outright.

"She doesn't let me call her Lena."

"Maybe because you call her Mrs Tits," Mem pointed out.

Two sets of impossibly blue eyes turned on her, both of them delighted at Mem's nerve. It made her flush. Thea stepped into Mem's space and reached around to squeeze her backside.

"Cheeky," she murmured, dangerously.

Mem grinned and leaned even closer. Thea's smile was vicious.

Lena's eyes flicked between the two of them.

"So. Are you Indian, Memona? Pakistani? Muslim? Hindu?" Lena filled a floral plate with glazed honey cookies. The rose-covered crockery was an interesting contrast to what Mem had seen so far. She was abrupt in the way of older generations but Mem didn't mind. She put a hand on Thea's arm when she rolled her eyes at Lena's old-fashioned assumptions.

"Second generation British," Mem explained. "But all those things are in my heritage."

"I thought you might be able to help me cook roti properly," Lena sniffed. "Mine don't puff up."

"Racist," Thea muttered.

"I can definitely give you some tips with that. Making roti just the right way is something my grandmother insisted on."

Lena suddenly looked as dangerous as Thea. "I'm not that old, my dear."

"Oh. I didn't mean—"

Thea came to her rescue. "You're seventy! And you don't cook."

"What would you know?"

Thea placed three mugs of tea on Lena's kitchen table and popped an entire honey biscuit into her mouth at once. Lena pulled a face.

"Sit down, Memona. It's nice to see someone around here with some manners."

Thea spluttered around her cookie. "I just made you tea!"

Lena looked Thea square in the eye, picked up Thea's mug and poured it down the sink.

"The fuck?!"

"You don't want to get too attached to this one, Memona. Thinks she's king shit. And she steals my vodka."

"I don't!"

"You do."

"Unbelievable bitch." Thea put her hands on her hips and practised her breathing.

"I know. Thank you." Lena sat, smiled sweetly and offered the plate of cookies to Mem. "I can see that I'm too late anyway. Go away, Fyodora. Girl talk."

Thea looked positively murderous. "I don't think so." She laid a very protective hand on Mem's shoulder. Mem liked the feel of it there. Heavy. Promising.

"Oh, do as you're told," Lena drawled. "If the lovely Memona Swan likes you as much as you think she does, you've got nothing to worry about."

A swift flash of fear crossed Thea's face so quickly Mem wasn't sure she saw it, but the swagger returned in a second. Thea threw her shoulders back and tucked two fingers under Mem's chin. She tilted her face to hers and kissed her hard. Mem sighed into her mouth, knowing the sound of her need would provide the hit Thea needed against Lena's chuckle.

"Don't be too long, darling."

Thea caressed her cheek with one long finger, seized five biscuits from Lena's plate with a pointed glare and swaggered out the back door.

Mem used Mrs Tits' house or garden to sneak through to Thea's place almost every night.

Avoiding paparazzi was something Thea remained quite strident about, even though Mem was beginning to find her feet and becoming used to the whole circus. She wondered if it was Thea simply being gallant, or whether she wanted to keep Mem just for her own lens.

Mem didn't mind. Mrs Tits was a hoot.

Sometimes Thea met her at Lena's garden gate, an urgent lust in her hands, something unholy in her smile. They'd trip and giggle right through Lena's garden, then Thea's and straight up to Thea's bed.

Sometimes Lena called to her from her front door.

"Come in, Mem. She's still at Jasper's studio. Said she'll be ten minutes."

Lena's house was full of pictures from a past life – one clearly lived hard and fast. Mem examined them curiously over yet more cups of tea and Russian sweet cakes.

A forest of framed photographs covered the mantlepiece. Lena as a very hot twenty-something resting her hip against a red Porsche 911 parked in front of the Colosseum in Rome. Lena astride a motorbike wearing nothing but a crocheted bikini and some fuck-off amazing boots. Lena in a long winter coat and a fur hat standing in the snow at Berlin's Checkpoint Charlie. The West German side.

A few things clicked in Mem's mind. She frowned as she tried to remember some modern history dates.

"If you're Russian and the Soviet Union didn't collapse until 1991 and that bikini is definitely from the seventies—" She pointed at the pictures that were clearly taken in Paris, London and Switzerland. "I thought travel wasn't allowed in Soviet Russia."

Lena chuckled. "I could tell you, milaya, but then I'd have to kill you."

"Really?" Mem squeaked. She suddenly had no doubt that Mrs Tits actually could.

"Money buys privilege." She shrugged in a wry, mocking way that seemed quintessentially Russian. "Back then, no one asked where the money came from."

Another old photograph caught Mem's eye. This one looked familiar, as if she'd seen one taken at the same time – from the same camera with the same role of film. It showed a superyacht from the eighties where a bronzed but paunchy man reclined on its deck surrounded by a dozen bikini-clad women. They fawned over him in a grotesque cliche. Champagne and cigarettes instead of grapes and palm leaves, but the man looked like a smug little caesar in every other way. The keyhole harbour and white buildings of Monaco were in the background.

She'd seen another picture just like it on the internet.

It took Mem a moment to find Yelena in the photo. Blurry in the background, but fully dressed in a white pantsuit with incredible shoulder pads. She was tossing an inflatable beach ball to a small girl with straw-coloured hair.

Mem's heart stopped.

"Is that—?"

Lena peered in too. She gave a fond smile. "Hmm. Yes. I'd forgotten about that." Then she snorted. "Is it any wonder Thea turned out the way she has? She's always liked the pretty girls."

So that was Thea's father, Mem realised. An actual Russian crime baron lording it up amid the spoils. She looked at the kid in the background – carefree little Thea – and wondered what it must have been like to grow up in the shelter of a man who had run one of Europe's biggest drug and prostitution rackets. Did she know? Then? Mem considered the bikini'd women in the picture and how *expendable* they looked. Had anyone ever stuck around for Thea? Was that why she and Yelena Titov were neighbours now? Mem felt her heart clench for Thea and began to understand why she had such trouble trusting.

Lena took Mem's arm and led her to another photo on top of a piano. This was of a very young Lena in a military uniform holding what was most definitely a Kalashnikov.

"You do understand what you're getting yourself into, don't you?" Lena asked, mildly. "You must know you're not the first of the women who've used my garden to get to Thea's bed."

Mem nodded. She knew that. She also knew the way Thea sighed and gazed at her when she thought Mem wasn't looking.

"Did you really use that thing?" Mem tilted her head at the photo.

"Could strip it down and reassemble in forty-six seconds," Lena said, proudly. "That's pretty impressive, mind you."

It certainly explained Yelena's relationship to Thea's father. And Thea.

The closest person Thea had to family – her only constant since childhood – had been an employee. A bodyguard.

It gave a sharper edge to everything she knew about Thea's life before now. She thought of honey-glazed biscuits on floral plates, the easy, teasing banter between Yelena and Thea, and learnt another important lesson about trust.

"I know," Mem said, and they both knew she was answering Lena's first question. "I like her. I think she likes me."

Lena smiled an upside-down smirk that was cruel, amused and affectionate all at once. It said it all. "I think she likes that you like her games."

That warmed Mem from the inside.

Lena saw Mem's blush. "Oh darling, you must be fun to play with. Don't worry. She's gone for you. She's never actually introduced me to any of the others." She squeezed Mem's arm and drew her away. "You know she'll be an arse about it, though," she warned.

Mem knew that too. Thea might appear aloof and complex to the rest of the world, but there was a simple aching truth at her heart. The ice was a facade. It hid a lonely child.

She nodded.

Lena gave her a warm smile. Mem had passed some kind of test.

"Roti," Lena pronounced when they were back in the kitchen. "Tell me your secrets. Show me how it's done. Though, if you tell a soul other than Thea that I *will* have to kill you. I have a reputation to uphold."

Mem grinned. They were deep into the finer points of kneading, rolling and searing on a bare flame, a sabzi masala simmering on the stovetop, when Thea arrived looking for Mem.

"I should get you in an apron in my kitchen, darling," she murmured into Mem's ear, pressing her against the kitchen countertop with the full length of her body.

Mem felt a rush of heat that had nothing to do with cooking and tilted her hips back against Thea's groin.

"Anything else?" she whispered.

Thea looked triumphant. "No. Just the apron."

There was a rude noise from the other side of the kitchen.

"You two are sickening," Lena drawled.

Thea stuck her middle finger up.

"Stay for dinner, *devochki moi*. It will be nice."

"Now who's being sickening?"

Mem laughed. She realised she loved them both. "Oh, stop it, both of you. Lena, plates please. Thea, cutlery. Sit. Now! Hands to yourself! Oh my god, you are evil! Sit down!" The last bit came out as a squeal.

To her immense surprise, Thea did, though not before giving Mem a searing kiss that hooked onto something deep inside Mem's core and tugged hard.

Lena's dry chuckle was merciless. "Simp," she shot at Thea.

"Fuck you," Thea hissed back.

They both buttoned their lips when Mem put her hands on her hips and tapped her foot, her head cocked to the side. She knew she wasn't fooling either of them, but she served the meal, and they ate and talked and laughed until late into the night and Thea's patience utterly ran out. When it did, she took Mem's hand, kissed her fingers, and thanked her and Lena very prettily for the meal.

Then her eyes darkened.

"Time to go, darling."

Lena's laughter rang all the way up the garden.

Mem taught them both to cook.

Well, she tried. Thea couldn't seem to follow a recipe if her life depended on it, and her concentration always crumbled whenever she saw Mem in an apron. *That* was a ludicrous stereotype that Mem tried teasing her for, but teasing only made Thea's gaze more dangerous. Mrs Tits sat at the counter, drank vodka and laughed at them.

Evenings in Thea's kitchen became a sanctuary of laughter and honest company far from the glare of the spotlight. Mem began to understand how the terms 'reclusive' and 'celebrity' went together after all, and found herself longing for the easy comfort at the end of each day.

Sometimes she'd arrive through Lena's garden to find her and Thea elbows deep in the preparation of a chicken tandoori, a loud argument in the air between them, usually over the finer points of the recipe Thea refused to read.

"I wrote it down for you," Mem laughed, waving the paper under Thea's nose.

"Meh." Thea's hands were covered in marinade. She snatched the paper from Mem's hand with her teeth, spat it to the floor, and chased Mem around the kitchen island until she could pin her against it for a kiss.

Once, Thea strode in late while Mem and Lena were preparing a biryani with a korma on the side, Lena telling old stories about Moscow in the 80s. Thea paused at the door and leant against the frame watching them – watching Mem – her arms folded and her gaze heavy. She'd been working for Jasper and was in a maroon suit that utterly worshipped her figure, a gold scarf tied tight around her throat, a heavy gold chain tangled with it. She stalked on heeled boots that did magnificent things to the line of her thighs.

When she sat at the counter she looked tired, though she smirked when Mem set a wine glass in front of her and poured her a glass. Took a long sip and couldn't drag her eyes from Mem's either. Mem left Lena at the stovetop and stood behind Thea to massage her shoulders, digging her thumbs into muscles that were knotted and tight. Thea leaned back against her, dropping one hand down to reach around and squeeze Mem's thigh.

"Mmm, I'll have more of this later, my darling," she murmured, greedy and needy, and Mem shivered at her tone, eager to provide exactly what Thea wanted from her. "Your touch is magic."

It made Mem warm, from somewhere between her legs to somewhere deep in her chest, when Thea's need spilled out so keenly like that. To be wanted by this strong, powerful woman melted her bones, but to be the one who could dissolve Thea was just as addictive. She could already tell it was going to be a long, hard night.

"What are you cooking?" Thea asked, her head falling lazily back against Mem's chest, her lust simmering like the pots on the stove.

Mem chuckled. "The recipe is literally right in front of you." She pressed harder with her fingers and got a slap on her thigh for her cheek. She loved it. It only made her giggle more.

"I don't read," Thea declared, proud and stubborn, magnificent and childish all in one.

"She's bolshie like that," Mrs Tits said.

"Well then, you'll find out when I serve it to you," Mem said pertly and moved to go back to the stove, but Thea grabbed her wrist and pulled her close again.

"Keep doing what you were doing," she murmured. It didn't sound like an order, it sounded like a plea, and she tilted her face up for a kiss, too weary to be overbearing, too soft to be proud. Mem liked this side of her as well and worked hard at those taut muscles until the woman was putty under her hands.

The gentle mood lasted until the meal was done and Thea sent Mrs Tits home with an urgent order.

They never managed the washing up. Something about Mem with her hands in the sink drove Thea insane.

Chapter Sixteen

Thea's house became Mem's favourite place, and Thea photographed Mem naked in every room.

"For my exhibition," she said, when Mem protested.

In the mornings, the sunshine streamed into the kitchen through the conservatory windows and Thea caught the sunlight on her face. She'd slowly strip the kimono from Mem's shoulders and snap its fall with her camera, fascinated by the brush of the satin against her skin or the curve of her hip through the silk.

Other times, with steel in her hands and something urgent in her eyes, Thea would place two fingers on Mem's shoulder and push her to her knees. Mem would kneel gladly, excited as always, until that smugness and Thea's bloody camera drove her to distraction and her own patience burst.

On those occasions, it was Mem who became greedy, unbuttoning the belt on Thea's pants and eating her out on her knees in her own kitchen until it was Thea who was sobbing for mercy, her fingers twisted in Mem's hair, her head thrown back with abandon.

She was beautiful like that – her softness a gift Mem drank from like an addict, a gentle, caring devotion that placed Mem at the centre of her world like a goddess. Like that, it was hard to tell who was worshipping who.

And some nights, they scratched home cooking altogether and ate takeaway Chinese on the couch in Thea's lounge room, drinking red wine and laughing like idiots, until they ended up in each other's arms, Thea sprawled between Mem's legs, leaning against her body, her face buried in the crook of Mem's neck.

Mem padded around the house, in their quiet moments, examining the art on Thea's walls. The house had three storeys and a converted attic, and its rooms had high ceilings and sash windows that made the hundred-year-old place seem airy and spacious. The middle floors were lush with polished wood and mahogany furniture. It was a blend of Victorian history, Thea's obvious wealth and her own casual but edgy style. Mem wondered how many people saw those upstairs rooms of Thea's life. Her kitchen was for entertaining and business. The studio was for working and art.

According to Mrs Tits, who shared her gossip gleefully and showed Mem the perfect view of Thea's garden she had from her own upstairs windows, most of Thea's previous women never made it past the studio.

The bed in the studio was for fucking.

These quiet upstairs rooms held a more intimate version of Thea.

There was art on all the walls.

Some were paintings. More evidence of money, Mem realised, when she leaned in to examine the signatures. There were some very prominent contemporary artists in Thea's collection, but the pieces themselves were dark. Moody. They made Mem slightly uncomfortable.

One room on the second floor, furnished as a second sitting room but with the look of being barely used, was full of black and white photographs. They were all portraits. Mem was beginning to recognise Thea's style as well as some repeated models amongst Thea's work. That woman there, she noticed, was the same as the portrait downstairs in the kitchen – an older woman, a small scar on her cheek. She was vaguely familiar, Mem thought again, though she couldn't put her finger on why.

Other portraits turned out to be from artists as famous as Thea.

"Diane Arbus, Dorothea Lange, obviously. Original prints," Thea said, waving a casual hand at two framed photographs. "You'll like this." She pulled Mem over to a portrait of a woman seated sideways on a wooden chair. She wore a casual suit and cloche hat, and her eyes interrogated the viewer. "Berenice Abbott was American, a lesbian, and a fucking master of composition. This is one of only twenty from her Parisian series in the 1920s – almost all of her subjects were queer. Look at the clarity in that—" she pointed. "You can see the wool of her jacket, the light on the very tips of her eyelashes. She did that with a camera that was essentially a wooden box and a glass plate. Genius."

Mem was more entranced by the awe in Thea's voice, the softness of her expression as she shared the joy and magic of her craft.

"Look at this one," Thea said, drawing her over to stand before a picture of a ballerina in an inelegant panic tying the ribbons on one shoe. She was in a crumpled heap on the floor in the wing-space of a theatre, the only light slanting in between a gap in the tall, velvet curtains. The woman was beautiful, but there was a frown between her brows, and her teeth bit into her lower lip. The image had the warm, sepia tones of the 1930s, and the gold foil, press-letter print beneath it read *Premiere ballerina, Great Theatre, Moscow.*

Mem leaned against Thea and watched the way she studied the picture.

"Tell me about it," Mem whispered.

For a second, Thea looked as if she might give Mem a dispassionate lecture on light levels, film grain and technique, but her arm slipped around Mem's waist and held her a little closer.

"This is by Margaret Bourke-White – another trailblazing American woman – taken in 1931 in Russia. Or the Soviet Union, I guess," she murmured. Her eyes flitted over every inch of the photograph in front of them, even though Mem assumed Thea must already know it well. This was a collector's piece. It had the photographer's signature in the bottom corner with 3/50 scrawled in fading pencil.

"She was pretty ballsy for the times," Thea went on. "First woman photojournalist embedded with the US military forces in World War Two. She was the only western photographer in Moscow when the Germans invaded. She was shot at, torpedoed in the Mediterranean, strafed by the Luftwaffe, she photographed Gandhi four hours before he was assassinated—"

That was all very impressive but Mem was more interested in the dancer in front of them and why Thea was still staring at her. Mem tapped her ribs.

"Why do you like this photo?"

There was a long silence.

"My grandmother was a ballerina. In Moscow," Thea said, eventually. She pressed her cheek against the side of Mem's head. "My mother too, but she stopped dancing after my brother and I were born. I never knew her – my grandmother – but Mama had a box of old photos she'd pull out when she was"—there was a huff of breath into Mem's hair—"when she was drunk and miserable. Beautiful old photos of her and my grandmother in glorious costumes, dancing in the spotlight. Or dressed in stylish evening gowns at parties. Shaking hands with Khrushchev and Brezhnev."

Mem frowned. "Is this your grandmother?" She nodded at the picture.

"Oh no. Just some random ballerina, I suppose," Thea sighed. She sounded as if she was a million miles away. "My father threw that box of photos on the fire one night after Mama was gone. Said he was clearing up her shit. Something he should have done ages ago, he said."

There was a bitterness in her tone that made Mem's heart ache.

"Gone?" she asked, gently.

Thea went very still in her arms. "Shot herself. In the head, apparently, though I only found that out from newspaper reports, years later."

"Oh god, Thea! I'm so sorry."

"You don't need to be."

Mem pulled her tighter. "How old were you?"

There was a tiny sniff. "Seven. We were on my father's boat, somewhere near Corsica. Her body washed up near Nice."

"Oh."

There was another silence while Thea looked at the photo and saw something that wasn't there. Mem didn't know how to comfort her.

She also thought of that photo with the bikini girls in Yelena's house, the pic of Yelena with the machine gun, and the sheer number of news reports surrounding Thea's father's arrest in London all those years ago, and wondered if even Thea knew the full story.

"I don't blame her," Thea said, suddenly, defensively. "My father was a monster and she was beautiful. It wasn't her fault."

It was the strangest defence Mem had ever heard. The guilt in Thea's tone was unmistakable. She turned in Thea's arms to offer her a proper hug.

"Of course, it wasn't," she murmured.

For a tiny second she thought Thea might melt into her and take the solace Mem was ready to offer her.

"It wasn't your fault either," Mem said. "You were just a kid."

Thea's eyes hardened and that infuriating smirk returned to the corner of her mouth. She shrugged.

"Ages ago, darling. Hardly matters now. Come and look at this."

And she tugged Mem to a trio of photos on the opposite wall.

Thea's eyes danced at her.

"That's Annie Leibovitz!" Mem exclaimed. "And that's you!"

Thea chuckled. "We did some shit-stirring for Vogue magazine. They wanted to do a feature on two queer women of art, so we gave them the straightest portraits ever. She did me and I did her."

The two portraits were almost identical. Both women in black turtleneck sweaters, their bodies dissolving seamlessly into an inky background, stared directly at the viewer. In a dramatic contrast, a pitiless white light illuminated their blond hair and pale skin, their faces laid bare to the lens. Every contour, every imperfection was highlighted, yet it was the depth and intensity of their eyes that anchored the viewer. The power of their gaze – the eyes that were generally hidden behind a camera – turned full force on the viewer without the modifying influence of the lens and they took Mem's breath away.

She knew what it was like to be looked at like that. Thea did it to her all the time.

It consumed her.

The third picture was completely different.

It was a wide angle shot of Thea's studio. A simple paper drop was deliberately crooked, an old wooden ladder stood under a broken light and unplugged power cords hung down from above. Cables, gels, lenses and curls of film littered the floor, and the two world famous photographers stood back-to-back in the centre of the chaos. They wore suits, their arms folded, their smiles smug.

And a dozen beautiful, naked women lay in a tangled writhing mess at their feet.

Mem spluttered out a laugh.

"We didn't give Vogue this one," Thea said. "This is one of only two prints."

"You are a tease," Mem said.

Thea's voice dropped an octave.

"You only just figure that out, darling?"

There was a white room at the very top of the house – an attic, utterly empty except for an old leather wingback chair. No pictures on the walls, an old Persian rug on the floor. Mem found it one evening and felt the mood change as Thea paced into the room behind her.

"This is my space, my muse." Thea's voice was low and dangerous. "A retreat. A refuge. I've never allowed anyone else in here."

Mem looked at the whiteness, the emptiness and understood. "I didn't mean to pry."

But Thea flung herself into the chair and hooked one knee over its arm.

"Strip for me."

Mem blinked. They were waiting for dinner to be delivered, but when Thea's voice hit that tone, when her gaze darkened and turned lazy like that, Mem knew what was coming. Her body did too. She peeled her clothes off and shivered. Not from the cold.

"Serve me."

A cushion was tossed to the floor just in front of the chair, but Mem settled down on the rug, knees wide, and slipped a hand between her own legs.

Thea's cry of outrage stopped in her throat, her lips staying open as her eyes followed the increasingly frantic movements of Mem's hand. Neither of them knew when it happened, but suddenly Thea was beside her on the rug, urging her on, her phone catching filth and heaven and lust in all the same shots.

"Come on baby. Come on. You gorgeous thing."

And then Thea was tearing her own clothes off and settling herself over Mem's face, her mouth landing on Mem's core with a ravenous hunger. They came together, locked in a shared ecstasy, sweaty, shaky and grinning foolishly.

"I won't be able to think of this room in quite the same way ever again," Thea admitted.

Mem was pleased. They rolled around on the rug, tickling each other mercilessly, until the vibe deepened again and they fucked until they sobbed.

Dinner went cold on the front step.

Chapter Seventeen

Thea Voronov was in danger of falling in love.

If she thought about it, she'd known it from the beginning – from that first moment Mem Swan walked into her studio and proved all the promises her photographs made.

Thea had always thought she was above things like love. Once her stupid heart had figured out that Kate only wanted her for fun, she'd never truly believed she'd find anyone else. She had what she needed: money – far too fucking much of it – and the respect of the industry. She made the art she wanted to make. She did just enough work for Jasper to ensure she always had a friend in high places. And there was no shortage of women who were happy to be tied to her bed for whatever other pleasures took her whim.

What else was there?

She watched Mem now, holding her hand. She was tugging her over the footbridge at Camden Lock to find the perfect spot to sit along the edge of the canal. Her smile danced back at her, her fingers were sticky with ice cream, and they discussed the relative merits of pistachio and hazelnut gelato over the brighter flavours of raspberry and lemon.

What frivolous bullshit was this?

Thea couldn't stop grinning like a fool.

"Under the willow tree?" Mem asked as if contentment, peace and joy were tangled in its branches.

Who was Thea to deny her? A smile like the sunrise was her reward.

Oh, Thea took what she wanted from Mem, certainly. Their nights at London's finest establishments were a dizzying blend of luxury and sensuality. Opulent five star restaurants with private rooms, soft jazz, dim lights and Thea's fingers in Mem's cunt under the table. All the best parties, where Mem moved with a grace and poise that left onlookers entranced. The way Mem carried herself, every gesture screaming her elegance and refinement, swelled something fierce in Thea's chest and made her proud to have her on her arm – even as Thea *knew* the clamps she'd put on the woman's nipples under her dress would be winding her up like a toy. And the envy on the faces of every other person around them? That was the sweetest bonus.

Behind closed doors, their dynamic only intensified. In the depths of their intimacy, Thea served out control and Mem gave herself over with a vulnerability that both thrilled and slightly unnerved Thea. She relished Mem's surrender, but the younger woman's willingness to submit and trust Thea so utterly was something she hadn't anticipated. While the tight, enthralling burn of domination was exhilarating, the weight of Mem's submission was humbling. It made Thea's heart race in ways she hadn't expected.

Mem wanted more from her.

Her curiosity was obvious. The minx went through Thea's toy box with far too much glee.

"Can we play with this tonight?"

She was kneeling at the end of the bed, and she'd pulled a strap-on and harness from the chest there. She dangled it from one finger with an impish smile.

Thea knew exactly how to shut that cheekiness down. She stalked slowly across the room until she was standing over the girl and watched her pupils dilate as Mem felt the mood change.

"It would be my pleasure, darling," Thea murmured, scratching her nails lightly against the nape of Mem's neck.

It was like a kick to the chest, all the air leaving her lungs, when she saw Mem had found a soft leather flogger and a crop too.

"And these?"

Thea almost didn't hear the plea over the blood rushing in her own head, her pulse loud in her ears and beating in her clit. She didn't want to hurt Mem. But, *god*, she wanted to watch her writhe so beautifully...

She knew kink was a game – fuck, she could play it better than anyone she knew – and yet Mem took everything she thought she understood about need and desire and twisted it until Thea was no longer sure what she wanted. It was that unutterable beauty staring back at her that messed it all up. That *perfection*. How could Thea play those same soulless games with this gorgeous creature? How could she use her, taking her beauty and exploiting it, just like the industry did to beauty wherever it saw it, like her father had done to all those girls so many years before...

"Please?"

It was better to avoid the matter for just a little bit longer. Which was easy to do when Mem was so very keen to obey.

"You're greedy, you wicked girl. How about you get on the bed and take what you're given?"

Mem craned her neck to look up at her and Thea saw the chemicals swirling behind her eyes. Mem leaned forward and pressed her cheek against Thea's thigh, her lips falling open as Thea tightened her fingers in her hair.

The heat of her cheek burned against Thea's legs.

"Clothes off. On the bed. Hands and knees."

Mem whimpered but she didn't move. Thea knew she liked being where she was – kneeling at Thea's feet devastated the girl. It nearly destroyed Thea too. She had to smother a chuckle when she noticed Mem pressing her thighs together, fidgeting and squirming like she could come just like that, without Thea even touching her.

The woman surrendered more completely than anyone Thea had ever known.

She fisted Mem's hair and pulled her upright, kissing her hard and licking into her, tilting her head back to go deeper. Her heartbeat fluttered under her fingers, her moan filled Thea's senses. She could drown in this, in the utterly perfect way Mem's body moved under her touch.

"Strip and get on the bed, my darling muse. I won't ask again."

And she turned away knowing exactly the effect that would have on Mem. She knew because she felt it too.

Clothes sailed around the room.

Mem wanted more from her, and some part deep inside Thea wanted it too. A tiny voice in her head whispered that Mem might be the one to make her whole – the perfect woman who wanted her for all the right reasons. Those whispers led her to the edge of her longing and showed her the view – Mem's body, open and inviting, her heart just the same.

She could be herself. She could relax and know she'd be held. She could dance that thin line between what she needed and what she feared, and Mem would hold her hand and dance with her, both of them lush with Mem's desire and its sweet, intoxicating call.

She mastered herself by devoting her art to her muse.

Deadlines loomed for both of them. They were like walls Thea couldn't see past – her own exhibition in just two weeks was a tired necessity that bored her, except that the collection held some pictures of Mem she was particularly pleased with. The premiere of *The Wolverton Diamond* was a week after that – and then everything would change for Mem.

Thea wondered if it would change Mem too.

Fame and money had changed Jasper and Kate. It was only logical that Mem would fall into the machine and be corrupted by it as well. Thea wanted to steal her away from it, she wanted to tie her to her bed and never let her out in the world. She was in awe of the woman's bravery and resilience in the face of the yawning, baying greed of the industry, and she was keen to see her soar with the sophistication and elegance that raised Mem above the whole wretched lot of them.

She wanted to hold her, cradle her against the soul-destroying misery of it and be the one to kiss away the inevitable tears.

She wanted every moment to be just like this one.

"There's a woman with the two most adorable kids at the refuge at the moment," Mem said. She leaned against Thea's shoulder and licked her ice cream. "They're two and four. I hung out with the play therapist today and we did finger painting."

It was late, maybe eleven if Thea cared to look at the time. She didn't want to move to find out. She had no idea what 'the refuge' was. She should ask. She should do the research and learn about Mem's charity. Get Lollie to read it all to her. But the line of Mem's throat was *just there*, and her body was perfect against her own.

They were both in drab clothes – baggy jeans and shapeless hoodies, Mem's hair tucked under a beanie.

"I look like a teenage boy," Mem had protested.

She could never look like that.

"A trick I learnt years ago," Thea told her. "Hunch your shoulders, look at the ground. No one will see us."

"I'll see you." Mem gazed at her with that intoxicating worship that both lit Thea up and terrified her. She curled against Thea and slipped her hand into the back pocket of Thea's jeans. Mem squeezed her arse with a filthy smile, then giggled with delight when Thea promised her a spanking later. She slung her arm over Mem's shoulders and led her out into the streets – to a dowdy pub in a seedy part of town where they could grind against each other as they jumped to some band they didn't know with a heap of people who didn't care.

They bought ice creams on the walk home and dangled their legs over the edge of the canal in an absolutely ordinary moment as precious as diamonds.

"When you think about it, probably every kid has done finger painting," Mem mused. "Well, either mud, or paint, I guess. But you don't remember it, do you? It's not until you do it later – *if* you do it later, that you actually experience it. Kids see things differently."

She fell silent.

"I sense something profound is coming?" Thea nuzzled into her beanie, breathing in the moment. She'd never been so patient.

"I'm just thinking." Mem dipped her finger into Thea's hazelnut gelato suddenly and painted a line down Thea's cheek. Thea raised an eyebrow at her audacity, but Mem leaned in and licked it off, her tongue hot, her smile pure sass. "It's all in the way you look at things, isn't it? I always thought my beauty was a curse, but now I can see the good I can do with it. I always imagined being a movie star would be some crazy kind of hell, but now I'm working my way through it step by step and it's not so bad." She kissed Thea's cheek, looked her dead in the eye and blushed, then grimaced at her own embarrassment. "I used to be so vanilla I didn't even know what that meant, and now I—"

Thea locked her arms around her waist and pulled her closer. "Now you—?"

"Now I want to submit to you in every way possible, and wholly surrender to all my kinky desires."

Thea snorted gently in her ear. She was adorable.

"Whose kinky desires?" she whispered, loading her tone with danger. She bit the girl's earlobe and held her while she shivered.

"Yours," Mem admitted. "Whatever you want."

It was too much, Thea thought. Mem was warm and trusting and perfect – and Thea had hardened her heart against that kind of bullshit years ago. The girl would do whatever she asked, and she knew that was dangerous – for both of them.

She hadn't broached the subject of the brand ambassadorship or the movie sequel with Mem since Jasper's party, and his irritating lordship shouted at her about it almost every day. But she knew with the deepest, sinking certainty that if she simply ordered Mem to do them, she would.

And that wasn't right.

So, Thea suggested finger painting – a different kind of kink – and she watched genuine happiness and laughter light up Mem's eyes. They bought more ice cream, strawberries, raspberries and chocolate sauce, and ran home with it all, giggling like idiots. And it was a shining, terrifying, simple joy that Mem wanted exactly what Thea did.

She wondered if maybe, just maybe, she could let herself fall.

Chapter Eighteen

"But this is Louis Vuitton."

Thea didn't even turn. "I had Delphine send it over for you yesterday," she said, breezily, as if the vice president of LV was a personal friend. For all Mem knew she might be. "Put it on."

She was fussing with her camera and doing something on the screens in the corner of the studio. They were in there – again – for another photo shoot that they both knew full well was going to end up with Mem naked and both of them exhausted on the bed in the other room. Mem wasn't sure why they even bothered with the designer dresses.

Last week, it had been Dior. A few days before that it was a run of English designers – Jenny Packham, Temperley London and Erdem. Gorgeous, sumptuous, amazing gowns, and Mem felt a million dollars in them. She looked a hundred times that in the photos Thea took of her – more, if you counted the diamonds Thea invariably draped over her body as well.

Being Thea Voronov's muse definitely had its advantages.

Thea bought luxury gowns and jewellery for her as if they were pocket money. The things she could do with light and shadow would have made even the cheapest high street frock look amazing, but Thea insisted. Mem surrendered. She knew Thea was working on images for her exhibition.

Mem couldn't help but think of all the good the money Thea was spending on these designer dresses could do at Heart and Grace House.

Mem slipped on the gown.

Two warm hands landed on her hips as she struggled with the zip. Thea was behind her, pulling their bodies together.

"Allow me," she murmured into her ear. Mem held her hair away and Thea kissed the nape of her neck. When she didn't stop, Mem tried to turn in her arms. The kiss turned into a nibble and then a needy sigh.

Mem smiled. "You okay back there?" she asked.

"Hooks and eyes," Thea mumbled, her lips still on Mem's skin. She sounded very distracted. "Tricksy things."

There was more diamond jewellery too. It was all from CreatedDiamonds, Mem noticed, but less ostentatious than the enormous rock they'd used in *The Wolverton Diamond*. Thea seemed to be developing an obsession with the way diamonds refracted light and spilled it over Mem's skin. It was all rainbows in the hollow of Mem's collar bones, a choker of white stones draped over the curve of her hip, or a diamond ring balancing on her lower lip while she sprawled in a sea of rose petals.

Thea paid for them all and insisted they belonged to Mem.

She wouldn't hear it when Mem tried to object.

"I can't buy my muse beautiful things?" she asked.

"It's just that—"

But Thea's eyes darkened. "Not that you need such trivial things to enhance your beauty," she murmured. "Every shot I take is a masterpiece when you're in it."

There was no hiding her desperation when Thea spoke like that. Mem stifled a nervous giggle.

"Silly," she tried.

Exactly as she'd expected, the word flew straight to Thea's ego. She drew herself tall again – that towering swagger that Mem adored – and flicked a finger under Mem's chin.

"Cheeky."

Thea's eyes lingered a fraction longer and Mem smiled triumphantly.

"Assume the position, Ms Swan," Thea drawled, and grabbed her camera. She was talking about the pose they had decided on for this particular shoot – an old-fashioned rope-and-wood swing hanging from the ceiling of the studio against a stylised rose arbour as a backdrop – but the comment was corny enough to make them both snort-laugh. Thea smacked her arse as she turned to go, and Mem poked out her tongue.

Thea's chuckle was way too pleased with itself.

The shoot ended up in bed, after all.

Two days after that, Piper showed her the account Thea Voronov had opened at the Marks & Spencers just up the street from the shelter.

"It's in Heart and Grace's name, though," Piper explained. "A monthly spend capped at three thousand quid." She gave Mem an appraising look and rubbed her hands together. "Three thousand pounds *per month*! Holy shit! Well done you, though. This is what we were talking about. Donations and sponsorship from your network exactly as we were hoping."

Mem smiled back at her, but she was surprised. Thea hadn't mentioned anything.

In fact, when she thought about it, she'd told Thea she had 'a project', a 'charity' – she hadn't told her what it was.

Thea must have done some research, she supposed. About her.

That thought shot the usual burning heat to that perfect point right between her legs, but a warm, full feeling hit her somewhere higher too. In her chest. Exactly where her heart was.

"You're welcome. I know your project is important to you," Thea said, later.

They were naked and tangled in the sheets of the bed in the studio, Mem flat on her back and dozy after three long and drawn out orgasms, the photoshoot Thea had planned forgotten in the other room. Thea lay with her head propped up on her elbow looking down at her. Her fingers trailed a lazy pattern over Mem's breast, circling her nipple in a way that kept a permanent tingle vibrating through Mem's body – if only she wasn't too damn exhausted to rise to it.

"It's a very generous gift. Thank you."

Thea gave an odd half-smile and shook her head, brushing the thanks away.

"Very practical too," Mem pointed out.

That bit had puzzled her at first. An account at a department store was an odd way to gift a women's refuge – she and Piper had both expected benefactors would donate cash. But then she realised people seeking shelter often had to leave everything they had behind. They'd need clothes, underwear, a toothbrush... Thea's gift was incredibly useful.

Thea frowned and Mem reached up to cup her face and thumb it away. There was a small moment, then Thea leaned into her hand.

"Thank you," Mem said again, "but you didn't have to."

Thea's smile was lopsided and so unexpectedly sheepish it warmed Mem as much as what she was doing with her fingers did.

"I like that you have a charity," Thea said. "It's noble and principled, though to tell you the truth, I did ask Lollie to sort things out for me. I told her to tell Jasper about it too. Let's see if we can't squeeze some money out of his lordship and his media empire and put him to good use for once."

Mem wasn't sure how she felt about pressuring a brand new friendship with a demand for charity. Thea must have seen the look on her face.

"Jasper is loaded and so are all his friends," she said, wryly. "Your project will be nothing more than a tax write-off for them so you may as well take advantage of them while you can. You can be absolutely sure they're taking advantage of—"

She stopped. Pressed her lips together. For a split second, Mem thought she saw shame.

"Of?"

Thea tweaked her nipple and smirked. "Of you, my darling."

Mem's back arched of its own accord and Thea tickled her ribs and swallowed her squeal with a kiss. She climbed over her and straddled her hips.

"Hollywood's hottest new superstar. Everyone wants you," Thea murmured against her lips.

Mem stretched languidly and watched a hungry, hopeless greed cross Thea's expression.

"Well, they can't have me," Mem grinned. "I'm *your* muse. I belong to you."

There was a groan, then Thea attached her lips and her teeth to Mem's neck and blew her mind.

In the red half light of the darkroom, Thea showed her the magic.

"We develop the film first, then we make a print," she explained, pouring mysterious chemicals into tanks and ordering the workspace with a meticulousness that Mem hadn't expected. "Do you trust me?"

She was so eager and her smile was so warm, she barely waited for Mem's answer before she flicked the light off completely and plugged them into total darkness.

Mem felt Thea's body pressed against hers from behind, her arms slotted though around her waist to guide her hands. Her breath was in her ear, her lips tight in an obvious smile against her skin. Happiness radiated from her.

Of course I trust you," Mem whispered, though she didn't need to say it. They both knew.

"We load the film onto a reel and put it in the developing tank," said Thea.

Confident, clever fingers guided Mem's, and in the darkness everything was sensation. She could smell the acrid tang of the chemicals, the earthy dust in the corners of the room, the scent of sex, and the fragrance of herself on Thea's breath. The heat of Thea's body against her back burned through the silk kimono Mem was wearing. Thea hadn't bothered to tie hers, of course. The plush of her breasts was against Mem's shoulder blades, the tickle of the hair between her legs was against her arse. Mem was cradled in her arms, in her care and in her cleverness, and there was nowhere else she wanted to be.

Once the film was safely in the tank, Thea flicked the red light on again.

Washing and drying the film gave Mem time to look around the room.

She'd always thought darkrooms would be cramped, tiny things, but Thea's was spacious.

A room at the back of the studio she'd never noticed before, it was lined with bookshelves and filled with all the books on photography that Thea's house was empty of. Old, well-loved, creased and possibly thrifted, there were hundreds of them, spilling from the shelves, most with torn pieces of thick photographic paper stuck between their pages as bookmarks.

Two lengths of drying line hung above a centre table just like every darkroom Mem had ever seen in movies and a handful of images were pegged there. Thea pulled these down now as they waited. She pushed them into a messy pile and flung them to the edge of the table as if they didn't matter, then she kissed Mem on her way past to pull paper from another drawer. She set out trays, placing them in front of Mem like sacraments, her eyes black in the red light but her smile shy.

"I think you'll like this next bit," she said. "It's my favourite part of photography."

She gave Mem's body another searing glance and her fingers twitched toward her camera. She couldn't help herself, Mem thought, and just to stir her up she let the front of her robe slip open. It gave her another hit of the thoroughly addictive pleasure of seeing Thea's eyes catch helplessly on her body, her lips fall open.

"I don't use film often enough," Thea murmured.

She walked Mem slowly back against one of the bookcases, and gently and lovingly slipped her fingers around Mem's throat.

"You're extraordinary in this light," she said, tilting her hips against Mem's. Mem's pulse took off, utterly out of her control, and she hooked her thigh over Thea's hip, her core opening beneath her. Her head tipped back.

"And you are insatiable."

Thea chuckled into the hollow behind Mem's ear, moaned like she'd found heaven there, and slipped the fingers of her other hand into Mem's cunt.

Mem gasped, arched her back, and pulled Thea in harder with her thigh.

"You can take it," Thea told her.

She wanted to take everything Thea wanted to give her. She sighed happily.

"And so damned cocky," Mem added.

There was another laugh, then Thea's hand was in her hair, her fingers were deep, deep in her core and Mem was spiralling again.

Thea worked by feel as much as sight – Mem knew that intimately – but seeing her here in her element was like watching something primal. Thea moved unhesitatingly around her darkroom, her movements sharp and decisive in the low light.

All her softness was in her smile.

"This one," she declared, and fed the negative into a complex frame, brushing away dust with expert moves, spinning dials and snapping settings on a tall machine that simply looked like another camera to Mem.

Mem draped herself over her back as she bent to examine her work through a curious, curved magnifier. A sigh rippled through Thea's entire body and she paused for just a moment.

"You're very distracting," she said, and it was a warning, sly and promising, for all that it was delivered with longing and lust. "I'm working here, baby."

"And it's wonderful to watch," Mem teased, letting her hands wrap around Thea's waist. She flattened her palms against Thea's bare abs, her fingers trailing upwards to her breasts.

Thea indulged her for a few moments, then straightened with a sigh.

"Sit." She pointed to the end of the work table. "Behave yourself."

"I thought you were going to teach me," Mem pouted.

Thea's smirk was instant. "To behave yourself?" She turned in Mem's arms and swatted her backside. Mem flinched then shivered with delight. Thea had spanked her til she squealed only an hour ago and she wasn't sure she could go again so soon. As it was, she was already regretting the full day of sitting she had tomorrow as she and Kate endured another round of interviews.

She edged carefully onto the table and did her best not to wince. She sat. Meekly.

Thea's laugh tickled her spine. She kissed her fingers and turned reluctantly back to her work.

Thea had taught her so much – about sex, about pleasure, about herself – that Mem could barely remember the person she'd been just a few short weeks ago. Now, the mere thought of Thea whispering 'obey me, my darling muse' was enough to have her practically coming in her pants during boring meetings with Adiatu or with her eyes closed at the stylist having her hair done.

But there was so much more Mem was keen to learn.

She'd asked Thea about it – about the more risqué of the prints hanging in the upstairs rooms of Thea's house. They were artful images, exquisitely composed, but they drew her like a moth to the flame.

Mem wanted to know how it burned.

"Do they excite you?" Thea had asked.

Mem was staring at a black and white shot of a smooth, round backside welted with stripes and caressed with silk.

"That looks like it hurts," she said, dubiously.

Thea shrugged. "That is the point." Her tone was dry. Mem looked up at the sour note in it.

"But you... *did* this?"

Thea's lips twisted like she'd tasted something bitter. "This is something I can do, Mem. Something I'm quite good at. I can whip you pink and make you beg for more, but just because I can, doesn't mean it's always what I crave."

Mem tilted her head, trying to piece together what Thea wasn't saying. "Does that mean you don't want to do... *this*... with me?" She hid a grimace at how naive she sounded. And how regretful.

Thea didn't answer then – not vocally, at least. Her body gave her away an hour later when the sex that night was rougher than usual, her fingers hard and her eyes unrelenting. It set Mem on fire, her body singing under Thea's hands, her entire soul alive like it had never been before. Submitting to Thea like that thrilled her, and she wanted more. She'd begged then, and seen the fire flare in Thea's eyes before a bitter snarl twisted her lips and the woman pulled back.

After that, she was gentle. Respectful. Infinitely careful and attentive, and she kissed and licked Mem to one of her most monumental climaxes – and so Mem knew then that the problem wasn't her, it was something inside Thea. Because Thea had watched her with need writ large on her face, with a longing that nearly broke Mem's heart.

She was lost on Thea, though she could see the curl of self-loathing inside her and wondered why she couldn't kiss it away.

Mem's eyes fell on another picture on the wall in the darkroom, tacked to the wall but crooked and old, and half-hidden behind a bookshelf. Forgotten. It was a candid snap of Dame Katherine Cox, taken just out that door in the bedroom of the studio. Kate was easily ten years younger, on her knees looking up at the camera, and naked with her arms bound behind her back. The flesh of her breasts bulged between coils of black rope and there was an obvious bite mark above her collarbone.

But it was her face that held the image's focus.

She was laughing. Uproariously. Her eyes were crossed, her nose was scrunched and her eyes were stellar with exasperation. Mem couldn't stop herself grinning back.

Seconds later she was fighting down jealousy.

It was confusing.

Kink was clearly a big part of Thea's life, and yet she shared only the edges of it with Mem.

"Come here," Thea said.

She hadn't noticed Mem staring at the picture, and the eagerness in her eyes was enough for Mem to brush all those feelings away. Thea wanted her. She was almost childlike in her desire to show Mem the magic of her craft.

How could Mem possibly resent her when she'd already given her so much?

"Now we develop it," Thea said, slipping the paper into a tray of liquid and pulling Mem over to a bank of trays on a bench by the wall. She wrapped her arms around her again from behind, nuzzling into her neck like it was her favourite place. "Watch this. This is the best bit."

She pressed a pair of wooden tongs into Mem's hand and slotted her fingers over top. They rocked the paper gently to and fro and a ghostly image began to appear. Thea was holding her breath, Mem realised. She was excited. It made Mem dizzy too.

"Smells," Mem murmured, wrinkling her nose.

"That's the silver halide in the paper reducing to silver metal. It smells like magic."

She was like a kid at Christmas.

In a few seconds, Mem began to understand why.

"Oh! I can see it. That's me!"

"Of course, it's you."

"But— Oh, Thea. I look— You've made me look—"

Mem barely recognised herself.

She stared at the portrait slowly appearing beneath the liquid and the room around her shrank to the pulse of her own heartbeat and the hush of Thea's breath in her ear. In that suspended space, the image before her stole the air from her lungs – Thea had distilled her spirit onto paper.

The black and white contours of her profile emerged from an inky background, a vivid reflection of her features rendered with a tenderness that was almost tangible. Mem could trace the curve of her own cheek, the slope of her neck, and the cascade of hair that fell like silk threads against the deep, opaque backdrop.

A diamond necklace was a constellation at her throat, each stone set like a star in the deepest night – but it was her eyes that anchored Mem to the moment. Thea had captured them as if they were the very source of all light, an impossible contradiction in the velvet darkness that enveloped her figure. They shone with a depth and a brightness that transcended the grayscale, a beacon that pierced through the page right through to the viewer's soul.

It was raw, powerful and magnetic. The image was Mem, yet it spoke of more than just her physical form. It whispered of her laughter at the jokes they had made as they took the shot. It revealed the pride Mem felt when Thea looked at her with those heavy glances. It echoed the cadence of her voice and mirrored the intensity of her passions. Mem felt exposed, but not in a way that left her vulnerable. This image celebrated her entirety.

"Oh, Thea," she breathed.

"Do you like it?" For once, Thea's voice was very small. Hesitant.

"I love it."

Mem loved it for the truth it spoke, for the artistry it showcased, and for the understanding it implied. Thea didn't merely see her – she had seen into her. Mem felt naked under her gaze, stripped of pretence and laid bare.

She didn't want to be any other way.

Thea stirred suddenly into action. "That's it. That's perfect. Into the stop bath, quick!"

"The what?"

With an expert snap of her wrist, Thea flicked the paper into the next tray of liquid.

"Acetic acid, amongst other things. It halts the reaction. I have you just the way I want you."

Didn't she, though?

She guided Mem's hand with the tongs again. "And now the fixer. It makes the image permanent and light resistant. I'll keep you like this forever."

They rinsed the paper in water and hung it on the strings above the bench. Mem couldn't take her eyes off it.

"You've made me look—"

"Beautiful," Thea told her, her voice soft and still full of the magic she'd promised earlier. "My muse." She hugged her again, still standing behind her, a strong, firm presence Mem wanted to fall backwards into forever.

It *was* magic, Mem thought, whatever this was between them. She smiled at the brilliant, talented woman gently peppering the side of her neck with kisses, and marvelled at all the contrasts – the breathtaking art and the anxious child-like artist keen to share it. Mem's reluctance to take on the world, and Thea's unshakeable belief that she could fly. Thea's hard fingers and Mem's devotion. Towering arrogance, ability and ego, and Mem's contentedness to serve it.

Dominance and submission.

She looked at the picture again and pulled Thea closer.

Thea *saw* her.

"I love it," she whispered again, and Thea turned her carefully in her arms and kissed her.

And in that moment, Mem finally came to terms with the burden of her beauty, because Thea saw straight through it. The portrait was a revelation and a proclamation that through Thea Voronov's lens, the real Mem Swan was irrevocably, stunningly, and utterly seen.

Chapter Nineteen

She wasn't such a cold-hearted, uptight bitch that she didn't have two friends she could work through her insecurities with.

Vera Green put a child in her arms the moment she opened the front door.

"Ah, Fyodora, darling. Hold one of the twins for me. Mo and Chidi are trying to kill each other in the study."

She was gone.

Thea swung the kid onto her hip with an ease that surprised even her and navigated her way through Vera's hallway to the heart of the house – the kitchen. She stepped around shoes of all sizes, an armada of yellow toy trucks and three naked Barbies. The hallway was lined with photos of all of Vera's adopted children, so many Thea had lost count, though these were all photographs she'd taken herself. The kid in her arms was new.

In the kitchen, a small tornado of strawberry blonde curls squealed when she walked in. Sally wrapped her arms around Thea's thighs. Sally was seven and had lost her birth mother to an overdose when she was four. She'd lived with Vera and her husband ever since.

Sally was one of Thea's favourites.

The girl cleared some papers from a chair and pulled Thea toward it.

"You can sit here, Thea. Next to me!"

Thea sat. The kid in her arms shuffled onto her lap and stared at her. She looked about three, with solemn eyes that appeared far older. Her mirror image sat on a booster cushion on the other side of the table and regarded Thea just as warily. A glass of milk and a plate with two uneaten cookies sat on the table in front of him.

"Which one is this?" Thea asked Sally.

"That's Sana and that's Tariq. They're from Syria. They don't talk much." She wrinkled her nose. "I'm writing a story. Do you like it?"

She held up a page of childish writing, the words changing colour with every letter in a strict pattern that Thea could see reflected in the neat row of pencils on the table. She admired the attention to colour theory.

"Read it to me."

Sally looked pleased and cleared her throat. "Once upon a time there was a girl called Sally who was very beautiful and she was a famous movie star and she had lots and lots of diamonds and—"

It didn't make Thea feel better.

Vera reappeared. "Alright, Sally. Chidi is doing homework and Mo is playing Lego. It's your turn on Minecraft."

"Woohoo!" Sally tossed her story to the table and raced out of the kitchen. She stuck her head back around the door a second later. "Bye Thea!" Then she was gone again.

Vera sighed, kissed Thea on the top of the head and sank down into the chair Sally had vacated.

"Kids!"

"You love them," Thea told her.

Vera grinned, a smile like sunshine that Thea had adored since she was a kid herself.

"I do. You want me to take that one?"

Vera held out two hands to Sana, but the girl shook her head and held on tighter to Thea. She still didn't say anything. Across the table, Tariq watched them closely, then offered one of the cookies to his sister. Sana took it and pressed it against Thea's shoulder.

Thea knew better than to wear her favourite suits to visit Vera. She was in faded black jeans, a band T-shirt and a satin bomber jacket she didn't care too much about. Biscuit crumbs were nothing next to a kid who'd lost both parents in a war.

Like Vera, and Thea herself, all of Vera's kids had been through some kind of trauma.

Thea sometimes wondered if they could see the same thing in her. Maybe that was what made them like her.

She couldn't think of any other reason.

She pulled the usual envelope of cash from her pocket and placed it on the table.

Vera smiled at her.

"You don't have to keep doing this, you know," Vera told her. "Mike's business is doing really well now."

Thea noticed she took the envelope anyway. Thea's cash gifts had been supporting Vera, her husband and their gaggle of foster kids since Thea's first paying job and they all knew she wasn't going to stop.

"I have a duty," Thea said.

"Rubbish." Vera squeezed her knee. "I tell you every time. Your father was the monster, not you. It wasn't your fault."

Thea hummed. The two kids judged her.

"Maybe one day you'll even believe me." Vera smiled. "Do you have time for tea?" She got up again and bustled around her kitchen. Thea watched.

Vera had been one of her father's girls – the ones that came and went from any number of their houses around Europe. The ones that replaced her mother, though Thea had always thought they were children just like her. Older, of course, maybe sixteen, but still keen to play kids' games with her, still more pleased to play with her dolls than Thea was. Thea's father had called this one Veronika, though he made up names for all the girls. Sexier, he said, more exotic. He meant saleable, but it wasn't until years later, when Vera was long gone, as were the girls who followed, that Thea fully understood what that meant.

She found Vera again many long years later, well after that string of girls – the ones who survived, of course – banded together to bring Grigori Voronov and the other goons in his human trafficking ring to justice.

Vera had Mike by then, and Thea tried not to be jealous. They couldn't have kids so Vera adopted a stream of them.

"Turned out I have a bigger heart than I thought was possible," Vera said, "especially after all that shit."

Vera always believed in Thea's heart too. Thea scoffed. She'd been blind. It had all happened right under her nose and she'd never noticed. She had a lot to make up for.

"It's Chidi's birthday soon," Vera said now. She put a slice of cake that Thea didn't want in front of her. "You'll come and take pictures, won't you?"

"Of course I will. I've been taking shots of your rug rats for years."

"You love them," Vera echoed. She poked her tongue out. She was probably fifty now, but she was still beautiful. Even the scar on her cheek.

"Never said I didn't," Thea protested. "How are the rest of them going?"

Vera had a long list. Thea listened with half an ear and tried to tempt Sana with the cake. The girl regarded her suspiciously. The words 'Mem Swan' suddenly focused Thea's attention.

"What?"

"Glad to have you back," Vera said, dryly. "I said, Piper is busy working on her charity with her friend, Mem, who I know you know. She's pretty, that Mem Swan." Vera was sly. "Are you two...?"

Thea rolled her eyes. "We're having some fun," she said.

"Pfft. Looked like more than that, even in the Daily Mail."

"Fucking paparazzi. It's just—"

"You're allowed to fall in love, Fyodora, darling."

"I'm not—"

"I've known Mem Swan since we adopted Piper. They were both eight, I think. She's the sweetest kid."

Thea glared. "That's exactly what I'm worried about. I'm using her, Vera. Screwing her in order to get close to her, to talk her into another movie and a deal with a diamond company. I may as well be my father."

Sana finally took the cake, squished a huge handful into her mouth, and smiled a gleeful chocolatey smile at Thea.

Why did they do that? she wondered. Why did all the pretty things trust her?

Tariq reached for some too.

"Ya thalaaam!" he yelled, exuberantly. He smacked his palms on the table and looked perfectly and completely happy with the entire state of the world.

Thea blinked at Vera. "What does that mean?"

"No idea," Vera said, "but I think they like you." She paused. "And is she doing the other movie and this diamond thing at your word? Or is she a capable, intelligent woman making her own choices?"

Thea glared sulkily at the remains of the crumbled cake. She said nothing.

"Why don't you come for dinner one night, Thea? Get you out of that cold, empty house of yours."

"It's not empty. I have Mem—"

She stopped. Vera looked triumphant.

"Just a bit of fun, hey?"

Thea gave Vera her kid back.

"I have to go."

Kate Cox said much the same thing.

"The whole point was to seduce her, Thea. Stop being silly."

They were in one of Spectrum Media's studios, taking pics for Adore Magazine. It was one of Jasper's high-end mainstream rags and something that Thea barely cared about except that Kate looked particularly elegant at the moment.

She was in a dress that hinted at 1930s style but was undeniably modern. It was gold and reflected light like a dream, hugged her curves and the line of her legs as she dangled her feet from the edge of an old mahogany desk. The studio had been transformed into an old-fashioned, wood-panelled study, complete with leather-bound books, a Persian carpet, and a stained-glass lamp casting a soft pool of orange light.

Kate gazed at Thea's camera over the pages of an open book she held in one hand. She crossed her eyes and poked out her tongue.

Thea wouldn't normally tolerate such impudence from her but they had an audience, even if Lollie had banished them to the far corner.

"Mem has projects. She has her charity," Thea said, in a low voice. "Movies and diamonds are trivialities to her. Her goals and plans are important."

Kate blew a raspberry. "What? She's grander than the rest of us, then? More responsible? And you're going to stand for that? You're off your game, Thea. When have you ever elevated someone else's desires above your own?"

That hurt more than she thought it would. She tweaked an eyebrow at Kate and was gratified when the woman dropped her eyes.

Thea captured it with her camera.

"Sorry, darling," Kate murmured. "I need this too. Jasper's been in my ear as well. The diamond partnership will be good for all of us."

Kate brought the book up to her face and they played with some silly stylised shots of her peeking over it. Apparently, the title was important.

"Why do you want it so much?" Thea asked, curiously.

Everything was changing around her. Only a few short months ago, this shoot with Kate would almost certainly have ended with the two of them in bed, and Thea would have gladly screwed whoever strayed into her path for the money behind the diamonds and the prestige that would come with them. Not because she needed it, but because it was habit. That was the shape of her world. Now, she couldn't get Mem Swan's earnest gaze out of her mind and she was ready to blow all of this off just to get back to her.

She was so far off her game she no longer knew what it was.

"I'm getting on," Kate said, mildly. "It's all doddery grandmother roles for me from here on in. Who knows when my last movie will be? Maybe this will be the one when the public decides my beauty is gone, and thus, my worth."

"Rubbish."

"And I've pretty much squandered everything I've earned up til now." Kate laughed and waved a hand. "Turns out I didn't really need a chalet in Switzerland *and* an apartment on Park Avenue *and* a castle in Oxfordshire after all. I need to grow up."

"You've blown it all?" Thea was surprised. All this time, she'd thought Kate was the sensible one.

"You're not the only one who mistakes wealth and stature for contentment and happiness, darling," Kate said dryly. She shifted on the desk, lying across it on her side, a gorgeously sultry pose that Thea instantly knew would serve as a perfect spread for the magazine and cement Kate's status as a style icon for the next hundred years. Grandmother roles, her arse.

"To tell the truth," Kate murmured, with a quick side-eye at the circus of attendants in the corner, "I've fallen in love. And I rather think it's for real this time. Anwen doesn't have much, and her parents are old and ill. I want to settle down with her in a nice, simple place in Sussex and grow dahlias in the back garden."

She *was* telling the truth, Thea realised. She could see it through her lens.

It made Thea jealous. She could picture Mem in her garden, lazing on a picnic blanket, the sunlight on her naked skin. Thea would make her daisy chains.

"So?"

Thea snapped out of her daydream.

"So what?"

"So, convince her to do the sequel! We have a timetable, Thea. The London premiere is in two weeks. StudioOne is keen to make an announcement. You need to—"

"I don't believe you get to tell me what I need to do, Katherine."

They worked in silence for a few moments until Thea couldn't bear it any longer.

"I feel like I'm corrupting her."

"Bollocks."

"I'm using her. She was— *unspoiled* before she met me," Thea continued, her voice just above a whisper.

"Come off it. She's a grown woman. So, she turned out to be as kinky as you, darling. It doesn't mean anything."

"She's created an entire charity all on her own. *I* was part of an operation that sold her best friend's mother into sexual slavery—"

"You are being ridiculously overdramatic, you ninny. You were a kid. You had nothing to do with it. You—"

"And I use people, Kate. I always have. I'm using Mem now – to feed my craving, my need for beautiful things and beautiful people, to hide all the ugliness I grew up with. My art, this whole damned industry is based on exploitation."

Kate skittered around on the desk suddenly and swung her feet over the edge. The siren was gone in a moment, and a woman Thea couldn't deny cared for her reached out to tug her closer. Kate took the camera out of her hands and pulled Thea between her knees. It was tricky in such a tight pencil skirt, but Kate cupped Thea's face in her hands.

"You're worried you're going to infect the wonderful Memona Swan with the kind of darkness that surrounded people like your father?"

Thea looked at her. She nodded.

Kate's lips twitched.

"That is absolute horseshit, darling, and I think you know it."

Thea tried to look sulkily away, but Kate turned her face back.

"*Are* you using her? I know we told you to seduce her, but do you like her?"

"I think I could even—"

She just managed to stop herself. Kate looked delighted.

"What?! What am I hearing? I didn't even know you could say that word."

"You're making my case for me." Thea pulled away and smiled her best fuck-you smile. Kate grinned back. She was so very annoying.

"Oh, just say it. You love her. There's nothing wrong with that."

There was a long moment while they stared each other out. Thea was going to break first. That wasn't like her at all.

"I love Memona Swan," she whispered.

Thea shut her eyes.

God, that felt good.

"Ha! I *knew* it!" Kate slapped her thighs and pushed Thea away. She crawled back onto the table, all hips and boobs and triumph in her most provocative pose yet. She yelled across the room. "Lollie, call Jasper and tell him he owes me five hundred quid. God, I *love* being right! Thea Voronov is in love, and it's about fucking time!"

The shoot slowed down somewhat after that.

Jasper actually showed up in one of his own photography studios just as if it was ten years ago and he wasn't a pretentious executive type just like the ones they used to mock back in the day. He thumped Thea on the shoulder before pulling her into a rough hug.

That felt nice too.

Kate and Lollie laughed at her, and she had to swat Kate on the backside with one of the leather-bound books before she could get them all to shut up and get on with the shoot.

"Woah! That's a first edition. Careful!" Jasper retrieved the book with a worried frown, opened it gently and handed it back to Kate.

Thea was feeling light-hearted. It made her less cautious.

"What is it?" she asked.

Everyone on the set stared at her. Jasper shook his head and laughed. He stepped in to cover for her like a big brother who really cared, and she loved him for it and forgave him everything.

"And she's back," he drawled. "The genius soaring above the trivial details, so focused on the big picture she leaves the minutiae to us mere mortals." He slapped her upside the head – and she let him do it. "It's *The Wolverton Diamond,* Thea dearest. You know, only this wee little blockbuster movie Kate's been working on for the last six months. Nice to know she cares, isn't it?" he asked everyone.

"Get out, Jasper. I'm working here."

"Is that what we're calling it?"

"Fuck *off,* Jasper."

He grinned and the set became busy again, the moment glossed over.

But it wasn't enough to dull the warm, full feeling in her chest at the thought of what she'd discovered here. *She loved Memona Swan.*

She held the camera up to her face so no one could see the dopey smile that threatened to break out on her lips again.

She needed roses – dozens of them. She was going to lay Mem in the middle of all of them and love her so fiercely, and so gently. She was going to claim her, and offer herself. Thea was going to conquer her, and surrender her own heart.

She was going to *love* her.

Chapter Twenty

"So why do they bother with a gilt-edged invitation when the whole thing is planned by everyone's agents anyway?" Piper asked.

She was spinning an expensive rectangle of embossed linen card between her fingertips, having plucked it from the fridge. They were waiting for the coffee machine and the toaster in what passed for breakfast before rushing out the door. It was the first morning Mem had been home for ages. Thea had sent her home last night.

Mem had pouted. Thea walked her back to the wall and kissed her pout away. Then she'd groaned and wrenched herself back to work. She had a hundred things to do preparing for the opening of her exhibition. She swatted Mem's backside as she went.

"The superficial world of show-business," Mem supposed.

"I've seen ads for this all over the Tube. This is huge," Piper added. "Look at you though – the opening night red carpet as a personal guest of the artist, ooo!" She poked out her tongue at Mem, who poked her own out right back. They grinned at each other.

Mem was in a brilliant mood. She was so excited for Thea's exhibition. The artist herself was playing it cool, but Mem knew it was going to be amazing.

She had a schedule of priors Adiatu had set up. She scrolled through it and hummed.

"Apparently, I've got a dress fitting at three and jewellery is by CreatedDiamonds. Nice. Then I've got an appointment for hair and makeup at half four." She pulled a face.

"Sucks to be you," Piper said. "Pass me the jam?"

"A car is picking me up from Adiatu's stylist, and dropping me and Thea at the red carpet at six."

"The amazing Thea Voronov doesn't need a stylist?" teased Piper.

Mem's mind immediately went to the thought of Thea all glammed up for the opening night of her latest exhibition and immediately flushed.

Piper pointed and laughed. "Hoo, girl!"

"Shut up." Mem grinned. She took the jam back and smeared a generous slather over her toast. She was going to need the sugar.

"You know this will make it official, don't you?" said Piper. "You and Thea? The two of you stepping out of the same car together in front of all those photographers, all those other celebrities? There's no way that isn't going to be all over the socials in seconds."

"Yeah," breathed Mem. Funny thing was, the thought of doing it at Thea's side definitely calmed her nerves. "No going back after this."

"And you're ready for that?"

"Media attention is part of the job."

Piper pointed at her with her toast. "That's not what I meant and you know it. I mean, are you ready for the whole world to know you're in a relationship with Thea Voronov?"

Mem couldn't stop her smile.

Why hide it? As far as Mem was concerned, she was all in with Thea Voronov. In fact, she was ready to go deeper. She could see a hunger in Thea's eyes whenever they were together, when Mem was on her knees, or tied to the bed, or being fucked into the mattress – Thea wanted more from her too. And Mem would be so glad to give it, to surrender utterly, except that Thea always pulled back. She knew her eagerness tore Thea's self control apart as well, even though the woman was expert at concealing it with a casual order or a greedy kiss.

Maybe this was what Thea was waiting for – for everyone else to know too.

After tonight, everything would be perfect.

"She has got – erm – quite a reputation," Piper added, suddenly looking shifty. "Have you thought about what that might mean for you if the whole thing falls apart and the world decides you're—" She stopped.

"What?" Mem felt the happy bubble in her chest wobble a little.

Piper mumbled at her toast.

"If the world decides I'm what, Pipes?"

"Easy."

Mem blinked at her. "Are you kidding me?"

Piper jumped right in with only a hint of shame. "Sorry babes, but what if Thea moves on and you're left looking cheap and slutty?"

"Seriously?"

"I just mean—"

"Piper! What the fuck? Are you protecting my honour or airing your stereotypes?"

Mem *knew* Piper was only looking out for her, but... *really?* She scooped a tiny amount of jam onto the spoon from her coffee and flicked it at Piper – just to show she wasn't angry. She was a hopeless shot. The jam landed on Piper's collar and her friend simply pulled a face at her, stuck the cloth in her mouth and sucked it off.

"Gross," Mem snorted.

"Cow," Piper mumbled.

There was a moment, then Piper tried again.

"I'm kinda serious, though," she said. "It's just that there's a big difference between having a two week fling with some rando from LesGo, and having the whole fucking internet know you're boffing the world's most infamous photographer just because Thea Voronov crooked her fingers. Social media, babes. It changes everything."

Mem didn't say anything. As much as she wanted to dismiss Piper's point as sexist 1950s bullshit, she had to admit it was fair. The harsh light of social media was pitiless. She wondered if StudioOne and CreatedDiamonds had considered the potential impact of a scandal with Thea Voronov on the saleability of their brand new movie star. Then she mentally smacked herself. She could already see Adiatu's fangs lengthening at the mere thought of a media pile-on involving her and Thea. Everything was fodder for the machine.

Nothing was private. Nothing was sacred.

Mem's whole life was fair game.

She thought of Thea sneaking her out through Mrs Tits' garden and avoiding the paps who prowled Thea's street. She thought of that aloof and alluring pride that curled Thea's lip when they dined at exclusive venues together. She hugged herself and grinned at the thought of their hopeless disguises and wandering the streets in freedom.

Thea cared. She was protecting her.

All of this warmed Mem from the inside. She *liked* Thea being greedy and gallant with her. When Thea looked at her with ownership in her eyes and hardness in her hands, Mem felt everything from her pussy to her knees turn to jelly. If Thea wanted to parade Mem on her arm through London's most exclusive events, Mem would be happy to do it naked just for her, just to see that glorious swagger in Thea's shoulders, that smug twist to her lips – that raw, immediate need that she did her utmost to hide.

Mem wasn't sure what that said about her but she was drowning in a sea of lust and hormones and she didn't care. If Piper thought she was throwing her a lifeline, she was a damn fine friend who didn't deserve to be wiping jam from her collar.

"I like her, Piper," she said and smiled. It was that simple. "Thea's the most incredible woman I've ever met. I can't describe it, but she *looks* at me differently. I mean, she's fucking sensational in bed and so domineering – which I didn't even know I liked but—"

"Woah!" cried Piper, holding up her hands in mock alarm.

"—but when it's just her and me, quiet together, she looks right through all *this*"—she waved a hand at her face—"as if she doesn't even care about it. She looks at *me*."

Piper breathed out a big sigh and shook her head. "Lots of people see the real you, Mem."

"No one I've ever dated."

"Poor little princess."

"And I don't even care if that makes me cheap and slutty—"

"I totally didn't mean that!"

"—but I'm ready for this."

Piper nodded. There was a beat then two decades of friendship bubbled up in the sookiest way possible and they were grinning like kids again.

"Hug?" asked Piper.

"Yeah."

Mem squeezed her tight. She was probably more nervous about tonight than she wanted to admit.

"I'm happy for you," Piper said when they pulled apart. She poured her coffee into a travel cup and pushed the rest of her toast into her mouth. "You're a braver woman than me," she said around it. "Which is lucky, coz you look a whole lot better in a frock too. You'll send me pictures, right?"

"Sure," said Mem, relieved.

"Gotta go. Interviewing a new social worker this morning, then I have to pick up the new twins from preschool while Mum has parent-teacher interviews for Mo, Sally and Chidi. Have an awesome time tonight. Don't do anything I wouldn't do!"

Mem waved her away. She couldn't keep track of Piper's siblings but was kind of jealous at the way the family pulled together when they needed to. Her own sister still hadn't sorted out those legal matters for her yet.

She remembered something just as Piper got to the door.

"Your uni enrolment!" she yelled. "Have you finalised it yet?"

Piper made evasive noises.

"Do it!" Mem said, catching up with her in the hall. "The enrolment deadline is coming up. I told you I'm paying your fees upfront, so get it done."

"Yeah, yeah."

"Yes, yes," Mem insisted. "Do it in your lunch break! Send me a payment link."

Piper backed out the door. She grinned in a way that suggested she was going to completely ignore everything Mem had just said.

"Have fun with Thea," she jeered. "Don't trip on the red carpet."

Mem stuck two fingers up at her and pulled a face at Piper's laugh.

She was a good friend.

***

The dress was amazing.

The young designer and her assistant seamstress practically sewed Mem into it, then stood back and smiled with delight.

Adiatu went overboard with superlatives and stern directions for Mem to mention the designer's name to every member of the press she met, but the designer herself just waved Adiatu off. She clearly had Sierra Leonean heritage as well because she ticked Adiatu off in Krio with a manner that impressed Mem hugely. It made Mem resolve to be tougher around her agent herself.

The dress was figure-hugging with a plunging V-neckline. Backless, it flared at a point just below her hips in a stunningly soft, emerald green satin. In it, Mem felt sexier than she'd ever felt in her life.

She knew one glance was going to dismantle Thea's mind.

Her stylists added a diamond necklace in a thick choker of sparkling white stones. A series of pendant diamonds tumbled down her chest like a waterfall of ice to a focal point directly between her breasts. It was nothing short of breathtaking. They added diamonds to her hair too – a carefully tangled and curled updo with a cascade down the middle of her back.

Not even StudioOne had dressed her quite like this before. Mem suspected Thea's influence in the arrangements.

She didn't mind at all.

Thea was in the sleek, black car that picked Mem up from the stylist.

Mem slid into the backseat beside her and felt the usual thrill when Thea dragged a slow, approving gaze all over her, her eyes lingering at her plunging cleavage. Thea's lips pressed themselves into a pleased line, twitching at the edges as she rested her hand palm up on the seat between them.

Mem slotted their fingers together and Thea's smile widened.

The car purred toward Southbank.

"Are you nervous?" Mem asked.

"Are *you*?"

Mem disengaged their fingers, swatted Thea's wrist primly, then slipped her hand back into Thea's. Thea chuckled. She didn't look nervous. Thea looked like a goddess.

"It's your show."

The red-carpet event filled the entire main hall of Britain's most iconic modern art gallery and the exhibition had been advertised all over London and the internet. Celebrities were gathering from across the world to see themselves in Thea's portraits for the first time. The guest list may as well have been the same as the Oscars. The world's art critics were circling too.

"Why should I be nervous?"

Mem felt a shot of desire pulse through her, then she burst out laughing.

"Oh, that's confidence! Very attractive."

Thea tugged Mem's hand closer and placed her palm on her leg. Mem could feel the taut line of muscle in her thigh and the heat of Thea's body. That stopped the giggles instantly. Thea smirked.

"Once I might have cared what the baying hounds think of my work," she said. She lowered her voice and leaned closer. Mem did the same. Thea brushed a delicate butterfly kiss on her lips – the merest touch – and seemed to have an incredible amount of trouble taking her eyes off them when she was done. "But I've got you now, Memona Swan. How could I be nervous with you at my side? I'm more concerned about you."

The car pulled up onto the Bankside Walk at one end of a literal acre of red carpet that graced the plaza between the Tate Modern and the River Thames. There were already a million people there – two banks of paparazzi with long-barrelled lenses all shouting at the celebrities who milled in the twilight.

Mem drew in a long breath.

"Last chance," Thea whispered. "The car can do another lap and let you out by yourself if you'd rather do this solo." Her eyes were kind but Mem knew her now. There was a tightness at their edges that said she'd be devastated if Mem said yes.

"I just need one thing," Mem said.

Thea covered her sudden panic with practised ease. "Hmm?" She tweaked one perfect eyebrow.

"Another of those kisses for courage, and then I'm all yours."

A wide grin cracked Thea's face and she was triumphant again. She gripped Mem's chin and attached herself to the soft spot at the top of Mem's throat, under her ear. She kissed – and then she bit.

"You're mine anyway," she said, ignoring Mem's loving indignation. "Come on."

Thea handed her out of the car and they were *on*.

A lightning storm of flashes forced Mem to keep her eyes down, but at a surreptitious squeeze of her hand she looked up. It was her first good look at what Thea was wearing.

It was a simple black suit, but fuck, it was so much more than that.

A superbly tailored jacket outlined the proud set of Thea's shoulders. It hugged her figure, showing curves but screaming power. She wore a white shirt beneath it, crisp and expensive, and unbuttoned all the way to her waist. Mem's eyes dragged down her front – all that alabaster skin, the swell of her breasts both tantalisingly hidden and shamelessly on display. A thick silver chain sat just below her collarbones, studded with diamonds, the clasp and its small extension chain offset to one side in a lazy manner, as if she had only bothered with the jewels because she had to.

Her pants were equally elegant – flaring over her thighs and flowing to the floor where she stalked on lethal heels. Her hair was sleek and smooth, though her bangs hung over blackened eyes with an aggressive idleness that was almost a dare. Her lips glistened.

The whole look was effortless and devastating.

Mem's mouth went completely dry.

Thea held up one hand – supremely arrogant, blisteringly entitled – and Mem knew her role. She slipped her fingers into Thea's palm and let the woman lead her along the red carpet. Thea plunged her other hand rakishly into her pocket playing the casual megastar like a dream, but everyone saw her mastery. This was her show. Everyone was there for Thea Voronov. She ruled.

Spotlights seared over the whole scene. Cameras flashed. Photographers called loudly for just her merest glance. Every eye looked her way.

And Thea only had eyes for Mem.

"Since we must do this, shall we have a bit of fun, my darling?"

Thea laid her hand deliberately on the small of Mem's back – not the slightest bit subtle – and there was a blizzard of flashes. The photographers loved it. So did Mem.

"What did you have in mind?" She leaned in, stretching up on tiptoes to place the whisper carefully in Thea's ear – and again the cameras went wild. She knew, the moment she did it, how deferential the move must have looked. How submissive. The soft chuckle Thea gave – only for her – was a wicked secret, a thrill, and the best part of the game.

"I'll start with this." She pulled Mem in for a scorching kiss.

It was deep and domineering, with Thea's hand sneaking from her pocket to Mem's throat where she wrapped her fingers carefully around Mem's neck. Mem had milliseconds to offer thanks to the gods of colour-stay lipstick, send profound prayers heavenward that her parents had not yet discovered how to view livestreams on Facebook, and then she surrendered, to the command in Thea's fingers and the ownership of her mouth. And the infectious sense of fun that was rolling off her in waves. It was all for show – she knew that – but she could taste the greed under Thea's swagger too. The cameras might have caught the performance, but Mem knew the reality.

Kissing Thea Voronov in front of the whole damn world made Mem thoroughly wet. As her fingertips rested on the skin between Thea's breasts she felt the skip and flutter of the woman's heartbeat.

This was turning Thea on too.

It was going to be a long, long night.

"You wonderful girl," Thea whispered, just before they pulled apart.

They grinned at each other. Thea's fingers brushed either side of Mem's lips, then lightly slapped her cheek.

Mem rolled her eyes.

And with a vicious smirk and a ludicrously cocky ripple of her shoulders, Thea hooked a finger into the necklace at Mem's throat and led her further along the red carpet.

"Alright you two, pack it in. It's a red carpet, not your own private porn set."

Kate Cox was on the arm of Jasper Fitz-Stewart, and it was hard to tell who was more elegant.

Jasper held out his hand and Mem shook it, but he was as cheeky and comfortable in the spotlight as Thea and Kate seemed to be, because he shifted his grip at the last moment and brought the backs of her fingers to his lips. He kissed her hand with a waggle of his eyebrows.

"Spectrum Media," he said, only a tiny bit apologetically. "Half that lot over there are mine and we have to give them something to work with. Image is everything, and all that."

"You don't think Thea's taking care of that herself?" Kate sounded jealous.

Thea smirked at her.

"Thea is a media hornbag," Jasper said. "Always has been."

"It's my show," Thea protested. She didn't look the slightest bit ashamed.

"But there are some things even you can't do on the red carpet." Jasper was a fool if he didn't think Thea was going to see that as a challenge.

"I disagree."

Thea pulled Mem close again with an arm low around her hips and bent her head to Mem's. With one hand cupped around Mem's ear – ostentatious with the secret – she whispered a long, detailed and filthy list of all the things she'd like to do to Mem right there in front of the cameras. Jasper hooted and pointed when he saw Mem's gasp, so Mem acted up to it, blushing and pretending at embarrassment. She batted her eyelids and leant her whole body against Thea's, seeking shelter in the hollow of her neck.

Thea's hand was on her back, heavy, each touch like she meant it, like she wanted everyone to know.

Mem whispered her own secret in Thea's ear.

"I'd crawl the length of the whole damn red carpet at your feet if you asked me."

Thea nearly stumbled. Jasper snorted with laughter, Kate looked resigned, and the gleam in Thea's eyes let Mem know she'd just earned herself a wonderful spanking later.

She couldn't wait.

"Enough! You're hogging the loveliest thing here." Jasper clapped his hands and shouldered Thea out of the way. "Memona, it is a pleasure to see you again and I hate to do this, but do you think you could be persuaded to tear yourself away from this cheap, talentless shutterbug here and take a turn with Kate for a while? My photographers are right there." He pointed.

Thea looked rebellious, but Kate slipped her arm through Mem's and squeezed.

"Come on, sweetheart. It's good practice for all our premieres coming up. Let an old trouper show you how it's done."

Kate was brilliant – so accomplished and generous with her time, both for the media and for Mem. She greeted photographers she knew by name, charming them with a cheeky joke at their expense. She pulled Mem into a short chat with an interviewer and then cleverly controlled its direction, keeping things light and casual. She deflected the more probing questions that were aimed at Mem and made sure everyone knew it was Thea Voronov they were there for.

It was a skilled performance.

"I've got so much to learn," Mem muttered as they strolled between photo stops.

"Pah!" Kate dismissed her worries with a squeeze of her hand and a broad smile directed out at the baying crowd. "It's just like acting. You'll notice I never actually *answer* their questions. I've got a set list of inanities and quirky stories and I stick to them just like a script. Red carpets are the most tedious part of the job, but they're nothing to worry about."

Ten minutes later, they were chatting with an A-lister so famous Mem was having trouble looking at him. She'd been watching him in movies since her own childhood. To be standing on the same side of a rope line with him now simply made no sense.

It didn't bother Kate.

"Ah, my favourite silver fox," she said, air kisses all round. "How is that brilliant wife of yours? Is she here?"

Kate manoeuvred the three of them into a group shot that Mem couldn't help but notice was right in front of Spectrum Media's cameras.

The actor himself appeared just as keen to be seen with Kate. He put his arm around her waist and, rather charmingly, asked Mem if that was okay before doing the same to her.

They all used each other, Mem thought. They barely even disguised it.

The paps went crazy. Mem wondered how many people around the world would see them here like this.

She knew Thea was back because a roar rose from the photographers like a wave of noise.

Thea, typically, ignored it all.

"Hands off, Nespresso," she said, mildly, her smirk wide.

The actor actually let go of Kate first and Thea's laugh was a tiny bit cruel. But Mem barely had time to even think about what that meant before Thea took her hand, brought it to her lips and nipped at her knuckles with her teeth.

"When you egotists are done showing off to the cameras, we might go inside and admire *my* brilliance for a while," she pouted.

Kate blew a raspberry and George Clooney rolled his eyes so far backwards he should have passed out. They both smiled.

Thea tucked Mem's hand into the crook of her arm and led her proudly into the gallery.

Chapter Twenty One

The Turbine Hall inside the Tate Modern was a cavernous space.

The building had been a power station once. Absolute madness, when Mem thought about it. It was just across the river from St Paul's Cathedral and the thought of it belching coal smoke in the very centre of the city seemed like heresy now.

These days, it was a museum and one of London's most sought-after galleries. The Turbine Hall itself was by far the most prestigious of all the exhibition spaces in the museum.

Thea Voronov's work filled the entire hall.

The ceiling shot nearly forty metres over their heads and disappeared into a red haze of dramatic lighting. Vast canvases hung on invisible wires so that they appeared to be floating in the room. They created a maze of images that guests strolled through pausing to clink their glasses, admire and praise.

A jazz band played on a raised platform in the middle of the space. Waiters wandered with trays of champagne and expensive-looking nibbles. The guests were an absolute constellation of stars, and the air tasted of their vanity – to say nothing of their relief and their greed.

Thea had made them all look incredible.

They burst into applause when Thea and Mem walked in and Mem felt it straighten Thea's spine, felt the quick, tiny squeeze Thea's fingers gave hers. Her artist stood tall in a sea of her subjects, every face turning to Thea's with gratitude. It was a triumph and Thea stood at the heart of it, unconquerable.

"What do you think, darling?"

She said it loudly, for the benefit of the guests around her. It was part of the act, but something about Thea's blindingly cocksure poise turned Mem on hugely. Mega-stars watched them, hanging on their performance, a curious blend of envy and avarice in their eyes. Mem took her cue.

She leaned closer. Thea's body was hot. It matched the heat building in Mem.

"It's amazing," she said, smiling up at her. "You're extraordinary."

Thea's hand was at her throat almost immediately and Mem let herself be kissed, greedily, hungrily in front of them all. This was Thea in her element – untamed, unapologetic, and undeniable. There was more laughter and applause.

"Thank you, my darling," Thea murmured in her ear, under the cover of it all.

"Friends and enemies – welcome!"

Jasper stepped up onto the platform and stole a microphone from the band. He held up his hands for silence. His bow tie was only slightly less dazzling than his charisma.

"I know, I know. Thea didn't want any speeches, but she's known me for twenty years now. When have I ever listened to her?" His eyes sought out Thea's in the crowd and twinkled at her.

She stuck her middle finger up at him.

"We all know Thea Voronov needs no introduction. Nor does her work. And indeed, those of us here lucky enough to have stood"—he broke off and pointed at a few people in the audience—"or *reclined* in front of Thea's lens will be forever in her debt." He let the knowing laughter bounce around the hall. "She makes magic, my friends, and it is all around us tonight."

Thea's fingers linked themselves in Mem's. Mem watched her profile, her chin up and her shoulders straight, but Mem felt her love in the thumb that tickled her palm, hidden between their hands at their sides.

"Of course, it's no secret that *I* was the one who discovered this extraordinary talent, nurtured it and put a camera in her hands in the first place, so you could say that all of this genius here is down to me." Jasper grinned widely at the hooting and jeering. "But I want to remind the artist herself of an anniversary that perhaps she is unaware of."

His voice softened and he looked at Thea seriously now. Kate crept up onto the stage beside him and took his hand. Lollie hovered in the background, a kind smile on her face. Thea's fingers were suddenly steel.

"Seven Dials," Jasper said, gently, just to Thea. "Twenty years, almost to the day, Thea dearest. You've come such a long way, and I'm so very proud of you." He smiled at Kate. "We're all proud of you."

Murmurs swept through the audience. Mem wanted to ask, but Thea stayed looking staunchly ahead, her posture now a little rigid.

Jasper smiled broadly again. "She'll take that out of my hide later, I'm sure," he told the crowd, and the easy laughter was back in a moment. "But it has to be said, my friends, the real art here tonight is not hanging from the ceiling, it's not on these extraordinary prints. It's standing right here amongst us – courage, talent and relentless pigheadedness all in the one annoyingly brilliant package. My friends, I give you Thea Voronov. Here's to her undeniable success!"

The applause was loud and heartfelt. Hands reached in to shake Thea's or pat her on the back. Jasper, wisely, exited the stage in a different direction, but the music swirled again and guests resumed their stroll through the exhibition.

A group of celebrities so famous it made Mem wince pulled Thea away to talk about their portraits – and Thea kissed her fingers.

"It's okay," Mem told her. "Find me later."

The look in Thea's eye let her know there was no doubt that was going to happen.

Mem looked around the exhibition.

Monochrome faces stared back at her from the artworks filling the Turbine Hall. Thea's skill had captured the souls of the world's most enigmatic figures, their eyes gleaming with the secret stories they'd entrusted to Thea's lens.

Mem looked at the nearest photograph – an elderly but very famous musician. His wrinkles were drawn in sharp relief, each one a celebration of a lifetime of laughter and heartache. Thea had etched the man's essence into permanence. Other shots spoke of glamour or refined reflection.

But as Mem wandered between the prints, she realised not every picture was of a celebrity. Certain faces – certain women – were repeated in Thea's work. Kate Cox, of course, but that wasn't surprising. Kate and Thea had been friends for decades.

Mem paused in front of a giant canvas.

This face was familiar. It was the same familiar face that was in the kitchen of Thea's house. An older woman. Something about it tugged at Mem's thoughts. The woman was not... not *attractive* in the traditional sense of the word, and Mem instantly hated herself for the thought. Of all people, she knew how superficial and meaningless mere attractiveness was. But with nothing else to do but sip her champagne and stare at the art, Mem interrogated her feelings about that.

In Thea's house, this woman's portrait had a nobility to it. Thea found the beauty inside everyone and displayed it to the world. But here, in a temple bursting with beautiful people, amongst a crowd who had amassed unbelievable wealth and fame all based on their exploitation of beauty, this ordinary woman was out of place. It was almost as if Thea had deliberately made her... plain.

Mem frowned.

She cast a quick glance around the exhibition again.

There were more faces like this one than she first thought. *There* was a woman in her eighties, smiling til her eyes creased up and almost disappeared. It was an infectiously joyous image and Mem couldn't look at it without smiling back, but then she noticed the woman was missing a front tooth.

Her eyes skipped across elegant and dramatic portraits of icons and superstars, and stopped on the next *odd* picture. A woman a little older than Mem – a kindness and generosity in her eyes that drew Mem in and wrapped her in warmth – but her lip was split. As if someone had hit her.

A few images over was a young man, hoodie pulled over his head, his face half in shadow but his smile wide. It was something in the background that gave the oddness away though — the corner of a cardboard sign, out of focus and cropped hard. It said 'home.'

Mem's suspicions crystalised. She would have put money on the rest of that word saying '-less.'

"You just figured it out, didn't you?"

Jasper was at her side. He held out his glass to clink it against hers.

"Well done, you. I doubt there's anyone else amongst this lot who will notice. I can see why Thea likes you."

He gave a dazzling smile. He was impossibly handsome in his tux, but there was a boyish cheekiness to his features too. He waved his glass at the crowd.

"Our esteemed guests are all too busy admiring their own images. And trying to figure out how best to leverage them for their personal gain. They're looking without seeing. Thea is going to be insufferable for days." He shuddered. "Weeks."

"What, exactly, has she done?"

"You tell me."

Mem looked around again. "She's juxtaposed commercialised notions of beauty with more genuine, honest expressions of grace and dignity. She's pitted everyday elegance against the thin facade of celebrity culture and— and I think the everyday images are more compelling."

Jasper laughed out loud. "Oh, I can see exactly why she likes you!" He held up his hand for a high five and it was so incongruous, so childish and delightful amid all the designer labels and matching egos that Mem couldn't help herself. She slapped her palm into his and laughed back.

"Our Thea is a shit stirrer," Jasper said. "It will be absolutely tickling her that none of these sycophants will notice. Tomorrow though, the show will open to the public. *Shadows Between the Stars* she's called it, pretentious twat that she is. Thea's Ugly Ordinaries shining out between the celebs. It won't take the punters long to figure out which is which. They'll love her for it."

Mem felt a surge of pride for Thea, mixed with something else – a simmering desire that was impossible to ignore.

She realised Jasper was watching her closely.

"Only question is, which category do you think your portrait fits into?"

Mem started. There was a picture of her here?

"Oh, bless. You're nothing like the others, are you?" He took her hand and led her through the exhibit. "Of course there's a picture of you. Memona Swan is public property now, my sweet summer child. You'd better get used to it."

He stopped in front of an enormous print.

It was her. It was one of the pictures they'd taken when Thea had draped her diamonds and they'd—

It was pretty clear from this image what they'd done.

Mem felt herself flush from her hairline to her feet pinched in her stilettos. She felt something throb hard in her core.

She also felt Jasper chuckling at her side.

It was a discreet photo, she supposed – head and shoulders. When she thought back to what they'd done together that night and the other images Thea had taken, she knew it could have been a lot worse. She throbbed again at the memory.

She was wearing the diamond – and nothing else – but she was head down on the sheets, her face turned to one side. The fist-sized diamond rested between her shoulder-blades, dazzling and bright, throwing tiny prisms of light onto her skin. Her back was bare, glistening with a sheen of sweat.

Three thin, red lines ran from the nape of her neck to the small of her back and the diamond sat in the middle of them. Fingernail tracks.

Mem tried, and failed, to smother a shiver as she looked at them.

In the image, her eyes were closed, her lips were parted and her hair was a mess. She looked content and exhausted. Dishevelled, used and beautiful because of it.

Jasper nudged her with his shoulder.

"Gee, I wonder what you kids were doing." He waggled his eyebrows suggestively.

Mem nudged him back. She liked him.

"You can't even begin to imagine," she told him, mock-primly. She grinned.

Jasper hooted.

A hand found the small of her back.

"Perfect answer, darling," Thea murmured into her ear. "Go away, Jasper."

Jasper smiled amiably and clinked his glass against Mem's. He sauntered into the crowd.

Thea stood behind her and they both looked at the picture. Her hands settled on Mem's hips and pulled her closer. Mem could feel the heat of her burning through the fabric of her dress. Thea's breath was at Mem's ear, a pleased little hum as Mem leaned back against her.

"Do you like it?"

Her voice was low and her lips brushed gently against Mem's temple.

"I do," Mem said. She paused.

Thea hips tilted upwards against Mem's backside.

"But?"

It was a hot whisper in her ear.

"But... but I know what you're doing here."

Thea nuzzled into her neck.

"And what am I doing?"

Mem couldn't stop a shiver.

"You're winding me up, for a start," Mem said, with a mini grind into Thea's groin. She revelled in Thea's low moan. "Please don't stop."

Thea chuckled softly. Her fingers tightened on her hip.

"I think it's clever," Mem went on. "The intent behind the whole exhibition. It's incredibly subversive and I'm impressed that you're getting away with it."

The whisper turned cocky again. "You're impressed?"

"I'm just not sure how you see me."

"Oh, Memona Swan," Thea murmured. "I can't stop seeing you. You are the most beautiful one here. *Look* at you." She nodded at the picture. Mem looked again.

All her life, people had taken photos of Mem. She was accustomed to seeing her beauty as traditional. Mem had learned how to smile for the camera before she knew how to walk.

She wasn't used to seeing images of herself that were... well... messy. Less than perfect.

She tried to see what Thea saw.

Her portrait wasn't a stylised glamour shot like most of the celebrity faces. Did that mean Thea saw her as she saw the other faces in her collection – the Ugly Ordinaries, as Jasper put it? But she looked again at the bareness and honesty in her expression. Without her smile, without the mask she always wore, she suddenly saw a kind of beauty she'd never seen before. Her pure and untamed self.

Her life had never allowed her the time or the room to see that before.

Thea had given her a gift.

She wanted to lay it right back down again at Thea's feet.

She realised Thea was watching her.

"I love it," she said. "Thank you."

Thea's cocky smirk slipped and tumbled into something far more intimate, far more genuine.

"Oh, darling. That's just the beginning." There was a world of promise glistening on her lower lip. "Kiss me," she ordered, proud again, like the moment had never happened.

Mem turned and tilted her face up to Thea's. Thea made no move to lower her lips to Mem's. Mem had to come to her. It flared through her blood, but she loved it, and found herself smiling against Thea's mouth.

Thea tolerated that for all of a second before she gripped the nape of Mem's neck and kissed her hard, not caring at all for who was watching.

She wiped her thumb across Mem's lips when she pulled away.

"Good girl," she whispered.

Thea took her hand after that and led her through the exhibition. The crowd parted for them as they strolled, knowing smiles and gossiping tongues following their path, but Mem didn't care. Thea was vibrant – so confident it was almost rude, but she pulled it off in a way that was ridiculously attractive. Mem just fell deeper and harder under her spell.

They stopped in front of a portrait of one of the Ordinaries – a woman blurred in mid-laugh, her head thrown back with tattoos wrapping her throat. The smudge on her cheek may or may not have been a bruise. Mem leaned in to read a caption.

"What does it say?" Thea asked.

There were just a handful of words there.

"It's your show," Mem laughed. "Didn't you write it yourself?"

Thea squeezed her hip. "Indulge me."

It *was* her show, after all. She was entitled to be smug. Mem read it to her and Thea immediately pretended to lose interest as another Hollywood giant stalked her down and cried her name over the hubbub.

"Voronov! Get over here and tell me about my good side!" he called.

There was a laugh at the heavyweight's attitude – just one more reminder of the strange, glittering realm Mem inhabited now, one that Thea navigated with effortless style.

As Thea left her side, there was a spark in her eyes, something a tiny bit predatory.

"Wait for me, darling," she purred.

It was an assertion of her claim, an assurance that even amidst this sea of her admirers, Mem was her chosen one.

When she was gone, Mem shivered with the sudden absence of her body.

Which Jasper noticed.

"Oh Mem," he said, appearing out of nowhere and topping up her glass. "You've got it bad."

Chapter Twenty Two

There was a balcony halfway up the far wall in the Turbine Hall.

It stood far above the exhibition, dimly lit and bathed in red light. Thea had been wanting to get Mem up there all evening and finally, she took her hand and sauntered with her past the security guard.

Two floors below them, guests still wandered between her photographs, their chatter rising up to Mem and Thea's level. An after party was planned for the rooftop terrace soon, but no one showed any signs of heading up there yet. Jasper would give the signal.

Mem – her beautiful muse and so much more – leaned against the balcony railing and smiled. So openly. So trustingly. The light was magic on her skin. The softness in her eyes was just for her. Thea tried to figure out how she'd gotten so lucky.

"I meant it," Mem said. "This is extraordinary, Thea. All of it. *You* are extraordinary."

Thea was feeling cocky enough to simply shrug, one hand casually in her pocket, her chin high, just to stir Mem up. It worked. Mem rolled her eyes with faux-exasperation and so much sass Thea found herself almost dizzy with glee. Her muse cupped her hands to her mouth and play-acted calling for the attention of the crowd below.

"Oh wait, everyone, there's one more photo you need to see. The very picture of modesty is right here—"

Thea spun her around and caged her against the railing, one thigh between Mem's, her body hard up against her.

"Cheeky," she murmured.

"Bighead," Mem tried.

Mem's giggle stalled the moment Thea slipped her hand inside the V of Mem's dress and squeezed her breast. She dropped her head to bite a sharp little row of kisses on the line of Mem's jaw and the giggle turned into a moan – one that was needy, amused and outraged all at once. There was no way Thea wasn't going to swallow that with a kiss.

She could taste the champagne on Mem's tongue and in the urgent little whimpers she made into her mouth.

How did she know Thea didn't need more hollow flattery? She'd had enough of that from the puppets down below. What she wanted now was some of Mem's worship.

There was a very strong chance this was real – that underneath all the costume and pretence Mem wasn't acting. Not like the hundreds of others before her who begged Thea just as prettily and took what she gave them and ran. It was taking all of Thea's courage but she could almost believe that Mem wanted Thea too, not just for her work, but for her.

Mem sighed into her kiss and draped her arms over Thea's shoulders, leaning as much of her body as she could against Thea's. The fabric of her dress may as well not even have been there – she could feel every curve of Mem's body pressing against hers.

God, she wanted this to be real.

"May I ask you something?" Mem murmured, when Thea let them stop to breathe.

"Mmm."

"What did Jasper mean when he said Seven Dials?"

There was such an intoxicating concern in her voice, like she cared – really cared – not just for the gossip. Thea's hands slipped down to the lush curve of her backside. She pulled her closer and squeezed.

Buried her face in Mem's hair. Closed her eyes. Breathed her in.

"Thea?"

Delicate fingers caressed the nape of Thea's neck. It was an exquisitely gentle touch – patient and unselfish. Not asking or demanding. Just letting Thea know she was there, ready to surrender whatever Thea wanted from her.

Thea pulled back to look at her.

"It was a long time ago," Thea murmured. "I was a different person back then." Was she? "A mess. A spoiled child."

Nothing had really changed. Though now, for Mem, Thea would do anything.

"Jasper and Kate found me at my lowest point and helped me when I didn't believe I was worth helping. I was overdosing in a gutter at Seven Dials."

She watched that hit Mem.

"Oh. You don't have to tell me, not if you don't want to." Mem's eyes were full of the most patient understanding anyone had ever bestowed on her, *ever*. It made her brave.

"It was a bad hit," she shrugged. "A dealer I was stupid enough to think was a friend sold me some shit that wasn't what he said it was. Some samaritan found my phone and Kate and Jasper saved me. Pumped me full of naloxone and took me to hospital. The kindest thing was that they emptied my pockets before they did, then lied to the doctors and cops about where and how they'd found me."

Mem looked confused. Bless. So that was what a happy childhood in the burbs did to a girl.

"So I didn't get done for possession of Class A substance," Thea explained gently. "Again."

"Oh."

The lack of judgement in her gaze was unnerving. Even Lollie had trouble getting through that story without looking prim. Thea guessed that was why she'd told so few people.

"I was already on probation and my place at art college was dependent on staying clean. I'd fucked up. Something I'm very good at. Is that what you wanted to know?"

That was cruel. A stupid habit she'd have to break. She looked over her cheekbones at Mem, kept her poise as proud as she dared. Mem seemed prepared to take it. She was still looking at her with those deep brown eyes that destroyed Thea's reserve. Why hadn't she run yet?

Thea shrugged and went on with her stupid sorry story. What else was there to lose?

"Jasper sorted everything with art college and, yes, as the smug bastard always likes to say, put a camera in my hands for the first time. And taught me how to use it." She waved a hand at the whole exhibition, at herself, and felt her lips twist in a bitter grimace. "All of this *is* down to him."

"Not one bit," Mem said, fervently. "All this magic is you, Thea Voronov."

There was a long moment.

She put a finger under Mem's chin and tilted it up. Mem obeyed her beautifully, and Thea saw *love* in her eyes, plain as day. It was even more addictive than her submission, and Thea wanted more. She wanted to take Mem home and forget this entire spectacle. She wanted to love this woman back with everything she had – a ridiculous notion that made no sense because Thea couldn't *love*. She barely even had a heart, not one that wasn't tainted with the monstrous ugliness of what she did for a living. She *used* women. It was in her blood. Sins of the father. She didn't love them.

Oh, but she wanted to love this one.

Her mind was swirling with a muddy mess of twenty years of self-loathing, the addictive praise from the idolaters below and Mem's tender submission, and the only thing that kept it clear was the trust in Mem's eyes.

"Thank you for telling me," Mem said, simply. "You know that doesn't change anything, don't you?"

Thea wanted to earn that trust.

"Thank you, beautiful girl," Thea murmured. "But that's not why I brought you up here. I want something else from you now. I want to give you something."

The impact of that took a moment to drop. When it did, Mem's blush was electrifying.

"Here?" she whispered.

"Right here. Where everyone can see."

Mem's eyes blew wide. "Really? But shouldn't I be the one, um, giving you... I mean, it's your show."

"Can't keep your hands off me, hmm?"

Mem chuckled. "Don't be smug."

Thea dropped one hand to her breast again and gave it a hard squeeze through her dress. Mem's chest lifted and Thea watched it hungrily. Mem was as eager for this as Thea was.

"You going to give me what I want?"

"Always."

"Face the room, darling. Elbows on the railing. Legs apart."

Mem smiled like the light of the sun and turned. Brushing her lips against the nape of her neck, Thea delighted in the shiver of desire that rippled her shoulders. She trailed her fingers down the gorgeous expanse of naked skin exposed by her backless dress, pressed gently and Mem bent slowly forward.

She was perfect.

Gathering up the fabric at the back of her dress nearly had Thea drunk on lust, and Mem skittered nervously on her heels. Thea didn't pause, not until there was nothing under her hand except skin and the lace of Mem's thong.

She pushed the lace aside.

Mem was slick like oil – soft, velvety and fucking incredible – and when Thea kicked the girl's ankles further apart, her gasp was like the voice of heaven. It set Thea's blood pulsing between her legs. It swelled something in her chest.

No, not something. Her heart.

She slid her fingers over Mem's clit and marvelled at the way her body twitched. She plunged her fingers deep into her wet heat and rocked her hard. Two beautiful eyes captured her own as Mem looked back at her over her shoulder, her lower lip caught between her teeth. Thea fucked her slowly, knowing her body well, leading Mem carefully and precisely to that sweet, sweet point where she clenched around her fingers, where she quivered and tensed—

Mem moaned.

"What was that, darling?"

"Please, Thea. Cl— Close. I'm— please, can I—?"

"Already?"

Thea suddenly hated her own smugness. She'd never enjoyed anyone's surrender as much as she enjoyed Mem's – she was so expressive, so responsive and it was impossible not to crave that – but Thea was doing this wrong.

She needed more.

She wanted to see Mem's face – all of it. She needed Mem's hands against her own body, the warmth of her palms that spoke of generosity and gentleness that was all for Thea. She wanted to see her beautiful Mem.

All those games she'd played with women in the past – they meant nothing to her now. That sense of power she craved, that she cultivated only to ward off something worse, it was nothing compared to the devotion in Mem's eyes. Love was pouring out of her now – *love*! Mem was a treasure and under her gaze Thea almost believed she could be... good. More than a cog in a machine that used innocence, sullied it and spat it out. More than the monster who dwelt in her blood.

Thea could be a *lover*. She knew that now, because Mem was her heart.

So she stopped.

She dropped a gentle kiss between Mem's shoulder blades and smiled at her desperate sigh. Thea nudged her upright and guided her around with soft fingers beneath her chin and finally let herself go, falling at last into those wide, brown eyes, into that soft, unfocused look that was just for her.

She could be demanding now. It was what she'd do with any other woman. She could hook Mem's thigh over her hip and thrust back into her again. She could keep Mem strung out on the edge of ecstasy, right there above London's hottest party, until she begged in just the right way. She knew Mem's body better than she knew her own. She could play this woman like an instrument.

And Mem would adore it.

She'd even love to beg.

But Thea wanted to give her perfect muse far, far more than that.

She tilted Mem's lips up for her gentlest kiss and smiled at Mem's sigh.

Then she dropped to her knees.

She didn't give her time to speak. Her dress was gathered up and pressed into Mem's hands, and Thea used her own to pull her lingerie aside, to thumb her reverently open. She buried her face in the home she found there.

The taste of Mem was better than champagne. Her scent, her warmth against her tongue – all of it spun through Thea's mind and she pressed herself closer, deeper, as deep as she could go. Her arms slid up the backs of Mem's thighs holding her up – Mem's legs were shaking – but Thea would carry her to the end of the world. She'd love her just as far.

She forgot herself then. There was nothing but the body beneath her lips, Mem's fingers in her hair and her cries ringing in her ears – Mem's very heart in her mouth – and a pressure that was growing and swelling and filling her and leading her to the same brink she was chasing Mem to—

The fingers in her hair clenched, Mem stumbled and Thea held her firm. A thigh hooked over her shoulder and pulled her in, fierce and hard, and Thea was content to drown, licking, chasing and drinking until the pressure against her mouth split and burst into ecstasy, a flash of infinite light that burned Thea's soul, exposed her naked truth and loved her for it. Thea smiled into Mem's core again, laughed at the shiver that shocked through her body, and licked her sweetly down and calm again.

She didn't want to get up.

An exhausted hand lost its grip on the dress and fabric cascaded around Thea's shoulders. Laughing, lost in it, she kissed Mem's thigh, placed her foot carefully back on the ground, and rose sheepishly to her feet.

Mem's eyes were deep and dark.

"That was—"

"Shh," she whispered. She kissed her beautiful muse – the woman who controlled her soul – and smiled against her lips when Mem hummed at the flavour.

They looked at each other for a long moment.

"Thank you," Thea said.

Mem gave a weak laugh. She cupped Thea's cheek in a way Thea wanted to make forever.

Her top was gaping where Thea had groped her. She straightened it carefully and adjusted the fall of her skirt. Mem wiped her thumb over Thea's lips and tweaked her collar. She trailed a fingertip down between her breasts.

Thea took her hand and kissed it tenderly.

"Jasper and Kate saved me at Seven Dials all those years ago, but it's taken me til now to really appreciate why."

She nearly died for the faith in Mem's eyes, for that sweet half-smile and dimple in her cheek.

"Now I know," she added. "I was waiting for you, my darling muse. Look what you've done to me."

On the roof of the Tate Modern the moon shone down on a whole new world.

Jasper had kicked the rooftop party into action, the cream of London society soaking themselves in yet more champagne and the throbbing beats of one of Europe's hottest DJs. Coloured lights and a million candles lit the glasshouse-style marquee, and, confident in their ascendency and confirmed by Thea Voronov's eye, the beautiful people of the world danced.

Thea hated them, but she had to admit they made a pretty picture – all that egoism shining with pretension. She didn't deny she was right at home amongst them, but she had Memona Swan on her arm now. She soared a million miles above them all.

St Paul's glowed like an orb above the glittering Thames, the river timeless and urgent all at once, and Thea was on top of the world.

She led Mem into the middle of the mayhem, bent the woman's body to her own and held her shamelessly. The music pounded and they danced, their limbs moving together, their senses assaulted by the sound and light, their sweat mingling until they were one. She saw Mem in a series of perfect snapshots created by the blinding lights – the sway of her hips, her arms in the air and her head thrown back. The look of abandon on Mem's face coiled a hot burn of need in Thea's chest. When Mem's eyes met hers, the need shot lower, harder, and Thea slung her arm low around the woman's waist and pulled her onto her hip. Through the thin fabric of the dress, she felt Mem's muscles clench around her thigh, and Mem moved as if Thea owned her.

She was divine.

They danced until thirst drove them in search of iced water and they found themselves outside in the cool air, gazing at London, Mem's head resting comfortably on Thea's shoulder.

Thea knew she needed to get Mem home soon – she needed to get this woman under her. She needed to watch her *writhe*.

"There you are!"

Jasper ambled up with Kate Cox in his wake. Kate carried her stilettos in one hand and her silk wrap in the other. She was leaving.

"I'm too old for this shit," she declared, cheerfully. Her cheeks were pink. She kissed Mem and Thea each on the cheek, and squeezed Thea's hand. "Well done, darling. A triumph, as always. But I've got someone at home warming my bed for me—"

Kate stumbled to a halt with a slightly guilty look – first at Thea, then at Mem, then at Thea again. It almost made Thea laugh – Kate had someone new and she felt bad for Thea.

Once, this would have been poison. Once, Thea had thought Kate might be hers.

But she had Mem now.

"Go on, then," Thea said, knowing her role. "Age should retire gracefully."

"Bitch." Kate shot Thea an amiable two-fingered salute. It looked fabulous on her. "See you soon, Mem. Don't let this evil woman lead you astray."

Thea felt Mem lean into her side again.

"Too late," Mem said, smiling happily.

Thea squeezed her backside.

Jasper pretended to puke and Kate left. Jasper didn't.

He leaned his hip against the railing and totally failed to catch the hint.

"What?" Thea said, pointedly.

"You've been hogging Mem all evening." He turned his ineffable charm on the woman at her side. "I want to talk business. We covered you in diamonds tonight for a reason, Memona. Tell me what you're thinking about the movie sequel and the brand ambassadorship, my dear. Inquiring minds need to know."

He said it lightly, cheerfully, and for a moment Thea's brand new heart nearly shattered in her chest. *This?* Again? Would it follow her forever, this endless, sucking, swindling deception? Would it always be exploitation? Could she never have something pure? Would she always be a souteneur?

Mem tensed under her arm. Thea saw her smile freeze before she steeled herself for an answer.

"I really haven't decided," Mem said. She poked her tongue out at his grumpy pout and for some reason it made Thea instantly proud – then radiantly happy. It made Mem part of the family. "There are some other things I want to do. Other projects I'm working—"

"Not doing the sequel?" Jasper exploded, all toothy smile and faux-outrage. "But, dearest, you must. What *will* StudioOne say? Have you told them?"

"I haven't, apparently, though I thought I had. I asked Adiatu to inform them but she said she's handling it. She's still trying to talk me into it too." Mem pulled a face.

"Good woman, Adiatu," Jasper said. He stroked his chin.

"Pain in the arse woman," Thea grumbled. Mem's fingers tapped her ribs under her jacket. Thea hid a smile. She was going to take that.

"I don't know why you're all so keen on me doing it," Mem said. "No one's even seen the movie yet. I might be dreadful. It might flop completely."

"Nonsense." Jasper looked keen again. "And the diamond deal? I think you'll be a fabulous brand ambassador. An influencer. An advocate for style and sophistication and piles and piles of gorgeous, glittering diamonds." He waved his arms extravagantly.

Idiot. Thea could tell he was drunk. He was still an adorable bastard, if a touch too cunning.

Mem looked uncomfortable again.

"Endorsing diamonds really isn't my thing." She wrinkled her nose adorably. "It feels wrong to promote that kind of ostentatious wealth when there are so many people suffering—"

"And yet you're wearing at least fifty carats right now." Jasper was suddenly sly.

"I am?" Mem blinked.

"She doesn't have to do anything she doesn't want to, Jasper," Thea told him, crisply. "Mem will make her own decisions, and I expect her agent may or may not inform you of her choices when she does." She gave him her best fuck-you smile. "Depending on whether it's any of your business."

Jasper smiled blithely. "Alright. Keep your hair on." He turned his charm back on Mem. "You'll think about it though, won't you?"

"Don't tell her what to do." Thea was losing her patience.

She knew what was coming the moment she said it.

"That your job then?"

She felt Mem's jolt against her body.

"Don't be a prat, Jasper," Thea replied, just as serenely. "Why don't you fuck off now?"

Jasper chortled merrily, shot Mem a jaunty wink, a shrewd look at Thea, and ambled away.

They watched the Thames for a moment.

"Sorry about Jasper," Thea said.

Mem squeezed her waist. "I'm a big girl, you know. You don't need to defend me."

It wasn't a reprimand. She said it gently with the hint of a cheeky smile, but for some reason, Thea was almost on the edge of apologising. That wasn't like her. Mem squeezed again. Her palms were warm on Thea's body.

"But I like very much that you do."

There was a beat. Mem's body pressed even closer. Thea could feel her need. Fuck, she needed to get out of here now.

"He's right, though," she said, and surrendered to the other thing about Mem that she adored.

Mem wanted her to use her.

She dropped her lips to Mem's ear. "It *is* my job. You'll do what I tell you to do, won't you?"

It wasn't a question. Both of them knew it.

Mem smiled at her, the world in her eyes.

"Of course, Thea," she whispered. "Order me."

At home, Mem stripped eagerly at Thea's word. She crawled naked up the stairs to the bedroom. She knelt between Thea's thighs and told every part of Thea's body just how extraordinary she was all over again.

Thea bound her in rope yet felt herself unravelling. Every command she uttered rushed with the usual swell of power deep within her core, but it was she who was left quivering under Mem's tongue. The sweet submission Mem laid at her feet had Thea flying, invincible at the top of the world, and yet she couldn't tear her eyes from the girl on her knees at her feet.

For the first time in a long time, and as she'd promised herself she'd never be again, she felt... frail.

She wondered who was controlling who, and then knew it barely mattered.

The answer was there in Mem's eyes, liquid, molten and burning for Thea, as she saw through all of Thea's hesitations, swept aside her guilt and licked away her self-loathing. She worshipped everything Thea pretended to be *and* the women inside.

Thea tightened her grip on Mem's hair and pulled her closer, though it was Mem who drew her in.

"Take what you want," Mem whispered, far too knowing. "I trust you, Thea. I want to be everything you need."

And for a moment, she was – her breath warm against her skin, their bodies slotted together in a perfect embrace, something raw and unfiltered on their tongues that tasted like love.

Thea wished it could last forever.

Chapter Twenty Three

"These images are sensational."

Thea reclined on the chesterfield in Jasper's office and didn't bother being modest.

"I know," she said. "Does the company like them?"

Jasper chuckled. "They love them. Thought they were going to blow something when they saw them." He smirked. "Maybe me. They were practically grovelling at my feet."

"You're disgusting, Jasper."

Jasper had summoned her to the executive suite in the Shard the morning after her opening night – actually, literally summoned her, like she was a recalcitrant child. Right now he sat behind his expansive desk like a smarmy Bond villain, steepling his fingers over a splash of glossy images of Memona Swan and Katherine Cox draped in created diamonds. They were for the London premiere of *The Wolverton Diamond* next week when the company would announce its joint campaign with both actresses as brand ambassadors.

Except that Mem hadn't signed yet.

Thea figured that was why she was there.

Jasper had been bullish and insisted she get the shots anyway – and she had. Gorgeous pictures of Kate draped in diamonds that she'd shot during a planned session. Devastating images of Mem she'd taken simply by demanding her muse sit before her lens.

The one Jasper was staring at now was some of her best work. Shot on film, Mem's beauty shining brighter than the jewels. It was a classic Thea Voronov shot, and she was cocky enough to know it would catapult the brand into the stratosphere and turn Mem into an icon. What could she say? She was the best.

She shifted on the sofa. Her arrogance almost covered her guilt. This was underhanded and sly, but as Jasper pointed out – almost daily – they were running out of time.

"So?" Jasper asked.

Thea aimed for idle nonchalance. "So what?"

"So, where's my diamond deal, Voronov? Memona Swan and CreatedDiamonds. I want the brand ambassadorship and I want the movie sequel— Damn it, you know exactly what I'm talking about. We've already got the images – thank you – but we need Mem on board. We've got one fucking week. If you could actually get your dick out and do what you're told for once, we'd have both deals in the bag already."

Thea pulled a face. Bloody Jasper. He was using her as much as he wanted to profiteer from Mem, and all to further his empire. It should hurt, she realised. Instead, she felt protective – which was a new feeling. She decided she liked it.

"I told you last night on the roof of the Tate. Mem's agent will let you know when she takes on either role – *if* she does at all."

Jasper's mouth fell open. It might have been funny if it wasn't so irritating.

"I'm not going to force her," she said.

"Why the fuck not?"

"She's her own woman. She makes her own choices."

"You agreed to this, Thea."

She folded her arms. "Not the way I remember it. You turned up at my house and gave orders. Brought Kate along with her big baby blues to hammer it in."

Mem's strength of character was why she didn't feel so monstrous handing over these beautiful images of Mem without her consent – even the perfect one they'd developed together in her darkroom. Mem had resolve. Thea hadn't corrupted her. She wasn't going to sign. No one but Jasper and a handful of CreatedDiamonds execs would ever see these images.

Jasper leaned over his desk. For the first time in a long time, he looked angry at her. She stared sullenly back and felt twenty years old again, when Jasper and Kate had stood next to her hospital bed and given her a stern but loving lecture about anti opioids and sheer stupidity.

Stubborn as each other, they stared like bulls – until the moment became stupid. Thea couldn't stay angry at him. They'd known each other for too long. He was a git – a fucking annoying one at that – but he was her git.

"Mem has principles—" she started, and was stunned when Jasper cut her off.

"Like you care. And not to put too fine a point on it, Thea old chap, but you do owe me."

That stopped her cold.

She *did* owe him. She'd be nothing without Jasper – a homeless junkie if not dead already. Twisting the arm of some grasping starlet should have been the least she could do. Except that Mem wasn't that.

"It's business," Jasper said, "and business doesn't have room for the principles of a Hollywood baby-star no matter how noble they might be. I have further agreements riding on the success of these ones. I have two-thousand people to employ, magazines to publish, influencers to bribe, clicks to fucking well bait. The industry doesn't stop just because you suddenly developed a conscience."

And there was the crux of it.

Thea had been just as happy to exploit whoever stood before her lens for all these years. She'd planned and schemed alongside Jasper and made her own millions. She'd manipulated the industry and the pretty young things who fueled it to the point where they were eager to prostitute themselves to her – for pleasure, sure, but for greed too. She felt her lip curl. For all these years, her crimes had been as ugly as her father's. She just printed it all on high-gloss with the worship of celebrities to make it shine.

But this new, fluttering, wonderful feeling in her chest made her think those days might be past. Mem Swan, with her beauty, her principles and her dignity, was going to stride right past it all. And the crazy thing was, Mem was holding out her hand. Thea was going to take it and rise with her.

There was a long silence.

"We made our first mag on a photocopier," Thea said, quietly, "using a stolen photocopy card from the Kentish Town Library. Who are you?"

He gave her a thin smile. "Same ruthless bitch as you, darling. And that was twenty years ago. Times change."

"She doesn't deserve this," she whispered.

"Who?" Jasper looked baffled.

"Mem."

It hit her again, like a revelation. She loved Mem. She *loved* Mem – a strong, determined woman who knew what she wanted and hadn't given in to Jasper, Adiatu or the overwhelming pressure of a Hollywood film studio. A woman unswayed by the allure of fame or fortune, who didn't see Thea's lens as a conduit to greater success. In Mem's eyes, Thea wasn't just a means to an end – she was a person to be cherished and loved in return. And the way Mem yielded to her, that deep, natural submission that mirrored Thea's own need for control, was something Thea knew she was always going to crave.

Mem didn't need the media machine – and suddenly, Thea found her liberation from it too. All she needed was Mem.

Thea was proud of her. Damn it, for possibly the first time in her life, she might even have been proud of herself. She may have let her friends down – Jasper and Kate weren't ever going to get that diamond deal – but she hadn't betrayed Mem.

She hadn't become her father.

Jasper's eyes narrowed. "Are you—?"

"What?"

It only confirmed his suspicions.

"You've gone soft!" He cackled suddenly and rubbed his hands together, his good humour completely restored. "I thought last night was just a damn fine show. Have you caught feelings?"

"Shut up, Jasper."

"Has the bullheaded Thea Voronov been seduced by those warm, brown eyes?"

"Fuck off."

"I didn't even know you had a heart to melt."

She had to give him that one. She hadn't known either until Memona Swan had stolen it.

"I'm not in love," she lied.

"Didn't even say the word."

They grinned at each other. A tentative truce.

"I'm happy for you, dearest, but I still want CreatedDiamonds, Mem Swan and Kate Cox, and a fucking movie sequel in the bag by the end of next week."

She stood up and walked to the door. Should she take those images back? No. It didn't matter. Mem had plans. A roadmap. Her charity and her principles. She wasn't going to sign. Let Jasper think what he wanted. Thea had never felt so light of heart.

She waved goodbye with her middle finger.

"Lollie has a whole photo shoot set up in Versailles just waiting for Mem to sign."

"Whatever."

"You need to fix this, Voronov," he called.

She didn't.

She had Mem.

Chapter Twenty Four

As *The Wolverton Diamond* raced towards its London premiere, Mem's workload only got crazier.

Adiatu filled her schedule with a million things – dress fittings, interviews, press junkets, a list of talking points Mem had to get her head around. Even etiquette lessons.

"You will be in the presence of royalty," Adiatu reminded her, for at least the fiftieth time.

The only time Mem and Thea got to see each other was in bed, but dreams woke Mem every night. Nightmare scenarios haunted her – tripping on the carpet at the Royal Albert Hall and landing flat on her face in front of hundreds of photographers, then waking and realising it wouldn't only be photographers – if she fell, it would be in front of the world. Thea knew just how to take her mind off it, but Mem didn't miss the hint of doubt in her eyes too.

The London premiere might have been a week away, but it was the two weeks of international appearances that followed that Mem dreaded with all her being.

"Do you want me to come with you, darling?" Thea asked. "I'll hitch a ride on Jasper's horrid little plane. He won't miss the LA parties."

The thought of doing the whole round of red carpets with Thea by her side was comforting – LA, Rome, Paris and Berlin, then Mumbai and Dubai, plus Tokyo, Seoul, Beijing and Sydney. But Thea had her own responsibilities here in London. She had a busy publicity schedule of her own after her exhibition had opened to rave reviews.

"I'll come," Thea decided, kissing her lightly on the temple. "But you know you'll be fine. You're already wonderful. Are you okay now?"

Mem loved her care.

Thea swatted her thigh under the sheets and pretended to be gruff. "Can we go back to sleep, then?" She rolled her over and Mem wriggled back against Thea's body, slotting her fingers between Thea's and wrapping her arms around her.

Thea sighed into the back of her neck.

"Thank you," Mem whispered.

Thea tilted her hips up. "Go to sleep."

Dame Katherine Cox was helpful too – when she wasn't crowing in triumph over Mem and Thea's new relationship, that is.

"You two were ridiculously hot together at the Tate the other night," she drawled, her eyes dancing. They were whispering together during a dull meeting where their agent and a world famous toy company were unveiling a set of Mem-dolls and Kate-dolls as their movie characters. "And I know exactly what you've been up to. You've got a glow that definitely doesn't come from yoga."

Mem pretended to be scandalised but she couldn't pull it off. Not in front of the queen of Hollywood. Besides, Kate had a curious look on her face – a blend of nostalgia and affection.

"You got her past her stroppy, sulky bitch stage *and* the little lost puppy stage. I'm extremely impressed. And a bit jealous."

Kate rehearsed her through their talking points. She taught her how to toss in cute little anecdotes from production and make them sound casual and new. She gave tips for deflecting pushy journalists who pressed for personal information.

"Use that power Thea has given you," she told her.

Mem blushed instantly and Kate's smile widened.

"Thought so. She takes your control, demands your submission and then hands you the world, right? How do you feel then?"

"Amazing," Mem blurted. "Confident. I mean, it doesn't make any sense, but once she shows me what I can handle, I realise I can do anything."

"Of course you can. Now just use that strength out in the real world, not just Thea's bedroom."

Mem squared her shoulders and conquered the talking points, and the ability to walk in four inch heels in a gown with a three-foot train.

They were driving to the filming of yet another late night chat show and got the giggles when their car stopped in traffic alongside a red London bus festooned with their faces.

"Thea took that pic," Kate said. "Remember? She got so cross at us for mucking around." She sobered for a moment and gave Mem a keen look. "Are you going to do this CreatedDiamonds thing with us, or not? We'll both be working with Thea again. It will be fun. Has she talked you into it yet?"

Mem frowned, but Kate didn't seem to notice.

"Persuasive, isn't she? God, I used to love obeying her orders. Tell me what she used on you, darling. A flogger? A cane? Oh, did she hang you from the ceiling all tied up in a thousand knots and whip you into tomorrow?" She gave a thoroughly indecent moan and smirked at the driver in the rearview. "Mmm..."

What? Mem felt suddenly defensive. Thea hadn't said a thing about CreatedDiamonds since that night weeks ago at Jasper's apartment, and she certainly wouldn't use the games they played in the bedroom to influence Mem's career.

Would she?

Mem was no longer sure Kate's relationship with Thea was healthy.

"I haven't decided yet. And what's it got to do with Thea? I can make my own mind up, you know." Mem sounded snippy even to her own ears. Why anyone thought she was a good actor was beyond her. But, it seemed to be going around because Kate pressed a palm to her hair and looked out the window.

"No need to be touchy." The finest actor of the age looked as guilty as hell. "The premiere is only days away. You might want to hurry up and decide is all I'm saying. And don't forget the sequel."

Mem hated this.

In a rare three hour break between engagements, she went to Heart and Grace House and made ten gallons of pumpkin soup.

There was children's laughter ringing through the building, the part-time cook they'd employed was a scream, and it was a relief to simply do something useful and productive, and gossip about women's football for a while. It felt better than listening to more of Adiatu's nagging about diamonds. They packed the soup into single serve containers and added them to the deep freeze. Cheap, hearty, healthy meals for the women who needed them.

Piper found her washing dishes.

"Hey superstar," she said. "Welcome back to our empire of good. Is Thea busy today?"

Mem blew a raspberry. "I came around to roll my sleeves up." She grinned at the cook. "We got heaps done."

"They're some pretty expensive sleeves," Piper noted slyly. "You always cook in Saint Laurent?"

"Sod off, Pipes. It's McQueen, actually. And you know I can't even tell the difference. Adiatu picked it."

The cook nudged Mem away from the sink and pointed to two cups of tea she'd laid out on the counter. There was a packet of biscuits too. They took the hint and carried their mugs to the office.

"Not that I'm not glad to see you here," Piper began, "but you could probably make better use of your time than making soup." She dumped the pile of paperwork in front of Mem and put a pen on top of it. "We're flat out at the moment. We have a totally full house and people on a waiting list. I know we can't help everyone but—"

Piper made a funny sort of choking noise.

"What?"

"But it fucking sucks having to turn someone away, Mem."

Mem looked up to see Piper wiping the corner of her eyes. *Shit.* She'd been a lousy friend. She pushed the papers aside and focused on Piper.

"What happened? Oh god, Pipes, I'm so sorry. I've just been so busy with—"

"I know – and it's okay. You've got heaps on your plate. I can't even imagine how you're feeling with the premiere coming up." Piper was trying to sound tough but her chin was wobbly. "It was just— The other night this woman turned up right on six when I was leaving. She had a bruise on her face and a toddler on her hip and nothing else. Said she'd heard about our place and finally realised she could be brave. That it was time. Except we had one room left, and a sixteen year old who's been on the street for three whole months knocked on the door too."

"Fuck." Mem bit her lip. "What did you do?"

"I didn't have any choice. I gave the sixteen year old a meal and let her have a shower, and she said she totally understood and she was fine, but— she was sixteen, Mem. A kid. I called a few other services to try to find her a bed for the night, but she took off. She was so resigned. She just wanted to sleep in a bed."

"I should have been here. I'm sorry you had to do that on your own."

Piper waved her off. "Rubbish. We all have our own skill set. Yours, right now, is making the money."

That hit a little harder than Mem liked, but Piper was right. Mem was seated at a table that served out opportunities like a feast, and yet there she was making subsistence meals in a designer suit with a price tag that could have the residents of the shelter dining on caviar. And there was so much more opportunity Mem could take advantage of. Both Kate and Thea, experts at the top of their fields, thought the sequel and the diamond ambassadorship were wise decisions. She'd be foolish not to listen to them.

Her phone buzzed with a message from Adiatu. The car to take her to her next engagement was out front.

She hugged Piper before she left.

"If I agree to this job with CreatedDiamonds, can you make it worth my while?" Mem asked.

Adiatu's head spun so fast Mem thought it might fall off.

"Four million pounds over three years." Adiatu said it so quickly Mem knew it had already been negotiated. "Will that work for you?"

Mem barely stopped herself from blurting 'fuck yeah' on the spot, but some new confidence inside her welled up and took over.

"How much is Kate getting?"

"Dame Katherine is an icon. She rules the fashion industry—"

"How much is she getting?"

Adiatu sniffed. "Nine."

"And the company wants both of us, right?"

Her agent regarded her with narrowed eyes. Mem ploughed right on.

"If you can get me five, I'll do it," she said.

"And the sequel?" Adiatu was relentless.

"I'll make a decision after the premiere. The box office take on the opening weekend should put us in a stronger negotiating position," Mem said. She didn't miss the approving quirk at the corner of Adiatu's mouth.

The woman was on the phone in seconds.

Somehow, Kate knew before she did.

"Yay!" she squealed, so girlish and playful it was like the Dame was twenty instead of her sophisticated forty-nine years. "I'm so glad. Wonderful decision, Mem. We're going to have so much fun."

Mem could also tell it was a bit of a performance because they'd just finished a photo shoot for a glossy weekend newspaper magazine and there was still a studio full of creatives around. She smiled back, then let Kate pull her into a hug.

"Really," Kate whispered then. "Good for you, love."

Jasper Fitz-Steward also seemed to know because he sent a congratulations message to her phone and Mem hadn't even known the man had her number. A massive bouquet of flowers turned up before Adiatu managed to tell her the good news. They were from CreatedDiamonds and came with a hamper of exquisite delicacies, as well as a silk shawl and a bottle of perfume from a brand so exclusive it made Mem wince.

Five million pounds over the next three years.

No decision at all, really.

An envelope tucked into the bouquet showed that the diamond company had also committed a hundred-thousand pound donation to Heart and Grace House, which was doubly confusing because Mem hadn't mentioned that at all.

"Jasper's idea," Kate laughed, squeezing her shoulders again. "You'll find he's very useful for things like that. And you're practically part of the family now, dearest girl." She bustled straight on. "Things are going to get super busy, though. We have to fit in a photoshoot with Thea now before the premiere. Yay and ugh. You could have given us a bit more notice, sweetheart – *four* days – but no one's complaining!"

And things certainly did kick up a gear.

Mem and Kate met the CreatedDiamonds executives in their offices in the Shard, just a few levels below Spectrum Media's corporate headquarters, and Jasper popped into the meeting too.

Breezy bastard, Mem thought, all handshakes and effortless charm, and throwing glossy prints of Thea's photos of Kate and Mem around the table like they were swap cards. She wondered where Thea was.

Adiatu was practically frothing at the mouth.

"Look at the dynamic she's caught in these images," she told the diamond execs. "Electric. So desirable. Utterly on point. Memona, our radiant new star whose beauty defies convention, and Kate, the timeless icon with her effortless, regal charm. They are the yin and yang of the cultural zeitgeist – the perfect balance for your exquisite diamonds."

She was laying it on a bit thick, but what would Mem know? Only a year ago she'd been a waitress.

Kate kicked her under the table. *Smile*, her eyes said.

"Under Thea Voronov's lens in Versailles tomorrow, Memona and Katherine will be the living, breathing embodiment of power, grace and allure – a heartbeat that resonates with the essence of your brand."

Versailles?

Mem had completely lost control of her life.

Adiatu turned to Mem and Kate. "Darlings, tell us how you, as creatives, can help contextualise the seductiveness of luxury diamond jewellery within a narrative of female strength, empowerment and modern elegance."

Mem blinked. The fuck?

Kate, damn her, her eyes glittering with the game, crossed her eyes and made a fish face at Mem before turning her charm on the marketing team at full force.

Great.

Now Mem had another aspect of her life to master.

Piper didn't take it as well as Mem hoped.

"But— but what about our plan? We had a *plan*, Mem."

It was seven at night and Mem had just stumbled in, practically braindead after a full day of facing cameras and journalists and not one single, genuine interaction. Piper was sitting on the floor, her laptop open, a bunch of papers beside her.

"I know, *I know*, but with that much money we can open a second shelter, and—"

"And?"

"And Kate and Thea both said it was a good idea. It will cement my reputation, which, of course, will make any future partnerships with benefactors more appealing—"

"Bullshit."

Mem didn't say anything. It probably was bullshit. The whole industry was. She still didn't want to do the sequel – not really – but she saw the logic of it.

Piper screwed up her face. She looked hurt. "One movie, you said. One movie and some sensible investments."

"I know, but—"

"Yeah, no, I get it. Suddenly your Hollywood buddies have more say in your life than your best mate?"

Mem pressed her fingers into her temples. Piper was right – and wrong – but they weren't really being fair to each other. She knew she hadn't been around for Piper and the shelter lately, what with the premiere and everything, but they'd always known this was coming. She missed her best friend.

She also hadn't seen Thea for two whole days.

"And the sequel?" Piper whispered.

"I'm thinking about it."

Piper put her hands on her hips and huffed out a long breath at the ceiling. They watched each other cautiously.

"There'd be some filming in LA, as well as Mumbai," Mem added.

"Oh, for fuck's sake!"

"I haven't decided yet, Pipes."

Piper turned back to her laptop. "Yeah, well, you let me know when you do."

It was a dismissal.

Mem didn't want to leave it like that.

"What's all that, then?" she asked lightly, raising her eyebrows at the papers.

"Uni enrolment. Like you told me to." Piper grunted sullenly, then burst into a massive grin. "Oh my god, pure mathematics is going to be so cool. I'm going through my text book now. It's really exciting."

Mem snorted. "Nerd," she teased, but she was glad Piper had done it. She had a talent she shouldn't waste.

"Dick," Piper retorted.

Mem felt their usual dynamic return.

"A second shelter is a good idea," Piper admitted. "You're my best friend in the world, Mem Swan. Just don't turn into a Hollywood asshole, okay?"

Mem laughed, weakly. "I'll try."

It was only then, amid the hustle Adiatu had subjected her to and the looming deadline of the London premiere, that she realised she hadn't told Thea about her decision. *That* was pretty Hollywood asshole, when she thought about it, but she figured Thea must already know. Jasper was flying them all to Versailles tomorrow for the CreatedDiamonds shoot. They needed promotional images for their big announcement at the premiere. Thea must know.

The woman's name popped up on her phone.

Just her name sent a thrill through her. Electric and undeniable, the kind of jolt that kickstarted her heart, melted it in her chest and caused it to drip like mercury and pool in a burning lust between her legs.

—*Darling. I need you. Use the back gate*—

Mem smiled, her body already tingling at the thought of Thea and what she might need from her.

And suddenly, everything was clear.

She knew what she wanted.

She wanted Thea.

Chapter Twenty Five

"*This* is what you needed me for? Cooking?"

Mem strolled through the back door of Thea's house like she owned the place and slipped straight into Thea's arms, tilting her head up sweetly for a kiss. Thea decided to let the sass slide and lost herself in the cheek of her smile. The woman could stride around her home like she owned it any time. She practically owned Thea's heart.

"Are we calling it cooking?" Yelena Titov's disrespect was a different matter but Thea had given up on that front ages ago. She emerged from Thea's walk-in pantry with an obscenely shaped sweet potato and a filthy expression.

The kitchen looked like a disaster zone but there were two dishes bubbling away on the stove that Thea was quite proud of. There had been a few arguments with Google complete with Lena stabbing a chopping knife at Mem's recipes for emphasis. Thea insisted Lena read them out loud for her over and again, but she'd wanted to cook them herself. She wasn't above admitting her limit, though. Or Lena's. They needed Mem for the roti.

"You actually made these yourself? I didn't even know your kitchen had food in it." Mem leaned over the stove and eyed Thea's chicken karahi like she was genuinely impressed. Thea stepped up behind her and swatted her backside. Mem nuzzled back into her.

"You think I'm all expensive restaurants and fancy suits? Now I have you, my kitchen has love in it," Thea said into the divine spot under Mem's ear.

Lena made puking noises.

"What's wrong with a home-cooked dinner with my favourite women?"

"*Pfft.* Always knew you were gone for me, Fyodora," Lena preened. She touched an ostentatious palm to her hair.

Thea's heart was so fucking light it was floating up near the ceiling. "Shut up, babushka." She even grinned when Mem slapped her wrist and Lena tossed a carrot end at her.

They watched as Mem rolled out the roti, an expert flick to her wrists, and Thea dipped her fingers in the flour specifically to leave a hand-print on the tight, dark blue jeans that hugged Mem's gorgeous backside. She loved the look of it there – entitled, a definite claim on her territory – and it took Mem another ten minutes to notice it. Thea and Lena snickered like children the entire time, and that was fun too. Thea almost didn't recognise herself.

Mem squealed with outrage when she finally saw it and their laughter rang through the house filling Thea's chest with feelings she hadn't ever known could be hers. Mem swiped at Lena with a wooden spoon, but she chased Thea into the pantry with a deliciously wicked glint in her eyes.

Thea pressed her back against the shelves, wrapped her fingers around her throat and squeezed the thigh that hooked so naturally over her hip. She kissed into the girl like she was devouring her.

"I know what you're doing in there," Lena roared.

Mem rested her forehead against Thea's and giggled – and for some wonderful, incomprehensible reason, Thea did too. Yelena Titov knew nothing. This was magic.

They sat down to the best meal Thea had ever cooked in her life and the fluffiest roti in the world. Mem had flour on her cheek and a light in her eyes that was just for her, and Lena dropped the shit for once in her life and smiled her blessings on them both like she really was the family matriarch. Thea pulled the cork on a bottle of red and they clinked their glasses across the table.

"You did all this for me?" Mem asked around a mouthful of aloo gobi. "It's not bad."

That was cheeky. It was absolutely delicious, even if Thea said so herself.

"She didn't follow your recipe," Lena grunted.

Thea ignored that. "I felt we were all due a little low-key perspective between my exhibition opening and the night after tomorrow when the madness of your premiere schedule descends. How better than with a meal prepared with love?"

"Gross," said Lena.

Thea flipped her the finger but kept her eyes on Mem's. Her own exhibition had been extremely well received by the critics and the punters. She was in love with an angel and a muse. The most beautiful woman to ever stand before her lens shone with an integrity and nobility so bright it even cast a little decency onto Thea – not to mention hope! And Memona Swan looked at her with love in her eyes. Not avarice, not expectation, but love. Thea would be proud, in just two evenings time, to stand admiringly at her side when her perfect muse triumphed on the red carpet for one of the year's biggest Hollywood movies.

Life, for the first time in a long time, was wide with potential.

"Two days of freedom left, my darling. How shall we spend them?"

Mem gave her a happy, goofy smile, and then a hiccup as something occurred to her.

"Well, one day. Versailles tomorrow. But I love this. Thank you, Thea. I love that you've—"

The whole scene stalled.

Versailles?

Thea didn't hear the rest. The view before her flashed bright and over-exposed. The lens, so focused on Mem and her beauty and that softness in her gaze that seemed just for Thea, suddenly zoomed out.

"You signed?" she heard herself say.

What had happened to her plans? Her integrity?

"Paris! A shoot actually *in* the palace! I'm quite excited about it, even though I know it's going to be exhausting. Adiatu secured a really good deal for me and Kate said—"

Mem was babbling. Thea watched the filters fall away.

What had she missed? *Had she been wrong about everything?* She thought Mem was incorruptible. It was what set her apart from the whole grasping industry. It was what made her different. Pure. Special.

Unless, of course, she wasn't different at all. Unless Thea had been fooled by a pretty face and some fine acting. She wondered what they'd offered her.

The rich hues of trust bleached into a stark monochrome of doubt.

She wasn't in the slightest bit surprised when her phone rang.

Jasper's irritating face.

"What?" she sighed into the phone.

"Ready for Versailles tomorrow? Just want to run a few things by you." She was silent a moment too long and Jasper wittered on. "The CreatedDiamonds shoot. Your girl came good. Well done, Thea darling. Last bloody minute though. Thank god for Lollie. She's had the whole thing organised for weeks, hanging on a hair trigger. Have you even looked at the schedule?"

Thea looked at Mem. Saw the light in her hair, the hush of her skin, and the lie in her eyes.

"You signed with CreatedDiamonds?" She ignored Jasper. She needed confirmation.

Mem swallowed a rapid mouthful of curry. "Sorry I didn't get a chance to tell you, but it got mental as soon as I agreed." She shrugged. "I took your advice. Decided I can take the money and put it to better use—"

Thea hung up on Jasper. She stared Mem out.

"How much?"

The girl's grin was a mile wide. "Oh my god, *so* much. Adiatu was amazing—"

"How. Much?"

"Thea?" Mem stretched an arm over the tabletop reaching for Thea's hand, but Thea snatched it away. "Is everything okay?"

"Answer me."

"Five million," Mem said. Puzzled. Her fingers stretched out for Thea's then curled into a loose fist when she couldn't reach them. Thea looked at it sadly.

Five million. Thea had to admire that. Adiatu *had* done well for her.

Yelena Titov delivered the second blow.

"CreatedDiamonds, hmm?" she said, watching Thea far too closely over the top of her champagne glass. "I saw all their glossy paperwork on the end of your kitchen bench. The bullshit those marketing people come up with. British company, my arse. The money behind that one is Russian. Vassily Kirov."

The room was closing in. No matter how she tried, she couldn't regain focus.

"I know that name," Thea murmured.

Lena snorted. "I should think you do. Friend of your father's, at least until he testified against him for a get out of jail free card of his very own. Ugly guy, right to his soul. Surprised you're working with him."

"I didn't know."

Dinner was curdling in her gut. Mem was looking at her with those beautiful eyes Thea had only just decided were the only genuine thing in her world. The monster inside Thea stretched and yawned like a cat and told her she'd made a mistake – another stupid, terrible mistake.

She snatched up her phone and spun away from the table, out to the conservatory where Mem and Lena couldn't hear her. She stabbed at Jasper's name.

"Vassily Kirov!" she spat, when he answered. It wasn't the main source of her pain, but it was somewhere to start. "CreatedDiamonds. You're backing a company built on my father's money? Built on—"

"He was never convicted, dearest. You should know that." Jasper was so infuriatingly breezy Thea wanted to hit him. "And besides, he's a British citizen now."

"That's hardly the fucking point." She spun on the spot, dragging her hand up through her hair. How could she not have known this? "Why didn't you tell me?"

Jasper reached the end of his patience. His voice hardened. "I handed you their prospectus myself. Weeks ago."

"And you knew I wouldn't read it. You total bastard."

"Wouldn't or couldn't, darling?" Jasper was smug. "If you'd actually cared, if you could have been bothered to look past your own ego for once in your life, the very least you could have done was get Lollie to give you a bloody summary."

Thea was in no mood to admit what was actually a fair point. She could kick herself for her stupidity. There she'd been – a love-drunk fool – thinking she was being noble by standing aside and letting Mem make up her own mind. She *hadn't* forced Mem. She hadn't influenced her at all. She'd had *convictions* for the time in her life – born in the warmth of those treacherous brown eyes – and, like an idiot idealist, it had felt right to stand up for them. Of course it had been too good to be true. She didn't know why she was surprised to find Mem had dived right in behind her when she wasn't looking.

Everyone had a price.

She could feel Mem and Lena and the wreckage of their cheerful meal at her back, and she wondered how much of it she could salvage. Not the damn curry, but that fragile happiness she thought she'd captured.

Jasper was on a roll.

"You can't keep drifting through life and letting ignorance excuse your moral laziness, Thea. At some point—"

She barely resisted slinging the phone through the glass of the conservatory.

Back at the table she tossed Mrs Tits out. She shook off the hand she laid on her arm.

"Try not to ruin this," the woman muttered in Russian as she went, tipping her head at Mem.

The resignation in her tone didn't help Thea's mood.

"Get out."

"Talk to her, you stubborn fool."

"Out!"

Mem watched them with those endless, wide eyes. They were so brimming with concern that Thea almost surrendered to them right then. She could drown in them, she supposed, summon the girl to her arms in the full knowledge that she'd slip into them and bend her body to Thea's touch with perfect compliance. And it would be arousing and addictive as always, warm and comforting, and maybe she could pretend that was all she needed. Maybe she could bury her face in the sanctuary of Mem's shoulder and close her eyes to everything else.

She'd lived a lie the rest of her life.

It was telling that it was Mem who made the next move. She rounded the table and stood before Thea with a worried half-smile. Found her hand. Tangled their fingers together.

It felt so good.

"Thea? What happened?"

She wanted to believe her muse was perfect.

She knew the odds of Mem actually being the pure, unspoiled goodness Thea craved all her life were laughably low. Thea Voronov was a monster. This was always going to be exactly what she deserved.

She let the girl tuck herself under her chin. Felt the divine press of her body against her own. Felt the moment Mem's natural deference nudged at her own ego until she pulled her closer and held her hard without thinking about it. They fitted together so perfectly.

That had to mean something, didn't it?

Mem started the sway. Thea could feel her soft hush of her smile against her neck, the girl's misguided confidence that the good side of Thea that she so trustingly sought was actually there. The sway turned into a gentle two-step and Thea let herself be led until they were locked in an exquisite slow dance, turning helplessly on the spot.

"Are you angry that I signed with CreatedDiamonds?" Mem whispered eventually.

Thea didn't stop their dance. She didn't want to answer.

"I thought you'd be happy. I thought you and Kate and Jasper all wanted me to do this."

A sneer twisted Thea's lips. She couldn't help herself. "Is that why you did it?"

Mem stiffened slightly in her arms. "I did it because five million pounds is an incredible amount of money.' *It was always the money.* "You know I don't care about my career, but there is a lot of good I can do with five million pounds."

Her breath was warm against Thea's neck. It almost hushed her monster back to sleep.

"For your *charity*?"

Mem pulled back. Peered a searching, pained look into Thea's eyes and quailed a little at what she saw there.

"Yeah," she said, evenly. "For my charity."

"How very virtuous of you."

The hurt in her face stung Thea too. They watched each other for a long moment.

"Thea?"

Thea pulled her back under her chin and resumed their dance. Her thoughts were a mess. She could feel old tendrils of self-loathing curling up from the depths to drag her under once more. She clung to Mem like a lifeline, wholly aware of the irony – that the one she'd thought would save her was the one who would finally drag her under. A two-faced, lying, grasping socialite just like all the others.

"Don't mind me," she murmured, bravely. "Some personal issues with Jasper have made me grumpy. Nothing to do with you. Forgive me for ruining our dinner."

The resistance in Mem's body proved she wasn't as convincing as she'd hoped, and they only had another minute together before Mem said the words that shattered things completely.

"Kate said a weird thing today," Mem whispered. She said it softly, stealthily, stringing the words out like a tripwire. "She made it sound as if she already knew you were going to talk me into doing the diamond thing. And the sequel. Like it was *you* who—"

Sprung. Her monster crowed in triumph.

Thea spun away. Strode back to the table and put it between them. Picked up her wine and sipped at it carelessly.

"Big day tomorrow, darling. You should go. Get your beauty sleep."

"Ouch."

"You'll need it if you want to look your five million pounds."

Mem made an awful sobbing noise. Thea turned her back.

"Thea, please tell me what's wrong."

Thea waved her glass, then slugged the whole thing back in one go. "I have work to do, my muse. An entire shoot to prepare for tomorrow. One that nobody bothered to tell me about. *You*"—her voice broke and she covered it with a cough—"didn't tell me. Lollie didn't tell me—"

Her muse appeared at her side with Thea's phone in her hand. She held it in front of her face. "I told you it was an insane day – and I can see the notifications from Lollie on your phone. Look at them, Thea. *You* haven't opened them. Don't get cross at me just because you didn't—"

"I don't read text messages," Thea spat. "Lollie knows that. I can't r—" She stopped herself at the last second. "I can't be bothered with—"

"You're being silly, Thea."

"Silly?" Thea felt the ice freeze in her blood. Felt it lift her chin and twist her lips into a smirk. It was as familiar as it was cold. "My muse is being far too bold. She needs to drop the attitude if she thinks she can get away with that."

Doubt and confusion flickered across Mem's face for moment. Thea could see her deciding whether this was a game, whether some of that beautiful submission might thaw Thea's ice – and she saw the moment when Mem straightened her shoulders and decided to call Thea's shit out for what it was. Thea was glad. It made what came next so much easier.

"No, actually, get out," Thea said. "I have work to do."

"Thea—"

"Go!"

Mem stood there, as stubborn and stupid as she was, and so it was Thea who swirled away, out the back door to her studio, slamming the door as she went.

But not before she caught a glimpse of Mem's face. Those endlessly deep brown eyes and all that beautiful fucking care within them. Those lips, crushed between her teeth. That gorgeous, gorgeous skin.

Fuck.

She should have known.

Chapter Twenty Six

Thea barely hung on to her fear all day.

She put on her usual defences – tight black leather pants and a red silk shirt. Her smirk for those she cared about. A sneer for everyone else. Her saving grace was that everyone in the group was so excited by the shoot – in the Hall of Mirrors, for fuck's sake – that they were completely fooled by it.

Almost everyone. Her darling muse was more observant than even Kate and Jasper. How had that happened?

"Are you okay, Thea?" Mem squeezed her hand.

"Of course I am, darling. Why wouldn't I be?"

A tiny frown creased Mem's perfect forehead and Thea wanted to kiss it gently away, with her softest kiss – but they were on display, lounging on the cream leather sofa in Jasper's private jet, and a more impressive show was required. She gripped Mem's chin and kissed her mouth instead. Hard and greedy, just like the Thea of old and not caring who watched. It burned through her blood like it always did – nearly erupted when she watched Mem's eyelids flutter as she pulled away. The lost, drunk look on her muse's face fired her up like it did every time.

It wasn't quite enough to squash down her fear and doubt.

Thea was acting right now.

Was Mem?

Lollie had done an exemplary job of organising the day, not that Thea would ever thank her for it. She bustled everyone aboard Jasper's plane with her screen in her hand and politely presented Thea with a contract the diamond company, Adiatu and Jasper wanted her to sign. Thea took no pleasure in learning her talents were worth considerably more than Mem's. Kate stood behind her with her hand on Thea's shoulder and pointed to the dotted line with girlish happiness. Jasper grinned in triumph and Adiatu's eyes flashed with dollar signs.

What choice did she have? Thea signed the damned thing and pretended she didn't care.

She flopped moodily down on the couch again next to Mem and realised she was crushing the girl's excitement.

"First private jet, darling?" she asked, smooth and smug and owning her role. "I'm sure it won't be your last." She linked her fingers in Mem's and struck as indolent a pose as she could manage.

Mem smiled with relief.

"Of course it won't be," Kate called. "There's no way we're flying commercial to LA next week. Jasper? Are you going to cough up for your two favourite stars, or am I going to have to rent a PJ myself?"

Thea couldn't be bothered waiting for Mem's answer and simply kissed her again – hungrier this time. She should take what she could before this came to its inevitable end. Mem tipped her head back obediently and allowed herself to be kissed.

"You're not going to do that the whole way there, are you?" Jasper grumbled, very put out to discover the lounges were both taken and he had to sit in a single seat. "It's my bloody jet," he whined, but no one paid him any attention.

In the Palace of Versailles, Lollie contrived to throw the general public out of the Hall of Mirrors for the day. An entire studio had been set up in the space, everything just the way Thea liked it. Tash Kirov-White from CreatedDiamonds arrived with cases of the most spectacular jewellery the place had seen since Madame de Pompadour, and a rack of astonishing gowns awaited the two beautiful models.

Thea strode into the middle of the space and surveyed it with her hands on her hips and a shrewd look of artistic calculation on her face. If she had to do this...

She clapped her hands.

"Let's get to work!"

She swatted Kate on the backside as she headed past her to get changed. What the hell, she slapped Mem's arse too. To her irritation, both women laughed.

She fell into the work.

It wasn't hard – hell, it wasn't even necessary. CreatedDiamonds had already approved the images she'd taken of both Kate and Mem – the ones she'd given to Jasper over a week ago. The ones she hadn't yet told Mem about, and probably wouldn't now her muse had shown her true colours. They were already printed larger than life, waiting to grace the red carpet at the Royal Albert Hall tomorrow night. *These* images wouldn't hit their campaign for a few weeks yet, but when they did… Thea already knew they were going to be sublime.

Kate was always iconic – every move she made was at the service of Thea's lens. Thea had trained the woman well. But it was Mem who truly startled Thea now.

She put on a stunning show.

Thea wondered what drove it. Was it Mem's natural beauty and talent, or the time she'd spent as Thea's muse? Had Kate's mentorship and Mem's determination honed her skills? Was it the excitement of being in Versailles, amid history and luxury with the promise of fame, or was it the rush and thrill of what they were doing? Perhaps the girl was simply having fun, and it was only Thea who was the grump.

Perhaps it was five million pounds that made her eyes glitter like that.

Whatever it was, it rendered Thea almost unnecessary. She gazed down the lens at Memona Swan, at the confidence, elegance and sophistication that shone from the very heart of her, and realised the muse had surpassed the artist.

All Thea had to do was point the camera at her.

She was beautiful.

During a short lunch break, she had Kate follow her to one end of the long, glassy hall and made her read the contract aloud to her. She watched Mem and Lollie laughing together as she did.

"Five years?" she muttered.

"It's not so bad," Kate told her. She looked so young and alive, Thea knew she'd never let her down. She'd still complain at every opportunity, though. It was an old dynamic, worn and tired after the new thing she'd thought she'd had with Mem. But familiar.

"I hate you," she sighed. "And Jasper."

Kate put a hand on her knee. "No you don't. Stop being dramatic. All that shit with your father was years ago, darling. Don't think about it."

Mem sauntered the length of the hall toward her in a sheer, golden gown, poise and courage in the swing of her hips, and Thea had never seen anyone so perfect. When Mem held down a hand to raise her to her feet and pull her back to work, the spark in Thea's cunt that always burned when they touched flared as fiercely as ever. Thea gripped her camera as they worked and couldn't make the composition balance. She'd thought Mem was that rare, beautiful, authentic soul who valued integrity over commercialisation. Now, Thea was terrified it was just an illusion, a trick of the light.

A performance.

Her muse had sold out.

Thea felt the door of the dark room inside her soul slam shut. Her own cynicism developed the image with chemicals of betrayal and Memona Swan was cast in stark contrasts of shadow and greed.

She still managed to turn out some of her best work.

"Oh, Thea," Kate breathed, when she saw herself in the images Thea threw to the main monitors as proofs. "You bloody genius. Thank you."

Thea felt cruel. "Did the best I could with what I had to work with," she said, flashing an utterly sublime image of Mem to the screen, but everyone seemed to think she was being funny.

The diamond executive nearly cried with gratitude. Mem watched her from the corner of her eye, and Jasper shook everyone's hands magnanimously, as if the hard work had all been his.

Lollie's ruthless schedule packed the whole circus back into flight cases, and they flew home.

Naturally, her clever muse saw right through her shit.

"Would you like to tell me what's wrong now?" Mem asked, softly.

They were home and Mem poured her a glass of something red and pressed it into her hands with a tentative smile. Mem heated the remains of last night's dinner, left over after Thea's tantrum, and they ate it at the kitchen counter then trailed through to the lounge room. Thea's shoulders ached, and she wanted to order Mem – damn it, she wanted to *ask* Mem – for another of those wonderful shoulder massages but she was no longer sure they were freely given. Everything was transactional once again. Her bones were sore, but they didn't ache as much as her heart.

"Nothing's wrong." Thea was a liar. She knew how to make it convincing though. "You were extraordinary today." A compliment, a dash of arrogance. Piece of cake. "No sign at all of the timid thing who first crept into my studio. You've come so far. I'm proud of you."

She was. Which only made this whole thing more unfortunate.

Mem eyed her suspiciously. She was knees up on the couch, hesitant about leaning into Thea's body, and Thea tried not to read too much into that.

"And yet you've been grumpy all day."

Thea let her wine glass dangle from her fingers with as much indolent laziness as she could muster. "I'm an artist, darling. I'm supposed to be prickly and mercurial."

Mem gave a soft snort.

Thea's fuse burnt down. "Is that attitude, my muse?"

That beautifully wicked lopsided smile nearly dragged Thea in and doused her fire. The twinkle in Mem's eyes almost set her fizzing and sparking again. The girl was hot and eager, and Thea would have plunged into her – a dark, depthless pool of desire or boiling sea of lava, Thea no longer cared – if only she could be sure this was real.

"And if it is?" Mem simpered. "Will you take me upstairs and spank it out of me?"

She shifted closer, her knees against Thea's thigh, her fingers reaching out to the buttons of Thea's shirt. Playful. So, *so* beautiful.

Thea flicked her hands away.

Mem thought it was part of the game.

"Oh, today was wonderful, Thea! Amazing. Incredible." Mem's eyes were like diamonds. "*You* were amazing. You were so fucking hot, striding around a palace like an actual emperor, I spent the whole day soaked for you. I need you so badly right now." She jiggled on the couch, squeezing her thighs together in obvious desperation. It was cute. "And my premiere is tomorrow. *Tomorrow!* Ugh! Can we celebrate? Can you take me upstairs and celebrate the fuck out of me? Please, Thea? I need you."

It was so tempting. It took a long, hard breath to calm her own desire.

Her cunning, clever muse tried a different approach.

"Or if you're still such a grumpy pants—"

Fuck, that adorable pout.

"—why don't we play something hard tonight? You can take that mood out on me. I want you to, Thea. *Please?*"

The bratty whine almost had her undone.

"What are you suggesting?"

"You know… Maybe we could…" The girl bit her lip. Thea watched it, plump around her teeth, and wanted to bite it too, wanted to taste its sweetness. She wanted to bury her face in her and consume her entirely.

But she quirked an eyebrow and sipped her wine like she didn't care. Watched Mem shiver as she did.

"You'll need to use your words, sweetheart."

And her wonderful muse did. She asked for exactly the kind of dominance that Thea was no longer sure she had the heart for. She wanted her heavy hands, her belt, she wanted a crop or a cane and her hands tied above the bed – hell, Mem wanted all the things that would have driven Thea insane at any other time, and Thea was a burning, pulsing mess at the thought.

She could push this girl to her knees right here, buckle her belt around her throat and make her crawl to the bedroom – and Mem would do it. She could tie her arms behind her back, cross the rope over her breasts until they bulged and swelled, and then she could bite them like the lushest fruit – and Mem would groan with need. She could whip her gorgeous arse, kiss the burning lines she'd left there, spank them again – and Mem would beg her for more. She could drag every orgasm from her, slowly, fiercely and demanding until Mem's throat was hoarse with crying and Thea's cunt was aching for her tongue – and Mem would be so *with* her, so present and loving and perfect.

And Thea would be a mess.

The wine was bitter in her mouth, but what wasn't? The girl's movie premiere would expose everything. Tomorrow, Mem would stride the red carpet toward the fame she'd obviously been angling for all this time, using Thea on her way – and at its zenith she would learn how transactional Thea had been in return. It was far too late to pull those images now. The machine was set to devour. The monster would have its prey. Five million pounds would never be enough to make up for it.

And it would be plain to the world. After all, Thea Voronov had a reputation. She used women and exploited their beauty for wealth. Smile for the paparazzi, darling. Mem would hate her.

And that would be fair.

But Mem was still looking at her with those eyes that saw through to Thea's soul and cradled it so softly, and the tiniest, most hopeless part of Thea still wanted to care.

"A thousand cameras and a billion eyes will be on you tomorrow, my darling muse," she said, helplessly. "I have to be gentle with you. I can't leave any marks."

Mem's pout collapsed her mind.

She stood and pulled Mem to her feet, a smile just managing to surface as Mem frowned at her in confusion. An arm low around her back pulled Mem closer, and Thea leaned against her as if she could absorb these last moments of sweetness and innocence through the length of her body. For a moment, they swayed together, warm and gentle – everything Thea wanted – and then she felt impatience ripple through Mem's body once more.

So she kissed her, one hand fisted in the hair at the nape of her neck, the other slipping under her shirt and squeezing her breast hard. Mem's mouth opened automatically, welcoming, feeling like home, and Thea pushed into her, swallowing her whimper.

"I have a better idea," she murmured. She tangled their fingers and led Mem upstairs.

"Watch."

A full height mirror in Thea's room leaned back against the wall. It was a free-standing thing, a metre wide, two metres tall, with a massive gold frame, all carved wood and filigree. She stood Mem in front of it and shucked off her own jacket tossing it over a chair, rolling her sleeves. Mem's eyes followed her hands.

"The mirror, my darling. Not me."

The mood had changed considerably. Mem had finally picked up on the darkness at the edge of Thea's soul and exchanged the brattishness for obedience. They both liked it that way, though Thea noticed she was still cheeky – she watched Thea in the mirror.

"I want you to see what I see." Thea stepped in close behind Mem and placed her hands on her hips. "What everyone will see tomorrow when you walk the red carpet and shine in front of the whole world."

Mem giggled. "If what I'm hoping is about to happen is really about to happen, I don't think I want the whole world seeing that."

Thea slapped her thigh and bit her ear at the same time and felt her heart rate pick up at the way Mem twitched against her. "Cheeky," she whispered. Mem hummed. "Safeword?"

"Milf."

That earned her another slap but Thea secretly adored her sass.

"Helmut Newton."

This time Thea chuckled. A photographer known for his erotically charged, striking black and white images of the female form. Her muse had been doing her homework. She tugged Mem's t-shirt over her head and trailed her fingers down her sides while her arms were in the air. She undid her bra and slipped it off her shoulders, spilling her breasts from the lace, cupping them again with both hands.

"Watch," she said again, her lips at Mem's ear, her nose deep in her hair, drowning in her fragrance. "Watch what I do to your body."

She stripped the rest of her clothes from her slowly. Usually, she tore at Mem in a frenzy, mouths locked together, hands groping and grabbing – or she made Mem strip for her, conducting the show with quiet instructions, deliberately dragging each moment out if her muse showed any signs of impatience. But right now, she wanted to stretch their time together out forever. Make it last. Savour it. Sear the girl's perfection into her memory. She undressed Mem like she was a goddess until she was naked before them both in the mirror, leaning back against Thea still in her leather pants and shirt.

Thea watched her own hands over Mem's shoulder. One tickling and teasing a nipple, the other slipping down between her legs, straight into the wet heat she already knew was there for her. She pinched a clit that was already hard.

Mem's head thudded back onto Thea's shoulder. She held her breath.

"Don't stop breathing."

Mem's own chuckle was ragged. "Tricky when you're doing that."

Thea swirled lazily circles around her clit as if she had all the time in the world – and she wished she did. Mem's hips bucked and her knees trembled, and Thea dug her fingernails into Mem's breast, just hard enough to make the girl's entire body jolt against her. She huffed a sad little sigh.

"Oh, Memona. I'm just getting started."

The shiver that rippled through Mem's body nearly sent them both to their knees, but Thea held her up, one hand in her cunt, the other at her breast. Mem squeezed her eyes shut and whimpered.

"*Watch.*" She swirled harder with the fingers. "If you don't do as you're told, my sweet, I'll stop."

Desperate eyes locked onto hers in the mirror and a gush of liquid flooded Thea's fingers. The girl was panting, closer than Thea had expected, and she decided to take pity.

Just a little.

She walked them backwards until she was sitting on the bed, her thighs wide with Mem perched on the edge between them.

"Put your legs over mine," she ordered, and Mem's scurry to obey swelled the hole in Thea's chest. The pose opened Mem to the mirror, to the perfect view for both of them, and Thea couldn't take her eyes off her. Memona Swan was magnificent, utterly divine and everything Thea had ever wanted.

And she was urging Thea on, clenching her thighs, lifting her hips to push herself against Thea's fingers. All of it filled Thea's mind, drugged her, set her reeling.

"Please, Thea. *Please.*"

So she plunged into Mem like she wanted to drown – two fingers, three when Mem heaved back against her with a grunt – and the rhythm she set was merciless. Everything about Mem threatened to tear her apart.

The heat of her, the clench around her fingers, the sobbing, urgent need as she willed Thea on.

"Deeper, Thea. Harder— H— harder. Oh god, Thea, *harder, please.*"

The way she leant back against her with complete trust, the way her eyes met Thea's in the mirror, matched her darkness and didn't recoil. The way one hand flailed out, found Thea's thigh and gripped it hard, the warmth of her palm collapsing Thea's brain even as she ploughed deeper and deeper into the girl between her legs. The way she tipped her head back, exposing that glorious throat – and the lost, degenerate moan she made when Thea wrapped her other hand around it.

"Touch yourself," she ordered, astonished at how cool she sounded.

Mem sobbed with gratitude and obeyed instantly, her fingers working at the same speed as Thea's, her peak rushing toward them both like a hurricane, a constant noise buzzing in Thea's ears like a plea, one that she didn't even realise was her own.

"*Watch!*" she cried, and Mem snapped her eyes back open. She lasted only a second before the sight sent her over the edge, goosebumps rippling over her whole body, her core clutching at Thea's fingers, her spine drilling back against Thea's – and suddenly Thea couldn't hold her up, couldn't hold both of them together.

She slipped sideways, tipping Mem down onto the bed and looming over her, still driving her hard, barely noticing when Mem's thighs wrapped around her hips and pulled her in. She locked her lips to Mem's throat and sucked at her pulse, drinking the ecstacy from that perfect place beneath her chin, calming her panting breath as she settled softly down.

She nearly crumbled then. Nearly toppled down onto the woman beneath her. Nearly rested her cheek on her heaving chest and found peace in her heartbeat.

Nearly.

"I love you," the girl whispered.

Thea's sigh was pure despair. Of course she did.

She pulled her fingers out of Mem and wiped them on the bedcovers. Slapped Mem's thigh to let her go.

"Thea? I love you."

A stellar performance. Almost convincing.

"You should go," Thea said. It killed her to see the confusion in Mem's eyes. "You have such an important day tomorrow. Your London premiere. The biggest Hollywood film of the year. You need to rest."

Mem laughed weakly. "After that there's not much else I can do."

Thea's lips twisted. "Go and spend time with your family. With your friends. Everything changes tomorrow." She stood up and found her blazer.

"Thea?"

"Go spend tonight with people you care about."

"What?! What does that mean? I care about you, Thea. Didn't you just hear me? I love you."

Thea turned her back. She had no idea anymore if that was actually true. Her muse had become such a fine actor, such a poised model. She was about to dazzle before the whole world – a true successor to Dame Katherine Cox's iconic status. And everything *was* about to change. Mem was about to see Thea for what she truly was. There was no point holding on anymore.

"Just go," Thea said. "I'll see you on the red carpet tomorrow night."

"Wait—"

But Thea strode away, out to her studio, to lose herself in images and art and the bitterness of her own stupidity.

Chapter Twenty Seven

There were some things a girl had to do alone.

As it turned out, arriving on the red carpet at the premiere of your own movie was one of them.

Mem stepped out of the sleek black limousine into a cacophony of noise. Photographers buzzed behind the rope line like a swarm of angry meat flies, the shining eyes of their lenses all pointed at Mem. They bayed for her blood, but Mem could do this now. As Kate had told her, red carpets were a performance just like any other. Mem squared her shoulders, sucked in her stomach, and gave them an eighty-percent smile.

It was all they needed.

She was proud of herself for knowing that now.

It had been a lonely morning, despite being surrounded by people all day. A hundred well-wishes popped up on her phone – friends, family, people she was beginning to recognise as 'networkers' – but nothing from Thea. Piper gave her a hug and a curious look when she explained she'd just needed some downtime at home last night to get her head in the right space for the premiere.

"Are you and Thea okay?"

Her tone was odd. If Mem had to guess at it, Piper sounded guilty, and that made no sense.

"Of course we are," she said, though she wasn't sure about that.

She had no idea what had happened last night.

There'd been stylists, hairdressers and she'd literally been sewn into her dress. Catching up with Benny for make-up had been a bright point and she was consoled by the thought of Kate going through the same rigmarole. They met up at Claridge's hotel – laughed together at how ludicrously OTT the whole thing was – and ate a minuscule meal that wouldn't disrupt the lines of either of their gowns. Then they were bundled into separate cars for their grand arrivals at the Royal Albert Hall.

She missed Thea, but this first part of the event was just for the stars. They had almost an hour of staged photos with the director, producers and their co-stars to get through, standing on a field of red carpet in a twilight held at bay by massive lights. The whole scene was dwarfed by enormous prints of the stunning images Thea Voronov had taken that first day in her studio. Mem's feet were already beginning to ache when the entire noisy circus was moved to line the long walk up the stairs and terraces to the doors of the grand hall.

Then evening fell, the other guests arrived, and the mingling and the step-and-repeats began.

Royalty strolled by and Mem wondered how on earth this had become her life.

Jasper sauntered in the king's wake, utterly unfazed. He had Tash Kirov-White and another CreatedDiamonds exec with him, both eager to be snapped with the star. There were air-kisses and smiles and promises of more pics further up the carpet in front of the CreatedDiamonds branding material, and Mem did her best work looking keen and interested.

"Where the fuck is Thea?" Jasper muttered in her ear, his smile never leaving his face.

A roar went up when Dame Katherine Cox kissed her girlfriend in front of the world's cameras. Mem craned her head to look at them and smiled at their obvious happiness. A slightly goofy, lovesick grin looked adorable on Kate's lips and Anwen's wide-eyed panic at being in the spotlight was calmed by Kate's fingers twisted in hers.

When she looked past them, there was Thea.

The sight of her made every cell in Mem's body ignite.

She'd straightened her hair again – a subtle fuck-you to the effort everyone else had put in – and her eyes were rimmed in black. The look was 1970s rock goddess – a tight silver metallic suit with nothing under the jacket but a tangle of chains between her breasts. Her pants were low on her hips and flared at her four inch heels. Oversized silver rings on all her fingers made her hands lazy and heavy.

The woman swaggered up the red carpet like she owned it – infinitely proud, gloriously entitled. She totally ignored calls from photographers and directions from the attendants. She threw a shameless wink at Kate as she passed. Laughed when Kate rolled her eyes.

But something simmered in her, in every angular line of her body – something taut and sharp and glittering, and something Mem suspected no one would recognise except those who knew her best. She had the sudden feeling things were about to go very, very wrong.

When Thea saw Mem, the whole act faltered. Just for a second, but it stuttered and glitched in a horrible mess. Thea gaped, staring at Mem like she was the iceberg and Thea was helplessly sunk. A flash in her eyes, a stricken terror on her face that twisted with loathing – and instantly she was blithe again, one hand in her pocket and a vicious, gorgeous smirk just for Mem. It made Mem throb for her even if she still wasn't sure what was going on.

And then Thea was on her.

"Sorry I'm late, darling." She didn't sound it. She sounded smug – far too smooth. She stepped right into Mem's space and leered down at her. "You look ravishing. Is your frock made entirely of diamonds?" Her sneer was both beautiful and heartbreaking. She put a possessive, grasping paw on Mem's hip and pulled her closer.

A million cameras flashed.

Mem's gown *was* made almost completely from diamonds – created diamonds. They'd been sewn into a dress designed by Armani. Long ropes of them gathered at her throat and cascaded over her breasts, skin coloured pasties her only modesty. They wove into a skirt that hugged her hips and thighs, then flared in a glittering train that swept the ground. It weighed a tonne, though Mem liked the heaviness of it on her body, much like the weight of Thea's hands, and until just a moment ago she had felt strong and powerful in it.

Now, with a dash of disdain and a curl of her lip, Thea made her feel like a walking billboard.

Which she was, she supposed. She should have thought about it more. She shouldn't have just done as she was told.

"Shall we give them something to earn their money?" Thea drawled, tilting her head at the photographers. She didn't give Mem time to answer before she slipped those heavy fingers around the nape of Mem's neck and kissed her hard.

"You're on the wrong side of the rope, Voronov," one of the photographers called.

Thea pulled away and left Mem panting like she didn't care. She knew him.

"Fuck you, Henry."

She stuck her middle finger up and a blizzard of flashes flared again.

What was wrong with her?

Mem wished they were anywhere but here. She wanted to hug her close until Thea felt safe enough to tell her what was wrong. She longed for the quiet of those perfect moments, when they had both exhausted each other, and Thea was pressed against her, her strength and her power both draining Mem dry and lifting her high. She wanted to wrap her arms around her and let Thea snuffle into her neck in that way she did when she was too proud to admit she needed to. She wanted Thea to conquer her. She wanted Thea to whisper how it was Mem who made her surrender.

She wished they simply had *time* to talk.

Thea swayed with so much nonchalance she almost toppled over.

"Are you drunk?" Mem whispered.

Thea pinched her hip. "Does it matter? Let's get this over with, shall we?"

And she draped Mem's hand over her arm and led her closer to the entrance. Mem fought to keep the smile on her face. Her eighty percent slipped to sixty.

"Get it over with?" she muttered through gritted teeth. "Even you said this was important yesterday. You said it was my big day. Fuck it, Thea, this *is* my big moment. Why are you being so—"

"Something you need to see, my darling muse. It will change everything." Thea wasn't looking at her. She was weaving between other celebrities stopped for photos and her chin was high, gazing at the signage that lined the paparazzi parade. Finally she stopped near yet another enormous image of Mem – this one right next to the CreatedDiamonds logo. An image of Kate in diamonds was next to it. She put her hands on Mem's shoulders and angled her so she could get a good look at it, that awful sneer still twisting her lips.

Mem was vaguely aware of Jasper and Kate urgently making their way closer too.

"What do you think, darling?"

Mem couldn't think. The image was beautiful. Black and white. A close up of Mem's face with a diamond necklace at her throat.

"This isn't right," she managed. She was painfully aware of every eye on her. "This isn't one of the pictures we took in Versailles. This isn't—"

Thea's laugh was cutting. "Of course it isn't. Did you really think we could bash up an entire campaign after just a few happy snaps yesterday?"

"But this is—"

"This is five million pounds, my muse. Worth it, do you think?"

Thea looked smug, then disgusted – like she was gagging, hating everyone and everything there to the depths of her soul – then completely blasé again. She spun Mem by the shoulders, bringing her face to face with the line of cameras. She even held up her hand, presenting her to the crowd in an awful charade that twisted something painful in Mem's chest.

Because it wasn't an image from Versailles. It was the one they had developed together from film in Thea's darkroom – Thea with her arms around Mem's waist, guiding her hands, whispering and sighing and laughing her love in her ear. It was the one that had proved Thea really saw her, and really loved her, because it was all captured there in the image. And it was the one that had made Mem love Thea too, because to be looked at like *that* could only mean one thing.

And here it was as *advertising*.

Her smile dropped through fifty to thirty percent. She knew her lower lip trembled.

"I can't believe you did this," she hissed.

Thea ignored her. She called out to some photographer – jokingly, colleagues and vultures together. "Did you get her good side, Anton?"

"She's way too good for you, Voronov."

"You didn't even ask me," Mem said. "I thought this was ours. I thought it was private and— *special*, Thea."

"You gave this to me."

Thirty slipped harder. "I don't think I did. I might be pretty, Thea, but I'm not property. I'm not your property. You can't just—"

Thea rounded on her in a flash. Her voice was low and hard. Her eyes cut slashes through Mem's heart. "You gave this to me, my muse. You gave me your body and your beauty and I took these pictures."

"Exactly! You *took* them."

"As I remember it, you were very willing."

It took everything she had not to snatch her hand out of Thea's. "That doesn't make any difference. You used me."

"As you have used me."

"What?"

But Thea lost her patience with the whole thing just as Jasper and Kate closed in on them. "Want to catch something priceless, lads?" she called.

"Don't—" started Kate, but she was too late.

Thea put her lips to Mem's ear and whispered while Mem felt her smile crash to zero.

"They paid me to seduce you, you pretty thing. Convince you to sign on as brand ambassador for CreatedDiamonds and order you to do the sequel. Just my luck you like to do as you're told. You made the job too easy."

And she thrust her hands into her pockets and strode away without a backward glance.

A million flashes burnt Mem's skin and blistered the tears from her eyes. Her heart was screaming but she was glittering. She was a star, the most beautiful woman on the catwalk, living the kind of fairytale innumerable girls dreamed of – and she hated every second of it.

Kate took one look at her face and swore. "I'm going to fucking kill her."

Apparently, Mem wasn't quite pulling it off. She put her chin up, sniffed, and with as much dignity as she could muster, stumbled blindly along the rest of the runway, into the shelter of the Royal Albert Hall.

She didn't remember the movie but *The Wolverton Diamond* was a resounding success.

There was a standing ovation, more photos next to Kate and the director in front of a rich, red velvet curtain, then she was stumbling through back corridors, crashing into flight cases, half-blinded by tears.

The worst part was that she still caught herself craving Thea's touch. She still wanted her arms around her. She still longed for the comfort they'd found together over the last few weeks.

The stupid corridors in a round building simply led her back out to the red carpet, where she stumbled to a halt again at the sight of Thea chatting with Jasper, a young, pretty blond woman already on her arm. Mem was so miserable she found Adiatu right then and there and told her to announce that she'd do the sequel. Kate held her up while the cameras stole away her soul again, and Thea's eyes turned blacker.

It turned out that leaving the premiere of your own movie was something a girl had to do on her own too.

Part Three

Chapter Twenty Eight

Somehow she got away from the circus.

She called Piper from Claridge's hotel as soon as the security guards disappeared with her diamond dress.

"There are paps outside the hotel," she cried.

"They're here too. At our house! Some prick just hammered on the door and scared the shit out of me. It's nearly midnight. Wanted to know if I was expecting you home."

"Fuck. Fuck, fuck, *fuck*, Piper. What do I do?'

"I'm already on my way. Stay where you are, babes. Just make sure your posh hotel will let me in."

Piper showed up twenty minutes later with a bag of shapeless clothes and an enormous hug. Mem simply fell into her and cried.

"Oh god, Mem, you poor baby. It's all over the socials already. Don't look. Please don't look. What an absolute arse of a thing to do to you. What did she say?"

"She said— She said—"

Mem's brain stalled every time she got close to the words Thea dripped in her ear. She could still feel her breath on her skin, the brilliance of a thousand lights beating down on her eyelashes. She could still taste the contempt in Thea's tone, the way it froze her blood and hollowed out her chest. The awful, ugly sneer that distorted Thea's face as if she was in pain still gouged at her soul.

The dagger had stuck in both their ribs, though Thea had torn hers out almost immediately and tossed it to the floor, while Mem's was still wedged in her heart.

"This is all my fault," Piper murmured into Mem's hair as she let her cry into her shoulder. "I should have told you—"

"You did tell me," Mem hiccuped. "I knew all about her reputation. I just didn't listen. I just thought— I just thought she lov—" A fresh wave of tears stole those words away too and she let Piper hold her while she sobbed like a child.

Thea *did* love her. She knew that. As much as all that posturing and posing on the red carpet had tried to hide it, Thea had hurt herself as much as she'd hurt Mem tonight. She was just infinitely more stubborn, with a well-established background of monstrous, ugly behaviour to fall back on.

It was only Mem who looked like the innocent fool.

She eventually became aware that she was dribbling and snotting into her best friend's neck.

"Sorry," she sniffed, pulling back. "Let's get out of here."

She changed into the hoodie and sweatpants Piper had brought for her and they escaped through the back alley behind the hotel, Mem doing her best not to think of the times Thea had taught her to avoid the paparazzi like that.

They went to Heart and Grace House – it was a shelter, after all – and Piper ordered her to crash on the sofa in the office while she took the couch in the common room.

But Mem couldn't sleep. She watched the sun rise and made some decisions. When Piper found her the next morning, she was already on the phone.

"Because you're my sister, because you've had three months to get your shit together and because it's the right thing to do," she snapped, giving Indira the serve she should have given her ages ago.

Piper put a mug of coffee in front of her and sat down to watch with raised eyebrows. The legal matters for Heart and Grace had been dragging for far too long.

"My manager will be in contact with your office later today and I expect the matter to be wrapped up by the end of the week— I'll be in LA. No, Indira, you'll be doing it gratis, thank you very much. Me being able to afford it has nothing to do with it. Your firm will be helping women in need. And no, I don't want to talk about it." She paused for a moment. "Love to my nieces." She hung up.

"Wow," said Piper.

"You'll see that our manager chases that up?"

"Sure, but—"

Mem's phone rang in her hand.

"Thanks for returning my call, Adiatu. Yes, yes, I have the schedule. I'll be ready. But I've emailed you a list of things I want added to my rider. Shall we go through it now? Benny, to do my makeup for every appearance— Just hire him Adiatu and get him on a plane. Every promotional image of me – and I mean *every* image – needs my approval before publication. Non-negotiable, I'm afraid, and you're lucky I don't fire your arse for that stunt you pulled last night—"

Adiatu was surprisingly meek. She should have stood up for herself like this from the beginning. She wasn't sure why she hadn't. Pretty didn't mean timid.

She watched Piper staring while she went through the rest of her demands, her best friend's eyebrows climbing higher up her forehead, her mouth hanging open.

"Hardly know you, babes," she said, approvingly, when Mem finally let Adiatu go. "Insisting every journalist asks you about Heart and Grace House was a nice touch, though."

"If I'm doing this, I'm going to make it worth it," Mem said.

"Look at you, all hard of heart and business-focused. Brand new day, hey?"

It *did* feel strong, but Piper was only mostly right about Mem's heart. It was hard. It was as hard as diamond – but it was shattered in a million glittering pieces, still scattered on that red carpet.

A black car picked her up a few hours later to take her to the airport and on to the two week media tour of premieres and appearances around the world.

Kate was inside.

"Oh, darling girl," she murmured, her arms wide. "You're a bloody trouper."

Mem sobbed all the way to the airport.

Chapter Twenty Nine

Needless to say, she wasn't travelling to Los Angeles and onwards with Mem.

What a misty-eyed fantasy that had been.

She worked. A few formulaic shoots for Jasper in his absence. Failed to find beauty in any of them.

She watched Mem on the Hollywood red carpet, though. All vivid and bright on the socials and so, so beautiful. Hung on her every word as the special guest on late night talk shows, vibrant and elegant like a goddess. She was just about to curse her out in vodka-slurred Russian as the consummate actress when she looked again.

Those weren't Mem's real smiles. Not the ones she'd gifted Thea when love shone from her eyes. They weren't her real laughs, when they'd bumped their foreheads together and giggled til their sides ached.

Mem wasn't happy.

She called Jasper up. Dragged him from some LA celebrity party.

"How could you have bullied her into doing the sequel, you arsehole?" she railed. "You knew she didn't want to—"

Jasper hung up on her.

Lollie was beside her, hanging back after work when she should have left hours ago. Some bullshit about spreadsheets but Thea got the feeling she was watching to make sure she didn't drink herself to death. Lollie could fuck that.

"Mem signed up for the sequel of her own accord, Thea," she said, evenly. "Maybe because she wanted to get out of London. Maybe because she wanted to get away from you after you were so awful to her at the premiere."

The talk show host was asking after Mem's charity.

Thea flicked it off and flung the remote across the studio.

"Wuh—?" squawked Lollie.

"Her *charity*," Thea growled. "I won't waste my time listening to her bollock on about saving fucking polar bears with her money, like *that* was the reason she used me—"

"Polar bears? What? She's opened a women's shelter, you idiot. A refuge. For victims of domestic violence and— Christ, Thea, I would have thought you, of all people— Did you even talk to her?"

The air turned heavy.

A women's shelter? A refuge? That's what Mem's charity was? *How had she not known that?*

But there was something else she wasn't inclined to tolerate.

"Me '*of all people*', Lollie?" she asked, dangerously.

Jasper's ugly mug flashed on her phone. Lollie was lucky.

"No, damnit," he barked. "While I'm pissed at you, what the fuck is this shit you sent me yesterday, Voronov? I sent you the youngest, prettiest thing on my books and this is what you give me? A five year old could do better with a fucking iPhone. Get your head together."

She hated herself.

She went out – baggy jeans and a hoodie pulled low over her face. She took a camera and told herself she was working, catching up with the homeless around central south London. These were her people – the ones she'd slept rough with all those years ago, and for so long too. All her old haunts. Under the bridge at Waterloo. Right up against the pollies at Westminster. The skatepark in the Southbank undercroft, even if it felt a bit touristy these days.

She stayed away from Covent Garden, though. Seven Dials. She wasn't that stupid.

A woman with a collection of putrid blankets and some milk crates gave her a smile some time close to midnight. She was set up under the railway between Southwark cathedral and Jasper's gleaming bloody Shard building and it made sense for two women to share the corner for the night. Thea gave her her camera. Told her what it was worth too. A mirrorless Hasselblad. She should have been able to get twenty thousand pounds for it.

The woman told her she was stupid.

A message from Mem appeared on Thea's phone and she nearly gave that away too.

Then she remembered what else was on it, and she took it to the Millenium Bridge and dangled it above the Thames.

She could see the Tate Modern from there, where her exhibition was still running.

She could see the rooftop where she'd kissed Mem's mouth and the heaven between her legs and known peace for the first time in forever.

She'd been so, so wrong, but it was too late now.

Her phone buzzed again and slipped from her fingers into the muddy water.

This, she believed, was exactly what she deserved.

Lollie found her five evenings later in Southwark near Borough Markets. She was in a car Thea recognised as one of Jasper's, complete with a suited driver.

"Get in."

Thea didn't want to. She stuck her fists in her pockets and her shoulders up near her ears. "How did you find me? I threw my phone away."

"You're stupid," Lollie told her.

That wasn't wrong.

They stared at each other through the open window of the Jag. Once, Lollie would only have spoken to her like that because she knew it would land her in Thea's bed. For a whipping. Now, Thea had the distinct feeling Lollie did it because she cared – *and* that Thea might just be reaching the limit of that care. Both those notions curdled in her gut.

Lollie blew out an explosive sigh, got out of the car and held the door open for her.

"You're still Thea Voronov." She held up her own phone. "Twitter. X. Thingy. You're all over the internet. Did you really think you could just disappear?"

"I did before."

"Twenty years ago, idiot."

Thea's head snapped up, a touch of her old self flashing to the fore. "Watch your tone, whelp. You were still in nappies."

"I was eight, thank you, your majesty, and I know that story. You put more effort into it last time. Anyone would think you want to be rescued now."

"I have no idea what you're talking about," she sneered as coolly as she could but secretly she had to concede the point. She was too old for this shit. Her bones ached after five nights on the street. She wanted her bed. She wanted Mem in it. She got in the car.

"Ugh. You stink." Lollie settled in next to her and nodded to the driver. Thea wondered when she'd lost control of her life. She crossed her arms and pressed herself back into the seat.

"Drugs?" asked Lollie.

"No."

"Really?"

"Fuck you."

"You pronounced that wrong. It goes '*thank* you.'"

There was a tense silence. Thea relented. "Really." She dialled back the snark a little. "I made a promise."

Lollie snorted softly and shook her head. "You're welcome."

Lollie took her home and ordered her around in a way Thea would never have tolerated before. She threw her in the bath.

"You're disgusting. Did you sleep in a dumpster?" She didn't leave. As if the whole episode wasn't undignified enough, Lollie sat on the lid of the loo and watched her. "Want me to help wash your hair?" she asked.

"I'm not a child."

"Going to stop acting like one then?"

Thea splashed her. She only intended it to be a flick of bubbles but she must have been more disconnected from herself than she thought. A wave of water surged over the edge of the bath and drenched the leg of Lollie's pants. The linen stuck to her skin. Her toes swam in her Jimmy Choos. They both looked at the soaked fabric. Thea couldn't meet Lollie's eyes.

"Not yet, hunh?"

Thea slid down until the water was just below her nose. It didn't quite hide the thin angry line she pressed her lips into. It didn't hide the tears that were threatening to spill either.

Lollie stood and collected up Thea's filthy clothes. She paused at the door.

"I've taken a job with CreatedDiamonds. Jasper secured it for me. Publicity manager with my own posh office in the Shard."

Thea didn't say anything. She wasn't surprised. She'd always known Lollie would leave her in the end. It was inevitable. But a job like that would suit her. She'd been selfish, keeping Lollie to herself, restricting her talents and insisting she serve her. This new role would give her far more responsibility and more scope than Thea had ever offered her.

It hurt a little that Jasper had organised it, but she could live with that. Harden her heart again. Find another pretty assistant to train. None of it mattered.

"I'll work a month's notice, if you like. Help you find someone to—"

"Just go. I don't care."

"Geez Thea. You say the nicest things."

"Get out."

Lollie sighed. "I'll order us some dinner."

When Thea got out of the bath, she found Lollie had laid out some clothes on her bed and left a new phone there, all set up to mirror her old one.

There was a message from Mem on it.

Thea stared at the letters.

M. E. M. She whispered each one, sounding the word out carefully. She loved the way it sat on her mouth, tingled on her lips, hushed out and returned to a gentle hum. She loved the full, round feeling that swelled in her chest when she thought of the girl. She even made herself love the wrenching cramps that twisted her gut when she remembered the look on her face on the red carpet when Thea revealed the extent of her betrayal.

She'd get used to that, too. Learn to live with the bitterness. Use it as fuel to push the pain away.

It was too late now.

She thumbed Mem's message away and used the phone for something else.

She was almost feeling herself again by the time they'd finished the cheap and cheerful Chinese Lollie had ordered in. She flicked her fingers to indicate Lollie should clear away, shot an eyebrow when the woman looked rebellious, slapped at her arse as she carried away her plate.

Lollie actually complained.

"Do you really think that's appropriate after falling in love with—"

Lollie was lucky the doorbell interrupted that remark because Thea would have been keen to make sure she regretted it if she finished it. As it was, they both looked at the black and white surveillance screen over the intercom button. At the front door, a young woman in a crop top, mini and fuck-me boots turned a well-rehearsed pout on the camera.

"Who—?" began Lollie. Then it dawned. Disappointment and contempt hitched her hands up onto her hips and she shook her head. "For fuck's sake, Thea."

Thea shrugged. She got up and hit the button.

"Just a moment, kitten," she told the hooker at the door. "Someone will let you in. There'll be paperwork to sign." She raised an expectant eyebrow at Lollie.

"Are you kidding me?" gritted Lollie.

"I'm still paying your wage, aren't I?"

Lollie flounced out. "Like father like daughter, hey Thea?" she flung over her shoulder.

Fuck.

That landed.

Five minutes later, when neither Lollie nor the hooker came to find her, she went to the door herself. Outside was a scene from her worst memories.

At least ten men with cameras mobbed on her front path. Lollie had taken off her light pink blazer and draped it kindly over the hooker's head. She had her arm around the woman's shoulders and was giving the paparazzi a solid mouthful about invasion of privacy and getting off Thea's lawn. One tiny part of Thea's mind had room to consider how decent that was of her, but when all the cameras turned to her, the rest tumbled into panic-mode. In one stupid moment she was seventeen again, wide-eyed and terrified on her father's doorstep. Just like then, her world was falling apart. Just like then, she had no one to turn to. No one who loved her.

It lasted a second before the monster inside her breached.

She roared.

She had no idea what she said but from the startled look on Lollie's face, it wasn't good. She yelled at Lollie, she yelled at the hooker – who she'd already fucking well paid for – and she yelled at the paps – who only intensified their focus with glee.

Lollie was clearly torn between protecting the hooker and managing Thea's outburst.

"Get inside, Thea! You want them to see you being self-destructive?"

Thea was beyond caring. When she pushed Lollie's hands away, she pushed too hard – or Lollie's shoe was still wet from the bath – or the hooker pulled her over – or a nudge from one of the men toppled her balance – Thea didn't know and didn't care, but Lollie tumbled down the front steps, taking the hooker with her and knocking two paps like skittles as she went. There was the definite sound of a very expensive lens cracking on the path – and then the uproar started in earnest.

Thea was more than happy to swing the first punch – she should have done this when she was seventeen – and she was still yelling. Fuck Lollie, fuck Jasper, fuck the stupid paparazzi. Fuck the whole fucking lot of you—

A gunshot tore through the air and everyone froze.

Yelena Litvina Titov had a modern black sidearm in one hand and an AK-47 strapped across her chest. She reached calmly down and took Thea by the ear.

"One picture of this hits the internet and I will find you," she said, mildly, into the silence. "Now, leave. All of you."

She dragged Thea all the way through her house, through their gardens and into her own kitchen before she let go of her ear.

"Idiot," she said, and kissed her hair.

Thea sat at her table and sniffed.

Mrs Tits put a shot of vodka in front of her and the bottle within reach. She'd clearly been cooking.

"Look at this," she said, proudly. "Perfect fucking roti."

The dam broke and Thea sobbed inconsolably.

Chapter Thirty

It was exhausting, but strangely, no worse than Kate had told her it would be.

She simply pulled her old beauty back on again – not the strange, honest, raw beauty Thea had drawn from her, but the standard smile she flashed at the cameras and felt soulless behind. It worked fine.

Mem had expected – now that her heart was broken – that putting on her best face for the world might have been tough, but either she was mastering this whole celebrity schtick, or her heart wasn't broken at all. It was just cold and adamantine. A lump of created diamond in her chest.

She suspected it was a combination of both, which was a disturbing sign too. The romantic in her would have proclaimed it was her heart and cried at the pain, but she had an inner pragmatist as well, and it was hard to deny Mem now had show business down pat.

A premiere in New York: bam! Red carpet in LA: smashed it. Late night talk shows with big name presenters: charmed them, flashed them her 'you're my best friend smile' and won hearts across the world. Parties? Memona Swan networked like a boss. Even scored some impressive donations for Heart and Grace House.

She wasn't blind to the careful layer of protection Kate, Jasper and Adiatu wove around her. They cleverly deflected questions and changed the subject whenever interviewers got too close to that moment in the spotlight in London. Adiatu earned her fee by ensuring the name Thea Voronov was never mentioned in her presence, though Mem could see they were all dying to ask.

It was busy – it was insane – but she liked it like that because it meant she didn't have time to think about Thea. It was exhausting, but it was cleansing.

Cleansing? her pragmatist mocked.

She was empty.

By the end of the first week in the States, Jasper was over it.

"I'm heading back to London. Some of us have to work." He grinned, winningly, then ducked as Kate aimed a bagel at him. They were all having breakfast in Kate's suite at the Beverly Hills Hotel. "I know you girls are off to Tokyo next, but I could fly you home if you're missing Old Blighty."

Kate did the maths and pulled a face. "It would only be for a day. Think I'd rather lounge here, frankly."

"Mem?"

They both looked at her. It was a look with depth, as if they wanted to ask her about Thea Voronov too, but also didn't want to tip some precarious balance. She both loved them for their care and hated them for their complicity. It wasn't hard to figure out who Thea had meant when she'd poured that vitriol into her ear – '*they* paid me to seduce you.' Kate and Jasper were just as guilty. But they hadn't dumped her with a callous mouthful of bile under the full glare of the world's media, and they'd been nothing but considerate since.

It was a mess.

"Give me a minute?" she asked.

She called Piper. It would be a relief to talk to someone who didn't want something from her and she'd give just about anything to sit on the sofa with her best mate and eat too much ice cream.

Wasn't that what you were supposed to do when your heart was broken?

Piper sounded distracted.

"I'm at uni! Me! A university student. I can't believe I put this off for so long, and babes, you're fucking brilliant for pushing me into this. I totally owe you for the rest of my life."

Mem felt her heart stir as a genuine smile slipped onto her face for the first time in a week.

"You're enjoying it then?"

"Oh my god, it's only been one week but it's amazing. My professor is freaking fantastic – totally hot too – but the way her mind works! She gave us these quizzes to see where we were at and apparently I aced them, so she had some of us come back for a second round, and I aced those too. So then there were, like, five of us left. Five puzzles later – in her office, mind you – and I was the last man standing. You are talking to the professor's newest research assistant and I just skipped two whole years of study and—"

"Breathe!" laughed Mem.

"Thank you so much, babes."

"Told you you were smart."

Piper's chuckle was dry. "Yeah, you did. No need to be smug though!" Then she gasped. "Oh, babes! How are you doing? Here I am crapping on about me, and you're—"

"I might be able to come home for a day," Mem interrupted. She didn't need Piper to go there. "Just tomorrow night really. But I thought I'd check if you were busy first. I just wanted to—"

Piper was clearly still on a high. She laughed again. "Of course! Though, let me check my calendar – I've actually got one now! The professor has me attending her evening lectures as well with the aim to knock this degree over in six months so we can crack on with my doctorate." She paused. "Oh."

"Doesn't matter," Mem said quickly. She struggled against the sting of rejection and tried to be happy for Piper. "How's things going at Heart and Grace?"

Piper sounded shifty there too. "Good. Um. Yeah. I've been so busy with uni. But the manager's reports have all been good. Haven't they?"

Mem hadn't looked at them either. That was what they'd employed a full time manager for, wasn't it?

"Enjoy school, Pipes," Mem said, the lightness in her chest freezing into diamond once more. "I'll stay on this side of the world then. See you next week when it's all over. Love you."

"Love you too, babes. Wait! Have you heard from Thea?"

Mem swallowed. Just her name hurt. It made her glad Adiatu was doing her job.

"I don't really expect to," she murmured.

"She's not doing so well," Piper said, gently. "Maybe you should call her."

It wasn't until after they'd ended the call that she wondered how Piper knew.

Kate found the evidence of just how well Thea wasn't doing when they were in Jasper's jet a week and a bit later. Tokyo, Sydney, Mumbai and Dubai were under their belts. They were finally heading home.

"Oh Christ, Thea," she muttered – and then couldn't deny she'd said it when Mem looked at her. She passed her phone over with a sigh.

It was a full-on performance. Thea was swinging punches at a mob of photographers on her doorstep and hollering obscenities in two different languages. She looked wild – still impeccably dressed, though her hair was wet and tousled. She punched like a boss but there was something desperate and lost in her eyes. Not the lost and bewildered, enthralled look she turned on Mem when she submitted utterly to Thea's touch and dragged Thea's surrender from her too, but doomed. Fallen. Thea looked wretched.

Mem didn't know if this awful little charade was about her, but she did know she hated seeing Thea miserable like this.

"She thinks she's a monster," Kate said, suddenly. "She thinks it's in her blood."

Mem was startled. "What?"

"You loved her, didn't you?"

Kate patted the lounge next to her and held up the blanket. Mem slipped in beside her and noticed Adiatu and the rest of the team retreat to another section of the plane.

"I did," she sighed. *There* was her heart. Right now it was a rock in the back of her throat, choking her. "Fuck, Kate— I *do*. I still do. What the hell is wrong with me? And she loves me. I know she does." She tried to swallow around her heart but her nose was suddenly running too and she couldn't see— She gasped out an awful, sucking sob, an appalling noise she tried to smother with the back of her hand, but Kate didn't seem to care. She pulled her under her wing and Mem shivered there, grateful, torn and confused, as desolate as Thea looked. "Or she did," she mumbled.

"Did you google her?" Kate asked. "You know what her childhood was like?"

Mem nodded.

"You got the newspaper version. The bare facts brushed over with a thick layer of sensationalism. The woman I know is even more messed up than that."

"Oh, so you mean a whole heap of trauma to excuse her behaviour?" Mem's inner pragmatist was still feeling belligerent.

Kate didn't look impressed. "What she did to you was unconscionable and you are entitled to be bitter, dearest. For a while. But Thea is a complex, damaged and wonderful human being. Are you going to demand perfection from her – which she might not be able to give you – or will you love her as she is? She tried very hard with you, you know."

Mem pressed her lips into a thin line. She knew that was true. Kate nudged her with her shoulder.

"Her father was a KGB operative. Ruthless, apparently, with an uncanny ability to get what he wanted. The Voronovs were already rich and privileged before the fall of the Soviet Union, but he capitalised on the chaos that came next and brought Thea, her older brother and his trafficking ring to London. You probably read about the scandal that swallowed him—?"

Mem hummed.

"It swallowed a hundred girls, at least – and that's only the ones they managed to pin to his network. From what Thea says, working through her memories later and from what her own investigators have managed to track down since, it was far, far more. After her mother passed, every woman who ever came into Thea's life was sold into slavery in some way or other." Kate paused and gave Mem a heavy look. "It swallowed Thea too."

"She ended up on the streets. Had an overdose. She told me," Mem whispered. She remembered the proud, defiant tilt to Thea's chin when she did, owning her misery and daring Mem to judge her. Terrified she would.

"Yes, but I'm not sure if you fully understand why."

"She was homeless—"

"It was an incredible scandal and it wasn't just the UK. For a few months there was barely a newspaper across all of Europe that didn't have the Voronovs on their front pages. Her father went to jail, but it was Thea who had to live with the scandal. Every newspaper in the country screamed that her old man and her brother were monsters – oh, and they were – but the media was convinced Thea was too. I mean, how could she have lived right in the middle of all that luxury and not seen what was going on? How could she not have known?" Kate shrugged. She grimaced as if the memory was sour in her mouth too. "I didn't know her then, but I remember the news coverage. I thought she was as guilty as her father. Everyone did. It was a different time, a different world."

"She was seventeen!" Mem protested.

Kate thumbed at her phone and pulled up an article from the time. *Voronov kid guilty in father's sex ring,* the headline screamed over a paparazzi shot of a seventeen year old Thea jostled between two bewigged lawyers. Mem's chest clenched for the girl Thea had been.

"She was rich beyond imagining and utterly spoiled. And Russian. The perfect plaything for the media. They had a field day. You know what it's like now, the full glare of the media spotlight, hounded by reporters who shout intrusive, abusive questions at you from every angle, their cameras poised to revel in your fall." Kate cast a sly sideways glance at Mem. "How do you think a sheltered seventeen year old handled that?"

Mem looked at the picture of teenaged Thea. The girl looked scared.

"I imagine it would have taken a toll," she admitted.

Kate's snort was harsh. "One she still battles with, darling Mem. She strides around with her nose in the air because she's still pushing back that fear and doubt. They convinced her she was evil too, just like her father. *He* got thirty years. She had to arrange her own punishment. She ran from anyone who tried to help her, filled her body with drugs and sold it to anyone who wanted it – just like the women her father had ruined. She felt it was her destiny."

"Oh, god." Mem discovered she was crying.

"And she still sees exploitation in everything she does." Kate was merciless. "We exist in an industry that churns through young women and profits from their beauty. And Thea Voronov rules it." She rolled her eyes with genuine affection. "God knows why she chose a career like this, but she craves beauty and gentleness, then goes on to hurt it and destroy it because she doesn't believe she deserves it."

Mem's breath shuddered into her. That explained so much. It explained the lofty arrogance Mem loved. The tangle of emotions on Thea's face that had been so confusing at the beginning made complete sense now. That cruel little sneer that Mem had found so thrilling, so sexy, so *powerful* – it had never been directed at *her*. Thea hated herself. She hid her true self behind a veneer of dominance and disdain – but Mem had been honoured with the real Thea too. Those deep, worshipful stares when she looked at Mem like she couldn't believe her luck.

"She loves you, Mem. I know she does." Kate pulled away and crossed the cabin to fetch Mem a tissue. She pushed it into Mem's fingers but she didn't return to their warm position on the couch. She stood opposite Mem and looked extremely uncomfortable.

The hum of the plane matched the turmoil vibrating in Mem's chest and she didn't understand why the most elegant and sophisticated woman in the world was now crouching at Mem's feet – not quite kneeling – but looking up to catch Mem's eyes. Definitely begging.

"Then why did she say all those things at the premiere? Why did she—?"

"Because we asked her to corrupt you," Kate said flatly. "If you want to blame anyone, blame Jasper and me. I didn't see it at first. Thea Voronov? Fall in love? The notion would have been fucking hilarious just three short months ago. But then she met you, dearest, and *we* asked her to use you."

"Why?"

Shame was ugly on Kate's face. One shoulder lifted in a bitter shrug. "Money? What other reason is there? Jasper worked out exactly how many millions CreatedDiamonds was good for and we all wanted our cut. You were just a cog on the wheel."

Hearing it confirmed so blatantly didn't make it hurt any less.

"That's really awful, Kate."

"Hey, I'm not proud. You would have been compensated too, and for all we knew, you might have been just as shallow as the rest of us. That would have eased whatever conscience I have left. But then I realised Thea was gone for you." Kate put a hand on Mem's knee and suddenly couldn't meet her eyes. "The part that really blackens my soul is that, even knowing she was in love for the first time in her life, we still insisted she persuade you to do the diamond deal. You were the most beautiful thing she'd ever laid eyes on, you loved her too, and we heartlessly manipulated her into *being* the monster she thinks she is. I'm so sorry, Mem."

"But—" She'd reassess what this meant for her friendship with Kate later. Right now, there was still one huge, gaping, glaring discrepancy in all this. "But she didn't," Mem said. "She didn't corrupt me – or whatever melodramatic shit you think that is. *I* chose to do the brand ambassadorship. It was *my* choice."

Kate actually brushed that away. "No, darling, we *insisted* Thea get into your pants for one reason—"

"Shut up, Kate! I'm telling you, after one mention of the diamond deal and the sequel on the rooftop at Jasper's party – *one* – Thea never said a word about them again."

Kate sat back on her heels, perplexed. "She didn't?"

"Not once. She didn't talk me into anything. It was me."

"Really?"

"She's not a monster."

Kate frowned, interrogating Mem's gaze for a long second, then she stood and slapped her thighs. Wholly exasperated. "Well, of course, she's not. Oh, for fuck's sake, the stupid woman." She flopped back down on the couch beside Mem. "You're going to tell her that, aren't you?"

"That she's not a monster?"

"She might even believe it, coming from you."

"I would tell her, if she'd answer my calls." Mem gave Kate an arch look. "You could redeem yourself by getting her to talk to me."

Kate regarded her shrewdly. "Fair," she said, eventually. "I will try.'

Something else suddenly became clear.

"That's why she's always been so reluctant to, um— you know, play hard when we're in bed," Mem said. "I've always wanted to take things further with her and she—"

"She's been gentlemanly?"

Mem scrunched her nose. "Yeah."

"Ha! Knew she loved you." Kate grinned triumphantly. She was infectiously charming even when she was guilty as hell. "You are the one who can submit to her, hold her close and love her while she straddles that mess between what she needs and what terrifies her. Please say you'll fix things with her."

Mem wanted to with all her heart.

"Why is she so dominant then," Mem asked, "if she's so scared of being monstrous?"

"Just the way she is, darling. Delicious, isn't it?"

"Yeah," Mem sighed.

"And it's just the way you are. You do know there's nothing wrong with that, don't you?" Kate gave her a very motherly stare, despite the subject matter. "You two are meant for each other."

They were quiet for a moment. It was late, and it had been a long, long two weeks.

"Mem?" Dame Katherine Cox was timid. "Are we good? You and me? I'll completely understand if you say we're not."

Mem pretended to consider it. "If you apologise to Thea, I think we'll be fine."

"Very fair," Kate said. "You're too good for the lot of us, dearest. You'll be just right for our little family."

They both tried to get some sleep after that. Mem stared at her phone for ages knowing her last calls and messages had been ignored. She just wanted to be home, talking face to face. Something else Kate said sifted through her brain.

'*Her own investigators...?*'

Mem was guilty too. She'd been so eager to play with the proud, beautiful, domineering artist, she'd overlooked the complex, needful woman within. There was clearly so much more to Thea that she didn't know. She couldn't wait to get to know her properly.

She tapped out a message.

— *I've been thinking about you and hoping you're okay. I'll be home tomorrow and I'd like to see you. May I come to yours?* —

She didn't expect an answer but she hoped it was a start.

Chapter Thirty One

After an endless flight, she touched down into a busy London afternoon with a new sense of perspective.

Thea turning her back and walking away from her on that red carpet had been the lousiest acting Mem had ever seen, and she and Thea had been far, far too good together to give up on each other now. She was going to find the proud, silly woman, pin her the hell down and talk this out.

But she was knackered by the time she got home.

It was late afternoon. Thea hadn't replied to her messages and Piper was at uni. Her parents and her sister were at work, and Heart and Grace House was ticking along smoothly and didn't need her. She tried not to feel like the conquering hero returning home to an empty castle, but she had to admit it was lonely and anticlimactic. Hollywood's newest, brightest star was still a Nigel No-friends.

She went to Thea's house.

When no one let her in the front door she walked all the way around the block to Mrs Tits' house, only to find she was out too. She hovered at the gate between the two gardens for a moment, then pushed through to Thea's studio.

The door was open and the place was a mess.

In the main studio, a paper drop lay in a crumpled pile on the floor, one of its stands fallen on its side. Lights and reflectors had been kicked into corners – there was the crunch of broken glass under Mem's feet. At the workstation beneath the screens, the tabletop was bare, as if someone had swept its contents aside with an angry arm. In the second room, the bed was a messy tangle of sheets.

In the darkroom, things were worse.

The floor was littered with photos. Hundreds. Every portrait that had been hanging from the drying lines had been torn up. The poster-sized images from the walls had been shredded. That funny picture of Kate that Mem had admired had been ripped from the wall and scrunched into a ball. Bottles of chemicals rolled around the floor. A tray of liquid had been up-ended on the table, every photograph it touched now a soggy mess.

"Oh, Thea."

Mem covered her mouth with her hand, dismay threatening tears again. She should tidy up, she thought. Straighten some things.

She stooped to pick up the first photo beneath her feet and realised it was one of her. She scrabbled for the next and saw her face again. On her knees, gathering every picture toward her that she could reach, she discovered they were *all* of her.

Thea had developed a hundred photos from their last shoot, and then tossed them all to the floor.

Mem fought back a sob. *What did that mean?*

Thea still loved her.

In fact, there was only one photo still on the wall, and even that was torn at the edge as if Thea had stopped herself from ripping it down at the last second.

It was a picture of that older woman – the same woman who was in the large print in Thea's conservatory that Mem had noticed on that very first day. The woman whose face was repeated in numerous photos around Thea's house, who had starred in Thea's exhibition too. The shadow between the stars.

The woman who looked so familiar, even though Mem had never been able to figure out why.

Mem gathered up a handful of her portraits from the floor and headed out to Thea's house. She found the key under the pot plant and let herself in.

A similar mess greeted her inside. Take-out containers littered the kitchen countertop and the bin was overflowing. Vodka bottles stood empty like a crystal forest on the bench. A camera sat on the table, its old-style film back open, the film ripped from its roll and curling in a long, overexposed ribbon.

A single portrait lay there too. Her. Mem. Blown up so large the grain of the film textured her skin. It was moody and moving like all of Thea's portraits – one of those strange, non-commercial views of her beauty.

Only Thea saw her like this.

In Thea's eyes, Mem didn't simply feel beautiful – she felt loved.

Mem bit her lip as she pictured Thea selecting it from the thousands she'd taken, carefully developing and printing it in the darkroom.

Then bringing it here to stare and stare and stare at it.

They couldn't possibly be over.

Every other picture in the room had been pulled from the walls and was face down on the floor. All except for one. That same older woman who looked down at Mem now with motherly wisdom. Mem narrowed her eyes. The woman looked *so* familiar...

She pulled her phone from her pocket and called Thea again. She left another message. Then another. Stopped herself from sending a third because coming over as a stalker wasn't going to help.

A note! Thea had to come home eventually. But Mem roamed through the kitchen, the pantry, the study and the lounge room and utterly failed to find a pen, a pencil or anything she could write with – which was completely fucking crazy. In the depths of her own bag she found a pen she hadn't used in years and coaxed it back to life.

Thea, sweetheart, I'm home and now I'm really worried about you. Please call me. Please let me see you.

She wrote it on the back of one of her pictures and stared at what she'd written. Her heart wanted to say so much more.

I don't understand what happened to us, Thea, but I know that what we had was so damn good, I don't want to let it go. I still love you.

Ugh.

And I know you love me.

It was needy, desperate and hopeless, and completely revealed she'd violated Thea's privacy and broken into her house, but Mem was past caring. She just wanted to find Thea and wrap her in her arms, wind back the clock, and make everything better.

She left the note on the table next to her portrait and went home. She crawled, jet-lagged, into her bed and worried about Thea. She watched her phone and hoped.

By morning, there were still no replies to her messages.

She stared sadly at the blank screen of her phone and refused to listen to the abject and desolate part of her soul that told her to give up. That Thea clearly didn't want to see her. But she knew how proud Thea could be. She knew the stubborn, unbending perfectionist inside Thea – the monster the woman thought lived within her – wouldn't allow her to come crawling to Mem. If Mem wanted this fixed, it was up to Mem to do the work, as unfair as that seemed.

Otherwise it would be nothing.

She called one more time, knowing it would ring out, then set off for Thea's house again.

Unsurprisingly, she found it empty. Using the pot plant key again revealed the same scene of devastation inside. If Thea had been home, she hadn't cleaned up.

On the table, Mem's note had been moved.

So, she'd seen it!

And done nothing.

That twisted Mem's heart again, but she wasn't giving up now. Running through the garden to Mrs Tits' house, she didn't find any assistance from Lena.

"Oh, I've seen that girl throw some top shelf tantrums in her time, but these last two weeks? Off the scale. I'm glad you're back, *milaya*."

"Do you know where she is?"

"Not her keeper, sweetheart, but wherever she went, she took a camera."

That wasn't much help but Mem refrained from rolling her eyes. Yelena Titov was in her bike leathers and sucking down an espresso before rushing out the door herself. She had a look that suggested she'd snap Mem in half herself if she didn't find Thea and make amends, now!

Kate hadn't heard from Thea either. In desperation, Mem tried Jasper.

He gave her a list of pubs. When Mem growled at him, he expanded it to include some kink clubs in Soho.

"It's Sunday morning, Jasper," Mem gritted. "I know she came home last night. And if you think she's out getting trashy at ten a.m. on a Sunday and you're not doing anything about it, you're not being the friend she needs right now—"

"Steady on, old chap!"

"—and you should be ashamed of yourself."

There was a silence, then a long sigh. "You're right." Jasper's voice was low. "You're right, Mem darling, of course you are. Give me ten minutes and I'll get back to you."

When he called back, he sounded far more contrite.

"She's with one of her rescue women," he said, "taking pics for a kid's birthday party. She's okay, Mem."

"Tell me the address."

"She's fine—"

Mem was close to reaching through the phone and shaking him. "Tell me the fucking address, Jasper, or I swear to god—"

He chuckled, pleased. "That's what I like to hear. Good to know you have what it takes to be the right woman for our Thea."

"You are a manipulative arsehole, Jasper."

"And so damn charming you can't help but love me," he sang.

"It's a thin line, old man."

Jasper's laughter was rich and warm. Bastard. He was too loveable for his own good.

"Give. me. the address, Jasper."

He sent it to her phone, his laugh still ringing in her ears.

When she looked at it to call an uber, Mem couldn't quite believe what she was seeing.

She knew this address. She'd known it since she was a child.

It was Piper's childhood home.

Piper's mother let her in, and the moment Mem saw her, it all made sense.

"Come in, Mem. It's so good to see you. How was LA and Sydney and Dubai and— Oh, sweetheart, you look like you've seen a ghost!"

Mrs Green – Piper's mum – was the woman in Thea's portraits. How like the inestimable Thea Voronov to turn a face Mem had known all her life into a piece of art so powerful Mem didn't recognise her. The large picture in the conservatory, the torn poster in the darkroom, the ones at the exhibition – this face was everywhere in Thea's life.

"*Rescue women*," Mem breathed, nonsensically. That's what Jasper had said. *She's with one of her rescue women.* "You're Russian, aren't you, Mrs Green? Were you one of the trafficked women from—? Oh god, is that why you couldn't have kids? Why you've adopted so many?" She slapped a hand over her mouth and stared at the woman she'd known almost all her life with her eyes bugging out. "I'm so sorry – that was so rude. I'm just— I mean, I've just figured something out and I—" She stuttered to a halt again. Her best friend's mum was regarding her with a gentle, lopsided smile. "Is Thea here?"

"Wondered when that was going to click, my dear." She slipped an arm around Mem's shoulders and led her down the hallway. "Surprised Piper didn't explain everything."

Piper appeared suddenly at the end of the hall as if she'd been attracted to the sound of Mem's voice.

"It wasn't my story to tell, mum," she said, exasperated and flicking a quick look at Mem. "You GenX-ers and your casual disregard for everyone else's stories, I swear. Did you really think I was going to tell Mem the love of her life was part of the human trafficking ring that sold you into slavery when you were sixteen years old?"

They both looked at Mem. It was dark and quiet in the hallway, a sanctuary from the usual chaotic madness of the Green-family household. So many thoughts collided in Mem's head, but one stood out.

"Love of my life," she whispered.

Piper chuckled. "Glad that's the thing you're focusing on, babes." She stepped forward and gave her a hug. "How you doing, megastar?"

Mem was still reeling.

"Thea was never part of any of that shit, except by accident," Mrs Green said. "Her father may have destroyed me, but Thea Voronov saved me. She's been supporting me and my wonderful, enormous family ever since. She looks after all the girls who managed to survive Grigori Voronov's hell." She gave Mem a sly, sideways look. "She just needs someone to look after her."

Mem wanted to be that person. She wanted that so much.

It was too soppy for Piper, though. "Ew, mum," she groaned. "Manipulative much? Not to mention cheesy."

Vera Green laughed and swatted her daughter on the arm. "Come through, darlings. It's chaos, but it's Chidi's birthday and Thea always takes photos of my kids on their birthdays." She strolled away through to the kitchen.

Piper and Mem regarded each other warily.

"You knew her all this time and you didn't tell me?" Mem wasn't sure how she felt about that.

"Tried to." Piper shrugged. "It was just a photoshoot at first, and then it looked mooshy as hell. I also had the ridiculous notion that two women who were shagging like bunnies might have actually talked to each other about things—" Mem poked out her tongue. "But of course, I underestimated just how hopeless lesbians can be about this shit—"

"You can shut up now."

"I kinda did try to warn you."

"You did," Mem admitted.

"You still love me though?" Piper grinned.

"Maybe." Mem squared her shoulders and tried to prepare herself for whatever she might find in the middle of Piper's family. "You might be a maths genius but you're rubbish at everything else."

Piper cackled, slung her arm over Mem's shoulders and they were best mates again.

She didn't expect to find the world's leading photography artist bouncing on a trampoline.

Mem couldn't believe what she was seeing. Thea Voronov was in the garden surrounded by at least twenty six-year-olds all dressed as superheroes. She was jumping with five of them as if she didn't have a care in the world.

She was wearing those sinfully skinny black jeans Mem loved and a purple silk shirt rolled to her elbows, though her boots were in a pile of kid-sized trainers at the foot of the trampoline. Her hair was tousled and flopping around her face as she bounced, getting in her mouth as she laughed. A camera was in her hands – as always – and she was on her butt on the canvas, catching shots of the kids as they pretended to fly above her like Ironman and Captain Marvel. Mem had the impression the kids had figured out how to 'bounce' the adult, and Thea was being jostled around like a rag doll.

From the look on her face, she was loving every second.

God, she was beautiful.

The parents and the rest of Piper's grown up siblings reclined on garden chairs and watched the show, or gathered around the large-screen TV in the sunroom. It was scrolling through a succession of photos Thea had already taken, and Piper was in control of the gear, arranging for pics to be distributed to parents' phones. They seemed awed that the famous Thea Voronov was photographing their kids and that they now had a priceless work in their hands.

The pictures, of course, were extraordinary. Innocence, laughter and potential all captured with grace and a master's eye, the black and white lending an artistry that made the future look bright. Mem found herself smiling back at the faces of kids she didn't know, her heart drawn into the images by the deft touch of the photographer.

And suddenly, there was Thea on the screen! She'd passed a kid her camera and been snapped while explaining how to use it. In the next shots she'd performed – eyes crossed, tongue poking out, a bug-eyed fish face – then her head thrown back and laughter tumbling from her lips. Mem stared. She looked joyous. She was magical. Mem wanted her so much.

"I think she comes here to play with my kids and enjoy the childhood she never had."

Vera Green stood beside her, arms folding, watching Thea on the screen too. Her smile was soft.

"I'm glad she has you," Mem murmured.

The woman nudged her shoulder. "Piper told me you two aren't together anymore. I hope you're here to fix that. I think she really loved you."

A familiar laugh behind them was cut suddenly short.

"Love?"

Thea had two kids at each elbow and a smile that was rapidly fading from her features. It took the kids a moment to catch the mood change, and one jumped, grabbing for her camera. Thea let him take it, her eyes locked on Mem's. The kids scurried over to Piper already pulling the data card from the camera's innards.

There were twenty people in the room and no one but Mem and Thea.

As Mem watched, the playful softness in Thea's body was pulled taut and tall into the proud, overbearing swagger Mem knew and loved. Her eyes hardened.

"Why are you here?"

"I was worried about you," Mem said. That wasn't even the half of it.

Thea tossed her chin. "Is that all?" She spread her hands. Smirk. "I'm fine."

The slight wobble of her lower lip proved she wasn't.

"You didn't answer my messages," Mem said. "You didn't even look at some of them."

The smirk turned into a sneer. "And that didn't tell you anything?"

Mem was vaguely aware of the others in the room shifting uncomfortably. Mrs Green bustled the kids out with the promise of lollies. Most of the adults followed them.

"Please don't be like this, Thea. I know you. I know you loved me – you still do! And you never said you didn't on that red carpet—"

One perfect eyebrow arched upwards. "Presumptuous, my muse."

"So, I'm still that?" Mem's heart leapt.

For a split second, Thea's look was hungry – ravenous – with all the greed Mem lived to see in it – then her eyes flicked away. Shamed.

Mem took a tiny step forward. "Kate told me what she and Jasper asked you to do – but you and I both know you didn't do it, Thea. So why—? You only said those things at the premiere because—"

"—because you took those deals like any other vacant, pretty thing, greedy and shallow, chasing fame and fortune and using whoever was in your path."

Thea spat it.

The naked hurt in her voice punched the air from Mem's lungs. Thea thought Mem had used *her*. This was a stupid, tortured mess. "You know that's not true," she breathed.

"Five million pounds." The twist of Thea's lips was ugly. "Good to know your price." She tossed her chin again, but she had trouble meeting Mem's eyes.

It was almost as if she didn't believe it herself.

Suddenly, Mem was infuriated. Exasperated, but loving the woman's dignity, her stubbornness, and her ego, and wanting to smack the whole lot out of her. She wanted to squeeze her. Kiss her. No, damn it, she wanted to smack her. She nearly laughed at the thought of her gloriously domineering artist allowing that, but she put her hands on her hips, threw her tits out and put on her best brattish pout. She knew what worked on Thea Voronov now and she was ready to give her everything she had. This stupidity had gone on long enough.

"Five million pounds to fund a women's shelter, you self-absorbed idiot—"

"Careful, darling."

"—which you would know if you had actually bothered to ask."

Thea's eyebrows shot so far up her forehead it was almost comical.

"But I forgive you, Thea. I know why you didn't ask, and that's okay."

Her stare became lethal. Her nostrils flared and her lips fell open.

Mem brought it home. "You were so busy shagging the fuck out of me you didn't have time to ask about things like that. And that's completely okay because I know you can't keep your hands off me. And that's *one hundred percent* okay because you, Thea Voronov, are utterly, hopelessly and irrevocably in love with me."

Thea stumbled forward, her lips in a snarl, her chest rising and falling with the violence of her breathing. Mem stepped in to meet her. They were millimetres apart, Thea's eyes darting between Mem's, urgently searching for the truth she hoped to find there.

Mem gave it to her.

"But the best part of all that is that I love you too. So much Thea," she whispered. "And, to be fair, I was so busy shagging the fuck out of you, I never thought to talk about it properly ti with you."

The corner of Thea's mouth twitched.

There was a long moment while relief, glee and lust built slowly and steadily in Thea's eyes.

"Say that again," she ordered, low, her eyes on Mem's lips.

Mem giggled and leaned her hips in, experimentally. Thea's hands fell to her waist as naturally as breathing and pulled her in. Mem doubted she even knew she was doing it. Thea's smirk blossomed.

"So busy shagging the fuck out of you—"

Thea slapped her thigh, just below her hip. Mem smiled. *There* was her woman, just the way she liked her.

"I love you, Thea Voronov. Absolutely and completely."

One hand crept up to Mem's chin. Those long fingers Mem adored tilted her mouth up to meet Thea's, and those deep, possessing eyes bored into hers—

"Oi! Kids' party, you two!" Piper sprang up beside them like a literal jack-in-the-box. "You are so not having make-up sex here. You'll gross out the six-year-olds."

Mem and Thea jerked apart.

"Fuck's *sake*, Pipes!" Mem aimed a punch at ex-best friend's arm and Piper cackled gleefully.

"You've always been my least favourite of Vera's kids, Piper," Thea growled, but the flush of her cheeks gave her away.

Piper threw her arms over both their shoulders. "Not even true, Voronov. And you can drop the ice-queen shizz. You don't scare me." She propelled them toward the hall. "Now, take Mem back to your place and go shag the fuck out of each other there. I don't want to see either of you again unless it's to help with the U-Hauling. Ow!"

Thea seized Mem's hand, tweaked her eyebrows with the slightest warning, then dragged her out to her car as if her life depended on it.

Chapter Thirty Two

They stumbled in the front door. Thea kicked it closed, not even pausing to separate her mouth from Mem's throat. She slammed Mem against the wall of the hall, keys thrown into a bowl on the side table, a vase of flowers teetering precariously.

They'd been here before – almost at the very beginning. Mem remembered what she'd done then and hooked a thigh over Thea's hip. A groan, a hand up under her shirt, a squeeze of her breast – hard – and Mem was groaning too.

"I need you, Thea. Please."

"That's beautiful begging, darling. Give me more, baby. What do you want from me?"

Thea's whole body leaned against her, her face was buried in the crook of her neck – there wasn't anything else Mem wanted. But she knew her poor artist still needed convincing.

"You, Thea," she begged. "I want you. All of you. Everything you want to share with me. I love you."

It seemed to be the wrong thing to say. The frenzied pawing stopped and Thea's forehead pressed against Mem's. Her eyes were closed. Her expression was tortured.

"You can't love me." It was so soft that Mem had to strain to hear. "You can't. It's impossible. I'm a monster."

"You're not."

"You must hate me."

"I don't."

"But I—"

"Oh, Thea." She untangled their bodies and kissed the woman's forehead, as softly and lovingly as she could. "What happened to you?

Why don't you believe me? I sent you a hundred messages. I told you I love you. I even left you a note—"

Thea made a miserable choking noise. "I can't—" She swallowed and tried again. "I can't—"

Mem waited.

"I can't read."

Of all the things she expected Thea to say, that wasn't it. She also knew how delicately balanced this admission was for Thea's dignity. One false move...

She took her hands and drew her into the lounge room, pushing her gently down onto the sofa. They sat sideways, facing each other, their knees interlocking. Thea had trouble meeting her eyes.

"Tell me," Mem begged.

"Never went to school," Thea muttered. "My mother was drunk the entire time I knew her and my father was a criminal. They didn't care about my schooling. I can read Russian – a little. My father's women taught me – the girls who—"

Mem squeezed her fingers. "That makes sense. And what about when you moved to London?"

There was a bitter snort. Thea was still looking at their hands. "I had a few years at some snooty private girl's school where my lack of academic standing was covered by my father's money. I got good at pretending. The only thing that held the humiliation at bay were the parties I threw at my father's expense." For a moment, that towering ego shone like a beacon again. "All the girls wanted me then."

Mem swatted her thigh. Thea looked startled, then dangerous, then miserable again.

"Until?" Mem prompted.

"Until my father's empire crumbled and I was nothing." Thea turned the bitterness of her failings on Mem. "So, I couldn't read your messages of love because I'm—"

"Don't you dare finish that thought, Thea Voronov! You're not nothing. You're everything to me." Mem put a finger on her lips and nearly laughed at the outrage that flashed in her woman's eyes. The Thea she loved was still in there, simmering just below the surface. Mem knew how to draw her out. "Just because you couldn't read them, doesn't mean they weren't still full of love. Let me show you instead."

She pushed Thea carefully backwards until she was leaning against the cushions and had only just settled herself between her legs with her hands on her belt when Thea figured out her plan. Thea moved like a cat.

"Oh no, sweetheart," she said, reversing their positions with ease. "I'm the one who hurt you, in front of the whole world. Let me apologise for that."

She was gentle. Deliberate – and greedy. Their time apart had been agony for Thea too – Mem could see it in the way her tongue traced her top lip as she slowly undid the buttons on Mem's shirt, in the infinite black of her eyes as they blew wide and lost focus when she pushed Mem's bra up and out of her way. Mem went to wriggle out of it all, but Thea's firm fingers stopped her, framing the bunched clothes around her breasts like a picture before tipping helplessly forward and capturing a nipple in her mouth.

Mem whimpered – couldn't stop herself – and Thea huffed out a laugh. Their eyes met, that bone-melting arrogance flaring once in her gaze before softening again. She planted a wet, wide, open-mouthed kiss right between Mem's breasts and set to work on her jeans, tugging them down and freeing just one leg.

"Eager?" teased Mem.

Thea nipped the inside of her thigh, then kissed the same spot, sucking hard. "That's my line, darling, and you have no idea." She hooked Mem's leg over her shoulder and her smile was an unholy mess of lust and heartache, shame and desire, but it was the craving that won out. She needed Mem – and so Mem opened wide for her and pulled her in.

Thea locked their eyes and dropped her mouth to the place where Mem wanted her most. She was panting in seconds, pressing her head back into the cushions, but holding Thea's gaze like it was a lifeline – the only thing she needed in the world. Thea's tongue was hot and skillful – she knew Mem's body utterly and didn't hesitate to give her what she needed – a devoted, worshipping focus on her clit and a look in her eyes that hooked deep into Mem's soul and bound them together. Her hips twitched upwards, pushing herself harder against Thea's mouth. She clutched at her own breast, then moaned and nearly shut her eyes when Thea grasped for the other one and palmed it hard. But she blinked and held on tight to Thea's gaze, eyes that watched her up her body as if she was the most precious thing in the world.

But there was still a hint of doubt behind her eyes – something that still looked awfully like shame and fear – and Mem knew they still had a lot of talking to do. When Thea slipped two fingers inside her, as easily and commandingly as if Mem's body was just a toy for Thea's desire, everything began to spiral. That thrill – that delicious, mind-numbing, all-consuming ecstasy that always filled her when Thea took control – began to circle around her spine. Thea saw it – she *knew* it – and she pushed deeper, harder, finding that spot and curling her fingers ruthlessly. Mem clung to her gaze, to the brilliant, breathtaking woman with her face between Mem's thighs, and realised it was all tangled together – Thea's power, her ego and her fear, Mem's newfound strength and the peace she found on her knees. It was love – it was complicated and confusing and they had so much still to sort out, but—

"I love you," she said – and suddenly it was the right thing to say, because Thea drove her harder, locked her lips around Mem's clit and did something sensational with her tongue.

Mem was instantly lost, straining off the couch in an agonising arch. Thea lifted her higher, holding her there, drawing the moment out forever in a brilliant flash of light and still, *still* watching her with the same love burning in her gaze. She cradled her, kissed and licked and sucked and thrust until Mem was empty and used, fulfilled and complete – and then she let her gently down, reluctant to lift her mouth from Mem's core, a beautiful, aching devotion in her eyes.

Mem pulled at her weakly. "Come here." And Thea crawled over her, let Mem kiss herself from her lips, then settled down half beside her, half on top of her, her head on Mem's breasts. She looked sheepish. Mem stroked her hair.

"It all got messed up in my head," Thea said a long while later. "The games we play and the deals Jasper wanted me to extract from you. It felt mercenary. Cruel. Like I was using you for both."

Mem tapped the nape of her neck with soft fingers. She could feel Thea's eyelashes tickling her skin. "You're not a monster, Thea," she whispered. "Do you believe me?"

Thea twisted until they were looking at each other again. Her eyes flicked back and forth between Mem's searching for redemption, and when Mem smiled at her softly – her *silly, wonderful* artist – they filled with tears and finally overflowed. Thea wriggled forward, buried her face in Mem's neck and sobbed.

"Oh, my sweetheart," Mem murmured, stroking her hair and feeling her heart burst for the proud, lonely woman in her arms. "You're never a monster. You're my heart. You're everything I want. You're my love and you're perfect."

The sobbing grew messier, sniffling and hiccuping, her whole body shaking against Mem's. Mem could feel tears on her shoulder and, for some reason, they made her smile with happiness. Everything was going to be fine now.

"You do believe me, don't you?"

Thea nodded against her neck. She sniffed, hugely.

"Use your words, darling," Mem teased.

There was a weak laugh. Just as she'd hoped, there was a gentle slap to her hip too.

Thea was fine.

They stayed like that for a while longer. Cuddled together. Perfect.

Something else ticked through Mem's mind.

"They're not games." She waited for Thea to catch the reference.

Thea's body stiffened slightly. The lofty arrogance crept back in and Mem was glad to see it return. "No?"

"No," Mem said, firmly. "To me, what we have is natural and perfect. You are a strong, dominant personality and I am fulfilled in every way when I submit to you – that's not a game. That's simply the way we are. We compliment each other. I love our dynamic."

Thea pushed herself upright. She was still a mess of tears and smeared eyeliner, but Mem saw her accept the role she was being handed. She saw the gratitude there too. The strong beginnings of that bloody smirk. "What dynamic?"

She was a tease and she knew it. Mem rolled her eyes.

"Don't make me say it."

"Use your words, darling."

"I hate it when you do this."

"No you don't." Thea's chuckle was glorious. Mem knew exactly how to conquer it.

"The dynamic where I need you to possess me completely and use me for your inspiration."

Thea's mouth dropped open and her pupils shot wide. "Oh, my darling, beautiful muse."

It was Mem's turn to chuckle. She knew she wouldn't get away with that for long. Thea gave her one questioning eyebrow then her full, towering, glorious domination broke free when Mem nodded yes. Mem was pulled off the couch and stripped properly naked in no time. When Thea kissed her – both hands entwined in her hair, the softest of grateful moans into her mouth – Mem leaned against her pride and felt it set her on fire. *This* was the Thea she loved – domineering and gentle, unrelentingly strict, and helplessly gone for her.

"Undo my belt," Thea murmured, not letting go of Mem's cheeks, not letting a millimetre's distance grow between them.

Mem reached down and slipped the belt from Thea's pants. Thea gave her one more stupendously gentle kiss and took the belt. When she held it up, Mem knew exactly what she wanted. She nodded, and Thea buckled it tight around Mem's throat, that beautiful wildness darkening in her eyes as she did.

She held the end. Turned and hooked it over her shoulder. The look she threw back at Mem was pure wickedness.

"Shall we go to bed, darling?"

She tugged and Mem followed her up the stairs in absolute contentment.

They took Piper up on her offer only a week later.

"Yeah no, totally fine, completely understand. I'm pretty sure both of you can afford removalists a million times over, but no, I'm good for carrying boxes. What are friends for, right?"

"Hush your whinging and carry this to the truck," Mem told her. "Just think, you have the joys of finding a new flatmate after I'm gone."

Piper grumbled, but she helped Mem move her things into Thea's house clearly happy for both of them.

"Useful, isn't she?" Thea remarked, as Piper struggled past with a box labelled 'Books and precious things.' "Think she'd make a good photographer's assistant?"

"Not in your wildest dreams, Voronov."

Mem giggled. "Sorry, Thea, but Piper's got her own hot woman to assist. How's your maths professor, babes?"

"You can carry your own boxes, you know."

They finished the day with pizza and beer, Mrs Tits coming over to poke through Mem's things and welcome her 'home'. Piper laughed way too uproariously at Lena's stories, which only encouraged the woman further, and Thea lay sprawled on the sofa with her head in Mem's lap, utter contentment on her face.

Mem fished through the box of books and precious things until she found exactly what she was looking for.

It was Sunday evening. They'd spent the day trying to unpack Mem's things, though they'd been waylaid time and delicious time again and, in the end, had simply stayed in bed. By evening, hunger had driven them downstairs and they'd cooked together – something simple and homey. Or rather, Mem cooked and Thea stood behind her with her chin on her shoulder, nuzzling into her neck and watching the process with assessing eyes.

"I want to learn to cook more things," she whispered.

Mem knew better than to voice her surprise. That was a brave admission for Thea – to relinquish her pride and admit the need to learn at all, to step out from behind the aloof persona and ask Mem for help.

"Will you teach me?" she asked.

Mem hid a smile. She twitched her shoulder.

"*Please.*"

"Of course I will."

The pride was back in a second. "I just need to be better at roti than Mrs Tits."

Mem spun in her arms. "Oh, I see how it is. There was I thinking—"

Thea tickled her ribs, smirked until her face split, then stopped Mem's mouth with a kiss.

After dinner, Mem took both the precious things she'd found to the lounge room.

"Sit down," she told one of them, pointing to the couch and plumping the cushions.

Thea flicked one eyebrow. It melted Mem's spine like it always did – they both knew it. Mem let her eyes flicker to the ground, then slowly back up, biting her lip as she met Thea's eyes. The rest of her bones melted at the darkness she saw there.

But this wasn't the time.

"Sit down, please," she said. She held up a book – old, worn, dog-earned and much loved. It had been her grandmother's, carried all the way from India after Partition. "I'm going to read you a story."

Puzzlement, indignation and realisation chased themselves across Thea's face in an almost comical procession until the woman simply seized Mem around the waist and pulled her down into the sofa with a beautiful, childish, unbounded glee.

"Alright, alright!" Mem squirmed as her ribs were mercilessly tickled again. But Thea simply tangled herself around Mem and pulled her close, Mem between her legs. She watched the book over her shoulder. Mem felt her heart might actually explode.

At the last minute, Thea seemed to remember Mem liked her imperious and domineering. The tickle turned into a nice, hard pinch.

"Very well then," Thea tried. "Read."

Mem rolled her eyes and tilted her head back for a kiss. She received a very impatient one and a pointed stare at the book.

It was hard to read for smiling.

"The Wolverton Diamond," Mem began. "Once upon a time…"

Epilogue

One year later

"If the illustrious Dame Katherine Cox would kindly focus on the task at hand and pay attention to her work, we could finish this fucking job," Thea drawled, as politely as she could given the circumstances.

There was that girlish giggle she loved and then Kate's eyes were back on hers. Thea jammed her finger down on the shutter button.

Impudent wench.

Thea had far more important things to be doing right now.

They were in her studio in the middle of what was hopefully the final hour of camera work for the second year of CreatedDiamonds' advertising campaign with Kate and Mem. These were Kate's solo shots, and if the infuriating woman would stop making eyes at her girlfriend in the corner of the room, Thea would be done already. If Kate's girlfriend wasn't behind her watching the whole show, Thea could also be a little more demanding in insisting Kate give her what she wanted. As it was, the almost sickeningly sweet lovelorn look that came into Kate's eyes whenever they slipped to Anwen's was exceptionally adorable and pure gold down the lens, so Thea couldn't really complain.

She was happy for Kate.

She flicked her fingers to indicate Kate should change her position – that private language the two of them had developed over the years – and Kate poked the tip of her tongue out at Thea's presumption. Thea snapped a shot. Poked her own out in return.

Thea was happy too, happy in a way she'd never expected would be hers. She even tolerated Kate's laugh and the eye roll that followed.

It had been a year since Memona Swan had moved into Thea's life full time – a year to the day. And Thea had plans.

It hadn't been an easy year.

Mem and Kate had filmed *Wolverton 2*, the schedule taking Mem out of her life for weeks at a time. New York, Mumbai, two particularly cold and miserable weeks in January when Mem had been filming in one of Jasper's mansions in Scotland and Thea had been stuck in London working on some celebrity's portrait series. Her friends were seeing more of her girlfriend than she was. But Mem returned home to her arms and her bed with an eagerness that made each separation almost worthwhile and chased all of Thea's doubts away.

Mem was absent again, but she was due home later that evening. If the renowned Hollywood superstar currently *wasting her time* would show just the tiniest bit of professionalism... She growled at Kate again.

Being happy to the depths of her soul didn't mean Thea was going to stop being queen of her own photographic studio, thank you very much.

Kate saw right through her attitude.

"Oh, she'll be home soon enough, blue balls. How about you focus too?"

Thea shook her head at the shit she was prepared to let slide these days and handed her camera to her assistant. She had what she wanted. She was just enjoying having Dame Katherine Cox semi naked in front of her again.

"Put some clothes on, you old tart."

Kate's laughter was rich, warm and the foundation of Thea's world, and she loved it. She'd never believed it until Mem had melted her heart, but she had a family. She'd been surrounded by one all this time and never known it. Now, with Mem by her side, it had grown wider and more loving, and she was inviting them all into her home this evening.

"Caterers say they're on their way. Everything's on track." Josef put a screen of proofs into her hands and she approved them quickly. They were excellent, of course, and they'd begin the work of processing them later. "I'll pack up here. You go," Josef added.

Josef was her newest assistant, but she'd already decided this one was a keeper. She'd met them through Heart and Grace House, which Thea had thrown her efforts into as wholly as Mem. Not simply financially, though with her assistance Heart and Grace House was now a network of eight shelters across London, but also personally. Thea ran photography workshops for the guests at the shelters. It turned out a photoshoot was a very powerful way to return dignity to a person who had lost everything, but she also ran classes that put cameras in participants' hands, that they might heal through art, or learn a new skill. Josef had been one of those in need of healing – a young person cast onto the streets by a family who couldn't accept their gender expression, but who was burning with potential.

They almost surpassed Lollie with their organisational skills and their ability to wrangle celebrities and agents – the things Thea had even less patience for than ever.

She'd been doing far less work for Jasper lately, and the freedom from purely commercial gigs further lightened her heart. If she took the work, she used it as a training opportunity for Josef or another of the talents from her Heart and Grace classes. Jasper grumbled at not having Thea Voronov's eye one-hundred percent on the job, but she told him to shove it and – incredibly – he accepted that. She still did celebrity shoots, but had added a new clause to her contract that insisted the celebrity in front of her lens donate massively to whichever charity Thea specified. It hadn't slowed down the demand for her work at all – if anything, the celebs were just as keen to be seen doing the right thing.

"It's still so transparent and superficial," she griped to Mem, curled up in bed together on a rare quiet evening in Mem's filming schedule. "They shouldn't need me to make them share their wealth around."

"It's half a million pounds," Mem pointed out, gently. "And we're happy to take it from them. Think of the good we're doing with it."

"But—"

"Shush," Mem whispered, and kissed her jawline.

Heat swelled hard and hot between Thea's legs whenever Mem spoke to her like that, and she rolled the girl over easily and straddled her thighs.

"What was that, my muse?" she asked, playfully. Her usual dangerousness was off – they were both tired – but Mem's smile made the swelling move up to her heart where it filled her chest so utterly Thea was at risk of falling into the girl beneath her and losing herself in love forever.

"That was me asking for trouble," Mem murmured.

Thea bent her lips to the bare breasts below her and sucked hard on a bruise she'd left there earlier. Mem arched into her mouth.

"Wicked, wicked girl." Thea nipped at a nipple with her teeth and grinned at the delighted yelp that startled them both.

"Wicked enough for round three?"

Thea laughed through her exhaustion. This girl was going to kill her. She wanted to die in the best way.

Thea's own art had taken an even sharper turn towards highlighting inequality over the previous year. Her most recent exhibition had highlighted homelessness across the UK and she hadn't even bothered to disguise it between gratuitous shots of the ultra-wealthy. If anything, the show had been more successful than her last one. And the collaboration with the photos' subjects had led to the creation of another of Thea's own new projects.

After shamelessly bullying Jasper, he'd provided a small premises in Camden and fitted it out with some truly vintage copiers and antique letterpress printers. With her own gang of talent from her photography workshops and some impressively creative people from the street, they had started an old-style street mag, just like the old days. Street art, street news, all the issues and vibes important to the community who slept rough, all cranked out on paper with gear that captured eyes dulled by the digital. She was the first to admit she was out of touch with that world that used to be hers, but she loved the edginess of their creations and the excitement that glowed in their eyes.

Of course, she had to learn to read in order to fully appreciate what they were creating.

That wasn't going quite so well.

Oh, Mem was a wonderfully patient and encouraging teacher, but an undeniable part of Thea's psyche objected strongly to the slightly schoolmarmish tone Mem's voice sometimes took when Thea's obtuseness exasperated her. That sort of presumption couldn't go unpunished and it was a fact of her new life that most lessons ended up in bed.

Mem even laughed about that, and took her authority way too far for Thea's liking.

"Hands off," Mem would say, totally failing to keep the delighted grin off her face.

Thea rarely obeyed.

"What did I tell you about touching this body *before* you mastered that spelling list?"

Thea let her eyebrows climb her forehead in the way she knew destroyed her woman.

"D. O. M. M. E," she said, archly, pointing to her own heart. She turned her finger on Mem. "S. U. B."

"Not even on the spelling list," Mem protested.

"Correct, though," Thea crowed.

"P. L. E. A. S. E. They're not even hard."

She was giving it to Thea on a plate. "I'll give you hard, darling."

"Wuh? Oh, you—ooooo!"

Mem's voice shot up two octaves as Thea tore the list in half and tossed it over her shoulder. Mem squealed and ran.

"I'm going to devour you," Thea promised, once she'd caught her, carried her to their bed and deposited her in the middle of it like her queen.

Mem stopped her with her bare toes on Thea's chest. "Spell it," she ordered.

Thea's grin was merciless. "D. E. V. O. U. R, my pretty muse. You are so mine."

Mem was due home in just over an hour.

Thea invited the rest of their family into their home where they joined Kate and Anwen already putting a fine effort into the champagne. Jasper strode in with air-kisses for everyone and a handsome young man on his arm who Thea hadn't yet met. Lollie bounced past wearing way too much diamond jewellery and making a beeline for Josef. Thea had no doubt they would gossip about her shortcomings for the rest of the evening. Piper arrived with her fingers entwined in the hand of an older woman and a shy expression that dared Thea to say anything, and Mrs Tits breezed in looking more glamorous than everyone else there. She thoroughly inspected the catering before giving a nod of approval.

"Thought you'd cook now you're all homey and domesticated," she smirked in Thea's ear.

"Fuck you," Thea said, affectionately.

Vera Green and her husband arrived with five of their children and Thea gave the kids polaroid cameras each and strict instructions.

"You're our photographers for the evening. You have to catch the important moments, the precious times. Do you understand?"

A flash went off in her face.

She was crouched on the floor talking to a seven-year-old, explaining the finer points of her art to a five-year-old, and one of the twins was smearing what was possibly avocado onto her leather pants. And she was happy.

She looked at the photo the kid had taken.

Yeah. They understood the brief just fine.

Just the 'congratulations' banner to hang and they were ready.

"Surprise!"

Kate yelled it like an idiot and everyone joined in, but it wasn't a surprise. Mem knew she was coming home to a party, but all the same, Thea loved the smile that cracked her face when she saw everyone there.

"The conquering hero!" Jasper called and raised a glass, but Mem ignored them all. She slid straight into Thea's arms, just the way Thea liked her, supple and soft, moulding herself against Thea's body, sighing with the pure relief of being there.

"Missed you," they both murmured at the same time.

Mrs Tits made retching noises into her glass.

Thea tilted Mem's face up and kissed her – god, those lips that she loved, their taste, their fullness, the way they opened so perfectly just for her. They both ignored the cheers that went up around them and pressed their foreheads together and grinned.

They only had seconds before Kate pulled them apart.

"Well?" she drawled. "Don't keep us in suspense."

"How was Geneva?" Piper asked.

Mem's eyes slid sideways to Thea's and her fingers sought hers out. Thea marvelled once again at how far her beautiful muse had come from the shy woman who crept into her studio over a year ago. Now Mem was no stranger to the world stage, holding her own with celebrities, politicians and diplomats around the planet.

But she would always seek out Thea's dominance.

"Geneva went great. New York went even better," Mem told the group. "My speech was very well received, I think—"

"You think? It's all over the socials already, dearest." Jasper waved a glass magnanimously. "You were triumphant. Eloquent and sophisticated. A voice of reason amid—"

"Shut up, Jasper!"

"Let the woman speak. It is kind of her point."

"Did you get it, Mem?"

Mem looked at Thea again and gave a shy, brilliantly happy smile. Thea squeezed her fingers. She already knew. She was so, so proud of her she could have wrapped an arm around Mem's waist and flown them both to the moon like a superhero. She tipped her chin at the group. A gentle, loving order. *Tell them.*

Mem took a deep breath. "You are looking at the new Ambassador to the United Nations Office for Gender Equality and the Empowerment of Women," she breathed.

The roar was deafening.

Thea lost her grip on Mem's fingers as everyone stepped in to hug her at once. *Her* Mem, leveraging her fame to advocate on the global stage for women's equality and safety against violence. Thea was so proud.

"I do feel that it's probably you who is putting in the most effort to make up for the evil attached to the Voronov name," Thea had whispered, months ago when Mem had first been approached for the role.

But Mem wouldn't hear of it. "Nonsense," she'd said, kissing Thea gently. "And you promised to let go of that – that guilt that isn't yours to carry. Your father is dead. For me, the Voronov name means love."

That idea was taking a lot of getting used to, but Thea found that she liked it.

She hoped Mem liked it too, because after dinner, she had a question.

They'd all pushed back from the table with that full-bellied contentment that came with fine food and good company. Thea was on her feet filling glasses – because that was her style these days – and rather than sitting back down again, she nudged Mem out of her chair and tugged her gently to a spot in the room where everyone could see them.

She made furtive gestures at the kids too. Their signal. They grabbed their cameras and sat in a row at their feet.

Mem turned a puzzled, but trusting, frown on Thea.

Thea faced the crowd.

"A year ago, I did an awful thing," she announced. "I whispered in this woman's ear in front of a hundred cameras and the eyes of the world, and I nearly ruined the best thing I've ever had in my life. As almost all of you delighted in telling me – and you were completely correct – I was an idiot."

Mem's head tipped to one side. She watched Thea carefully.

Thea slipped her hand into her pocket. She pulled out a small box containing a very special ring. It wasn't a diamond – fuck, Thea could go the rest of her life and gladly never see one again. This was something completely different. An emerald set in pitch black metal, the band engraved to look like a strip of film. *My darling muse* carved carefully on the inside.

She wasn't going to get down on one knee. Not in front of this lot.

For Mem, later, she'd fall to both knees and worship her properly.

"I'd like to stage a small re-enactment," she said, "and whisper what I should have said the first time."

There was a collective gasp from around the table, but Thea only had eyes for Mem. She held the ring carefully in front of her, then leaned in to whisper in Mem's ear.

She nearly drowned in that sweet, sweet spot beneath her ear.

Nearly lost herself in her scent, in the hush of her hair, in her breath and in her presence.

"My darling Mem. You are my life, my soul and all my happiness in the world. I love you. Will you marry me?"

The kids clicked their cameras. A blizzard of flashes captured the joy on her lover's face, and Mem said...

"Yes."

~ The End ~

About the Author

Jolie Dvorak likes to write steamy, angsty romance featuring women who fall hard and love harder. When her first book was released, she revealed that 'Jolie Dvorak' was, in fact, the pen name of another sapphic romance author and challenged readers to guess who. This led to some very lovely compliments and quite a few long, funny conversations, but Jolie's true identity remains a secret. If you think you know, send an email to hello@joliedvorak.com with your theories. Gold star if you get it right.

Jolie wrote her first book on a yacht in the Whitsundays and the second in a fixer-upper in Sapporo, Japan. Her adventures writing this book have taken her to a charming (though slightly crooked) windmill in the tulip fields of the Netherlands. Access is only by bicycle, so she and her wife have purchased a tandem, complete with a basket on the front for the cat.

Days are spent combing local flea markets in the hopes of finding a lost van Gogh. Evenings are a whirlwind of writing, fueled by strong Dutch coffee and stroopwafels. The cat dozes amid the windmill mechanics and fails to catch mice.

Of course, Jolie doesn't actually exist, so all the above is yet more of her alter-ego's fantasies.

instagram.com/jolie.dvorak

amazon.com/stores/Jolie-Dvorak/author/B0B9L5317H

Also by Jolie Dvorak

The **She Demands Perfection** Series

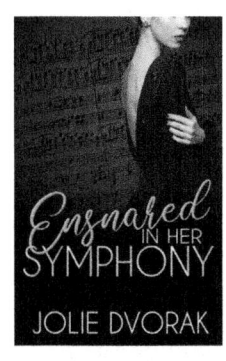

Ensnared in Her Symphony

Maestro Virve Vintinen is at the very top of her game. She's the principal conductor of the Berlin Philharmonic Orchestra – the classical music world is hers to rule and she does so in style. She has a reputation, sure. She's been known to make entire brass sections cry with one raised brow. She's reduced the harshest music critics to tears of rapture. She is widely regarded as one of the finest musicians of the age. And she likes to be in control – on the podium and in the bedroom.

Sabina Harper is the acting concertmaster of the London Symphony Orchestra but her career until now hasn't been stellar. Previous rivalries and jealousies have made her wary of the limelight, and with a sick niece to help care for, she doesn't find herself burning with ambition.

When a freak accident leaves the London Symphony Orchestra without a conductor just days before their European tour, Virve steps in to assist. Sitting in the first chair looking up at her is the delectable Sabina Harper. Ms Harper is hot, talented and she plays music that fuels Virve's soul.

Which is odd, because Virve thought she'd thrown her soul – and her heart – away long ago.

As the tour begins, Sabina Harper proves herself to be eager for exactly the kind of pleasures Virve likes and they make an arrangement to enjoy each other on the tour. But Sabi's music, her luscious body and her searching brown eyes threaten to crumple Virve's steely resolve.

Maestro Virve Vintinen might control the music, but who controls her heart?

Enthralled in Her Design

Their attraction is instant, their connection undeniable.

Syrene Harkman likes to be in control. She heads an award-winning global architectural firm, she designs things of beauty, she pays for the finest pleasures. When she loses one of the biggest jobs in her company's history and turns forty-five on the same day, she does not appreciate the cheap, tacky, dive of a strip club her friends drag her to. With a half-decent whiskey in her hand, she decides to stay. What's the worst that could happen?

Burlesque dancer and stripper Beatriz Rose has bills to pay, her grandmother to support and dreams of one day doing something more with that art-school degree than just repaying the student debt. She never expects true love to strike when she's at work, but when it does, it hits her hard in the form of a steely, demanding and outright gorgeous woman. Bea breaks her own rules and finds herself in a client's bed.

They're perfect for each other but their worlds are a million miles apart. In the aftermath of a one night stand that flares hotter than either expected, the two women decide they're meant for each other—but real life has other ideas.

Society tells them one night to forever is a fairy tale. What are they prepared to surrender to prove that fairy tales can come true?

Available on Kindle Unlimited and on paperback at Amazon.

Dear reader,

If you've come this far, thank you! You are wonderful.

Please let me express my heartfelt gratitude to you for diving into the world I've created in this book. Your support means the world to me, and knowing you're out there, somewhere, makes this simple writer very happy. It's readers like you who keep our vibrant community of indie publishing alive and thriving.

If you've enjoyed your journey through these pages, I would be incredibly grateful if you could take a moment to leave a review or rating. Even the briefest feedback makes a significant difference. It not only helps this book gain visibility but also supports me in continuing to do what I love most – writing stories for you.

I also invite you to join my newsletter community. I confess to being thoroughly rubbish at Facebook but email is a good, old-fashioned way for us to stay connected. I'll send you updates about my upcoming projects, exclusive content, and behind-the-scenes glimpses of my writing process, and I promise to keep our emails interesting! You can sign up on my website.

And, in the spirit of always improving, if you happen to come across any errors or typos within these pages, please do let me know. Your keen eyes help me polish and perfect my work. Feel free to drop me an email – I appreciate your help immensely.

And lastly, if you ever want to reach out just to say hello or share your thoughts about the book, I'd genuinely love to hear from you. Hearing from readers is one of the greatest joys of being an author.

Once again: thank you. Your support is the lifeblood of independent publishing, and it allows authors like myself to continue sharing our stories with the world.

Happy reading and warmest regards,
Jolie Dvorak

Printed in Great Britain
by Amazon